FLIN

ARIES RISING

By the Same Author

ARIES RISING

ARTHUR HERZOG

RICHARD MAREK PUBLISHERS
NEW YORK

Library of Congress Cataloging in Publication Data

Herzog, Arthur.
    Aries rising.

    I. Title.
PZ4.H58Ar   [PS3558.E796]   813'.54   80-12835
ISBN 0-399-90088-8

Printed in the United States of America

For C.D.

Acknowledgments

The author wishes to thank the following people for their generous help in providing information on and ideas for:

ASTROLOGY: Charles Emerson, vice-president, National Council for Geocosmic Research; Laura Maas; Debra Mieghan.

OFFSHORE BANKING: Richard Jaffe; Jacques Gorlin, office of Senator Jacob Javits; Professor Franklin Edwards, Columbia University; Stephen Friedman, Robert Stankey, Department of the Treasury; Herschel Clesner, counsel, subcommittee of the Committee on Government Operations, House of Representatives; Ian Giddy; Richard Straus.

GAMBLING: William Conway; Denis Gomes, Silverbird Casino, Las Vegas; Jeffrey A. Silver; Walter Tyminski, "Rouge-et-Noir"; David Bernstein.

SMUGGLING AND EXPORT-IMPORT FRAUDS: Marcella Martinez, United Nations; Angus Hone; Professor Jagdish N. Bhagwati; Remy de Haenen; Frank Hughes, International Monetary Fund.

COUNTERFEIT CURRENCY SUBVERSION: Robert J. Parra, Irving Friedman, Citibank Corp; Tom McCoy.

COMPUTER CRIMES: Donn Parker, Roy Price, Stanford Research Institute; Carol Browne; Beldon Makus; Professor Julien Hennefeld.

CRIMINAL BEHAVIOR: Dr. David Abrahamsen's book *The Psychology of Crime.*

THE CARIBBEAN: the Honorable Christopher Nascimento, Government of Guyana; Jill Bobrow; Lillie Townsend; E. Nascimento.

YACHT AND SEA BATTLE: Rainer and Hilary Bruns; Yaakov Adam.

ASTROLOGICAL BANQUET: Gael Greene.

FLYING: Jim Greenway, Arnold Zone, John Emmerling, Piper Aircraft.

VISUAL EFFECTS: Diana Hydock.

EDITORIAL: Don McKinney.

AND FOR WORK ON A DIFFICULT MANUSCRIPT: The Inside Address, Bridgehampton, New York.

Nectanebus, King of Egypt, was driven into Macedonia by fourteen nations in rebellion and later he wished to teach astrology to King Alexander, who, they say, was his son. Alexander gave him a push and knocked him into a pit, where he broke his neck. So it would have served him better to have watched the earth than the heavens.

—Nicole Oresme, from *Livre de Divinacions*

The interrogation chambers lay in the basement of the presidential palace on Revolution Square. The prisoner wore a faded set of denims and no shirt. Except for some swelling about the eyes, his body was without marks, though his inner organs must have hurt because of the rubber truncheon that had been skillfully applied during the night. So far, the prisoner had said nothing.

Despite the early hour, the room was already hot and the President had removed his jacket. Only rarely—he couldn't, in fact, remember the previous occasion; it had been years ago—did the President conduct an interrogation personally. Still, he had to hear the answer with his own ears. Not that the prisoner had been at all forthcoming; the rebels' resistance to torture was notorious.

"Raul, my patience is thin," the President said. "I am not accustomed to rising at dawn and I have had no breakfast. I *must* know how you got it. Where did it come from? There must be more. How did your group obtain them?"

Raul had the thick, stolid face of a *mestizo*. The President regarded it with contempt. Manipulating the racial fears of the major population groups had helped keep him in power all these years, yet the President had a strong sense of white superiority, which he concealed.

"Raul, I am your leader. Your president. Your general. Remember? I appeal to your patriotism. Think what will happen to our country if we have full-scale civil war. That would destroy us. The North Americans would come again. They might never leave. Raul?"

The man's eyes had closed as if he slept. He did not, of course; he merely conveyed his hatred for the President's authority. Hector Hernandez understood that.

"Raul," he said almost gently, "I want you to open your eyes. I want you to look at your good strong body. It is intact, no? You may leave here with your body intact. No one need *ever* know that you have talked to me. You can say you denied the gun was yours, and that you were reprimanded—nothing more. At the same time I shall release several of your fellows, to show the government seeks to be conciliatory. I will go *that* far to provide you with a cover. Agreed?"

President-General Hernandez wondered what he would do if the man told. Release him, as promised? Yes, he thought. Why not? But the other rebels—never. In that case, the guerrillas would certainly kill Raul on the theory a deal had been made. It was the same as Raul signing his life away. Perhaps it would be better for Raul to stay in prison for a time . . . but the guerrilla maintained his quiet.

"I can make you talk. Believe this." Actually, the dictator would have preferred to avoid force. Carter and the OAS were making noises about "human rights," an empty phrase Hernandez detested. Somoza, his friend and international neighbor, had been attacked for the use of torture. The threat of sanctions made things difficult. In extreme cases like this one, where the third degree seemed more and more imperative, the prisoner could not be released until obvious injuries had healed, and medical care in prison posed many problems. All in all, it was better to kill a rebel after he talked. Even so, that could not be done too often, because of the Department of State. . . . Hernandez realized how much he had come to dislike the North Americans. In that, at least, he was one with his people.

"For the last time . . ."

The torture technique, Hernandez' own idea, though he hadn't tried it yet, had come to him when he stood with an official from the World Bank on the beach in front of a hotel he owned, watching the gringo tourists reddening in the tropical sun, basting themselves with worthless oils. The World Bank had turned down the tourist-development loan. He had anticipated the refusal, which had just come, but he had been angered anyway. He turned his rage on the *mestizo*. "Take him," he ordered.

The man would talk, he felt sure. The astrological portents were favorable. The Pisces sun would burn; Mercury, which governed speech, would be overhead.

That the guerrillas obtained modern weapons was no surprise; the easy flow of arms throughout Latin America kept insurgents in business in many countries, including his. But this rifle was different. The serial number identified the M 16 as property of the army of which Hector Hernandez was commander in chief. It had left the main arsenal not two days before, Hernandez knew, because he had sold the guns himself. But to have them used against *him!*

The consignment of two thousand M 16A's—a light automatic rifle ideal for jungle warfare—had brought a good price, or would have: close to one-half million. The guns had been destined for white Rhodesia, to travel by freighter to South Africa and then overland. Payment would have been made directly into Hernandez' seven-figure personal-contingency numbered bank account in Luxembourg under absolute secrecy. The President would then have paid out $100,000 to the account of his associate who had arranged and implemented the transaction. The Americans would be duly informed that the guns had been stolen (the removal of the M 16's had been made to look like theft) and that they must be replaced for public safety. The Americans would complain, but comply in the end. They had to—Hernandez' country was too vital in the Central American configuration.

Now Hernandez had to learn what had gone wrong and, if possible, retrieve the M 16's. Though there was no sign of a conspiracy, one had to exist: that he had understood from the moment the *mestizo* had been captured with the weapon in a suburban house. The *mestizo* was a Gonzalista, which meant the rebels had begun to issue the guns. Where did they come from? The freighter had left port on schedule. It was to have made no stops under any conditions. Could the rebels have hijacked the ship at sea? Nonsense. They had no such capability. The freighter must have surreptitiously put in to shore down the coast and continued to South Africa with the rest of its cargo. The police had been lucky to find the gun so soon. Whoever masterminded the scheme probably had gambled on having more time, which meant an all-out military effort against the government might be starting.

Hernandez was almost certain who had perpetrated the heist, but he had to be utterly sure. Much more might be involved. That was why he had to crack the terrorist. The *mestizo* was high enough in the organization to know the truth.

The man had fair skin for a part-Indian. Good. The weather report said hot for the season, zero chance of precipitation. No clouds. Good.

The guerrilla was taken to a remote field on the President's estate near the capital. The high steel fence around his property—erected at a cost of millions—prevented access. His personal staff had been instructed to stay far away. Nobody was there except a handful of secret police and the prisoner.

The prisoner removed his clothing, as ordered. Every hair on his body was shaved off, including his beard, eyelashes, and eyebrows. He looked like a mannequin. A pinion embedded in heavy concrete was placed on the shadeless ground. A cuff went on the man's ankle. The pinion and the cuff were chained. The secret police repaired to an outbuilding for coffee. It was eight o'clock.

Now and then a secret policeman inspected the prisoner. By ten A.M. pink spots appeared on the shaved areas. These virgin areas had turned crimson by eleven. By noon, with the flaming sun overhead, his newly hairless places were molten, the rest of the body pink. Blisters rose at the ankle where the hot metal held. Squatting, the man had tried to brave it out, face impassive as usual, but to leave the bald head exposed proved impossible. He clasped his skull. He rolled on the ground, ridiculously—as if trying to shade himself with himself. The swollen penis was purple, the buttocks incendiary.

Water was given. The terrorist must not die—yet.

By telephone from his air-conditioned office, Hernandez dictated the next move, the one inspired by the tourists. Johnson & Johnson baby oil was kneaded into the wordless man's screaming skin. Olive oil would

have served as well, but Hernandez liked that touch. He envisioned a
sort of boiler, with the grease on top of the meat.

The terrorist returned to prison that evening was the color of the
boiled Caribbean crayfish Hernandez loved so much. His penis had
retreated almost completely into his body to escape the sun. His eyes
were bright pink, with aureoles of yellow scum. His tongue licked
cracked and bloody lips.

If it hadn't been for the slight protection offered by his *mestizo* skin,
the terrorist would have been ready to talk. Since he would not, he was
left alone to stand in his cell, because he could allow nothing to touch
his body. At midnight he still refused to speak.

Hernandez was weary of the prisoner's obstinate silence. The dictator
showed the bloated man a paring knife. Starting at the wrist, so that the
man could see, he deftly removed a strip of skin all the way to the elbow.
Silence. Working the knife around the bicep, he detached a circle of skin
and slid it down to the wrist. "Like your bracelet? Raul, I'm going to
skin you alive."

Clucking at the man's bravado, he began work on the crotch.

The rebel whispered, "The Tall One."

"Find the Tall One," the President ordered the head of the secret
police.

PART I

1

So much to say, no way to say it; so much to tell without the right words to tell it in. Very well, begin. But where? Beginnings, endings, which is which?

Within a day of arriving on a Carribean paradise, Philip Castle told a harmless lie that changed his destiny forever.

It started with a plane crash soon after he landed. A complete stranger was killed; even in death he intervened in Castle's fate. Our paths cross in unexpected, surprising ways. Not even the most rational philosophers can disagree with that assessment.

Had Castle *foreseen* the accident? He was tempted to believe it. Anyone landing on the short field for the first time, like himself, would have morbid thoughts; when a plane actually crashed, he was bound to ask if he had anticipated the event. There was a murky term for that— *déjà vu.*

Flying Windward Air from St. Martin, where the Eastern 707 terminated, took a mere fifteen minutes. Glistening yachts riding in turquoise bays, lush little valleys, neat terraced plots, pink hamlets—St.

Jean exuded serenity. No wonder the rich and privileged regarded it as almost a private preserve. Philip listened as passengers gushed about the wealthy families who owned the fabulous houses nestled on hillsides or rooted on rocky points. One house had a swimming pool shaped like a free-form "5"—somebody's lucky number, no doubt. Philip Castle wasn't feeling very lucky just then.

The high-winged, twenty-seat De Havilland Twin Otter overflew the only town of any size, headed out to sea, banked sharply, and returned, radio silent—there couldn't have been a control tower at the strip. But a small radio antenna loomed alarmingly close. It stood on a hill, and another hill, topped with a white windmill, rose on the other side, so that the plane swooped down the cleavage between two earth breasts. After shuddering in an updraft, it dropped abruptly, leaving Philip's stomach at a higher altitude. Passengers squealed in fear, though not him. Seeming barely to clear cars on the road, the plane dipped to asphalt. Damaged aircraft were scattered around the squat terminal. Even a STOL like this one needed a good deal of the runway; white sand beckoned through Castle's window as the plane turned.

The heat, moist, clinging, vaguely oppressive even in March, was the Antillean antithesis of the cryogenic cough from Lake Michigan. Clearing customs was a mere formality. He had only to carry his bag from the plane and hand his passport to the short-sleeved gendarme who glanced at it without looking at Philip to compare his face with the one on the photograph.

"No stamp?" Philip asked, surprised.

"Go to the police station if you want one," he understood the man to say.

An Australian jeep called a Minimoke had been reserved. There was nothing to sign or show. A few minutes later, Castle was following a hand-drawn map past a graveyard, along the beach, by a modest hotel, and up a steep hillside.

White with a red roof, surrounded by tropical verdure, the house seemed larger outside than in because of the expanse of terrace, reached through spacious doors, with a glorious view of half the island. There wasn't a telephone—a blessing! The place was prettily furnished, and Castle was almost glad his friends the Wallers had forced him to come— almost, because he dreaded being solo in paradise.

A female voice sounded through the water in the shower. "Be right out," he called, emerging in the living room in shorts and a T-shirt. A woman in a plain dress stood there, with a dark, sharp-featured face. She told him her name was Sansa, and he remembered: Sansa took care of the house. The Wallers had telegraphed her about his arrival. She lived down the hill, near the landing strip, and must have seen the plane come in.

They probed for a common tongue. Sansa spoke Spanish as well as French, but not much English, while he spoke no Spanish and only a little French that he'd learned in high school. French and English, then—Franglais.

Sansa had brought him food because he was a stranger and this was his first day, generosity doubtless meant to be remembered at tip time. The cold chicken was ample for two. Her glance shifted to the bedroom, from which no sound came. Yes, he felt his face indicate, he was by himself. Her eyes widened, her expression changed. No wife? He said not really. She giggled as though to acknowledge the absurdity of the answer. You're either alone or you're not. She looked younger when she laughed. She was quite pretty, with a nice trim form. How long would he stay? He didn't know. Probably not long. The Wallers had lent him the house for a month, but he doubted he'd last a week. Too bad! St. Jean was so beautiful, the most beautiful place in the world. Yes! For him, it already had a magical quality, like Prospero's island.

The woman usually cleaned the house in the afternoons, but occasionally she preferred mornings. Would he be disturbed? Philip shrugged—disturb what? He was too old to want to masturbate. How discerning women were. She tuned in the moment sex crossed his mind. She responded by spreading her feet ever so slightly, smoothing the material around her hips. She could return that evening to serve his supper if he liked. She desired so much his visit be enjoyable. If she could help.

So Sansa was a light hook! The Wallers would have told him, had they known, but why would they be aware? Philip was tempted. He hadn't been with a woman in he wasn't sure how many weeks, but for whatever obscure glandular or psychological reasons, Sansa didn't move him. Even if she had, he wouldn't have done it. To pay for sex in his present mood would have been giving up, and he was too close to that state already. He changed the subject to mosquitoes, already attacking his pale ankles. Sansa found black coils that resembled slender snakes. He should light them in his bedroom before he slept, and use the netting above the bed—she showed him. Like a bridal canopy without a bride.

After Sansa walked down the hill, he examined the coils. No matter how far you went, you couldn't escape mosquitoes, any more than you could escape pain.

Or astrology. He had Jamaica on the radio. "What's your sign, girl? Is it compatible to mine?" a rock singer blasted, after which the announcer shouted, "Aries, Taurus, Gemini, Cancer, Leo, Virgo, Libra, Scorpio, Sagittarius, Capricorn, Aquarius, Pisces, Pisces, Pisces, all of them, and you, right here on radio—" He switched over to classical music on the St. Jean frequency. The airline magazine on the way down had had an astrological column, a piece on preparing horoscopes and an ad for astrological toilet water. Twelve variations, each for a sign. "Smell like the sexy Scorpio you were meant to be." *Meant.* By whom? Jesus!

The bar contained a haphazard collection of near-empty bottles that must have been left by the previous tenant—the Wallers rented the house except in March, when they usually used it. This was the first of the month—people had probably gone yesterday, maybe that morning. He poured gin over ice from the fridge and searched for vermouth. Drinking and gloom were handmaidens—he hadn't learned yet to handle either in moderation. What would he *do* on this island of only eight square miles? Try not to get tight in the evenings. Go to bed early. Force himself to exercise. In the last few months he'd gotten slack. If he slid any more, he'd have a hard time recapturing muscle tone—he'd reached that age.

Philip was lapsing into the familiar inner debate about how to live the rest of his life without Ellie, interspersed with admonitions not to feel sorry for himself, when the sound jarred him from self-preoccupation. He had heard the sound of a plane in trouble before. The roar of emergency power being applied was completely different from normal engine noise. He listened intently, putting down the drink. Ominous silence followed a hollow slap. He thought quickly of the "premonition" he'd had when the Windward Air flight was landing.

He rushed to the terrace. The landing strip was in clear view below.

Before it lay a plane in the water, belly-up. It looked like a toy. He seized the binoculars that hung by the door. The twin-engine craft was of fair size, maybe an Aero Commander. People ran down the beach, but the water around the wreck was empty. Philip was utterly certain someone inside the cabin had died.

Castle wasn't squeamish. If he resisted going at first, it was because of a habitual caution about involving himself in matters that weren't his business. You never knew what the outcome might be. And did he wish to avoid confirmation of his dreadful hunch? But the wreck beckoned and he swung into the jeep, reconstructing the accident as he drove. He had been vaguely aware from the sound that a plane had landed. The pilot must have touched down, discovered a navigational error or a mechanical failure, and tried to take off again with a desperate burst of power. The plane had lurched skyward, failed to achieve sufficient takeoff speed, stalled, and flipped over as it struck the sea.

The road by the airstrip was already filling up with cars. Parking, he walked down a short path through beach grass. People rushed in every direction without any purpose that Castle could discern—left, right, back and forth, screaming in high-pitched French. An elderly woman cried, while an elderly man comforted her. Did they know anyone on the plane? For some reason Castle doubted it. Someone shouted in English, "How many are on board? Are they alive or dead?"

The plane was a silent universe unto itself, lying forty feet from shore in perhaps eight feet of water. The white underside bobbed slightly in a light surf. Swimmers in face masks converged, crawled on the belly, took turns diving and struggling to open a door submerged in a filmy sea of oil. If there had been passengers, they would have been seen inside the debris-darkened cabin. Men carried rope from a nearby shore restaurant; they waded the rope to the wreck and tied it to a horizontal stabilizer. Forming a line in the water, men pulled without result, yelled in frustration. The rope slid off and was retied. The frantic tugging began again.

Another set of would-be rescuers appeared with a large hammer and a metal wedge, and clambering aboard the plane, began to cut a hole in its tough aluminum skin. Philip's stomach contracted as he put himself in the pilot's place. Suppose the man (or woman) was alive? If so, he probably was trapped in his seat, conscious or not, feet up, head down, body held tightly by the seat belt and shoulder harness. The only reason he still breathed was the air trapped in the cockpit. But water must be sloshing in, rising toward his face. *Faster,* Philip urged the men on top the plane. *The poor devil may be drowning a stone's throw from the beach.*

The voice, speaking in distinct French, startled Castle. "He shouldn't have flown. He was warned." The American turned sharply to find a tall young woman with long orange-red hair, exquisite features, high coloring, tiny freckles and a slender body. A thin blouse revealed full breasts under a bikini top.

He asked in English, "Warned?"

Startled brown eyes with gold flecks jumped toward him. Evidently she'd been thinking out loud. "I . . . meant nothing." She pointed at the rope. "Why aren't you helping?"

"Tail section's stuck. The plane can't be budged that way." He looked at his Timex. "Anyway, whoever's in there's dead."

"You're right. He must be dead by now."

"Only the pilot on board?"

"I think so."

"Most likely he was killed on impact."

"You know about planes?" she asked.

"Something."

"Are you a flier?"

"I used to be. Why?"

But she walked off, mouth pensive. He watched her rear bunch beneath the bikini—she moved with the grace of a wild animal. The sensation in his crotch felt welcome, but of all times! He forced his attention to the wreck. A tractor had appeared on the runway, and a heavier rope was brought to the plane. A diver with tanks disappeared below the surface; rising, he shouted to a companion aboard a rubber dinghy, who motioned. The crowd on the beach went still, as though it sensed confirmation of what had to be true.

"Everybody back! Everybody back!" People moved away from the tautening cable. The tail section rose slowly, bent, ruptured. The diver went down again. A body floated to the surface. Facedown, arms limp in the water, the corpse was dragged aboard the dinghy. Outboard engine whining, the rubber boat sped toward shore, where a battered ambulance waited.

People stampeded, Philip too, impelled by an overpowering curiosity, an instinct, almost, to see the victim with whom they identified because sudden death lurked everywhere, and yet to reassure themselves that they still lived. Castle had a glimpse of the dead man's pallid features. *My God, without the curly beard, he'd look like me!*

As if to expunge its presence, the body was rudely shoved inside the ambulance, which careened back over the runway while the cable pulling the plane to shore crushed it with primitive vengeance. They'd never find out what caused the crash, Castle thought. Unable to witness further destruction, he perused the beach, but the girl with the gold-brown eyes had vanished into the twilight.

2

Back on the hill, Philip Castle had his gins, nibbled at the cold chicken Sansa had left, tried to read a mystery story, poured himself a liqueur and, on the terrace, settled restlessly in a lounge chair. The plane wreck had shaken him, and so had the brief encounter with the girl. He didn't want to think about either.

The moment he raised his eyes to the bright stars spangling the black velvet sky the argument about astrology flashed into his mind.

Ellie hadn't really left him because of an astrologer—he knew that. Astrology had been an effect, not a cause. But that she'd let stargazing—Castle's estimation of astrology—come into their lives at all annoyed him anyway.

"An astrologist!" he said in disbelief when she said she planned to consult one.

"Astrologer."

"Who gives a damn which it is?"

"Look, I understand your attitude, given your mother and all." Castle's mother had been a devotee of astrology and he hated the subject. Ellie went on, "But I have more respect for astrology than you do. I have to make a decision and I need help."

The decision was whether to leave him, go off with Richard, get a divorce. It was almost that cut-and-dried. Richard had been Ellie's boyfriend before Philip entered the picture and hadn't forgotten her in all those years. They'd started seeing each other in earnest while Castle was away at a conference, and one thing led to the next, she finally admitted. Philip, once he'd absorbed the shock, concluded that Ellie was kidding herself. He'd begged her to see a therapist—not him; you didn't treat your own wife—but she'd refused. He thought he knew why, too: therapy might have exposed Ellie's real motives. That she was approaching forty and feared losing her good looks. That the attention of a rich bachelor—Richard had never married—flattered her.

And now that she was intent on breaking up, she wanted to be told what she wanted to hear.

"Zoltmann will clarify my future," she was saying. "He's supposed to be terrific."

"Zoltmann?"

"Frederick Zoltmann. He's Richard's astrologer."

"The deck is stacked, Ellie."

"Be patient. Maybe it'll work out between us yet."

He wished he were capable of giving her a firm ultimatum—him or me—but, as always, he reacted judiciously, even when he sensed that Ellie wanted him to stand up to her. He'd accepted the affair as the temporary price of not losing her, hoping she'd return to her senses. The torture had been doubly painful because he'd endured it for nothing.

She timed the announcement for the Christmas holidays when their sixteen-year-old son, David, was visiting her parents in Oregon. She'd hardly eaten a mouthful at dinner. She dropped her fork and said, "I've decided." He tensed. "I've been to see Mr. Zoltmann. More than once, in fact."

"I'd forgotten about him," he lied.

"According to Mr. Zoltmann, this is the right time for me to make a move. He predicts it will be successful. I want to do it. I'm leaving you." Her frightened eyes seemed enormous. "Mr. Zoltmann's terrific, as I said." She paused and smiled slightly. "Though he likes to cop a feel."

"Oh, Lord."

Ellie went on carefully. "The signs in my horoscope point to Richard. I'll spend the rest of my life with him. Married."

"Ellie . . ."

"Please don't tell me I'm out of whack because I'm having a life crisis of some kind. Of course I am! I'm seeing things as clearly as I ever have. You were right for me once, and Richard wasn't, but people change. I admit he doesn't thrill me like you do sometimes—I mean, when you stop working long enough to let yourself go. But I'm not a girl anymore. I need a different style. That he's rich doesn't matter, but Richard can give me what I want. I've given my best years to you and David. What's left is for me. Richard and I will do things together. Like *we* never do. Richard plans to retire."

"*Retire?*" Richard was the same age as himself.

"He can do it, believe me. Next summer we'll travel to China." She paused, but before he could collect his scattered thoughts Ellie said brusquely, "I'm tired of writing copy. I'm tired of bosses younger than me and clients who make passes. I'm tired of household chores. All I ever do is work. With Richard I'll have a maid. I don't want to be stuck in a rut like you and everybody else."

To argue with her stubborn chin was useless. "When are you leaving?"

"In about an hour. Richard's coming for me. We might as well get it over with. Phil, I'm sorry." She didn't cry.

On the terrace a mosquito coursed by his ear and he flailed at it futilely. Everything had seemed futile after that. Ellie had moved into Richard's swank near-Northside apartment. David decided to live on a commune in Oregon at least until summer—to hell with school, he said, and couldn't be budged, not even when Philip flew west to see him. Philip was shocked to learn that he didn't care. That was a real blow—to learn he didn't care about his own son. Or about himself. Or about his career. The bottom simply dropped out one morning, when it didn't seem to matter whether he left his bed.

Under the detached expression he offered the world Philip hid his emptiness. He tried to explain it as the postpartum depression authors often experience when they turn in their manuscripts—he'd spent several years on *The Psychology of New Nations*—but that wasn't the answer. He could hardly bring himself to correct the galleys—he didn't have the energy. He saw fewer and fewer patients because he wanted to shout at them; he was frequently late to his classes at the university or didn't appear at all.

He'd wondered what would happen to him this year or the years to come. He considered relocating, but if he did, he'd have to take himself along. He began to drink. He was pretty drunk when he threatened Zoltmann. Maybe he'd laugh at the incident someday, but certainly not yet. He was just too low.

He had to stop brooding. *Get up. Go out.* He was sick of self-pity.

In the Moke, he drove down a winding road that brought him to Pointe-de Mer, the town he'd seen from the sky. It had a well-protected harbor dotted with expensive yachts from which music floated across the water. To cruise about the Caribbean in the middle of winter must be some life, Philip thought enviously; well, he'd never have a chance to try it. The town consisted of several one-way streets running around the harbor, lined with smart restaurants and duty-free shops. Next to the main pier was the inevitable French fixture, a café, which a sign announced as "Le Boucan."

He ordered a Cointreau from the balding middle-aged black man behind the bar and took in the surroundings. Le Boucan was open at one end that overlooked the beach. Banana fronds covered the ceiling; green vines spread across them and worked their way down wooden pillars. The tables were rough wood, bleached white from being scrubbed clean. On the walls were announcements of yachting races, old photos. One showed a smiling round-faced black with a keen expression. Curios like conch shells lay in glass cabinets along with piles of cigarette cartons and liquor bottles with labels familiar and strange. From a far corner came the clinks, clanks, lights, and noises of an old pinball machine. Country music played.

Castle had to smile a little at the eclectic assortment of things collected behind, over, and around the bar: post cards, T-shirts and towels, on which was printed *Kastar Aldrig In Handduken; What's the Use of Getting Sober When You Know You'll Be Drunk Again;* a balloon made like a bee; a Toronto Maple Leafs pennant; an electric clock that said Miller High Life; a calendar from the Banque Nationale de Paris; a message to "Pay When Served"; a plaque for Cape Cod; bank notes from a dozen lands. It looked like the motley of the world had representation in that place.

Philip listened to the multilingual chatter around him. The talk concerned only one topic—the crash. In the babble his ears strained for information. Aero Commander . . . from the Cayman Islands . . . pilot used the airstrip before . . . should have landed safely . . . quite mysterious . . . mechanical troubles or . . . French . . . known to drink before flying . . . *trop de vin peut-être* . . .

The heavyset black man behind the bar said abruptly in a bass voice, "How are you?"

"Fair. I'm a friend of the Wallers. They said to tell you hello. You're the owner, aren't you?"

"Yes. They won't be down, then?"

"No. Herb Waller's stuck in Chicago this winter. They lent me the house. I'm Phil Castle." He put out his hand and the other took it.

"I'm Joseph Martinez. Call me Joe. Fine people, the Wallers. I shall miss them. They frequent my place when here. I knew you'd arrived. I should have been insulted if you'd failed to visit, but you came promptly."

Philip grinned at the flowery speech. It felt strange to grin, like moving a limb that had been immobilized. "How'd you know I was here?"

"Oh, I'm aware of most things that happen on this rocky island. A surprising place when you understand it, Philip."

There it was again. People always called him Philip. He was just too stiff for "Phil."

"Sansa told you?"

The black man made a disparaging face, for no obvious reason. "Sansa loves to talk. Sansa talk too much. And that's not all."

"I gathered."

"Sansa likes money. There is such a thing as liking money too much."

"I feel the same way, which is helpful, since I don't have a lot of it."

"Yes, it is hard to make ends meet, especially when you have fourteen children, as have I." He took a new-looking photo from the wall and showed it. Ten of the fourteen were boys, ranging from their early teens to their twenties, all big like their father.

"I don't know whether to commiserate or applaud."

"Both, I suppose."

"Do they all live here?" Philip asked politely.

"Yes, fortunately and unfortunately. They have a habit of getting into trouble. They're a little rough."

"Is Sansa native to the island?"

"Sansa's from El Parador, in Central America. She's East Indian."

"*East* Indian?"

"Millions of East Indians were imported to the Caribbean as indentured servants when slavery was abolished. They were slaves, too, for all intents and purposes. Sansa came to St. Jean as a little girl to visit her uncle, and never left, though she goes home from time to time. Sansa has close ties in El Parador, I believe."

"And you? Are you a native of St. Jean?"

"*Me?* Heavens no. I speak French but I was born in Guyana when it was a British colony. My parents immigrated here—not easy, for blacks." Joe Martinez lowered his voice. "They are more racist than you might think. They keep black people out. You've noticed how few blacks there are?"

"Yes."

"There was little cultivation of sugar—the island's too small. Few slaves. That's why this island is almost entirely white."

"Do you resent that?"

Keen eyes searched his. "Some days."

Joe neither offered more information nor moved. Castle asked for a refill, then said, "What does 'Le Boucan' mean?"

"You must know history, friend. It is more than odd that a decent history of the whole Caribbean does not exist—that says a lot about how little importance is given to the area. Once there were French settlers who lived on Hispaniola—now the Dominican Republic and Haiti—and ate dried beef, *boucan*, in French. The Spanish hunted them with bloodhounds, and pushed them out. They went to smaller islands, took to the sea, and retaliated by raiding Spanish settlements. They were the first pirates—the buccaneers, so-called because of their staple, dried beef. Other adventurers joined them. Errol Flynn made them famous. The swashbuckler. Errol Flynn was how people pictured the buccaneers. Do they still show his films?"

"On TV."

"Do you watch them?"

"I don't watch TV much," he said, not liking to think of those late movies he'd watch until he drank himself to sleep. "But I see a Flynn flick from time to time."

"My favorite isn't a pirate picture, actually. It's *Dawn Patrol*, about the First World War. Seen that?"

Philip smiled. "Last month."

"Boy, that part where he takes David Niven's place and goes on the raid all by himself. Blows up the arms depot. And the dogfight! He loops-the-loops and shoots down two Huns before von Richter finally gets him." Martinez playfully put his hands together, waving them, in an imitation of wings. "I loved that bit." Joe Martinez gleamed teeth. "Errol Flynn was bigger than life. Well, any man that enjoys Errol Flynn is okay by me. And you're a friendly fella, Philip. You don't have airs, like the yachties."

The proprietor busied himself with the customers, and Castle studied them. "Yachties" had to mean people from the big yachts, tanned and carefree-looking in expensive casual clothes with vacuous faces. Ellie, he thought, would have loved the atmosphere. It would have appealed to her innate snobbishness. They used to fight about wealth. Castle had a bias against the rich.

The few locals were easy to pick out. They were pale and plain and their square faces looked rather alike. When they smiled they showed missing teeth. On a little place like this—the permanent population was only several thousand, the Wallers said—intermarriage must be frequent. The natives struck Castle as simple honest folk, and he wondered what they did for a living. There couldn't be enough farmland for all to till. They fished, he supposed, or worked in the tourist trade, though the Wallers claimed tourism wasn't much of a business here, and the islanders even discouraged it by permitting only a handful of small hotels. There were no casinos, golf courses, or discotheques, so why would ordinary tourists come? . . .

He hadn't stopped hoping, he realized. He had been watching, in fact, a particular bare foot with red toenails that stuck out from behind a post in the corner. He'd thoroughly inspected the place; if the foot didn't belong to her, the girl from the beach wasn't there. The foot vanished, and he saw her the moment she rose from the table. She started out, followed by two dark-haired muscular men, both young. She wore tight linen slacks and a gauzy blouse tied below her breasts, leaving her tanned belly exposed. If he hadn't been drinking he might not have had the nerve to push his way from the bar. Seeing him, she halted abruptly. Moonlight shone on the water behind her.

"How do you do," he said.

"Hi there. Enjoying yourself?"

"I'm not sure yet. My first trip to the beach wasn't exactly fun."

She frowned. He put her in her mid-twenties. "No, it wasn't. I'll avoid that beach for a while. There are plenty of others."

"Which do you prefer?"

"I choose a different one every day, for variety. Each beach has its own personality—you'll see." She seemed to avoid his gaze. "Tomorrow I'll be at Cul de Sac. I'll go in the morning. Nobody comes there until afternoon. So long."

She trotted away gracefully, followed by the swarthy men, who ignored Castle completely.

He returned to the bar and asked Joe Martinez, "Who's she?"

"Name's Marie-Celeste."

"French? But she has no accent."

"She's French, though, at least partly."

"Where is Cul de Sac?"

Martinez must have overheard the conversation. "I expected you'd ask. The far end of the island. If I was you I'd stay away. Cul de Sac means dead end."

"Why? Too young?"

"Too taken."

"By anyone of those guys?"

"*Them?* God no! A much older man."

"She's very pretty."

"Beauty is skin-deep. You wouldn't like her friend. He might not like you, either, I warn you."

The girl on the beach had said that the dead pilot was warned. They seemed to do a lot of warning down here.

3

The full account of late-twentieth-century international finance may never be written because the facts will not be complete.

A gaping hole lurks in the statistics—the extent of misrepresented or unaccounted-for money generated by the drug trade, tax evasion, unlawful currency exchanges, skimming, export-import frauds and other crimes loosely labeled "white collar," though collars may have been bloodied.

The quantity of dirty money—"dirty" because illegally obtained and/or sequestered—is believed to be staggering. In offshore Atlantic banks—so-called because the majority are located on islands off mainlands, which seek to attract capital—hundreds of billions of American dollars are said to be hidden from the IRS. (Offshore banks operate almost without restrictions.) By one count, there are fifty billion dollars' worth of lost, missing, or stolen securities. An estimate puts the practice of double invoicing in Latin America as equal to twenty percent of its total trade. Though mostly unreported, the new and burgeoning crime-by-computer has serious potential. If economic crimes in the western hemisphere are added up, type by type, the crude sum of dirty money that has been accumulated, mostly from or in the United States, would appear to be in the neighborhood of one trillion dollars.

Such a figure cannot be easily absorbed. A trillion is a thousand billion. A trillion dollars is nearly one-half of the gross national product of the United States. Effectively applied, a trillion dollars would go far toward ending the miseries of global poverty. If criminally obtained and/ or sequestered American dirty money was recaptured, and taxes paid by those who evade them, there would be sufficient funds to significantly lower the taxes paid by Americans for years to come.

Be it too high, or too low, as seems more likely, the figure underscores a foolish perception. When Americans think of crime, they imagine street crime, which, by comparison with economic crime, is a minuscule matter. Never before, law-enforcement and tax authorities agree, have economic criminals been so sophisticated. Those who believe that most of them end in jail are quite mistaken.

They were four.

By accident they found themselves at the same bridge table during a tournament at a Las Vegas hotel in March 1976.

Though each a superlative player, none finished the match, being far more interested in each other. No one remembered exactly how the communication had been made—what signals had been sent, what words had been dropped. If ESP were mentioned, it would have alerted them—all four believed in the unconscious contact between kindred spirits. They were soon convinced they had been destined to meet.

If not, why the many coincidences and parallels? Why were these particular people in the same room at the same time? Why did they represent the four cardinal signs of leadership? Why were their bridge positions—N, E, S, W—entirely appropriate? How come all four were in the crown line or keystone positions of the tarot deck? Why—gradually the facts emerged—had each suffered a grave misfortune in 1968? And why, exactly a year after, had all become . . . ? They smiled; why should four people at a bridge table turn out to be . . . ? If they were secretive, they had reason.

Once they had admitted to a common interest in breaking the law—or laws; they operated in various countries, had different scams—they displayed excitement. Never had they encountered professionals of their caliber and class. High-spirited, they admitted to liking their work, relishing the originality of it, enjoying their victories, delighting to fool others with their poses. They laughed at what amateurs they'd been at the start, though the youngest should be more careful about his gangland connections, the oldest felt. He held hoods in elegant contempt. He regarded them as vicious sharks. By comparison, the group at dinner in the posh private room had the majesty of killer whales, he said.

They toasted each other with the finest champagne; they shared a superior vision. Modesty and self-effacement seemed absurd. Why conceal their strengths, or, for that matter, weaknesses? The others at the table would have seen through them easily. And so they explained themselves as frankly as they could. They had followed their pathways with brilliant success. They were amazed to discover how much each had accumulated. Approximately, of course; complete candor about assets does not exist among rich people, even those who trust each other. Good taste, the desire to play up in order to impress, or play down to reduce risks, must affect claims to wealth. But each possessed a fortune. Together . . .

The temple tower, or ziggurat, had been built on the flat crown of an artificial hill. It symbolized the binding together of earth and heaven and provided an ascent. There were many stair temples around the city, overlooking the flat, lush plains. Through a slit in the tower roof, plump, dark-skinned men searched the nighttime skies of Babylonia, meticulously recording the movements of the seven planets that turned about the earth—Sun, Moon, Mercury, Venus, Jupiter, Saturn—and the stars beyond them. A complex system had been developed, with properties assigned to the planets: Mars-Nergal, the fiery god of war and destruction, the morning-rising Venus, giving birth to the day, symbol of feminine qualities, love, gentleness, procreation. . . .

The beneficent Sun was most important; the Sun's path was divided into twelve sections, the twelve constellations had been identified along its course, the elliptic, each corresponding with an earthly month. Aquarius, the water-pourer, delivered the heavy rains of January, for instance. In this way, natural forces could be explained; and, if the movements of stars could be reduced to regular patterns which could be understood and foreseen, the destiny of kings could be predicted. As above, so below. . . .

The Bible called the men who toiled in the temple-towers Chaldeans. When the oldest of the group in Las Vegas announced that he had been a Chaldean, a wise man, once, none of the others looked dubious. In other incarnations, he believed, he had lived in Egypt, Greece, Spain, and he continued to live: his destiny was not played out. Death had always intervened before he could achieve his dreams, but this time he hoped to succeed. He wanted power—of an unusual kind.

He was a magician—the ace of diamonds. Adolf Hitler had the same card. Many nice people do, too. But most of them share the desire to be rich, he said.

He'd been born outside Paris on April 20, 1916, at 4:08 P.M., of a family with a title but modest means. He was employed by a financial establishment when the Germans invaded. France surrendered before he was called up. He worked as a bank teller during the war, a job he chose deliberately because it enabled him to identify possible collaborators with the Gestapo by the size of their accounts. The names went to the resistance. He participated in several dangerous missions but did not fire a gun. To kill directly was not in his stars.

His legitimate career could be easily summarized: French consulate, Zurich, where he specialized in trade negotiations; the prestigious Banque de Paris et Pay-Bas, Geneva, where he was a commodity banker. He traveled extensively throughout the world. His title, fluency in several languages (natural for an aristocrat), composed manner, exquisite clothes, perfect discretion, won him important friends. Affable, keen, humorous when he wished, he always moved in the best circles.

He mentioned impatience with detail, however, as a fault, as well as a hot temper, which he tried to control. If he condescended to women, it was not because he regarded them as inferior (he was too smart for that) but to prove he could get away with it. He was unable to stop proving himself. He liked to win, more rather than less as the years passed.

He had a vigorous sex life but staved off marriage until 1964, when he was forty-eight. He wasn't anxious to be married then, either—men like him have great resistance to matrimony—but the opportunity was too good. The woman was beautiful and potentially very rich, her father being a leading French industrialist. The father objected strongly to the age difference (she was twenty-three; the aristocrat had always preferred young women), to his reputation as a rake, and to his motive. The industrialist assumed, correctly, that the aristocrat married for money and told him in no uncertain terms never to expect an inheritance. The aristocrat discounted this threat: the industrialist was old, the daughter his only child.

His bride urged him to quit his job at the bank and live with her on a grand estate owned by her father near Lyon—the old man couldn't say no to her. There, she surprised him, revealing that she pursued studies in the occult, by which she could read character and fate, she said. When the aristocrat demurred, she told him about himself. He had an unseen side which one day would emerge. He was destined to be a successful criminal. He would meet an archrival with a similar configuration who, identity disguised, might vanquish him. He had better be vigilant, since she wouldn't be there to protect him. *She* would die first. He took these tidings lightly.

In 1968, pregnant, she began to visit a gynecologist in Lyon. Independent as always, she insisted on driving alone, leaving him to study the materials she'd given him, in which, despite himself, he had gradually come to give credence. Her car skidded on an icy road and went over a cliff. The aristocrat had loved her in his way, and grieved. He was astonished by the accuracy of her prediction that she would die first, and wondered why neither of them had foretold that she should not drive on that particular day. He resolved to achieve perfection in the uses of her materials.

The industrialist kept his promise: The aristocrat inherited nothing. He was forced to leave the estate. He resumed his banking career in Geneva. Examining his life, he decided to get rich in his remaining years. Wealth would amuse him, take his mind off her, help him toward the goal he had finally set for himself. He perceived a golden opportunity, and hadn't his astute wife predicted he'd turn to crime?

Monetary investors are said to dream about their favorite currencies. The currencies of which they most frequently dream are the U.S. dollar, the Swiss franc, and the West German mark. These currencies are strong, or "hard." To dream in weak or "soft" currencies might bring nightmares, especially if you are an affluent person living in nations whose currencies are not freely exchangeable. Such people may be desperate to get their money out of the country so that it can be converted to hard money, but to do so may be a jailable offense.

In 1969, when the aristocrat entered white-collar crime, the lira had been a nightmare currency for years. Wealthy Italians worried that labor unrest, the powerful Communist party, extremists of all kinds, and other factors had made the lira an endangered species. If it could be removed from the country and exchanged, even at a loss, for a hard currency in Switzerland, say, the Italian who did so would have money abroad, hedged against inflation, tax-free, usable for investments or pleasure. The Italian government would have no way to know because of the secrecy of the Swiss banking laws.

His first role was that of a simple courier. It was done all the time, but he wanted to learn the problems firsthand. In Rome he hinted to a friend that, for a fee of ten percent, he would smuggle money to Switzerland. The Italian could have moved the money himself—bribing a customs official if necessary—but he was an important government official and couldn't take chances. For the aristocrat there was no risk at all. Who would suspect, much less search, a French banker with a title and so much poise?

A few more trips and he was established. But to repeat the operation too often would be foolish. Besides there was bigger money to be had.

Quiet questions led him to the villa of a Turin millionaire he was sure he could trust even if nothing came of it. After the usual pleasantries, the aristocrat looked out the window and said, in Italian, which he spoke as well as French, "One would think, since we live in the free world, that one would have the right to invest as one chose, including abroad, don't you agree?"

"Fervently," said the Italian. "Why, then, do you call it the free world?"

"Well, one is free to improvise. Kidnappings are common these days. A kidnapping might be useful."

The Italian recoiled. "Kidnapping?"

"Why not? I could arrange to have you abducted, or if you prefer, your son. Upon the payment of ransom, you or your son will be released. The police will not be notified unless word of the ransom reaches the government, in which case the kidnapping is the cover story for the payment, to which the government cannot object, even though the ransom money is carried over the frontier—covertly, of course. It will be deposited in a Swiss account, in your name. Failure is impossible."

After deliberation, the wealthy Italian put his life in the aristocrat's hands. There was something about the man he trusted implicitly. A huge "ransom" was promptly paid by his company, the manufacturer released, a numbered bank account created in Geneva. Other spectacular kidnappings, engineered by the Frenchman, were sometimes reported in the newspapers. Not a single "victim" was harmed.

Next came the pseudo-robberies. Plenty of Italians lacked liquid capital but possessed valuables—paintings, sculpture, tapestries, jewelry, stamp and coin collections. Faking a robbery was not difficult with the owner's connivance. The French nobleman selected the thieves, arranged the job, sold the objects after they had been brought over the border, for one-third the take, which was gladly given.

Using his special ways of reading character, he picked dependable accomplices and was double-crossed only once. He completely lost his temper, as he occasionally did. Contemplating revenge, he remembered a meal in a Taiwan restaurant. The Chinese adored the specialty of the house, though it was illegal. The table had a hole in the center. A bound monkey was placed under the table, its head shoved through the hole. The top of the skull was removed, and, with chopsticks one ate the warm brains of the still-live monkey. The revolting scene had stuck in his mind.

The man who had double-crossed him was brought to a Paris cellar and tied in a chair. An Arab, well paid for the work, sawed a hole in the top of his head. His brains were removed with a spoon and placed in his mouth. Word of *that* spread.

The aristocrat compiled a list of countries with the "right" set of problems—blocked currency, political instability, deep fears about the future. The list included the Union of South Africa, Rhodesia, India, Turkey, Jamaica, Argentina, Peru, Ghana, Guatemala, and later, Taiwan and Iran. There were people with money in all those lands. In Johannesburg, a South African couple begged him to remove 100,000 rand—something over $100,000. He shipped the money air freight in two boxes identified as bedroom slippers. The slippers in the middle layers were stuffed with banknotes. The auguries told him nobody would search the boxes. Nobody did.

The signs pointed to the Americas as the logical place to expand. The big drug dealers were there, and so were incredible amounts of U.S. dollars seeking to evade taxation. He established an elaborate organization designed specifically to make him almost impossible to trace— representatives in Liechtenstein whose bank secrecy laws exceed those of Switzerland, holding companies in Panama (where there are 35,000 registered companies, many simply mail drops), offshore banks in Bermuda and the Cayman Islands, a British crown colony 475 miles south of Florida, with a population of 13,000 and more than 300 private banks licensed to conduct limited business.

The aristocrat needed more capital. Back in Johannesburg—his energy was endless and he traveled constantly—he contacted the same couple for whom he had successfully removed 100,000 rand. He had a better proposition this time. Instead of paying interest, Swiss banks had begun to charge a fee for keeping foreign money there, so much had poured in. If the couple wished to take more money out of South Africa, he could suggest a bank in the Bahamas, owned by a trusted friend of his, which for a time deposit of one year, would pay interest of twelve percent, a figure high enough to be interesting but low enough to avoid suspicion. He would not charge his usual courier fee because he wanted a favor from the friend.

The couple gave him 250,000 rand in large bills. He took the money out in a cloth belt wrapped around his waist. In London a year later, the South Africans learned that the Bahamian facility was bankrupt. Pretending bad investments, the aristocrat had looted it, transferring the deposits to another of his offshore banks. The couple had no recourse. They had broken South African law, and to commence legal action against him would invite prosecution.

His international operations continued, but he concentrated on the United States, in search of a special kind of depositor. Dining out on his aristocratic credentials, he would acknowledge that he had foolproof ways to avoid paying U.S. taxes.

Like any salesman of life insurance, he had plans tailored to various needs. The source of income didn't matter—it might be drugs, stolen jewelry, political payoffs, hidden profits, concealed investments, skims, unreported fees, anything. A person came to him with $100,000—it was usually much more—in cash or negotiable securities, which he would transport to the Cayman Islands, flying from Miami, and open an account in his bank with a service charge of six percent. Nobody bringing money in was ever searched, and Cayman bank secrecy laws were a complete shield against the IRS.

A friendly offshore banker could be useful. He could suggest that the Cayman bank hold a person's stock portfolio to circumvent the requirement to report capital gains. For individuals who had even the vaguest connection with import-export, he might recommend founding an offshore company through which profits could be skimmed outside the United States. Among his clientele was a leading rock-'n'-roll group which transferred, through the Cayman bank, about five million dollars to dummy companies in the Netherlands Antilles, where banking laws were limp. The group paid no U.S. taxes at all. Or—he had so many "ors"—one could set up an offshore company, pretending it was foreign, and actually lend oneself money and deduct the interest from U.S. income taxes. The money could be used to buy property in Florida, say, again with tax advantages—in 1979, almost half of the five billion dollars' worth of real-estate purchases in the Miami area were by "foreigners."

The aristocrat, through fees and excellent investments, had done splendidly. His magnificent new home on a small Caribbean island was complete. Perhaps the new friends he'd just met in Las Vegas, where he'd come to scout for depositors, would like to visit.

His name was Raymond, Count de Vaucresson.

4

Exhausted, Philip Castle slept late, until finally woken by probing fingers of light through the wood blinds, as if the sun wanted to enter the room.

He ate a quick breakfast and set off hurriedly in the Moke. It was nearly eleven and he was afraid of missing the girl. He felt pleasantly adolescent—not that anything would come of it. He wasn't exactly a prize package—a disappointed middle-aged man who'd lost track of his life. What a glamor girl like Marie-Celeste would see in him, he couldn't imagine. But he had nothing to lose except ego, of which there wasn't enough left to worry about. Anyway, for whatever reasons, she seemed to have encouraged him. Or had she? He wasn't sure.

A crumpled ball of wire, metal, and glass, yesterday's wreck stood at the side of the runway like an advertisement against flying.

He found the beach called Cul de Sac. At the turn was a sign: "LE NUDISME EST FORMELLEMENT INTERDIT." *Formally*, yet. The road ran beside an abandoned salt pond, degenerating into rocks, then sand. Another jeep was parked there, a VW, larger than his, white, with a perky blue-and-white-striped canvas top. The olive-drab Moke was less festive. Maybe that summed up the contrast between the girl and him, if the VW were hers.

The curved beach was a crotch between two leglike promontories. Removing his flip-flops, Philip walked to the other end, disappointment mounting when he failed to see her. He was about to give up as, passing a great hunk of lava, he sensed a human presence.

Draped on a towel, she was minus a top. Her breasts, angled gently toward the sides of her body, were browned and gleaming with oil. Little beadlets of sweat extruded from her skin. Plastic disks joined at the center shielded her eyes. Her hair was in a bandanna. Afraid she slept, Philip coughed self-consciously.

Removing the disks, she sat up. "Sorry. I didn't mean to frighten you," he said.

"What's to be scared of?" she said. She made no effort to cover herself.

"Not me, God knows." He stood uncertainly. "Did you think I'd come?"

"Were you invited?"

"Well, you . . ." *Hadn't* she rather deliberately dropped the beach's name? "In any case, here I am." The eye protocol wasn't clear to him. Was he permitted—encouraged—to stare? Not to was hard.

"So you are. Did you bring a suit?"

He produced one from inside a towel. "I'll change behind the rock."

"You expected a cabana?" She had an impish laugh.

He emerged, feeling like a Victorian rotogravure with his white skin and long boxer trunks. "I must look like the Abominable Snowman."

"I wouldn't say abominable." She inspected him. "Just a little out of shape. Better be careful about the sun." She'd applied lip gloss in his absence.

"Yes, it's bright." He removed a leather case from his neatly rolled clothes and put on dark glasses with droopy lenses. He spread his towel next to hers. "My name's Philip Castle," he said as he sat down. He held out his hand and she took it. Her fingers were cool.

"I'm Marie-Celeste."

"The barman told me."

The young woman seemed slightly alarmed. "Joe says a lot of things. What else did he say?"

"That you were part French. The rest wasn't specified."

"The other half's American, though I think of myself as French. I had part of my education in the States."

"I wondered why you didn't have an accent, though maybe you do, just slightly." He was surprised at how easily they had started to talk, though the Wallers had told him everything was casual and friendly in the Caribbean. How beautiful it was: the sky, the gentle sea, the beach, the breasts, especially the breasts. He indulged himself in a good look— pointed, firm, ruby-nippled, large on her narrow rib cage. Half humanity had breasts, yet these two dominated his attention. How American of him! He wasn't used to seeing the naked mammaries of a stranger, though a European would be, he supposed. He wasn't European. Her breasts excited him. He sprawled on his back, as had she. "Live on St. Jean?" he asked.

"I'm spending a few months here as a guest."

"Good duty," he murmured.

"Duty?"

"It's what they say in the service."

"Service? Oh, *military* service. Are you in the military?" she asked.

"Years ago. Somehow you never quite lose the lingo."

"Were you a pilot in military? You said you flew."

"Yes, as a matter of fact."

"What kind of plane did you fly?"

"Jets. I was a fighter pilot."

"Wasn't it dangerous?"

"I guess so."

"You were in a war then?"

"The Korean one."

"Did you shoot down enemy planes?" she asked languidly from behind closed lids.

"Uh-huh."

"Did you win medals?"

"Yes. What does nudity mean here?"

Marie-Celeste snorted. "The signs are the work of the new mayor, the fool. Everybody's embarrassed about them. He's afraid St. Jean will become like Guadeloupe, where people go naked on beaches."

"But you . . ."

"Nude is bottomless. Topless isn't nude."

"I hope I get used to it. Women don't go topless where I'm from." He added, "Chicago."

"Topless on beaches means trouble in the States. It attracts voyeurs. What a strange country America is."

"Europe seems strange to Americans too," he pointed out.

"You've been there?"

"Once, briefly."

"That's not enough. I love Europe. What is your work? Are you an airline pilot? Those glasses . . ."

"They're left over from the war."

"The *Korean* war? You kept them all these years?"

"Yes," he said, oddly embarrassed.

"I bet you wear old clothes, too." He grunted. "I had a professor as a lover once and *he* always wore old clothes. I think you're a professor also."

"Yes."

"Of what?"

"Of psychology."

"At a university?"

"That's where you usually find professors."

"Is it boring to be a professor?"

"Boring?" Philip had never asked himself that question, though teaching *was* pretty unadventurous. "Not especially. I have patients, too. And I write, or did."

"Oh, what?"

"Well, pieces for scholarly journals." He added, "I have a book coming out."

"What's it called?"

"*The Psychology of New Nations*," he said, sorry suddenly he hadn't picked a livelier title.

The brief interest that had sounded in her voice faded. "It doesn't sound like something I'd read."

"It's not for the general public," Castle said resentfully.

"I bet you wish you *had* written for a big audience. Have you been teaching for a long time?"

"About twenty years."

"Nobody should do anything that long, unless you're an Einstein or a Freud. Are you a Freud?"

The query got to him. That was part of his trouble—the realization (Ellie's departure had caused him to examine everything afresh) that he was never to be a great or inspired psychologist. *The Psychology of New Nations* was carefully done and good enough. It might induce a few at the State Department and elsewhere to be more understanding about the problems of the Third World—to which Castle was sympathetic, or had been: the fire had gone out of him—but the book wouldn't really change anything. He avoided the subject.

"Listen, everything's boring sometimes, isn't it? We all go through periods . . ."

"Not me. I don't believe in boredom. Boredom is waiting for something to happen. I don't wait. I wonder if you've lost enthusiasm. Are you married?"

The question seemed inevitable, Philip had heard it so much the past few months. "Separated." Despite himself he returned his eyes to her breasts and shining lips.

"So that's it. Should I be sorry?"

"If you want."

She wiggled her skinny hips as though digging a hole with her bottom. "I kind of like breaking up. Then I can meet somebody new. Have you met somebody new?"

"Nobody who matters."

"Do you own a plane?"

"No. Too expensive a hobby. Anyway, I haven't flown in years. I . . . don't have time." He sensed a strange displeasure when she showed him the back of her head and was silent. "What do *you* do?" he asked.

"I live. In Paris. This winter I'm a guest here. Last winter I was a model. The one before that I acted some. The winter before . . . I forget," she said over her shoulder.

"You don't work in the summer?"

"Not if I can help it."

"You're lucky."

"Why are you here?"

"I needed a change of scene," he said, trying to seem casual.

"Oh." He feared she was falling asleep because there was nothing left to say. He was probably boring her already. He sat up and looked at the water. Cutlass-billed birds soared overhead. Pelicans. One crashed into the sea for a fish, reminding him of yesterday's accident. Why was she so interested in his having been a pilot? "Where were you born?" he heard her ask in a flat voice.

He hesitated. "A town in southern Arizona. Bisbee."

"How old are you?"

A signal light went on. "Forty-five."

"You look younger. What day were you born?"

Somehow he had felt it coming. Only astrology buffs asked your exact birthday—nobody else cared. He was trying to escape, but the question slammed him back to reality. "When were you born?" Marie-Celeste repeated.

The question rankled. It forced him to think of Ellie and his dead mother who had ignored him for astrology. He was irritated with the girl just as he had started to like her. Just for the hell of it, he lied. Castle's real birthday, March 21, was barely three weeks away, He made himself younger by exactly nine months. "December twenty-first," he told her. It was such a silly fib.

Marie-Celeste's intake of breath was audible. She whipped her head around. "That was somebody else's birthday, too!"

"One out of every three hundred and sixty-five people," he said, watching her carefully.

"Don't joke. I'm talking about the pilot. The one who died."

"It couldn't be true!"

"It is, though. That makes you two astrotwins."

"What a word," he said with disdain. "Well, it's a coincidence."

"Is it? He dies almost the very moment you arrive—that's a coincidence too? You even *look* a little like him. You were in the crowd. Didn't you notice?"

"So what?"

"*So what?* I'm so upset I can hardly speak."

"How well did you know him?"

"Not very. Recently, he began to fly in on business. His *own* business," she said in a tone that precluded questions. "I wish I knew what caused the accident."

"Could he have misjudged the field?"

"Him? He could have landed dead drunk or blindfolded, just about. Maybe he was ill, or it had to do with the plane."

"You said he was warned. Who warned him?"

"I did," she said sadly. "I prepared his horoscope when he was here last week. I told him not to fly that day. Boy, it was only yesterday."

"Well, you can't blame yourself."

"I'm not. I wish he'd listened, that's all. I have to stop talking about this. It makes me nervous."

"Fine with me." The conversation, strangely, made him edgy too.

She began tracing a design in the sand with a long forefinger. "What's that supposed to be?"

"A centaur. Sagittarius is the centaur, with a bow and arrow. You're a centaur."

"A horse's ass with a bow and arrow," he said, trying to be light.

She regarded him solemnly. "You're too hard on yourself. Come on, let's swim."

Marie-Celeste rose abruptly from her towel and loped toward the hard-packed sand on the edge of the gentle surf. He watched her for a moment without moving. Feet apart, she stood for a moment staring out to sea. Then she began to bend from one side to the other, stretching so far down that her hair almost touched the beach. He found her gracefulness strongly pleasurable, though he couldn't help thinking that she performed for his benefit. Why? She hadn't been flirting. She did a few more slow exercises that reminded him of a combination of yoga and classical dance, then turned, face placid, and signaled him to follow.

She raced into the sea, taking bold strokes, and he came gingerly, skin crinkling in anticipation of the first contact with the water. But the temperature was perfect—neither too hot nor too cold. He smacked the Caribbean with his palms, enjoying it, then swam out to her. Long wet tawny hair hung straight down both sides of her slender face. "You look like a lioness with that mane," he said.

A golden-brown eye winked. "Sure I do. I'm a Leo!" She lowered her head, brought her knees to her stomach, and executed a surface dive. Through water with the transparency of glass, he watched her cruise ten feet down among coral flowers.

"I bet you think it's more than a coincidence that I compared you to a lioness and you turn out to be a so-called Leo," he said when she came up. She nodded. "Aren't some things just plain chance?"

"No. At least I don't think so. There are no accidents for believers in astrology."

"I hate astrology, if you must know," he said, treading water.

"Really? How silly of you! Have you ever had your horoscope cast?"

"Me? I'm a scientist. I'm at the opposite pole from a mystic."

"Mystic! People who think something's far-out call it mysticism." Her breasts bobbed in the current. "Astrology's a science, too, the *real* science of personality. It's been neglected, that's all."

"Astrology's a parlor game."

"Why do you dislike it so much?"

"Because . . . because people shouldn't take it *seriously*."

"You're out of your depth, and there are freaky currents here. Let's go in."

"Any sharks?" he called in the same spirit.

"Mostly on land."

They lay silently on their towels for a few minutes. "What time were you born?" she asked.

"In the morning. How'd you get hooked on astrology?"

"A friend. But I'm no expert. You should meet one. Did Joe tell you I was taken?"

Philip nodded. "Who's the happy man? What does he do for a living? Is he married?"

Her eyes fluttered evasively. "He's not married. You're mighty inquisitive—that's a Sag for you." She pronounced it *Saj*. "Sagittarians think they have all the answers." Marie sat up and seemed to study him. "But you don't *look* like a Sag."

"I thought I resembled the dead pilot."

"Facially maybe a little, but that's all. Sag males are often big, beefy guys with muscles and powerful legs. How tall are you?"

"Just under six feet, unless I've shrunk."

"You seem shorter because you stoop. Turn your hands. See! Sag hands are wide and powerful, yours are slender. You have small feet, which isn't right for a Sag, either. Typical Sagittarians have florid complexions; yours is pale."

"I've been in Chicago all winter."

"You have too much hair except for your little bald spot, and not a bit of it's gray. Sags tend to get gray. And your face . . . it's too narrow for a Sag. The forehead's too high. Your eyes are hazel—they ought to be dark. Sagittarian men have full lips and huge teeth—you don't. You don't have enough body hair for a Sagittarian. You'll get a burn. Roll over."

Supple hands smoothed an ecstasy of coconut-smelling lotion onto his back. "I don't seem to be running true to form."

"You flew planes, didn't you? The Sagittarian arrow is a symbol of flying."

"That's all it's a symbol of?" He could feel himself pressing into the sand.

"Sag males can be Don Juans, but don't get any ideas."

"Suppose I do?"

"Don't."

"Am I too old for you?"

"Age doesn't mean anything to me. Anyway, you aren't old."

"But you don't find me attractive."

"You mean *you* don't find you attractive. You'd probably be quite attractive if you had a better opinion of yourself," she lectured from above. "You're kind of good-looking in an oddball way. And I like your mind. You have the mind of an Aries. There must be a strong Aries in the picture somewhere."

"An Aries," he scoffed, remembering he was an Aries. "Do you like Sagittarians?"

"Sagittarians and Leos don't usually get along so well. They're both fire signs and born free, so they compete. They can quarrel constantly. There's no real victor because neither's a cardinal sign."

"What are the cardinal signs?" he asked innocently.

"Aries, Cancer, Libra, and Capricorn."

"They're better?"

"The cardinal signs are born to lead, which doesn't mean a Leo can't stand up to an Aries, say. But Arians, hard-driving as they are, are generous, while a Sag tries to run all over a Leonine woman. He's not sensitive. He forgets how proud she is. She's royalty, after all. The Sag always tries to be the lion-tamer. He ignores the fact that Leo's a fixed sign—his is mutable. And he's too pushy sexually. Forget about trying to go to bed with me."

It was maddening to hear her talk that way and yet feel her knead lotion onto his skin. "You like Aries men, I guess."

"Aries are winners, above all. My companion's an Aries."

"How does that work out?" he said with a sigh.

"Between an Aries man and a Leo woman? They're both dynamic, exciting. She has enough dignity to keep him in control, and he likes to make a queen of her. She wants to be appreciated."

"I'd appreciate you," he said a little wistfully.

"Not like he does. When he's not too busy, anyway."

"Ha! So he ignores you!" He thought of how Ellie had accused him of the same thing. "I'll put a Sagittarian arrow through him."

"You Sagittarians, always clowning around. He's nobody to mess with," she advised. "He'd break you like a croissant. *Have* you broken, I should say."

"Oh? He doesn't like to dirty his hands?"

"He likes them clean."

"Where is this man?"

"Away on business. Tell me the truth. How good a pilot were you?"

He wished she would lower her breasts to his back. "Pretty good," he murmured.

"But you *could* fly again, couldn't you? It must be like driving a car. You never forget how."

"It's not so simple as driving a car, but I could fly again, yes."

"Maybe you should. It's in your sign."

"I don't want to fly anymore." He watched a crab scuttle down the beach.

5

Evasive, shifty, hard to pin down, he avoided close contact because he was vulnerable despite the armor he wore. He pretended to be bold and tough, but if the odds were not in his favor he would run. He was quick to take offense and slow to give praise. He never forgot a slight. Hostility permeated his wisecracks and innuendos. Women liked him because they sensed something fragile under his brittle shell, but he was durable, too, clawing back from defeats. Inventive, resourceful, he bubbled with ideas. His ethics consisted of a single credo: help thyself. He was the Eight of Diamonds—fated to be rich.

He might have been an empire builder, in some other time. He could easily have been a court jester, too. And he might have been murdered.

He was born in New York City on July 7, 1946, at 10:03 P.M. (His Las Vegas listeners automatically calculated his ascendant to be Pisces in Cancer.) No one could account for his delinquent traits—each parent blamed the genes of the other, but wasn't he utterly unlike his siblings? At five he was stealing candy and comic books before graduating to portable radios and money. He liked to trip old people on the street by

53

shoving sticks between their legs. Quick with his fingers, he was a precocious cheat at cards. Maybe if he'd been religious . . . But he wasn't. He hadn't been inside a synagogue since he was ten, when he had a fight with his mother about going to church. She was a domineering, demanding woman who tried to control the boy by withdrawing affection and even food. The more she punished, the worse he got. He became incorrigible, or very nearly, yet was clever enough to stay out of reform school.

Unable to secure or buy a deferment, he was drafted and sent to Vietnam, which probably saved him from prison. Because of his quarrelsome nature, his furtive efforts to avoid combat, his reputation as a soldier who raped village girls, he had few friends in the company, but, in the case of one, he chose well. His buddy was the son of a high-ranking Midwestern union official who ran its pension fund. The contact sounded promising and it was the sole reason he risked his life to drag his wounded friend to safety. Wounded himself, in the foot, he possessed a due card which at the right time he would present. He calculated everything.

That was in 1968. The soldier in the next hospital bed lent him books on a fascinating topic. A born gambler, he saw in this system a way to increase the odds favoring him. A hoarder, he saved everything he could find on the subject.

After his discharge he had changed his name—he'd always wanted one that sounded classier, and the name he chose fitted the ideas he'd learned in the hospital. In 1969 he moved to Florida and soon learned whom to hang out with. His connections led to a job with a group said to be controlled by Meyer Lansky. His function was to escort junkets for big Miami gamblers to Las Vegas. The casinos kicked back ten percent of the gamblers' losses to the organizers of the junkets. He knew, because he carried the bag to Florida from Vegas, wisely delivering every penny. The bag also contained IOU's which the gamblers, for a discount, paid in Miami, so that the money was never recorded on casino records. Many millions of taxable dollars were skimmed from Vegas in this way before the federal government cracked down, not very effectively.

Vegas was the place for him. Through the organization he got a job as assistant manager of a casino there. One of his duties was to stand guard at the count room early in the morning when management skimmed the take. Things were relatively straightforward in Vegas then.

His Nam pal showed up at the casino by invitation. They talked. "Listen," he said in his staccato fashion, "Vegas is going to boom. I don't care about the fucking recession here—it'll pass. This country *wants* to gamble and nothing will stop it, but the goddamn banks and insurance companies won't go near Las Vegas. Jerks! They think there's something wrong with gambling, or with us. The loot has to come from someplace else. I want to show you a building lot not far away. There's jerks here too, even the blackhats. This lot's supposed to be the wrong size and too small. It's long and narrow, just right for a casino. I want to build a hunnerd-fifty-room hotel over it—the minimum for the Strip. Are—and will be more—great big hotels around it. Bring in the business—it'll be like free advertising. The land is cheap, for this town anyhow. And inflation's coming. The time to build is *now*. If your old man's union would lend the dough . . ."

His Vietnam friend, who worked for his father managing the pension fund, was impressed. The father, aware of his debt to the son's friend, also thought the proposal made sense. And the veteran had no criminal record and therefore no impediment to licensing. But the young man was inexperienced, the union man concluded after meeting him, and maybe a little whacked up. Something about the eyes. The official would go along with the deal provided there were silent partners the union would select. The vet figured he was being used as a front, but what could he do? Plenty.

He began with kickbacks from the contractors building the hotel. That was standard in Vegas. When the casino was in operation, he started to skim. The first ones were too hazardous, he saw later, and would not repeat them.

Getting the cooperation of a few employees wasn't difficult—they were scared of being fired and were given a small piece of the take. The other man in the count room looked the other way when he wrote out an extra fill slip authorizing chips to be sent to a table and walked off with the chips, cashing them in through an associate and destroying the slip. That brought him $20,000. The hotel had a legitimate race wire; it was easy to past-post the race book and bet on ones that had already been run.

Every Las Vegas casino has an eye in the sky—one-way mirrors in the ceiling that look from the tables like mirrors or black glass. He constantly prowled the catwalk above them to make sure his dealers didn't cheat, except when he instructed. He watched his baccarat skim from the eye. For this game the casino gave big gamblers special buttonlike chips. Each button was worth one thousand dollars. A particular player, his accomplice, had markers for $30,000, of which $15,000 was in buttons. The dealers knew how to palm. During play the dealer palmed ten buttons. The markers were subsequently changed to $20,000, which was repaid. $5,000 in buttons, $15,000 in cash. Minus a cut, the missing $10,000 went to the man in the eye. The scheme was repeated many nights. Agents of the Las Vegas Gaming Control Commission, spying constantly, never spotted it.

He was pleased to have pulled off what he claimed was the first big-time slot-machine skim in Vegas history. He solved the traditional problem of how to get stolen coins out the door by simply eliminating that step. When emptied from the machines, the coins went to the count room and were weighed according to denominations—silver dollars, fifty-cent pieces, and so forth. The scale showed precisely how much value the coins had, so he fixed the scale to show less weight than there actually was.

Suppose, he explained to his new friends in the private dining room, a certain number of pounds equaled $100 in silver dollars. All silver dollars in excess of that weight were placed at the rear of the cart. The $100 worth of silver dollars went to the cashier, to be dispensed. The excess coins were placed in an auxiliary bank behind the cashier's booth. When the cashier needed more coins, they were supplied from the auxiliary bank, which employees assumed was part of the casino's normal operation. The cashier paid for the coins with envelopes of dollars, which were placed in a slot in the auxiliary bank. An accomplice periodically opened the locked drawer below the slot and removed the envelopes. For more than a year this scam took in $10,000 a day.

The signs told him it was time to stop. The next evening the Gaming Control agents arrived and searched the auxiliary bank, finding it bare.

The cancer-specialist hoax was pure genius on his part, he boasted. He knew his heavy-betting clients. The eminent East Coast doctor was in over his head when the Vietnam vet made a proposal. He would

destroy the doctor's markers—IOU's—if the man would provide names
and information on all prosperous cancer victims he treated. They had to
be terminal but still ambulatory. It was important for them to be on their
feet so that they wouldn't have been in a hospital if anybody checked
later on.

The doctor provided information about wealthy patients from various
cities, and people pretending to be these people arrived at the casino.
Having the proper identification and good credit ratings, the impostors
were given markers—for $100,000, say—and would duly lose some of
the money before cashing in. The markers would thus be reduced. But
they weren't repaid in full. He took the money instead, while the casino
kept the markers. When the patients died, the doctor informed him, and
he wrote off the markers as uncollectable because they were gambling
debts. This scheme earned for him more than a million dollars. He quit
when the omens told him to.

By then he had a wife and two children whom he never saw and
supported as skimpily as possible. He didn't like to spend except on
himself. He had a $70,000 car, a large collection of male jewelry, a
racehorse, and a bundle of cash.

There was an employee who threatened to squeal unless he was cut in
big. The man was found in bed the next morning with his chest crushed
in. *Crushed.* The Vegas police never learned what happened. (It had
been done with a sledgehammer, on his orders.)

His partners never caught on to his various tricks. A casino expects to
lose about four percent of the take in bad debts, since big gamblers
typically carry no cash, play with markers and sometimes don't pay up.
But he could tighten credit procedures and—though risking the wrath of
some steady customers—reduce the loss to two and one half percent, the
difference being enough to cover the skims. The overall gross wasn't
affected, since his partners kept the splurgers walking through the door.

One big spender was a rancher from Texas. The owner knew the man
would arrive in advance—he always knew, through the grapevine, when
drug dealers, sheikhs, Japanese exporters, and other ready dispensers of
money were due. He had a special room where the minimum bet, $100
or $500, was sufficient to discourage little folk. The numbers, on which
he relied, promised a spectacular night.

That afternoon the Texan had visitors, a tall girl with big breasts who told him he was a pansy and wouldn't withdraw the charge until he proved himself repeatedly; two girls of not more than nineteen who restored his ardor by giving him a show and then dared him to satisfy them both. Yippee! What a day! The Texan had never had anything like it. A bottle of Scotch, dinner, and wine arrived. Arm in arm, the three showed up at eleven, right on schedule, in the semiprivate room where the hotel men waited.

By midnight, Scotches later, the Texan was down $900,000 at roulette, a large but not extraordinary loss. The owner planned to make it one. The strange eyes glittered. He offered the rancher double or nothing. The broad-shouldered Texan had always thrived on dares. He bet red. The wheel turned, the ball skittered . . .

Although the owner foresaw he would win, he had nothing to lose if he didn't. The Texan would be even, ahead if you counted the girls and the dinner, but those were minor concerns.

. . . black, natch.

The next day, in the owner's office, the Texan confessed to an inability to produce readily almost two million dollars. But he owned a yacht, registered and moored in Panama, easily worth the money. As a tax dodge it had already paid for itself, and he never used it.

The veteran told the three new friends he'd met at the bridge tournament at the hotel about the yacht he had just won. The boat could be used to entertain stars who appeared at the hotel, to impress important gamblers. The eldest demurred. Why should the veteran tell his partners (or the IRS) about the yacht? It could be owned by a dummy corporation to circumvent taxes on it, and it might be useful. The rich Texan? The man must be impressed with the importance of keeping his mouth shut; if he didn't, he'd regret it as long as he lived, which wouldn't be long. The tall one nodded agreement, and so did the female, who was among the most beautiful women the Vietnam vet had ever seen, though a little old for him.

They arrived at a not-very-original name for the yacht—*Zodiac*. The new owner's name was Canfield Koster.

6

Philip Castle spent a haphazard afternoon buying a few groceries, a little liquor (not much: he planned to leave soon), and film for his camera. But whose picture would he take? And who would take his camera. But whose picture would he take? And who would take his? He sent a postcard to his son in Oregon. "Dear David," Castle wrote in large printed letters. "It's great down here. Wish you could see it. I'm fine. Hope you are, too. Love, Dad." It was all he could think of to say.

Sansa had come and gone by the time he returned. He drove to the beach below his house and ran on the edge of the surf to the airstrip and back—only a mile all told, but it winded him. He read more of the mystery story and took the book with him to a restaurant. Service on the island was painfully slow, the Wallers had said, but he, who had nothing whatever to do, got lickety-split treatment. Probably they wanted the table for more than a party of one, though he wasn't exactly having a party.

Over coffee he debated visiting Le Boucan again, but decided not. Marie-Celeste had firmly refused to dine with him, but he had a hunch, he didn't know why, that she might show up. She knew where he lived.

On the terrace under the stars, holding a Cointreau, he resumed the soliloquy of the night before. *Why* had he lost a wife of nearly twenty years? *Had* he been too passive, reined-in, throughout their marriage? She had told him before he was afraid to express himself strongly, and he *was* afraid of what might happen if he let his demons out. As with Zoltmann. . . .

Philip Castle hadn't smoked in years, ever since his son told him it wasn't fair because Philip would die young. He'd spotted a couple of filtered cigarettes in a crushed box inside the house, and he brought one back along with the matches and an ice cube to dilute the liqueur. He lit the cigarette, sipping the liquid to cool his throat. The smoke made him feel light-headed. Or was it the vacant expanse of night in which he seemed to drift?

The reels of his mind turned again. Yes, he'd gone a little crazy in his bitterness. Poor Zoltmann!

It was an early Friday evening. He'd had too many drinks at a bar—he had never frequented bars before. Acting on impulse, he'd looked up "Zoltmann, Frederick," under "Astrologers" in the Yellow Pages and gone there. It was close by. Zoltmann had a small shop specializing in occult materials—books, charts, posters, cards, cabalistic notions. A discreet sign in the window invited "Consultations." Finding the door locked, Philip rapped. A small, plump, middle-aged man with thick eyeglasses and pale skin finally peered out, and evidently satisfied with Castle's business suit, opened the door, though almost grudgingly.

"Yes?"

"Mr. Zoltmann?"

"Yes."

"May I come in?" He was surprised he had to make an effort not to slur.

"There is something you want?"

"Book."

Zoltmann inspected him uncertainly. "Come in, then. What book are you looking for?"

"A basic introduction to . . ." Castle stepped inside, trying not to lurch. Zoltmann locked the door behind him.

"You said . . ."

Philip wasn't at all sure what he wanted to say. If he'd known, he'd forgotten. Maybe he only wanted to set eyes on the man who, in his drunkenness, he held fully responsible for the breakup of his home. He should speak reasonably, inquire if Ellie still came for consultations, and if so, plead with Frederick Zoltmann, *bribe him*, to advise her to return. He still wanted her back, desperately, or he wouldn't have been there. He'd told her that on the phone, getting only silence as a response. Maybe he should . . .

"Yes?" Zoltmann asked impatiently.

"Zoltmann, you've done great harm."

They were out of sight of the street, alone. "Harm?" asked the meek man.

"You remember that you, how do you say it . . . *cast* a horoscope for Eleanor Castle? You told her it was in her best interest to leave her husband—well, I am her husband."

"Ellie? Anything exchanged between her and myself is strictly confidential."

"Confidential! What do you think you are, a goddamn licensed physician?"

"Don't become agitated, Mr. Castle. Please leave." The astrologer had moved toward the door.

"Where do you get off handing out advice? And charging for it! You've messed up my life, you little bastard. You . . . you even feel up your female clients. Fuck them, for all I know."

"I will call the police," screamed Zoltmann, becoming pink.

As he turned, Castle grabbed his shoulder roughly. Zoltmann was trembling. "I'd like to . . ."

"You are out of control, Mr. Castle. Please, get hold of yourself. You are drunk," Zoltmann quavered.

Castle was trembling too. He wanted to spread the smug astrologer's features across his face. He pulled up his fist, grabbing Zoltmann's shoulder with the other hand, and then he visualized the bloody fingers when, as a kid in Arizona, he had smashed the Indian boy's face, shocking himself with his violence, and he remembered Korea, when again he had given way to total rage. *No! Don't do it! Restrain yourself!* His arm ached from the effort of holding it back. He dropped it and used words. "You fucking quack. You take advantage of mixed-up people like Ellie with your asshole astrology. Listen, she believed you when you told her it was a propish . . . good time to make a move. Next time, you better be more sparing with your stupid advice or somebody'll knock your teeth in. You deserve a dentist."

With that he departed. Zoltmann locked the door behind him, shaking his head so that Castle would be sure to see the gesture. Philip felt good at first, as if purged, but a reaction soon set in, especially after Ellie called from Richard's as soon as he got home and told him that, but for her, Zoltmann would have had him arrested.

"You can't be arrested for calling somebody a quack." Philip had sobered up.

"He is *not* a quack. And you threatened him. He will definitely call the police if you approach him again. Phil . . ." He detected an odd admiration in her voice, ridiculous as his behavior had been. "You can't really believe this has happened because of Zoltmann. I mean, well, I told you I needed something else."

"You don't have to repeat."

"If only you had . . . Listen, this is more talking than I wanted to have between us. I think you ought to see a shrink, like you wanted *me* to."

"Maybe I'll try an astrologer," he said wearily.

Zoltmann was the first step toward St. Jean. Philip had leveled with a fellow psychologist about his drinking, despondency, aimlessness, vague notions of suicide. The other psychologist thought that an infantile streak had been bared by trauma. Philip was furious at being abandoned, as a child might be; depression was a sign of anger. Maybe, over the years, Philip hadn't permitted himself enough outlets, hidden his feelings, failed to assert himself with women. Pressure had been building up as it might along a geological fault. There could be an episode—by which the psychologist meant a breakdown. He advised, since Philip refused to go back into therapy, a complete change, no matter how brief.

His friends the Wallers reached the same conclusion independently. They'd never seen Philip like this. They hadn't rented their Caribbean house for March yet, and Jo Waller said she'd never speak to him again if he didn't use it. They wouldn't take a nickel. He was touched—he'd almost forgotten people cared for him. Even so, he stalled, trapped in the coils of inertia. But the prospect of breakdown terrified him, especially when he remembered his history and his sister's—she'd been in and out of mental institutions for years. *Go! Don't. Go! Don't!*

In the end he surrendered to fate. If the next bird that passed overhead flew east, he'd make the trip. (He was, he realized, loading the odds against his departure.) The bird flew east. He'd taken a month's leave of absence, and here he was, miserable in paradise.

Tired of his inner wranglings, he was about to put an end to them with bed, early as it was, when a car roared up the drive. It had to be Marie-Celeste; he had been right. She'd come. But why?

7

It had been she (she claimed), who ordered what came to be known as the Massacre of St. Bartholomew because it began, in Paris, on St. Bartholomew's Day, August 24, 1572.

She persuaded the king to authorize the killings—she suspected Huguenot leaders of conspiring to draw France into war with Spain. Before the bloodbath was over, some fifty thousand French Huguenots perished.

A comet that appeared in the skies of France terrified this same woman who engineered the atrocity without remorse. The comet, they said, was a demon that presaged the death of a queen.

On a late November night she, a middle-aged woman in a heavy coat, mounted the winding steps of a scarred tower in Provence where an old man waited in the turret. He traced a magic circle on the floor, seated her inside it, put before her a disk of polished metal on which reflections shone. On the disk appeared the figure of a crowned male, succeeded by three other crowned males, all four seeming to move around the disk. Was it done by the "science of mirrors," popular then, or did the pudgy woman imagine the event? No one outside the room would ever know, but the apparitions proved to her, at least, that she would live during the reigns of three successive kings, her sons. The fourth king, their cousin, would come to the throne after her death. And it came to pass.

Later, the old man would predict when and how her husband, the king, would die—from a lance, which seemed impossible, since the king of France never dueled. But, playing a ceremonial role at a tourney, the king was accidentally speared in the eye and died, fulfilling the prophecy.

She was Catherine de Médicis, queen regent of France. The sorcerer was known as Nostradamus.

In other lives she might have been a poet, given her love of balance and form. And yet her complex personality was in conflict. Wanting peace, she could be sullen, petty, mean. She desired proportion, yet mired herself in trivialities. Highly skilled at logic, she let emotion interfere with judgment. Boldly erotic, she was inhibited in her core, even with partners of her own sex. She believed firmly in honesty—for others. She was awash with contradictions, but not about the major theme of this life. She was determined to be rich. She was a wheeler-dealer, the Ten of Clubs.

She was born at 8:23 P.M. (Eastern War Time) on October 12, 1943, in Brookline, Massachusetts. Her well-off parents were socially prominent. Her father, a corporate executive, doted on the girl, but, fearing his wife (and his lust for his daughter), confined his attentions to tutoring. To get the daughter out of the house, her mother sent her to boarding school.

Nobody knew that she stole—first, books from the school, then clothes from stores. She had a compulsion to do it. She took herself to a psychiatrist who told her that the prevalence of kleptomania among women could be explained by penis envy. The stolen object was symbolic of the penis, and she took it in revenge because she didn't have one. It gave her a sexual thrill. She probably had an unconscious desire to be caught—to appease her guilt. She resolved never to shoplift again.

She graduated *summa cum laude* from college, using her logic and total recall when she did not understand a subject. (She'd gotten an A in high school trig by memorizing whole textbooks rote. She never learned to use a slide rule.) She thought she might become a scientist, but she couldn't make money in research or eduction. She went into a training program, deciding to become a business executive.

In 1968, fate took over, as she saw it. For her it was a typical lapse.

She slept with a man she hardly liked and whose name she couldn't remember not much later, yet neglected to use her diaphragm. She *knew* instantly that she was pregnant. Distrustful, fearful of her father's response, she asked no help. Alone, she arranged for an abortion without checking the abortionist's reputation. It was a bad job, resulting in an infection and interior bleeding. She was lucky to get off with a hysterectomy. She might easily have died.

During a long recuperation in her New York apartment she reached decisions. She didn't want to get married: having a child would have been the only point. Progress through corporate ranks would be too slow for a woman, even one gifted and glamorous as she. She determined, therefore, to become expert in a field that could be expected to grow. The selection was almost automatic, given her logical abilities: computers.

When she had been a girl her parents flirted with a special subject, even choosing her first name because of how it could be shortened, but had lost interest long since. She had a friend who owned a bookstore, and during her convalescence ordered a number of volumes to see what it was all about. She mastered the discipline easily, and reached the astonishing conclusion that she had been destined for crime.

Computers and crime—a brilliant combination. Before long *everything* would be run by computers, but nobody would understand the machines except specialists. She would be one. She returned to school, with her father's help, and after two years of diligent study became a qualified expert in computer programming. After a few jobs, she went out on her own as a consultant, charging $600 a day.

She cultivated a social life, entertained a great deal in her Park Avenue apartment. She knew many people through her parents and constantly enlarged her circle. A woman's magazine wrote her up as a "gal to watch," but the reporter failed to ask for her guest lists. The names were almost entirely male (wives or girlfriends were not recorded). Mostly they came from the upper echelons of big business, with a few gangland figures thrown in. She would sleep with these male friends if it seemed advantageous.

What she planned to do was impossible if you didn't know the tricks, almost easy if you did. Business executives were intimidated by computers, fascinated by the endless columns of data that could be ordered at will, convinced that errors were impossible. For them, tinkering with the gadgets was out of the question. Ignorant, they didn't realize that errors could be *caused*, and all traces of malfeasance could be erased from the reels. If a scam was to be discovered, it would have to be elsewhere than the computer room.

The computer lady was beyond suspicion, since she had been hired precisely to improve or correct a system. She could work totally out in the open, since nobody kept watch over her or would comprehend her activities if they happened to glance at the terminal where she punched keys, producing information on the screen. It was as though she read a book. She would look for the table of contents, then inspect the various chapters to see what was written there, learning what exploitable knowledge the machine might have.

Her first caper was merely a foray. On a consulting job for a large publisher, she noticed an order from the bookstore whose owner was her friend. It called for two copies of an expensive art book. On the morning the order was to be processed, she entered the master file, coded under "maintenance," and changed the order to twenty by adding a zero. By afternoon the computer had printed the orders, the twenty art books among them. Before 6:30 P.M., when a permanent record was made of the day's activity, she returned to the file and removed the extra zero. The books arrived—twenty copies for the price of two. It worked. The owner treated her to a fine dinner.

She began in earnest. Stealing money outright didn't seem sensible—too many controls existed for her, say, to issue checks via the computer under a bogus name. It was too risky. Better opportunities lay with companies that produced or handled valuable merchandise in quantities so big that thefts would not be easily or quickly detected. The objects had to have street value and be easily disposed of.

She would coolly analyze various items in terms of sales potential, then wheedle a consulting job, through her circle of contacts, in the proper place. Many women would have found a certain large wholesaler too dull: not her. She laughed at his jokes, awarded him one unforgettable night in bed, and was given the job of improving his computers. He handled cigarettes. A forty-foot trailer, loaded in Winston-Salem, held 500 cases of cigarettes, sixty cartons per case, for a total of—$30,000 cartons of mixed brands. The manufacturer's value was $75–100,000; street value, almost $200,000. How to heist the truckload? Nothing so strenuous as armed robbery. With ease, through her gangland connections, she learned about an abandoned warehouse in Hoboken, New Jersey. On the day the computer showed a truckload of cigarettes was due to leave Winston-Salem for New York, she penetrated the machine and changed the destination to Hoboken. At the cigarette company in Winston, the same order came through a computer terminal, and becoming a bill of lading, went to the loading docks. When the truck was en route, she restored the original destination on the computer records. Following instructions, the driver went to the Hoboken warehouse, where the cigarettes were peacefully unloaded by confederates.

When the truck failed to arrive in New York, its destination was checked—an empty warehouse. The cigarettes had vanished without a trace. The police weren't told of the crime—it was damaging to reputations, and would never be solved because there was no means to locate the perpetrator, evidently an employee. Her share was $75,000, not bad for tapping a few keys.

Another job found her in the Eastern computer room of a company that manufactured, in the Midwest, truck-type tractors, otherwise known as bulldozers. These struck her as salable merchandise. She located an accomplice in Amarillo who formed a company and ordered one bulldozer, which he paid for and sold. He ordered another, and this time she intervened, adding two zeros to the one inside the machine. A hundred bulldozers were delivered and sold all over the state. Serial numbers filed off, they couldn't be traced. The dummy firm that ordered them had gone out of business when the manufacturer investigated. Her share: two hundred grand.

Since, as a consultant, she might work for a particular company a day or two a week and had several clients at any one time, she had a certain latitude of choice. A job might last for months, so there was no need to hurry. She never moved unless the portents were absolutely right. She violated that precept once, when she tried to steal a 707 deadheading after a big storm to another airport. With a computer, she rerouted it to a faraway airport where a phony crew, hastily uniformed and assembled, would be authorized to fly it to Africa. She was sure a particular general would buy it cheap—negotiations were already under way. The "mistake" was discovered before the 707 left the United States. No one was held responsible, though she blamed herself, hating failure.

The signs were excellent for the Exxon job, a bold one, conducted at its refinery in Bayway, New Jersey. According to the computer, the barge belonged to a regular customer and the order had been processed. It pulled up and sailed away loaded with thousands of tons of gasoline. So far as she could find out—consulting for the company, she had to be discreet—Exxon never acknowledged the theft. The beauty of computer crime was that victims usually kept quiet.

The public-relations department of Gulf Oil insisted on silence when, as if by prestidigitation, hundreds of thousands of dollars in petroleum products vanished from its refinery in Puerto Rico. The SEC *did* discover that a Chicago manufacturer of medical instruments had inflated its stock by juggling the inventories on computer records, but she, who perpetrated the deal for management, was not connected with the crime. East-West Freight Lines, a common carrier, failed to publicize that somebody, using a telephone tie-in, successfully diverted a trailer filled with goods, including cartons of watches, en route from Mexico. Low-priced units, they were that much easier to sell; so were seasonal items—toys at Christmas, air conditioners in the summer; small stuff was worthwhile, though she did filch a medium-sized computer from IBM worth several hundred thousand dollars, and was very proud of it. She sold it to the mob, which was just beginning to explore the possibilities of tying into banks for valuable information. . . . A major railroad never confessed that three boxcars filled with Japanese TV sets arrived on the siding of a feeder line, no more than ten miles long, in the Midwest, and were empty when reclaimed. She'd penetrated the "train consist" file. . . .

By 1976, having amassed a fortune, she remained insatiable. What had she done with the money? the elegant, older gentleman inquired in Vegas. Jewels, rare antiques, paintings, gold. She had piles of cash sequestered in safe-deposit boxes under pseudonyms. She needed the services of a friendly offshore banker, said he with a smile. *He* needed a minicomputer for his Caribbean villa, she suggested back. She was about to lift a dozen of them from Wang.

"No, no," he demurred in his thick French accent. "I already have a computer in my bank. But our companion here, he might be able to use one on the yacht he just acquired."

She turned to the hotel man, who leered at her with his strange eyes. "Wouldn't you like a Wang on board? It's a marvelous, compact instrument. I could devise an occult program for you."

"You come with the computer?" he asked.

"It's for sale, not me," she said with a brilliant smile. "But since we have become such close friends, you can have the equipment cheap." She named a figure.

"Tell you what. Double or nothing."

"My dear man, I *never* gamble. I don't have the right signs," said Elizabeth Harris.

8

Tawny hair flowing free, Marie-Celeste burst in the doorway wearing a loose-fitting T-shirt with "St. Jean" printed across the front, a gold bracelet, and short shorts. Her feet were bare. She carried a plastic case.

"*Bon soir.*"

"Hello." He tried to keep his enthusiasm for her visit under control. "I was about to turn in."

"Already? I would have woken you. I *must* know the hour of your birth. You said only that you were born in the morning."

"Astrology again! You would have gotten me up for *that!* I can see giving you my bedtime but . . ."

"I assumed you were born around seven. That's a popular hour. Was I right?'

"As it happens."

"I *am* intuitive, aren't I? Thank God. If I'd been wrong, I would have to do it over. What was the exact time? Do you remember?"

"I'm not sure. Why?" he asked, afraid he knew the answer.

"I've prepared your horoscope." On the coffee table she spread out sheets of paper and four small volumes with battered covers. "I guess the precise minute doesn't matter for now. I can rectify your chart later on if necessary."

"Necessary to whom?"

Her eyes blinked rapidly. "Why, to you! Don't you want to know about yourself?"

"All right, all right. What's 'rectify'?"

"To trace back to the precise moment of birth by comparing your horoscope with major events in your life."

"Come on!"

"No, really! But to rectify a horoscope you have to have one. First you—"

"Do I *have* to listen to this?"

"Absolutely. First you use an ephemeris—*this* is an ephemeris— which tells you what was where in the solar system at a particular time. Then you can find the sidereal Greenwich Mean Time at noon of·the birthday—*sidereal* time is measured by the stars, not the sun, like ordinary time; there's a slight discrepancy. When you've got the ST and the longitude of birth, you *add* the right number of hours and minutes for births after noon or *subtract* them both for births before noon, and when you've done that, you calculate the exact positions of the sun, moon, and planets in ecliptic longitude and declination. And when you have the latitude of birth, you look at the table of houses—*this*—and starting from the mid-heaven corresponding to your local sidereal time, you find what degree of the zodiac was rising on the eastern horizon, which is called the ascendant. You put it on the chart, along with the descendant, mid-heaven, *imum coeli*, cusps of houses, positions of sun, moon, and planets, and you're all set to interpret the horoscope, though I may have left out a few steps. Simple, isn't it?"

Pure gibberish, he was thinking while he looked at her. The hairs on her arms were reddish gold. Attached to the bracelet, he saw, were gold charms studded with rubies. He touched one, shaped "♈." "What are those?" he asked, though he knew.

"The twelve signs of the zodiac, of course. The hieroglyph you're holding stands for Aries. See the ram's horns?"

"A present from your pal?"

"Yes. Isn't the bracelet darling?"

"Expensive, too, I bet."

"Sure. Now, interpreting the horoscope is the hard part. I mean, it takes *skill*."

He solemnly inspected her paraphernalia. The effort she must have expended learning that stuff would have gotten her through a course in graduate school. He wished she'd been his student. "So what did you find out?"

"Let's see. You were born at approximately seven A.M. December 21 in a small town in southern Arizona." Marie-Celeste opened a sheet of paper on which was a circle cut into twelve wedges, like a pie. Inside the wedges she had drawn, in different colors, were a variety of symbols. "This is your horoscope. You have Sagittarius rising. You're a double Sag because you have both the sun and the ascendant there, you know."

"I didn't," Philip said.

"It's unusual! Sags are often daring and fearless, but a double Sag is really brave. Your chart clearly shows your ability to fly an airplane, and your Mars is in Scorpio, meaning a warrior. It's no accident you were a fighter pilot during a war."

"You forget one little detail. There had to be a war for me to fight in."

"The war was probably inevitable," she said uncertainly.

"Did the stars arrange the Korean war just for me?"

She flushed. "I didn't mean that. I meant . . . well, things happen of a piece . . . everything's related to everything else. It's hard to explain . . . I wish I had help. . . ." Her finger traced a nonexistent line across the chart. "Weren't you awfully young for the Korean war? It seems so far back."

"It *was* far back, and I *was* young. I enlisted when I was just out of high school."

"Did you do dangerous things *before* the war?"

"Well, I played chicken a few times. That was really stupid—one of my friends got killed. I drove in stock-car races. . . ."

"*You?*"

"*Yes, me,* dammit," he said, raising his voice. "I barnstormed too, if you want to know."

"Barnstormed?"

"I flew in exhibitions on Sundays around the state. Stunt flying."

"How did you get into that?"

"How did I get into flying? Well . . ." He shifted uncomfortably. "We were pretty tough kids. Couple of guys I knew ended in jail, one for murder. I wasn't that bad, but just the same I was a ringleader. And we all stole from little shops. I wasn't much of a student until later on, you understand. I suppose I was trying to prove myself. Prove I wasn't chickenshit. That was the worst thing you could call somebody in Bisbee—chickenshit."

Marie-Celeste smiled tolerantly. "You sound like savages."

"We weren't nice. Well, there was an Indian kid—I remember his name even now: Eulalio—who hit some smaller kid on the back of the head with a basketball. I don't even know if Eulalio meant to. Anyway, I was the one who told Eulalio I'd meet him after school. He was alone and tried to sneak away, and I tackled him. My bunch stood there and cheered and Eulalio tried to fight. He looked tough but he wasn't. I kept pounding him until my hands were red to the wrists." He could see them through a curtain of decades. "I'll never forget it. It makes me sick even now. I always wondered what happened to Eulalio; he never returned to school. I hope I didn't hurt him seriously."

"I'm sure he survived," she said. "What did the fight have to do with flying?"

"Well, my temper frightened me. I was out of control and I didn't like that, you see."

"You're plenty self-controlled, if you ask me."

He ignored that remark—it had the earmarks of an insult. "And I began to wonder where I was heading. I took up with planes as a way out. There was a little airport, and the owner let me push planes around—polish, gas, and grease them. He liked me, I guess. I don't usually talk this much about myself."

"Go on."

"Well, the guy had an old Stearman used for cropdusting, and he gave me flying lessons instead of cash. I got pretty good. At seventeen I had enough hours for a license to pilot a small plane. I buzzed the countryside, drove people crazy, did aerobatics."

"Did you ever have an accident?" she asked with excitement.

"Couple of close shaves was all."

"Were you almost killed?"

"Not then." The question startled him: he remembered the row of ambulances covered with crosses lined up by the runway as his F-86 Sabrejet came in with holes in the wings, cockpit smoking, landing gear crippled. He shuddered inside. "I'd just as soon not go into it."

"You must!"

"Must I? Oh, well, all right." He moved her astrological wheel with his finger. "I enlisted in the Air Force, trained at Willy . . ."

"Willy?"

"Williams Air Force Base of the Tactical Air Command, near Phoenix. I thought I'd never master the cockpit of an F-86 Sabre. I didn't think I had what it took to be an ace—aggressiveness, consummate skill, cunning, they said."

"I wouldn't think so either," she remarked blandly.

"But I did! They sent me to K-2, a field near Pusan. My job was to fly cover for the B-26's patrolling the Eighteenth Parallel to stop MIGs from coming down. I was a 'hot' pilot. I had three kills. It takes five to be an ace."

"Really!" She was plainly impressed. He warned himself not to sound like an old fogy telling yarns from a couple of wars back, but she wanted to know and he hadn't talked of it for a long time.

"I didn't want to fly that last mission—I was pooped and about to be sent to Japan for R and R. Rest and Rehabilitation. I wanted it to be a piece of cake, but it wasn't. The squadron, four planes, got jumped by twelve MIG-15's. We didn't have a chance. I broke off to the right with the element leader—"

"Don't worry. I won't ask what that is."

"—leaving the flight leader and his wingman. I engaged and blew up a MIG. I looked around for my wingmates, but they weren't there. All shot down. Then I took hits. I dove for the deck—the surface of the earth—and pulled out just in time. A MIG followed me down. I guess he concentrated on me too much—he didn't make it. He crashed. If I'd gotten credit for that, I would have been an ace. My electrical system was out, and my hydraulics damaged. I went home, flying at five hundred feet by dead reckoning. I was gulping fuel at a fantastic rate. Finally I saw railroad tracks and a road—the one to Pusan. You've no idea how hard it is to get your bearings from the air. I didn't know whether to climb to five thousand and bail out or try to make it—fuel was nearly gone. But I stayed on my heading and finally saw those runways, glistening black. I jinked right and left, lined up for a straight approach, came in. The gear dropped out and locked . . . power on, speed up, I told myself . . . no flaps, no boards . . . a hundred thirty knots over the fence, and there I was. I nearly rammed a tree at the end of the runway."

"So you *were* almost killed. Yes, I saw it, in your eighth house of death," she said without emotion. He felt silly, like a showoff. Yet he'd liked relating the incident. She brought him up short when she said, "Now you're afraid of flying a plane, aren't you?"

"Why do you ask?" he said stiffly.

"It just came to me." She looked at him. "When did you fly during the war?"

"Nineteen fifty-three."

"Do you own a gun?"

"What's a gun got to do with it, for God's sake? The answer is no. But I used to. I was a hunter."

"Were you a good shot?"

"Hell, I had trophies."

"That all sounds typically Sagittarian, except you must have changed a lot."

"I had to."

When he said no more, she asked, "What was your greatest mistake?"

"You're supposed to give *me* the answers. This is sort of fortune-telling in reverse, isn't it?"

The jest didn't seem to interest her. Brow furrowed, she stared at the chart. "You're an odd combination. Brave, but not a leader. Astrologically speaking, you're loyal, trustworthy, dependable, security-conscious, a both-feet-on-the-ground guy."

"All four. I'm a centaur, don't forget." He realized he kidded more since she'd told him Sagittarians clowned.

"Substantial and yet . . . something about you bewilders me. It's like you *want* to be an Aries type, but don't have the high aspirations, the pioneering spirit, of a true Arian. You take directions, bend to the will of others," she chanted.

"You make me sound like a second-string man," he said. He had to remind himself that, as far as he was concerned, it was a parlor game.

"You have a hard time making decisions," she said, studying the circle before her.

"Sometimes. I had one hell of a time deciding whether to come down here. I flipped a coin or something," he admitted.

"You see! Quick and firm decisions are characteristic of a dynamic leader, which not everyone can be," she went on. "Some, like you, are born to follow orders. To take on the world like an Arian, you have to be ambitious, focused. You have to be able to handle your Neptune, which most can't. Neptune stands for the imagination, but all signs have positive and negative sides. Neptune also means fear. Your imagination scares you. You're confused."

"Want a drink?" he asked, getting up.

She shook her hair. He poured a Cointreau and returned. "I really don't understand you. It's as though you don't know who you are. That must be because Sagittarians sometimes have an intangible quality. They're hard to pin down." She stopped speaking, then asked abruptly, "Are you successful?"

"What do you mean by *successful?*" he said sharply. "I'm not famous, but my peers respect me."

"Do you have money?"

"I pay my bills on time."

"You could do with some real loot."

"I don't care about loot, as you call it. I never have."

"I'm not sure I believe you, but, if so, too bad. I only hang around with very rich people." Her laugh was shockingly brazen. "You could make serious dough with the right opportunity, according to your horoscope."

"Listen, I earned over fifty thousand last year. I could have made more except that I took too many charity patients."

"Congratulations," she said with a look that conveyed "small potatoes."

"I own a house in the suburbs! Ellie will get half of that, though, when it's sold, after I've repaid the mortgage. I don't know why I agreed."

"God, the middle-class hassles over a few bucks. Do you like adventure?"

"Who has adventures nowadays? Except maybe in bed, if you can call that adventure."

"You don't think bed is adventure! What's *wrong* with you? And there are other adventures, if you know where to find them. When were you married?"

"Nineteen years ago. Almost twenty."

"Do you remember the exact date?"

"Well, it was close to . . ." He started to say "my birthday" but caught himself. ". . . April Fool's Day. Which would have been appropriate. April 3."

"The separation is recent, I bet. That's a sore spot, isn't it?"

"Yes." He returned to the bar.

"You drink too much. You have Jupiter and the moon in water signs Scorpio and Cancer, which means buried emotion. All that water drowns your fiery sun ascendant in Sagittarius, creating steam. You use alcohol as a way out." He was silent. "About your marriage, the confusion I mentioned must have interfered—"

"Lay off!"

"You're angry because she left you. She *did* leave you, didn't she?"

"Please!"

"You feel sad without her? Lost? She meant a lot to you?"

"Yes! Yes! Yes!"

She inspected the chart. "You have pride, just like me, a Leo, though not as much."

"Who doesn't have pride? *Will* you shut up?"

The gold-brown eyes took him in. His humiliation was apparent, he knew. She opened another book. "Yours is the fifth path," Marie-Celeste droned. "You're a rolling stone. You crave excitement, novel experiences. You must have had a tough time as a professor. I want to check your tarot card."

"Tarot? People still mess with those?"

"I want to be complete."

"Is there a charge for this?"

She didn't take offense. "Maybe I'll ask a favor sometime. Ten of Cups. Hearts to you. You might be a powerful lover . . . maybe."

"But you don't think so." She nodded. "Why'd you come over tonight?"

"Well, I was interested in how your personality corresponds with the dead pilot's." She blinked rapidly—he decided the mannerism indicated uncertainty or lying. Yes, he was sure she lied to him—he had no idea why or about what.

"Isn't there anything compatible in our signs?" He was aping the song he'd heard on the radio.

"Leos are called the lovers. I'm looking for pleasure all the time. I'm lighthearted. I don't take things seriously, like you do. My rising Gemini is responsible."

"Oh?" He placed his hand on the small of her back; she didn't move.

"Don't you *understand?* There could be an attraction between us but it would turn out badly. Because of your strong Saturn in Aquarius— Saturn means limitations, too much control. You're much too guarded a person for me. Your big Saturn opposes my sun. And you have your moon in Pisces, a water sign, meaning emotional dependency. You wouldn't let me relax and enjoy myself."

"Try me," he said, emboldened by her slightly parted lips.

He had it, suddenly. The blinking eyes told him everything. Marie-Celeste was a little shy! Not terminally, but in instances of vulnerability she could pass the buck to the stars. He had her! He kissed her forcefully. Her shoulders stiffened but the mouth stayed open. Her resistance wasn't convincing. She put her hands on his chest, then his shoulders, then on the back of his neck. He touched her breasts with his fingers. All was bare beneath "St. Jean." "I could pretend to be an Aries," he whispered. "Aries attract you."

"Damn you!" The brassy self-confidence had vanished. "Please! Leos are terribly passionate. I don't want to say no, but I have to. My companion . . ."

The beautiful young women reminded him of a high-school girl begging for him to cease even as her elbow explored his crotch. "I can't stop," he pleaded, like a high-school boy.

She kissed him with such vigor he feared he might lose a tooth. He wondered if she was satisfied by her Aries lover. "All right. Let's make a bargain, Philip. I'll sleep with you, but after *he* comes back I can't see you anymore. It might be soon. No jealousy. No scenes. Okay?"

"Okay? How long?"

"Maybe a week. Listen, it won't work anyway. Don't be sad if it doesn't. I'm just a temporary."

"It'll work." He started to pull up her T-shirt, with urgency.

"No. Let's go outside," she breathed. "I want to see the stars. Put a pad on the deck. I'll be right out. Burn a coil in honor of the mosquitoes."

The little devil, he thought as he stripped and lay down on his stomach. Probably doesn't take the pill. She's inserting her diaphragm. She'd anticipated sexual relations all along. He wondered if she had a motive for being with him, beyond lust, but he fortified himself against his enemy, self-doubt. He wanted to be positive, like an Aries. "Where are you?" he called.

"Be patient," said her voice through the bathroom window.

He could see headlights on the road by the airport and lights from the shore restaurants and the dark yachts in water gleaming in the light from the creamy dish of the moon, like the outline of a breast. He saw sexual shapes everywhere. . . . *What have you been missing all these years? Hurry, woman!*

She glided across the deck, shining whitely. "Do astrologers make better lovers?" he said as she lay beside him.

"Oh, shut up. Sagittarians talk too much."

She consumed him. Not in his whole life had he had three orgasms in a row. When it was over she propped herself on one elbow, stared at him, and said, "I wouldn't have believed you could make me feel that way. It's not in your horoscope."

"Maybe astrology's faulty when it comes to sex."

"No, I must have overlooked something." She sounded puzzled. "I've got it! Your moon in Pisces falls trine to my Venus in Cancer. That's why I'm attracted to you." Marie-Celeste seemed pleased with her insight.

9

Even his closest associates—normal friendships he had none, unless it be his longtime wife, to whom he was faithfully devoted—found him hard to decipher. His truthfulness and rectitude attracted tremendous loyalty. He was factual, austere, unanswering, sober, somber, cold. His solemn countenance and height—he was very tall, especially for his people—contributed to his aura of leadership. His stiffness seemed natural for one with a mission. He guarded himself against being sentimental and soft, believing himself (wrongly) susceptible to such vices. He was certain that in another life he had been a general, perhaps in a holy war. Methodical, precise, confident, he had the gifts of good commanders and politicians, except that he found compromise difficult, being deeply opinionated. He would not hesitate to be ruthless if it aided his cause. In the tarot deck he was the joker— God or Satan or both.

He was born on New Year's Eve, 1934, at 1:22 P.M., in El Parador City, capital of El Parador. His father, an export-importer, was a member of the Rosicrucians, a secret society that studied the occult. He created his son's first name out of the last name of the famous chess player, partly because the name suggested a birth sign.

Following his instincts, he had entered a military school, where he met Hector Hernandez. Hector Hernandez was the son of Generalissimo Hector Hernandez, who had taken power in a revolution in the 1920's, and stayed there largely because of the United States. Generalissimo Hernandez, though he submitted to infrequent, rigged elections, was an absolute dictator, and so was his son, who succeeded him in the late 1950's. The younger Hernandez' main concession to democracy was to drop the superlative from his title.

The trader's son joined the army and rose rapidly to the rank of captain. He was unpolitical and blindly loyal to his friend, General Hector Hernandez. (He had a deep respect for authority.) Not so Ruiz, the captain's younger brother. He hated Hernandez and the poverty, exploitation, and squalor his regime represented. The Cuban revolution had shuddered Latin America like an earthquake. Dissidents sprang up everywhere, including El Parador, where they were called the Gonzalistas, after an early hero who had died in a skirmish with Hernandez' police.

Without making it publicly known, so as to not embarrass or endanger his conservative family, Ruiz joined the Gonzalistas. In 1968 Ruiz was in charge of a guerrilla training camp deep in the jungle. The rebels carried no credentials, and, though Ruiz was killed in an army attack, his body was never identified. The family claimed he had left the country and disappeared. Hundreds or thousands of people disappear on earth every day. Almost at the same time, hurried no doubt by grief, the captain's father died too. Suddenly, in his misery, the captain saw the condition of his country with fresh eyes. He wanted revenge for his brother, for his people. Resigning his commission (he made sure to stay on good terms with Hector Hernandez), he took over his father's business. He soon perceived a golden opportunity.

Always a way of life in the Caribbean, smuggling had become extensive. A liquor-store owner on a duty-free island like French St. Barthélemy, its warehouses stuffed with alcoholic imports, sold a quart of Chivas Regal to a smuggler for under three dollars. On Guadeloupe it brought twelve. At a profit of nine dollars a bottle, it was easy to see why two or three hundred cases were loaded late at night (though the authorities didn't really care) and sent to Florida, Jamaica, Puerto Rico, or Curaçao, where the liquor might be transshipped to Central or South America. Several duty-free Caribbean islands made a living out of smuggling liquor and cigarettes.

Cattle from the Dominican Republic were smuggled into St. Martin; price-controlled Venezuelan coffee slipped into Colombia; wine from French islands was smuggled into non-French ones. Machine tools were delivered to Jamaica without import licenses or the payment of duties. Pharmaceutical drugs (badly needed because of the American embargo) could be brought into Cuba. From Surinam, onions and garlic were smuggled into Guyana; diamonds and gold were smuggled out of it. Smuggled tropical birds brought huge prices in Florida. People smuggled from Haiti to the United States paid even better.

Arms were good. A general here or there might want to unload a store of rifles that the Americans had replaced with newer weapons. Ready markets for arms existed in the Middle East, Africa, South America, from all sides of the political compass.

The drug trade was biggest, dwarfing liquor smuggling during Prohibition—but the Colombians and North Americans had it pretty well sewn up. Still, to transport the stuff even a small part of the way . . .

But smuggling remained a cottage industry, with the traffic (except for drugs, which were more centralized) divided among hundreds of cutthroat competitors. To make it pay substantially required organization, sophistication, and a leader.

The Central American trader, soft-spoken, courteous in manner—he reminded people of a priest, though he had no religion in any conventional sense—hardly seemed suited for the role. But he had that ineffable quality called *presence* and an uncanny knack of predicting developments in the political world. His arguments for putting smuggling on a rational basis found adherents in the Caribbean islands, in Belize, Honduras, Costa Rica, Panama, Colombia, Nicaragua, Venezuela, Guyana. His contacts came from the trading business. He knew who the smugglers were, or he could find out.

What did he have to offer? His own credentials as a businessman and a former military officer; a legitimate business to serve as a front; a large network he was developing. He would fix the price, find buyers, locate suppliers, supervise the arrangements, choose the personnel, collect and distribute the take. Everyone would profit. But there could be no return to competition, or the organization would fall apart.

Those who refused to cooperate faced sanctions, including death. A smuggler with a small coastal freighter was known to be clearing $40,000 a month on liquor and cigarettes. He wouldn't join the network even after warnings that he must if he wanted to stay in business. Late one night his boat was boarded by armed men who bound the crew.

While they watched, a tall man with a morose manner gave him one last chance. The smuggler shrugged contemptuously—he was not the sort to show fear. "Very well, then," said the tall man in Spanish. He produced a bottle and said, "Drink."

"Drink? What is it?"

"It is rum from Guyana. One hundred sixty proof. Drink."

"That is too strong. I shall *not*."

A hand shot out, seized the smuggler's throat, squeezed. The man's eyes bulged. "Drink."

Rum of such potency can be taken only in tiny sips or heavily diluted with mix, though it can also be used as a disinfectant or burned in a chafing dish. The smuggler took a tiny swallow and wrinkled his face.

"More," said the tall man. The smuggler, whose hands were tied behind him, sipped again from the bottle the other held to his mouth. "More."

"I cannot."

"Drink."

"All right. I will join your organization."

The tall man said, almost apologetically, "I am sorry. It is too late. I would never be able to trust you now. Drink."

"Please!"

"Drink. More."

The smuggler threw up on the deck. The tall man said again, "Drink."

"Oh, God. Please," the smuggler mumbled.

"Drink."

"I am drunk. It is poison. . . ."

"Drink."

The smuggler became unconscious before the quart was entirely empty. He died on the deck in his own vomit. The Tall One bought the boat at a good price from his heirs, and hired the crew, which became slavishly loyal to him.

Another recalcitrant, a lemon smuggler (even lemons could be highly profitable in the complicated Caribbean world, where every country had different import and export restrictions), was told to remove his pants and squat on his knees. The Caribbean lemons, the size of golf balls, were shoved one after another into his anus and lower intestine until feces and blood came. The man writhed on deck until he died, though the Tall One hated filth.

When the smuggling organization thrived, the captain went to his friend the President of El Parador and offered to cut him in on a share of the profits if the dictator (who had no inkling of the captain's relationship to a dead rebel) would agree to permit a small port in the northern part of the country to be used as a base for smuggling into the rest of Central America. The omens had told the Tall One that the General, far from being outraged, would agree. He did. Hernandez also permitted a runway to be constructed in heavy jungle near the coast to be used by smugglers.

The trader had already begun to use his own profits to buy guns for the guerrilla group called Gonzalistas, who struggled to overthrow the dictator. The rebels trusted him completely.

The Central American conceived another role for himself in a practice that flourishes throughout the world, but especially in Latin America, where it accounts for many hundreds of millions of dollars a year. He didn't abandon smuggling, but the new venture proved even more lucrative.

Its purpose was to foil government controls over exports and imports. Export underinvoicing and import overinvoicing were the schemes primarily used, since the objective was usually to convert soft money from a currency-blocked nation into hard, dream money outside of it. You could overstate the amount of goods you *imported*, having obtained an import license and foreign exchange. Suppose you bought $100,000 of women's wear in New York. Your accomplice in the garment district shipped you $50,000 worth, and put the rest, minus a commission, into a bank account in your name. Once out of your country, the money was accountable to no one, and strictly for your own use.

Or, you could understate the quantity of your *exports*—twenty tons of coffee, say, when you shipped forty—and have your foreign buyer put the difference in your account.

These subterfuges required a foreign partner who took a slice of the money you moved abroad illegally. Often they necessitated slipping cash to a customs official not to examine too closely the merchandise you exported or imported, and bribing an executive of the national bank (who figured the value of your invoicess and/or provided you with foreign exchange) to look the other way. In Latin America such problems were hardly insurmountable. In the case of imports, you could also circumvent central bank regulations and tariffs by buying foreign exchange on the black market. You paid a twenty-percent premium for the currency, purchased out of the country by the local black marketeer, but you saved fifty or sixty percent in duties when your underinvoiced merchandise arrived.

The Central American became an expediter, for a fee, making arrangements, paying bribes, putting people together. To find North American connections who would wash money for Latin Americans was his reason for visiting Las Vegas in 1976. After his relationship with the French aristocrat began, the deals took a different turn. It was sometimes possible to eliminate real commodities altogether; a phony letter of credit from an offshore bank or a dummy bill of lading would serve to move money out of a blocked-currency nation. Or, if he disliked a dream-currency-hungry importer, the Tall One might obtain payment and deliver nothing at all. . . . What could the importer do? He had connived to violate the laws of his land.

The scams, the captain told his companions in the private dining room, were perpetrated for a single objective—to topple the durable regime of Hector Hernandez. The rebels he had supplied with guns were his tools. "But you see," he said in ponderous English, "there might be another way—faster and more effective in the end. I cannot accomplish this step alone, however. I had a suspicion, more than a suspicion—you know—that I would find the proper help in Las Vegas, and perhaps I have. This is how it would work. . . ."

When the exposition was finished, the older man nodded, eyes enthusiastic. "Why, it is absolutely brilliant. I believe there might be excellent reasons for assisting you."

The beautiful woman seemed enthralled, too. "For us the possibilities are endless."

"I dunno," said the young hotel owner. "It could cost a lot."

"Why, then, make more money! That's the easiest thing in the world," cried the elegant older gentleman.

"Yes," said the tall man, Capablanca Morales.

10

It was a bright day and Marie-Celeste stood over him. She'd left his bed at dawn, he'd been dimly aware, and she was back. He patted the sheet sleepily. "Come lie down." The mere sight of her instigated another erection.

When she perched, her unlined face came into focus. A pout lurked at the end of her wide mouth. If he hadn't known better, he would have thought his lioness was ready to cry. "It's over," she said. "Us, I mean."

He sat up quickly. "*Us?* Something I—"

"Always ready to blame yourself, aren't you? You have nothing to do with it—sorry about that. My friend's returning."

"When?"

"Day after tomorrow."

He sank back as dreams upended. "I'd counted on the whole week."

"You—we—can't have it. That's the reality. We have an agreement, yes?"

"Yes." As he stroked her sinewy arm, he thought drearily that it was happening again. Women leaving him. Two in a row. Ellie for Richard, Marie-Celeste for her friend. The similarity was far from exact, but close enough to be depressing. He had a sudden urge to fight for what he wanted instead of passively accepting the inevitable. "How'd you find out?"

"He telexed this morning." She stared at him lidlessly and added, "There's a telex at the house."

"A private telex?" he exclaimed. His shadowy rival took on a dimension.

"He uses it for business."

"Did you telex him about me?" Philip asked, simply for the sour drama of saying it.

"Too expensive." She laughed. "I'd be hung from my tits. Quit stalling—we don't have much time left." She started to undress.

"Two days," he said sadly. He hated his role as an expendable lover. "Does he change his plans frequently? Might he arrive later?"

"He rarely changes plans when he's decided something. It's sort of a rule of his. He's very determined. Philip, I'm sorry, but we don't have two days. He has people coming—three of them. They arrive tomorrow. I didn't know, honestly. He . . . doesn't keep me informed. I won't be able to get away. I have to attend to them. It's my . . . well, role. Today is it."

"What are you, his social secretary?"

She smiled into his ear. "Every second until dawn tomorrow I'm yours."

"Why dawn?"

"He usually telexes early. I have to be there. But he won't telex until then, and the servants have the day off. They've gone fishing and won't be back until evening."

Castle was beaten and knew it. Licked by a telex machine. He adored her, he decided while they were making love, relished her tight behind, tiny waist, tongue-sucking kisses, audible and visible ecstasy. How different sex was with her than it had been with Ellie. He remembered his departed—dead was how Castle wished to think of her—wife's determined pursuit of a single orgasm. This girl was like Chinese firecrackers that popped every second. Maybe Marie's multiple orgasms amounted to Ellie's single one in small bursts, but he doubted it. Marie-Celeste just got more out of sex. He started to wonder again about her lover, but pushed him out of his mind. It was Philip Castle she was with, and she seemed to enjoy him. A little later he took a deep breath and said, "Marie-Celeste, would you leave him? For me?"

"I can't. Don't ask. You couldn't afford me. Who's that?"

"I don't know." He went to the door, opened it, and peeked out. "Sansa, the cleaning lady. I forgot she might come in the morning. I'll tell her to come back—or don't you care if she sees you?"

Marie-Celeste was already slipping on a long white cotton shirt that reached to her thighs. She grimaced. "Sure I care. But my car's in the drive and I left my charm bracelet on the terrace. You'll never get her out until she knows who's here."

"Will she recognize you?" He had to remind himself that to protect the girl from discovery wasn't his concern.

"If she doesn't, she'll try like hell to find out who I am. But I don't suppose it'll get back to my friend."

They emerged from the bedroom together. Sansa's mouth formed an "o."

"Bonjour, madame. Ça va?" Marie-Celeste said sunnily.

"Oui, bonjour. Je regrette si je vous dérange. Si vous préférez, je peux retourner cet après-midi," Sansa said.

"Ce n'est pas nécessaire. Merci. What's for breakfast, Philip?" Marie-Celeste went to the terrace to retrieve her bracelet. Sansa's face was stoic.

Every beach on the island—some twenty of them—was different, each in its own way, Marie-Celeste rhapsodized. This one was less lush, more desert-islandish than yesterday's, which had a jungly feel. It was fringed with tall, skinny cacti and sheer black rock walls, and made Philip think of drinking water, though he wasn't thirsty. Flecked with black, the sand was coarser than that of the other beach, which had been smooth and dazzlingly white. The sea was even calmer here.

Philip slapped at his leg, pink now instead of pale. "The mosquitoes must go home at dawn and change into their fly clothes."

He liked her laugh. Ellie had never seemed to laugh at his jokes much. He'd almost stopped making them. He recalled his solemn manner as a therapist. He'd go to the double doors—double so that a waiting patient couldn't hear what was being said in his office by the patient; he himself spoke only infrequently, and then to ask questions;

treatment by him, as a Freudian, was nondirective—and solemnly usher the patient inside, motioning toward the couch, closing the doors behind them. "Good morning," he'd say—he taught in the afternoons—sitting down behind the patient's head, folding his hands. "Well, then, shall we begin?" How purposely dry the technique had been, in order that the transference—that was the goal, transference, the transformation of the therapist into a parental figure, so that the early experience would be recreated by the patient's psyche—could occur without the influence of his personality. It occurred to him that he might never treat patients again.

"Look at those birds," she was saying. "Free as. How do they fly without flapping their wings?"

"The gulls are riding something called ground cushion. At low levels the atmosphere provides extra support. It's the same for an airplane." But he wanted to avoid the topic of flying; an avid look came to her face whenever the subject came up. "Who are these pals you have to take care of?"

"One's a trader from Central America. The second's a guy who owns a hotel in Las Vegas. He's creepy. The third's a woman. She's a computer whiz. There must be money in computers, the way she dresses."

The sun shone pinkly through his eyelids. "I should ask about you. I don't even know your last name."

"Rombachet." She went on mechanically, "I was born August 15, 1953, in Bordeaux. My Gemini's rising, as I told you. Geminis are nervous, fickle, and unstable. Gemini is ruled by Mercury. He takes color from other planets but doesn't give anything back. Mercury, which influences me strongly, can make you a genius or a crook. My moon conjuncts Neptune in the fifth house of love affairs . . ."

"Oh, come on."

"Really! Leo's ruled by the sun, thank God. Old Sol has a good heart. So have his children."

"That's all?"

"You want facts? Okay. I am the only child of a French businessman and an American woman. I can't imagine why they married, because they always hated each other. They split up while I was a baby. My childhood was a little crazy. I spent every other year with a different parent. When I was with my father I was treated like a princess. I went to the best boarding school in Switzerland. That's when I met Raymond . . ."

"Raymond?"

"My friend. He lived in Geneva then."

"Ah, the lover. How old is he?"

"You Americans always want to know how old a person is. It's the first question you ask, that and 'What do you do for a living?' Ari—Raymond is called Ari—is in his early sixties. He's in banking. He has one on Grand Cayman, among other places."

She went silent like a dead radio. Cayman Islands . . . pilot . . . Philip wanted to pursue the connection but decided he shouldn't, not yet. It was too soon to ask for revelations. "You were speaking of your childhood."

"My mother was poor. Not trained for anything, like me. The only reason my father helped her at all was that she'd let me spend every other year with him in Europe. He was a wine merchant. So one year I'd hear what a bitch my mother was, bleeding him dry, he who had a town house, a country place, servants. The following year my mother would tell me what a bastard he was for letting us starve. Mother got so anxious about money she used to tremble. She'd wake up in a cold sweat in the middle of the night and couldn't go back to sleep. She had rings around her eyes." Marie-Celeste made a fist. "I never want to be like that."

"No wonder you like rich men, and I assume your friend with the telex is. What happened to your mother?"

"Oh, she's okay. She finally remarried. She had a tough time financially after my father died, though. So did I. He'd remarried long before. I never liked his wife, and didn't try to hide it. She contrived to get every penny. She was supposed to help me, but she stopped when I became twenty-one."

"Did you go to court?"

"No. It might have taken years, and I had other things to do. Besides, the signs said I'd lose."

"Did you hire an astrologer? Was it Raymond who hooked you on astrology?"

"Yes."

"Count Dracula. Did you live with him in Geneva?"

"Off and on. He traveled so much. Still does."

"Does he want to marry you?"

"What a question! The answer is no. I don't want to marry him either, or anyone." She added, "Ever."

"A lot of women *say* that. How can you be sure?"

"My horoscope. How did you know Raymond is a count?"

"I didn't. What kind of guy is he?"

"A wonderful man, kind and gentle, unless he's crossed. He has a mission in life. He has plans to help humanity. He will let nothing stand in his way. Do you want to help humanity?"

"I'm fresh out of ideas this morning. What kind of plans does this count have?"

"Something to do with new leadership." She blinked at him. "Come on, let's hit the water. Coral's wonderful. It's why I brought you here."

Philip wasn't accustomed to a long, spontaneous, meandering, carefree, poignant day, their first and last. He wished there were more to come.

He and Ellie had been to the Caribbean only once, because she didn't like the heat, and the sun gave her a rash. They'd visited one of the Virgin Islands, but the trip was so forgettable he didn't remember which.

Ellie. . . . More and more, he thought of her critically. Certainly he had loved her, certainly she had qualities he admired and respected, but his feelings for the lioness were sharper, more poignant, than those he had ever had for his wife. Because they were new together? No, he and Ellie had been new once too. This was not the same. Would it wear off? He suspected he could enjoy Marie-Celeste after a year, after ten. Was it chemical? Was it . . . no, no astral attraction. He wasn't becoming suggestible at this late date. But why ponder it? They had one day together.

Castle was a seasoned observer. People couldn't hide things indefinitely, he knew; little by little, drawing her out, he decided that out of bed M-C displayed two preoccupations: crime and Philip's prior experience with airplanes. Could there be a link?

They were in the Moke. Quitting the beach, they had driven on narrow paved roads up and down hillsides, past gorgeous houses and spectacular vistas, through a little village where women wore white bonnets and ankle-length dresses and sold baskets. He solemnly followed her into a cave, which, she said, had been used by pirates, and later smugglers. There had been so much crime on St. Jean that the French (who acquired the island from the Swedes, who got it from the British, who took it from the Dutch, who seized it from the Spanish, who stole it from the Carib Indians, who'd swiped it from the Arawak Indians) tried to return it to the Swedes, who wouldn't take it, she'd heard. Everything had been smuggled through here—booze, cigarettes, guns, pornography bound for the United States before it was liberalized, drugs. There was plenty of smuggling even now.

"On this peaceful place? I don't believe it."

"You don't? Come."

She had him drive down a side road that bottomed at a cove where there was a concrete jetty with a floodlight overhead. "At midnight here you'll find speedboats being loaded with booze and other things, which go to a freighter moored outside."

"What about the cops?"

"I told you Sagittarians are naive. The gendarmes don't give a shit. You think St. Jean makes a living selling baskets? Half the islanders are involved. A lot of people here are filthy rich. Isn't that great?"

"Great for them, I guess," he said dubiously.

She told him, with a quick hard glance, "Some stuff is moved through here by plane."

"Drugs?"

"Cocaine. From Colombia. Did you know that drugs exceed coffee as Colombia's number-one export? Pilots are always needed."

She was testing him, he decided. "Oh."

"Oh what?"

"Just oh."

"Do you like coke?"

"Never tried it. Bad for the nose. Do you?"

"Sure."

"Have you tried everything?"

"Not yet, but I will before I'm done. Do you disapprove of me?" She giggled naughtily. He did and he didn't. He suspected he'd be titillated if she told him all. "Do you want me to?" he asked without expression.

"At least you'd be taking a position. You never do, you know. You're always neutral, except in bed."

"I'm not neutral. I'm square."

"I wonder if you were really destined to be a square. People can get on the wrong paths. I see you, somehow, as a bolder spirit than you seem to be."

"I'm a college professor," he reminded her.

On top of a mountain lurked a tiny restaurant with a handful of outdoor tables. There was nobody outside but them. Porch umbrellas flapped in the gusts.

Far below on the hillside, houses with soft white walls and raspberry roofs clustered together amid lush green foliage. A long curved line of palms fringed the sparkling beach. Waves crashed on the blue-gray stone of the promontories, where a few gnarled trees managed to grow. The water in the lagoon was iridescent, blue in the center, pale green near the shore, with dark places that were coral. As the waiter opened a bottle of white wine, Marie-Celeste said excitedly, "It's so clear!" She pointed. "That's St. Bart. That one—no, *there*—is Saba. Nothing but an extinct volcano rising straight into the sky. There's always a cloud on top. That's St. Eustatius—Statia, everybody says. West is St. Kitts and Nevis . . . island after island, stretching all the way to South America. Wouldn't you like to see the whole chain?"

"Yes." He was contracting Caribbean fever because his resistance was low.

"I could spend the rest of my life here. Couldn't you?"

"It'd be nice, with the right company. What am I talking about? I'd get restless. And I have responsibilities at home."

"Don't you *tire* of responsibilities? When are you heading back?"

The waiter brought two *niçoise* salads. Philip took a bite and said softly, "When your friend comes."

"So soon?"

"There won't be much to hang around for."

"You don't want to go home, do you? I think you do a great many things you don't want to."

"True of all of us, my young friend."

"No, there are people who do exactly as they like."

"Rich people," he said with contempt.

"So get rich."

"Oh, sure."

"If something came along, would you take it?"

"Like?"

"I don't know. Maybe a new career." She added hastily, "I don't have anything specific in mind."

She was leading him on, he decided. Into the lion's den. "I'm open to suggestions."

"Here's one. After lunch, let's see what's happening."

"Where?"

"Guess."

The heat made them perspire until their bellies rubbed together like well-lubricated parts of a single machine. But there was no question of stopping, even of rushing. Pressure in him grew. He, usually silent, cried out. She whimpered. In pain, he suddenly feared, asking.

"Oh, no. God, no."

They dozed until a breeze from the terrace fanned them awake, and then she had him in another amorous vise, head thrown back, feet flat on the bed, keeping him within strict limits until she had tantalized his ardor to the point of ferocity, lowering himself until the coupling was total and a stunning simultaneous climax achieved.

"Talk about sexual athletes," he said after a while.

"Sexual athletes?"

"People who make out with each other lots of times a day for years on end. Then even do it at lunchtime. *What* are you doing?"

"Getting you ready."

"You *can't* be unsatisfied, unless you're a nymphomaniac."

"I am! With you anyway. Once we've started, I can't quit. Thank God we have the whole evening ahead."

Philip Castle groaned.

The sand in their hourglass seemed to flow faster as they headed toward dissolution, when they, as a physical unit, would cease to exist. He supposed it was always that way near the end of an affair—this was an *affair*, a torrid one, not a *relationship*, the uneasy word he always used as a shrink. He felt loneliness impending: tomorrow he'd have to confront the problem of his drab existence. She'd given him excitement, and he felt a perverse gratitude—perverse because he was angry. He'd honor the arrangement and back out gracefully, but he resented the count. He couldn't help it. If only he could supplant the old man.

During dinner in the rear of a restaurant where she hoped she wouldn't be noticed, Marie-Celeste Rombachet said in a slightly studied voice, "Tell me about your wife."

He had almost ceased thinking of Ellie—for the moment at least. "What's there to say? An ex is an ex is an ex."

"That *tone*. You're sorry for yourself. But I wonder how you really feel about her."

"I don't understand."

She showed her palms in rebuke. "Don't play naive with me. You've told me a little about how she picked up with this other guy and left you dangling—it must have been like having your balls cut off."

"It was," he said softly.

"And when she broke off with you, you were ready to throw in the sponge, weren't you?"

"I was pretty low."

"What was her name?"

"Ellie *is* her name," he responded through tight lips.

"I keep wondering if you mightn't have been *glad* to get rid of her, for all the grief."

"I won't have to pay alimony, at least."

"That's not what I mean! She doesn't sound so hot to me. I think you're lucky to be out. Maybe you do too, only you won't admit it."

"I *wasn't* glad to be rid of her. Why do you say preposterous things like that?" One of his feet gyrated nervously.

"How you act with me, for one. It's like you're starving for a good time. You didn't have much fun with her, did you?"

"Well, if we didn't have so much fun sometimes, it was because of me. I work too hard."

"You always blame yourself. Maybe you worked so hard because you weren't having fun with her. Have you thought of that?"

"Fun! That's your notion of life in a nutshell."

"I'm not ashamed of it, either," she flared. "You enjoy suffering. That must be why you let Ellie call the shots."

"Is that so!" he said. He pounded the table with his fist: silverware rattled and glasses sloshed. People looked. *Watch it. You're sore about losing Marie*, he warned himself, too late: the words were already en route. "When I want insights, I'll ask for them. Not that you have the slightest idea what you're talking about. Ellie's okay. She's a *woman*, not a twit like you." Marie-Celeste only smiled. "Look, relationships . . ." Oh, God, that word. ". . . have natural rhythms, cycles. Sometimes they just stop. It's nobody's fault."

"Oh, boy, you try so hard to sound reasonable. I think you're pissed with her. Pissed as hell." She was right, of course, but he wanted to cover his ears as she went on relentlessly, "I'd be pissed if I were you. You're pissed with me, too, and that's okay. I don't blame you. Script reads: you get involved with a pretty girl . . . I *am* pretty, you know."

"So people stare at you, you vain bitch!"

"I didn't order my appearance! It came in the package. It's kind of a burden—men *won't* leave you alone—not that I'm sorry. Far from it. Anyway, good-looking chick screws you to death, sort of falls for you, and goes back to her lover. You don't like that, do you?"

"No." He put his hands on either side of his lean face. "It's your fault. You got me into this—admit it. Why? What in hell do you see in me?"

"A man who should play his cards right if and when the time comes."

"Chinese-fortune-cookie stuff. I can't get over feeling you want to use me for something."

"I do. Let's get out of here."

"Know something? I could fall in love with you."

"You better get a parachute."

Once more their sex was wonderful. For him it had more of a "hello again" quality than "good-bye," but that was wish fulfillment, like astrology, he told himself as, arms around her, he tried to sleep. He had to accept the bitter reality that it was over between them. He *had* fallen for her, and didn't have a parachute. She'd reintroduced himself to himself, restored some confidence, no, more: she'd uncovered a vein he'd hardly known was there. He couldn't assay it yet, but it seemed quite unlike the Philip Castle he knew: a bolder, sexier, more exciting spirit. Without her, he'd quickly become a stodgy depressive again, he feared, moving through life with half his power on. He *had* power—he could sense it now. *So long, Marie-Celeste.*

PART II

11

El Parador
Area: 14,492 square miles (23,323 sq. km.)
Capital: El Parador City
People: El Parador is almost evenly divided among five basic groups, each comprising roughly twenty percent of the population: Amerindian (descendants of the original aborigine Indians); Caucasian (white); Creole (Negroid); East Indian (imported as indentured labor); and *mestizo* (mixed white and Indian blood). Though these distinctions are respected, formally and statistically, in actual fact miscegenation has been, and is, so extensive that the population is too intermixed to be actually separated.
Population: 303,084
Natural resources: El Parador's fertile soil and abundant rainfall make it one of the potentially richest agricultural countries in Central America, despite its small size. Development, however, has not met the targets of the government's five-year plans, of which the fourth is in progress. . . . Geology and minerals: there is as yet no Department of Mines, but the existence of significant oil deposits is suspected, and drilling has begun both offshore and in the steep Maya Mountains, which form the volcanic backbone of the country. Both gold and deposits of high-grade uranium have been mentioned in surveys, but not yet discovered. . . . Hydroelectricity: the Cachiquel Basin in the northeast part of the country is considered to have high hydroelectrical potential because of the powerful Nan River running through it. The World Bank

has not yet complied with the country's urgent requests for low-cost loans.

Geopolitics: El Parador's strategic coastal location makes it a key Central American power.

Currency: The unit of the monetary system is the pipil (P), comprising 100 centavos. It is valued at P-3 to the U.S. dollar . . . the amount of currency in circulation has a U.S.-dollar equivalent of approximately 100,000 million.

The Executive:

President: General Hector Antonio Juan Hernandez Garcia
Cabinet (Gabinete) with portfolio . . . Dr. Enrique
Cordova Astacio Sanchez, Minister of Finance. . . .
—from *The Caribbean Annual, 1978*

The president of El Parador did not conform to the stereotype of a banana republic's military dictator. He was short, spare, and had a clean upper lip. Rimless bifocals perched on his small nose. Instead of a uniform, he wore a snappily tailored Sills business suit, from New York. If the Minister of Finance had been clad in starched khakis, with epaulets, boots, and perhaps a pistol in a holster, he could have played the Latin-American strongman instead, being corpulent, red-faced, and sporting a handlebar mustache. Astacio, however, had a Ph.D. in economics from Harvard. The Finance Minister often regretted Hernandez' rooted ignorance on matters of national currency.

Each had called the other at exactly the same time, with an urgent message. The result was an instant meeting. Scheduled appointments had been abruptly canceled. The President went first.

It had been four days since the Gonzalista Raul had been persuaded to talk. Raul had since died of overexposure to solar radiation—why a *mestizo* would shave off his body hair and stay naked in the sun until his skin peeled off was beyond the comprehension of the doctors at the hospital near which he had been dropped. The secret police had sent alerts to the elaborate network Hernandez maintained, the most extensive in the Caribbean—certainly better than that of the CIA, which, stupidly to Hernandez, underrated the area despite Cuba, the

Mexican oil finds, and a ubiquitous revolutionary presence. Hernandez possessed a communication that had just arrived.

It was a letter, sent to the usual drop. Letters were slow, but safer than exposing information to rebel moles who, the dictator was sure, had infiltrated the telephone and telegraph systems, probably even the secret police. The letter concerned the Tall One, whom the secret police had been trying to locate. The Tall One had moved his headquarters to Costa Rica, with Hernandez' approval, to conceal the collusion between them, but he had dropped from sight, and an alert had been out for weeks. Hernandez feared the Tall One was hiding from him.

Even before the Tall One vanished, Hector Hernandez had been suspicious. It had come to him one day as he studied his horoscope that he might run into financial troubles because of an associate. The person who seemed to fit this description best was the Tall One, who was in an ideal position to cheat him. Hernandez had contrived to place an informant, a Venezuelan pilot whose background had to seem perfect to the Tall One, on the smuggler's payroll. In turn, the Tall One had lent the pilot to a European offshore banker who had him fly him to the island of St. Jean once in a while. The pilot was to fly again later that day, but without the banker. The pilot had written from Grand Cayman four days ago. The pilot was to carry a box that held, he believed, El Parador currency—a pipil note had dropped on the floor. He did not know where the Tall One was, but the European had a house on St. Jean. The pilot had been told to wait on the French island until the Tall One arrived, which would be soon. The pilot would then make a long flight, with the Tall One as passenger.

What did it mean? Hernandez wondered. A great deal to Señor Astacio, who produced a pipil. Named for one of the aboriginal Indian tribes that had inhabited the region, it was pronounced *piepull*. The note bore the national coat of arms—an elliptical shield, symbolizing El Parador's determination to defend herself at any cost. Emblazoned on it was an equilateral triangle, the three points standing for "Justice," "Equality," and "Liberty," which were written in Latin in fine print. Five volcanic rocks lay on the shield—volcanic for rugged strength, five for the principal groupings in the population. "República de El Parador en la America Central" circled the shield, and outside the words were white stars. The stars, supposed to manifest the galaxy of nations, had been introduced by the President when a new issue of notes had been printed a decade before. For him, they had another significance.

The note was signed by Hernandez and the Minister of Finance, Astacio. Both signatures were virtually illegible on paper reduced to pulp from endless handling.

"Do you see this? Do you see this?" Astacio waved the bill. He was one of the few people in the government the dictator could trust.

"Looks like an ordinary pipil to me," Hernandez said.

"As to everyone else. That is the trouble. The pipil is counterfeit."

"*What?*"

"I could not grasp what was happening. I finally had batches of currency subjected to chemical tests. The counterfeit paper is different, but not much. Of course, *knowing* the bill is counterfeit, one can detect small irregularities. The points of the stars are imperfect. But the counterfeit is hard to spot. An experienced bank teller would have trouble."

Hernandez polished his glasses with a tissue, a maneuver that gained time to cogitate. "It is most peculiar. Who would bother to counterfeit a pipil? A hundred-pipil note I could understand, perhaps."

"I have not found any counterfeit one hundreds, fifties, or twenties. Only tens, fives, and ones." Astacio took a roll from his pocket, tied with a rubber band, and placed it on the President's mahogany desk. "I did not wish to tell you until I knew what denominations were being counterfeited."

"Why have they not been spotted before?"

"They are hard to recognize, as I said, but also they have been flooding the market only comparatively recently, I suspect. This counterfeit note is no more than six months old. It *looks* much older, but it isn't. It is almost new."

Hernandez polished furiously. "Counterfeit an *old* bill?"

"The note was printed to appear old, then deliberately aged with acids and crushed. Yes, it could be done—I have checked. The workmanship is fantastic. I told you we needed to reissue our currency. You failed to listen, friend."

The bifocals regained Hernandez's snub nose. The eyes behind them were blank. "I would think that exchanging counterfeit one-pipil bills for genuine ones would be very time-consuming if serious profit were expected."

"I do not believe the bills were printed for reasons of profit. In my opinion they are related to the other problem."

El Parador had a host of problems, but the two that preoccupied the government were the guerrillas and the "other"—inflation. A barely tolerable one hundred percent before, the cost of living had jumped, starting about a year ago. In the last few months it had increased even faster. Now at an annual rate of two hundred fifty percent, it would soon reach three hundred. No economic medicine had proved capable of even slowing it down. Inflation was killing El Parador like a cancer. "I do not understand."

The Finance Minister said patiently, "I explained to you sometime ago that we had discovered a great expansion in the money supply. The Central Bank assumed people were removing their money from mattresses, or wherever they kept it, and beginning to spend, increasing national consumption as a percentage of disposable income. They are saving less because our money is losing its value. Indeed, that is part of the trouble. But it is impossible to know the total money supply—we can only estimate the amount in circulation: three hundred million pipils. That is what the figure *was*. It is a great deal higher now, and the increased money supply is the fundamental reason inflation is at its present frightening rate. The additional currency is counterfeit. I wish I knew how it enters the system."

"Skip the details! Why do you not remove the counterfeits from circulation?"

"We cannot. We lack a mechanism to do it with. We have to assume at least seventy-five *million* in counterfeit money is floating, mostly in small-denomination bills which are the bulk of our currency. Even if we made a public announcement, the repercussions would be staggering. Banks might fail if a percentage of their cash assets were declared invalid. Imagine how the peasants would react on learning their money was worthless. There is quite enough discontent already. That must be the purpose of the counterfeits: to bring down the government."

The President had taken a tranquilizer before breakfast and could consider the situation fairly calmly from his massive seat. He was being whipsawed. Combating insurgents caused inflation. Further inflation increased dissidence. More recruits for the rebels. And now this. "Why not recall the entire money supply and issue new notes?" He inspected Astacio's face. "What is the objection?"

Astacio sighed. "There are tremendous difficulties. Uncertainty about the future will be increased, adding to the flight of capital. And reissuing the currency would be an administrative nightmare; it would be unpopular. Finally, there is the matter of time. The new currency would have to be different. It would have to be harder to counterfeit. Drawings must be approved, plates engraved, money printed in the United States or Europe. It would take too long. Inflation might jump again if in the interim the counterfeits continue to pour in, as I'm sure they are all the time. The pipil note your agent discovered—"

"I *knew* it! So! The Tall One has not only stolen guns from me and given them to the rebels, but he also must be the source of the counterfeit money! I should never have trusted him. He must have been a Communist all along." The dictator had secretly hated the Tall One since military academy, where he had been known as the Short One, as though he were the Tall One's alter ego. "But why was the pilot flying counterfeit currency to St. Jean for a European offshore banker? And who is behind this banker? The CIA? No, they are on our side. The Russians, seeking to install the Communists here? But a major power would be wary of having the same trick pulled on one of their satellites, like Cuba. Maybe Cuba is responsible."

"You are avoiding the issue. We require a stringent program for removing the counterfeits without causing panic. We might consider increasing the national debt by replacing the counterfeits with genuine new money at the banks."

"The answer is to kill the Tall One. I would like to increase his height by several inches first."

"We need a program, I tell you," Astacio said.

"Yes, yes. Go ahead. Do something. When will the Tall One arrive on St. Jean, I wonder?"

When Astacio had left, Hector Hernandez summoned his secretary, a male who carried a gun. "Check with Records," he said. "I want the exact year and date of the birth of Señor Capablanca Morales Ramon. The time of birth, too, if they have it."

Later that day the head of the secret police ran in. Hernandez had an agent on the island of St. Jean, as in so many other places—a young woman who worked as a maid. Her services had been obtained—without great difficulty—as a result of threats against her family in El Parador. In complete violation of security, she had placed a phone call to the secret police, reporting that the Tall One had just arrived on St. Jean. Not too long before, he had been on the island in the company of an American woman, a French count who had a mansion by the sea, and another American whose yacht was expected. A pilot who flew the count to St. Jean had crashed and died on the island four days ago. The count was not on the plane.

"The Venezuelan!" Hernandez cried. "Could he have been murdered?" He walked around the room in agitation. "We must act." He removed his glasses and immediately put them back on his nose. "House by the sea. They will be staying there, which may make it easier. How long would it take my warship to reach St. Jean?"

"About two days."

"Dispatch it as soon as you can. Capture Morales. Bring the others, too."

"But the island is French, to say nothing of other difficulties!"

"It must be done at night, but make sure nobody identifies the ship. Cover its markings. Put the men in plain clothes—it'll look like a kidnapping. If the others are there, and guiltless—which I doubt—they will be released. We can say later that the Tall One was arrested as a threat to national security, the others possible accomplices. Exposing the counterfeiting scheme will take people's minds off the fact that they are foreign nationals."

Hernandez realized, pleased, that with the Tall One out of the way, he'd have the smuggling all to himself. Still, he would have to be careful. The currency hoax had been brilliantly conceived, and his horoscope had not forseen it.

12

So long, Marie-Celeste. Not quite, he decided when he woke alone the following morning. He was mightily curious about her friends. Raymond's notion of helping humanity consisted of picking its pockets. The count almost had to be a crook—a big-time drug dealer with a bank account on the Cayman Islands seemed likely. Maybe the others were in the drug trade too. For whatever reasons, the girl had gone almost out of her way to arouse Philip's interest, and he wanted to see the mysterious supercriminals in the flesh. She'd asked for it.

He had gleaned from her the arrival times and places of all four. Knowing it would annoy her (and partly because it *would* annoy her), Philip was at the airport, ostensibly to ask about flights out of St. Jean, when the Cessna Skymaster, with center-mounted fore and aft engines, circled the field and came in. Marie-Celeste's striped-top VW raced up. She had no time to do anything more than glare at Philip Castle, because "Cappy" was leaving the plane.

"Cappy" was what she called him. He was from El Parador, a backwater Central American country Castle had barely heard of before arriving on St. Jean. Cappy was *fantastically* rich, like the rest of the

110

"gang of four," as Philip had begun to think of them. Yes, Marie-Celeste was acquainted with them—they'd come to St. Jean earlier in the winter. The met four times a year, though this gathering was a bit ahead of schedule. She knew their astrological signs—Cappy was a Capricorn, which anyone could tell just by *looking* at him. His height could be accounted for by his sun in Capricorn trine to ascendant. Cappy was destined for greatness, she'd said. Someday Cappy would be President of his country and be an important Caribbean leader. A drug dealer as political hero? It sounded unlikely.

The man who crawled from the plane had to bend over double to pass through the door, taking the supportive hand of a neatly uniformed pilot. Easily six-five when he stood up, he wore a black suit (in the tropics!), a black tie, and a white panama hat, brim descending, which miraculously stayed on his head and hid his features. He carried a long cane, using it to favor his left knee, on which he limped. He was all straight up and down, like a column. He appeared to have tremendous physical strength. Philip put him in his late forties. Cappy was nobody to tangle with.

Head thrust forward, Cappy moved toward the little terminal with surprising speed, considering his limp and careful, almost hopping steps. When he reached Marie-Celeste, he removed his hat and bowed deeply. She leaned on tiptoes to kiss him, but he adroitly turned his cheek, so that she puckered empty air. *(The gesture of one who dislikes to be touched?* For no particular reason, Philip had begun to keep a mental record.) The hair was jet black, parted in the middle. Edged by large ears, the earth-brown countenance carried a suggestion of who could say how many racial origins. Under a wide forehead, with high-ridged bones at the temples, the face was small for the body, with dark eyes, set far apart, a broad flat nose, a square chin that added to the air of determination. A Capricorn face? Yes, Philip could see the likeness of a goat, but what Cappy captured for him were paintings of Latin-American peasants, with carefully controlled energies and secretive souls. That wasn't all. The straight-shouldered, martial back, the impassive, self-centered expression, the confident motions suggested a man who was proud, accustomed to deference, perhaps professorial, not easily persuaded to change course. As a leader, Cappy would be arrogant.

He spoke so softly Philip couldn't hear his voice, but Marie-Celeste was saying, "I have a wonderful lunch for you at the house." The man nodded uninterestedly, and carrying his bag, followed Marie, towering over her. She had acted as though Philip didn't exist.

Philip turned, to see another watching the Central American. It was Sansa, and her mouth was open. She didn't notice Philip; her full attention was on Cappy.

Castle had lunch at the bar at Le Boucan, with Joe Martinez standing on the other side. "I haven't had the pleasure of your company in the last few days," he said.

"I've been busy."

"How did you like Cul de Sac?" Joe mocked him with his eyes.

"I had a lovely time."

"I can imagine. I envy you—almost. Still, there are dangerous currents at that beach."

"Yes. I can see how it might get tricky. A man arrived this morning named Cappy. Know him?"

"We have done a little business together. He is in the export-import line. He knows the Caribbean well. He has many connections."

"I'm sure he does."

"He is a close associate of your friend's companion. But you are aware of that."

"Yes."

"There are many stories about Cappy. He's an exceptionally bad person to have angry with you. Are you still seeing the young lady?"

"No. At least, I don't think so," said Philip.

"It is very interesting that you had a . . . what shall I say?"

"Fling?"

"Fling with her. Nobody else has since she's been down here, I'm certain. That makes you sort of special, Philip."

"I don't understand it either. How did you find out?"

"I told you, little escapes me here."

"Sansa again?"

Joe Martinez shrugged.

"Marie-Celeste says Cappy has a future in Caribbean politics. Could that be true?"

"Depends what side he ends up on."

So Marie-Celeste hadn't been talking rubbish after all. "I don't know much about the players."

"Well, the Caribbean is a collection of independent states that frequently quarrel with each other," Martinez said earnestly, leaning forward and putting his elbows on the bar. "About whether to be pro-Soviet, nonaligned, or pro-U.S., for instance. But there are those who long for a single Caribbean nation, starting with smaller islands but one day including Jamaica, Hispaniola, maybe even Cuba, and then all the nations that line the Caribbean, including the Central American ones. It would be a strong state. It could stand up to the major powers. It could set prices for raw materials, like OPEC does. It could be a major force in the third world. Burnham favors this concept."

"Burnham?"

Martinez pointed to the photo of the smiling round-faced black man on the wall. "Forbes Burnham, Prime Minister of Guyana."

"And you're from Guyana."

"Yes, I am a patriot," Joe said proudly.

"Why don't you go back there and live?"

"Too lazy. Still, I believe in a united Caribbean too. Cappy has also made noises in that direction, but I don't know. I have wondered occasionally what his objective is. There is . . . something he does not say. You develop a feel for this after a time in politics."

"You're in politics, Joe?"

"In a manner of speaking. I play a role. I do not like it known. What are *your* politics, Philip Castle?"

"Oh, not much of anything. I'm the usual mixed bag. I'm what's called a liberal, but I don't like liberals, if you know what I mean. I used to feel strongly. I guess I've given up."

A summons came from the phone. When Joe returned he said, "Once more Sansa talked too much. She has telephoned El Parador. I think I know why. There will be trouble," Martinez muttered worriedly. Philip would have liked to question him, but he had to go.

He drove the Moke to the airport in time for the early-afternoon flight from St. Martin. Libby would be on it. So far, "Libby" was only an abstraction.

Marie-Celeste appeared and accosted him in a sharp voice. "You were here this morning!"

"I was getting flight information."

"Now?"

"Making a reservation to leave on Tuesday."

"Oh." The young woman's apparent unhappiness changed to resolution. "I *wish* you'd quit hanging around the airport. You make me nervous. Don't forget our deal."

"I won't."

Marie scowled, and went to watch the plane land.

Libby, Marie had told him, lived in a purportedly fabulous apartment on Park Avenue in New York. She had many friends, all stinking rich like her. She was exceptionally beautiful—like a Greek goddess, "not a ragtag beach queen with straight hair like me. What an actress she would make—Libras are actors, you know."

Philip's brain fired off associations. Cappy-Capricorn. Libby-Libra. Libby was last off the plane. Did people who took up the rear wish to cause anxiety in those who waited for them, since they'd wonder if the traveler was on board? But Marie-Celeste had been right: the two women were markedly different. He could imagine Marie as a model, but Libby was a beauty of a more special category. She was older—thirty-five perhaps—but age had nothing to do with it. Marie was the sort of female you eyed on the street. Libby was the one at whom you hardly dared look for fear she'd vanish in thin air.

He compared their movements—Marie-Celeste's prance, Libby's slow glide, as though she moved on a cushion of oil. When the two women stood together, the contrast was even more evident. Marie, a little taller, in an old shirt, denims, and bare feet, seemed almost boyish with her sharp features, pollen-dusting of freckles, mane of orange-yellow hair. Libby wore sandals of pale leather on which specks of embedded mica shone, slacks of tan wool, loose at the ankles, tight at the crotch and legs, a white cotton halter covered by a blue pastel linen safari jacket that matched her eyes. The breasts looked demure, perfectly formed. (Had he examined women this closely before? His sensibilities seemed heightened.) A large diamond glowed on the long index finger of the left hand, and the right arm carried an endless row of bracelets, white-gold, he thought. Her chain necklace was the same metal, and white gold

covered with tiny diamonds were the rings in her pierced ears, which led
the eye to her hair, a gleaming gold ball held in place with diamond-
topped pins. The skin was white marble; the wide-open eyes a clear,
luminous pale blue, large and wide open; the nose narrow and straight
with almost invisible nostrils. She had high cheekbones, a red bow
mouth, dainty dimples, finely etched cleft in her chin.

"With Venus as ruler, the female Libra has almost *got* to be a
knockout," Marie-Celeste had raved. "Libra-the-scales means balance
and harmony, and that's Libby for you. Libra's the only sign that's
inorganic: she's almost too perfect to *be* alive. Libra's an air sign, and
that's Libby too. She's sort of, well, ineffable, but she sure knows how to
use cosmetics, which is normal, since Libra's the sign for cosmetics.
She'll probably wear diamonds—Libran gems.

Castle saw in the beautiful, assured woman a master of color
coordination and unobtrusive makeup, suggesting to him that she was
principally interested in how others regarded her. A symptom of
narcissism? He made a wager with himself—not that he'd ever have a
chance to win it—that Libby was cold, or at least detached, as a sex
partner. (Imagining women in bed was new to him, too.)

He heard her tell Marie, in a firm but gentle voice, "Love, the trip
down here was a bitch. I've a pain in my lower back. Please, darling, let's
go to the house. I *must* lie down. Perhaps you'll give me a massage."

Late afternoon, Philip took his camera to the wharf where dilapidated
schooners from nearby islands brought fruits, vegetables, and lobsters to
sell. An American woman was there. She had an agreeable smile, lively
eyes, and a sensible face. She wondered at what speed he was shooting.
She wanted to talk and be friendly, which was fine with him except, as
he expected, a ship appeared in the harbor. He could read the name on
the bow: *Zodiac.*

The *Zodiac* dwarfed the other boats. She was a giant, with a
streamlined superstructure as though to shear the wind with the same
ease her keen prow sliced the sea. After she'd anchored; a gangway
dropped down the side and several figures descended to a small craft,
which headed for shore.

Canfield . . . Canny, for short . . . Cancer . . . crab. Philip
recognized Canny from Marie-Celeste's description. Canny was part-

owner of a Las Vegas hotel. He'd won the yacht on a *bet*. He moored it in Panama. The four friends—Canny was youngest, in his early thirties—sailed on it sometimes. She'd been on board once and couldn't get over the seagoing luxury. Canny was *really* smart but she didn't like his abrasiveness. He had a lot of sharp edges, made cutting remarks, could hurt. He'd pinched her ass. All that was typical of a male crab of a certain kind, the kind with Gemini rising. (Completely different from a female Libra with a rising Gemini, she told Philip.)

Canny wore a bathing suit and a captain's hat with a black visor. A crewman pointed the Boston whaler toward the dock, but Canny screamed at him in a high voice; he couldn't have cared what onlookers thought. He wanted to be delivered to shore. Maybe he didn't like climbing *up*. The dinghy went to where he directed, the wrong place, because rocks blocked the strip of sand he'd set his heart on. He scuttled over them agilely, reaching land with wet tennis shoes.

Did Canny resemble a crab? Perhaps, if Philip let himself be fanciful. The man had small feet and thin legs and *did* seem to walk sideways because he kept one shoulder forward, as though ready to ward off blows. The arms long and developed—Canny probably worked out with hand weights. He didn't have much of a neck. Philip placed his height at five-eight.

The round, grumpy face had a greenish pallor, as if this was a nocturnal creature that never saw sun. (It *was* amusing to convert Canny into a crab.) Between sandy-colored hair and eyebrows the bulging forehead, covered with acne scars, was a narrow band. Canny had a small nose but a wide mouth, both humorous and cruel. The badly shaped teeth were discolored, probably from cigars: he whipped one from a shoulder pouch and pretended to light the match on Marie's behind. The lips laughed but the eyes didn't, black, beady eyes starting out from their sockets, swiveling endlessly, staring without blinking, rolling on, seeing everything, always on the alert.

Marie-Celeste glanced at Philip just once; the strange eyes followed, seemed to find Philip, examine him. Canny snapped his fingers. Philip noticed an emerald ring.

The four of them were at a table in Le Boucan that evening when Philip walked in; liqueur in hand, he watched them surreptitiously, as did many others in the room. The quartet didn't look like they belonged there, or anywhere, perhaps. Canny wore a gleaming white uniform that could have belonged to an admiral, except the sleeves were too short and the buttons pulled. He fired volleys of jokes, it appeared from his gestures. Libby's bow mouth smiled tolerantly, though sometimes she frowned, as though Canny went too far. She wore a pale blue blouse with blue silk slacks. She'd swapped her diamonds for what Philip took to be opals: an opal necklace caressing her throat and opal bracelets on both wrists like ropes of bondage. Cappy was still in a black suit, but the starched white shirt was open at the neck in a transparent attempt to be casual. All listened when he spoke, because he was hard to hear or had authority or both: he was deferred to at all times. Marie-Celeste rarely talked. She poured white wine like a hostess.

When they left, Cappy stood abruptly, waiting stiff-shouldered for Libby to precede him. She glided out, lifting her chin slightly but looking neither left nor right, as if oblivious of the leers from tooth-missing locals. Canny took a different route, maneuvering between tables and chairs as though he moved through an obstacle course. Marie-Celeste went last. Reaching Philip, she stopped abruptly. Her eyes closed to slits as she examined the other end of the bar and the American woman Philip had chatted with on the wharf. He hadn't noticed her until he followed Marie's stare.

"I saw you with her this afternoon," Marie whispered. "You so much as talk to her and I'll . . . I'll . . ."

"Jinx my horoscope?" he said to irk her.

"As long as you're on this island you're mine!"

"Hey, play fair!" But Marie stalked off.

Martinez refilled his glass. "Tough customers."

"The big-eyed woman in blue?"

"Better believe it. I do."

"Cappy's in export-import, you said. Is that *all?*"

"You shouldn't ask questions like that."

"I did, though." He took a chance. "Smuggling?"

Joe grinned. "Depends on what you mean by smuggling. Running booze? That's for the little man. That guy is not little."

"Okay. Drugs?"

"Are you a narc, Philip?"

"Do I look it?"

"No. You're more like a college professor. I can see you in horn-rimmed glasses and a tweed jacket with pockets on the sleeves, smoking a pipe." The heavyset man chuckled.

"Except for the glasses and pipe, that's me—in real life."

"Okay. I wouldn't say they deal in drugs, no. Not as a serious thing, anyway. Those people wouldn't take that kind of risk."

"What, then?"

"I'm . . . not totally sure, to be frank. I understand Cappy's operation. Let's just say it's on a broad scale. But as for the group of them, there has been talk. They have incredible financial resources, I feel certain. Perhaps they believe the Caribbean is ripe for plucking, which it is. You Americans have weakened us, manipulated the prices of our raw materials, placed tariffs on our sugar for all your chatter about free trade. . . . We're going down the drain, no mistake about that." Joe's anger was real. "When are you leaving?"

"Day after tomorrow."

"I rather hoped you'd learn something. They're scum beneath their fancy trappings," Joe said truculently. He vanished and returned. "The lady down there . . . you just bought her a drink, on me. Show her a good time—she needs it. Forget about the other one."

Castle nodded as the woman mouthed thanks. She had on a flowered sleeveless dress more suitable for a garden party than the tropics. A leather cigarette case and a silver lighter were placed near her right hand. She smoked two cigarettes while he made up his mind to join her. He had another liqueur in the interval. When he stood by her he noticed her pump shoes and purse were color-coordinated. She wasn't wearing stockings. Her thickish ankles were covered with red mosquito welts. He had her story in ten minutes. Social worker . . . Hartford, Connecticut . . . thirty-four . . . divorced . . . no children . . . departing in the morning. She'd been on St. Jean for a week, met no one on paradise island, he guessed. She struck Philip as a level-headed person, only life had disappointed her.

He returned to her hotel, not having thought he would, but he was lonely already, or was he trying to get back at Marie-Celeste for being about to resume relations with the count? Probably, but it was too late for self-analysis. The woman and he had a nice time but there was no undersea eruption for him, as there had been with Marie. He woke at dawn, thinking of her. The American woman smiled in her sleep as he padded out. He drove to the house on the hill and watched the sun caress the bright bay. Too bad he had to leave.

13

If her friend planned to arrive by noon, he'd arrive by noon, barring disaster, Marie said. He was *so* precise. Philip arrived at the airport by 11:30, to be on the safe side.

It had been a busy morning. Sudden enthusiasm led to a half-hour's calisthenics, a long swim, a *three*-mile run back and forth on the curved beach, another swim. His tired body felt grateful.

At the airport he bought a lukewarm beer and settled down in an old plastic chair to wait. *My God, what are you doing here anyway? You don't believe this. Your hands are sweating and it's not just the heat. Jesus! If anyone had told you five days ago that you'd be lying in wait for the shadowy lover of your ex-lover, you'd have laughed incredulously, but not now.* He was fascinated by them and by his own actions.

As Philip glanced at his watch, a shiver passed through him. Soon he'd see the count.

What did he know about the man? ("Is a count an impressive title?" he'd asked. "It impresses me," said Marie-Celeste with sincerity.) She'd finally told him almost more than he wished to know. The count's young wife had been killed in a car accident, a tragedy. He'd changed his life, gone into a new business, something to do with currency exchanges, and had been so successful that he'd been able to open private banks all over the Caribbean. He had them in St. Vincent, Curaçao, Panama, plus the Cayman Islands. He traveled throughout the islands and the United States to meet with clients and arrange transactions. Suave, charming, he was very Old World and obscenely wealthy, naturally. "Naturally," said Philip, who detested the count even at second hand.

"Isn't it interesting." the girl went on, "that Aries, Leo, and Sagittarius are all fire signs? Astrologers call that the fiery triplicity. It contains spirited, princely, and generous natures. Memorable things happen because of it. You two might like each other if you met—which you won't."

"What happens if two Aries want the same woman?"

"Think of two powerful rams thundering across a field, horns ready," she had said with a little trill.

"I wish I were an Aries, not a goddamn stinking centaur. Can I change my sign?"

"The stars would take a dim view."

Ten minutes to go before noon, and still no count. It would be a close call. With uncharacteristic lack of remorse, Philip wished the count's plane would fall into the sea. (*No, no, you don't mean that,* his rational self told him. *You don't want him killed. You wish him to vanish. That's a big difference. Okay, vanish—but you wouldn't mind at all if he got killed.*) But the plane wouldn't crash, and he desired to see the man in the flesh, to have Marie-Celeste witness the count and him together. The man had years on him.

Marie-Celeste screeched in his ear, "Why don't you check into the airport and *live* here?"

"I like less noisy accommodations. I came to pay for the car."

"That's not what you said before."

"I have a right to change my mind, don't I?"

The gold-brown eyes narrowed. They looked like a cat's. "You were with that frumpy broad last night, weren't you?"

"What do you care? It's all over between us, you said."

"I *care*." She actually stamped her foot. "Confess!"

"How do you know? Did your horoscope tell you?"

"I *saw* how she looked at you. Joe Martinez pimped for her. She tipped him to do it. I *know*."

"You don't really," he said.

"It's a fucking good guess!"

He was mercifully spared further interrogation as a plane passed over the field. "Him?" She nodded. He squinted and asked, "How many Aero Commanders does the count have?"

"He *had* two." She looked away and muttered, "I didn't mean to say that."

The plane dropped through the V between the hills. "Marie . . ."

"I wish you wouldn't call me Marie. The name's Marie-Celeste."

"Okay, okay. Marie-Celeste. Celestial Marie. M.C.—the master of ceremonies. I guess this is really good-bye."

"I guess so. Take your hands off me quick."

"I can't. I love you. I can't believe it. I really do. I want a kiss."

She pecked him.

Would the count in some sense resemble a ram? A white-haired man, stoop-shouldered, emerged from the far side of the red Aero Commander. The creaky old count! *He's* able to rut with the lioness? *Ha-ha*. Philip's smile faded as the white-haired man opened the cabin door. The pilot! The count stepped easily into the sunlight.

Mother of God! Philip gasped as he approached. Raymond, or Ari—Ari, Aries—could easily have passed for fifty. About Castle's size, he had a lean frame that didn't need powerful muscles. Thick, graying reddish-brown hair with a widow's peak. Forehead high and arched like a proscenium, seeming to flow to semispherical eyebrows. Long nose slightly curved, flat planes of cheekbones, straight mouth, square at the ends. He strutted a little, quick, poised, impatient. . . .

"The perfect Aries," her voice goaded him softly. "Darling!" Marie-Celeste ran to the count and threw her arms around his thin waist, raised one foot, and lifted her face; the Count kissed her brow complacently and then looked up.

Philip felt battered by the bluff gaze. What did he see in those intense gray eyes with large irises? Curiosity? Warning? Sardonic humor? Malevolence? Just looking in his direction? No, there was something purposeful in the expressive stare. *He knows about me!* He dismissed another, more complicated thought that followed: *He has known all along!*

Philip was taking the late-afternoon sun on the beach when Marie-Celeste appeared, wearing a caftan. She sat on the sand, keeping her distance. "Listen, I told you I might ask a favor. Now I am."

"What, for God's sake?" He felt bitter, as though Marie were sequestered in somebody's harem, but not his. Self-pity had begun to seep into him again. He should never have gone to the airport.

She pulled up a long sleeve. "Look!" She pointed to her bicep. "I'm bruised! My jaw is sore, too. Is it swollen?" Tears seemed to lurk behind her blinking eyes.

Sweetheart. . . ." He was upset but something in her face made him draw back suspiciously. "What happened?"

"Raymond's terribly observant. When he saw you today, he sensed something. He made inquiries. Perhaps we weren't sufficiently discreet . . ." *Weren't discreet at all!* "He's aware I've been out with you. Aries are extremely jealous, like Leos, and hot-tempered, too. He lost his, became violent . . ."

Philip became skeptical. "You mean it?"

"Yes! He asked whether I'd *been* with you."

"You didn't tell him?"

"Of course not! But he suspects. He hit me! Several times! I don't bruise easily, so it doesn't show much. He was vicious. I hate him!"

"Really, Marie, you can't expect me to—"

"Believe me? Yes, you must. I've convinced Ari to do your horoscope. He's a master. But he insists on having the *precise* moment of your birth. Can you tell me? Please, for both our sakes. I don't want to feel guilty."

"Guilty?"

"About you. Those guys you saw with me at the bar the first night—they work for him. They'll beat you up. It's happened before."

"To other guys you've been with?"

She played with her toes, then stared at him intently. "Yes."

"Slut."

"I made Ari agree that nothing will happen to you if he approves of what he finds in your horoscope."

"And if he doesn't?"

She shrugged.

"This is bizarre. I'll go to the police."

"Oh, I wouldn't. The count owns considerable property on this island. Your influence is zero—or less. Can you swim to shore from ten miles out? Give me the exact time of your birth."

Philip could see no advantage in telling his real birthday—for all he knew, an astrological zealot like the count might take offense, *greater* offense. He was dealing with nuts. On the other hand, suppose Ari didn't like what he saw in the horoscope? "Would it be better for me if I were born before or after seven A.M.?" he asked cagily.

"I don't know." Her eyelids fluttered.

"Why are a couple of minutes, one way or the other, so important?"

"Because you're the astrotwin of the dead pilot," she blurted, a little theatrically.

"What difference does *that* make?"

"It does, really. An enormous difference to the count."

Philip decided to plunge. "Okay, I've given it some thought. My mother kept a baby book for me, with a flowered cover. I still have it somewhere. In it she recorded how much I weighed every week, how often I slept, you know. I tried to visualize the page, and, if I remember it right, I was born at seven-oh-six A.M." That was the truth.

"Thank God," she breathed. "From what I told them, they figured you'd been born after seven A.M. They will probably calm down. They wanted to be sure you weren't dangerous."

"*They?*"

"Yes. Ari, Canny, Libby, and Cappy all studied your chart."

"Jesus," he said, only half in disdain. He'd been more anxious than he realized. "Tell me, does the horoscope of one person ever closely resemble another's, born on a different date?"

"Only if the time of day is nearly the same and they are born within a few days of each other. Except for that, it'd be a real long shot. I suppose it could happen, though, even when the birthdays were months apart. Why?"

"Just wondered."

She rose.

"I'm getting tired of saying good-bye."

"Me too," said Marie-Celeste.

"Let's don't then."

"We'll see." She pranced across the sand.

It was his last night on St. Jean. Tomorrow the plane would take him out of here, and the strangest episode of his life would be over. A plane crash, a lovely girl, strange people, intimations of . . . what, he didn't know.

But tomorrow he'd be back in Chicago, buried again in responsibilities. Here he felt removed, relieved from the heavy concerns of the real world, but isolation couldn't last, and duty was inevitable. Perhaps he'd find a sensible woman like the American he'd slept with, marry her. If only he could drum up interest. . . .

That was the sticking point. Marie had been right on the beach—what uncanny insight she had: he'd lost enthusiasm. He thought again about relocating in San Francisco. He could easily get a teaching job there. No, no, it wasn't the *place*. He just didn't want to *do* anything, nothing he'd already done, at least. He needed a change, a big one. But it was crazy: you couldn't start out fresh at forty-five, lord, almost forty-six. He'd have to be satisfied with a future that was a continuation of the past.

Maybe he'd write an academic paper on astrological belief. Point: humans will always try to explain the world around them, if only for security. Point: they will gravitate toward cause and effect. Point: in the absence of other knowledge, they will find cause and effect even when none exists. Demons were the first causes, then stars, constellations, gods, astrology. Much later came the scientific outlook—his. No bootlegged causality permitted. But why did people persist in outmoded attitudes when far better answers were available? Or (to put it differently) when it was okay *not* to need answers for everything? Some people *couldn't* accept the role of uncertainty in human affairs. They built strange systems, had quirky views, interpreted reality eccentrically. . . .

The screeching of tires could only be Marie. As always, she burst through the doorway . . . hello, good-bye, hello, good-bye, *when* would it stop? But he felt like a kid with a reprieve from homework; he was glad to see her. "Philip! Raymond is intrigued with your horoscope. You're really unusual, he says. He wants to meet you!"

"As he wants to meet all your men?"

"Don't be jealous at a time like this! There's a great chance for a psychologist! These people are something else. You might learn a lot. Dinner tomorrow, okay?"

"Again the master of ceremonies."

"Leos *are* masters of ceremony. *Will* you come?"

"I'm leaving tomorrow, remember? My bag is packed."

"Unpack it! Anybody waiting at home? Are you expected?"

"No," he admitted.

"Why are you going, then?"

"I want to forget you, that's why! I don't want to *meet* your lover. . . . Do you love him?"

"I . . . That's beside the point. I'm . . . crazy about you."

"Invite somebody else."

"Listen, suppose I told you that we *might* be able to stay together a little longer? Would that grab you?"

Tonight she wore velour slacks and a flowered blouse, which she began to unbutton.

"You're trying to bribe me!"

She moved closer until her bare chest touched his. She put her hands on him. "Sure."

"What about the count and the others?" He could feel his body react.

"They're having a meeting. Don't worry—I won't be missed for a while." She was in his arms, and he held her hungrily. "*Will* you come? For dinner! Say yes."

Castle could almost see the count's gray eyes watching them.

14

She fetched him in the VW, claiming to be worried he might not find the house. Or was the count making sure that Philip showed up? Certainly the place was impossible to miss, even though it lay in a corner of the island Castle hadn't visited, perhaps because she hadn't wanted to take him there.

Flanking the drive, illuminated by spotlights, were two stone pillars topped by rams' heads with golden horns.

"He isn't modest about his sign," Philip said.

"Why should he be? Aries is the leader of the zodiac, the most intelligent of the signs."

The pool was lit up too, from beneath. It was the number five he'd seen from the air. "Why five?"

"Five's Ari's birth path. He considers it his lucky number. 'Five' people want to conquer the world."

"These creeps into numerology?"

"I wouldn't call them creeps—not to their faces. If you like yours the way it is."

"I just lost my appetite for dinner."

127

When she stopped the car, he tried to kiss her. "Not *here*."

"Later? I'm *definitely* leaving tomorrow."

"Are you?"

She got out and he followed her past several parked cars. Outbuildings flanked the main house, which stood on a hillside that dipped gently to the beach—a private beach. They entered through a domed structure of rock. "An old sugar mill. Ari imported it from Martinique," she explained. Inside was a cool tiled foyer with a splashing water fountain that shot an illuminated jet through an aperture in the roof. Another archway brought them into a chamber with white walls and exposed overhead beams. A dark-haired man waited, arms bulging in the sleeves of his waist-length cotton jacket. He was one of the two who'd accompanied Marie to Le Boucan. "This is Bob. You'll see Bill, too. We call them the Geminis—that's their sign, and they even look like twins, though they're not related. Bob, please get Mr. Castle a drink. Philip, I'm going to change. Relax. Nobody will bite."

He ordered a gimlet and Bob vanished wordlessly. Obviously for decoration, though the night was relatively cool, a tiny fire burned in a massive red stone fireplace with a mantel of dark polished wood six inches thick. Over it a rich tapestry hung. Heavy silver goblets, cups, and platters lay on glass shelves at the end of the long room filled with heavy, carved antique furniture a museum would have cherished. The paintings appeared to be genuine old masters. This was a Caribbean château.

Bob returned with the gimlet on a silver tray. The linen napkin bore the initials "RdV" in gold, surrounded by golden sunbeams. Philip heard footsteps on the stone floor and a clear baritone said, "Good evening. I am Raymond de Vaucresson, and I am pleased to make your acquaintance." Philip stood face to face with his rival.

"Hello. I'm Phil Castle." The count's hand was warm, lean, dry, strong. "I admire your furnishings."

"The antiques? They come from some of the finest houses in Europe." The count had a French accent but his English seemed flawless.

"And the paintings? Are they . . . ?"

Raymond displayed small, even teeth. "Fakes, I'm afraid. Still, as reproductions, they are quite good, aren't they? They should be. I commissioned them. I'm afraid of the humidity here, so the originals are in my vault in Paris. The paintings were chosen because of their themes. You have heard of my interest in astrology, I assume? Well, the Rubens"—he pointed a finger bearing an amethyst ring—"is a portrait of an unknown astrologer. That's a Van Gogh, of course. He painted another version of it called *Starry Night*, which is in the Museum of Modern Art in New York, but I prefer this one. The fire and passion of those stars! Arian qualities. Van Gogh was an Aries. Ah, you are looking at the astrological signs. Aren't they lovely? They were painted by Francesco del Cossa for the Duke of Ferrara. The girl there is March, for spring, sitting over Aries. Arians always attract lovely women. I don't own the originals of the frescoes, unhappily. I thought of, ah, extracting them from Italy, but it would cause a fuss. Perhaps you would like to see other parts of the house?" He smoothed his wavy hair.

"Very much."

The count wore a red velvet smoking jacket tied with a black sash, an ascot with a diamond pin on top of a white linen shirt with lace ruffles and cuffs, black trousers, patent leather shoes. Philip followed the shoes, thankful he had followed Marie's advice and put on his linen jacket.

"I didn't so much design this place as sculpture it," the count said. "I stood on the hillside to see and feel how the sun moves, the wind blows, the birds fly, the moon rises, the stars appear. I used lime to draw the design of the house on the ground. I wanted my little home to be organically one with the environment. There is no glass in the windows. I like the sea within reach. Much of the verdure—palms, *capa de oro*, rubber, cinnamon—does not normally grow here. I brought it in."

The house was on three levels sprawling down the hillside, with short semicircular stone stairways connecting them. Philip saw courtyards with gardens, a paneled library, an observatory with telescope and a glass bubble, sitting rooms in various colors. "Have you observed there are no right angles? Only wrong ones." The count chuckled softly. Corners were rounded, passageways arched; walls turned gently where they met tiled floors. "I don't like hard lines. Here, space curves, blends, flows together, as it should. Corners remind me of limits, the end of things, and we don't want things to end, do we? Nor do they have to end! They only *seem* to end because of the way we view them, stuck as we are with our faulty perspective. Human time is a formality, an inconvenience, don't you think? Someday we shall surmount our clocks, perceive that space and time are one, without boundaries. Heaven and earth are but two halves of a whole, totally interconnected and revealing endless correspondences, even in the smallest matters. The universe is organic and it lives forever in the ceaseless, vital struggle between stability and instability, symmetry and asymmetry, constancy and change. Perhaps we shall become eternal too, when we learn enough."

Pretentious phony-baloney! That the count feared death was the simple meaning of his foolish diatribe. Still, the man must be smart to have attained all *this*—to Philip's surprise he felt something akin to envy, he who'd thought himself immune to the lures of wealth. He'd have to keep a rein on his fantasies. He'd never be rich.

"You've met Mademoiselle Rombachet," the count said when they returned to the living room. Marie-Celeste looked gorgeous in a long bronze gown with a high neck and a back that swooped to her rear cleavage. She wore a big ruby ring. She grinned at him. "And this beautiful creature is Elizabeth Harris, aka Libby." Most people, he thought, have irregularities in their faces, or at least blemishes. Libby had none. He was pretty sure her body would be the same. Libby's blond hair was piled on her head; a diamond choker emphasized her long, slender throat. Beneath a calf-length lily-colored gown—he tried not to stare—her nipples were stiff. From excitement? Large pastel eyes stared at him impassively. Was there in those pools hints of prurience? "Mr. Castle," she acknowledged in a modulated contralto.

The man in black sat next to her on the couch, holding a salt-rimmed glass. A margarita. The cane at his side, Philip saw, had a bronze handle shaped like a goat's head. He wore a black onyx ring. "Señor Capablanca Morales Ramon. His parents were great admirers of the famous chess player Capablanca, and he was also a captain in the army of his beloved though poorly governed country, hence we call him Cappy." Using the cane, though with no sign of effort, the man rose five inches over Castle when he stood. He bowed from the waist without expression, dark eyes boring holes into Philip's brain. "Mr. Castle."

"How do you do, Señor Morales."

"We like soubriquets here. You may call me Ari if you wish," the count said. The square mouth became mocking as he went on, "This is Canfield Koster. We call him Canny because he is sharp, though he may not look it."

"Cut the shit, Ari," Koster said grumpily in a high, grating voice that was slightly feminine behind the bluster. He still wore nautical whites.

"Canny, I'm kidding. Must you take everything so seriously?"

"Do rams *kid?*" Canny shot back, and chortled. He extended a hand, which Philip took. It was thin and hard as a shell. "How you doing, Castle? Got a nickname too?"

"No."

"You're a Sag, aren't you? Maybe we can work something out along those lines. What's your middle name?"

"I don't use it." The wide-set, bulging black eyes seemed to have Philip in a crossfire. He answered despite himself, wincing, "It's Archibald."

"Archibald!" Canny clicked fingers. "Got it! Archibald! Sagittarius-the-archer! We'll call you Archy!"

Philip squirmed for comic effect, and the others laughed. If this was an audition, so far he was doing all right.

Dinner was served on a veranda with a thatched roof, above a sea spread with moonlight. A hurricane lamp flickered at the center of the round table.

"This is my chef, Fat," the count announced with a flourish as the Chinese man came from the kitchen. Fat wasn't exactly a midget but he couldn't have cleared four-ten without his lamb-chop holder. He reminded Philip of a yellow ceramic pot. His shiny round face crinkled with merriment when Raymond said, "Fat has several distinctions. He is the only chef I know of who has to stand on a box to reach the stove, and he is, in my opinion, which is worth considerable in such matters, one of the most original cooks alive. He has perfected a cuisine that is a combination of French, Creole, and Polynesian—Polynesia is where Fat is from. What is the menu, Fat? No, we shall be surprised. Fat has complete discretion in such matters. He is authorized to have flown in whatever he requires—so much is unobtainable on the island. Whenever you are ready, Fat." Fat departed. "I feel I have yet to offer Fat the supreme challenge in cookery. On the yacht, perhaps," the count continued.

"Oh? Fat is coming along on the trip?" Marie-Celeste said with animation.

"I believe he will. Canny's latest chef has quit. What is that, my dear Canfield, the sixth in less than two years?"

"The sons of bitches," Canny said moodily. He farted. The others did not appear to notice.

"Perhaps they don't like serving dinner at midnight. Canny's a nocturnal creature, left to his own devices. Cancer, his sign, is governed by the moon," the count said to Philip. He turned to Koster. "Going out later?"

"Yeah. All arranged. I'll pick her up at the café."

"Good. I'll be interested to hear what . . . her name again?"

"Sensa or something."

". . . she has to say." Philip looked at Marie-Celeste, who seemed puzzled.

"Are you interested in astrology, Mr. Castle?" Libby was asking casually.

"Please call me Philip—or Phil. It doesn't matter." He sat silently for a second, thinking his answer might be important. "Though I'm still not sure how useful astrology is, I'm trying to keep an open mind." Which wasn't true.

"Useful? My dear fellow, would I have acquired all this"—the count's global gesture included Marie-Celeste among his possessions—"except for astrology?"

"Well, maybe you would have."

"You never rely on portents when making a choice?"

"I don't think so," Philip said.

"I believe you told Marie-Celeste you had a difficult time deciding whether to come here," the count said. "How *did* you come to it? Tell me precisely."

"I weighed the alternatives, and this seemed the best one."

"Really?"

"I . . . ah . . ." He looked down. "Well, I almost forgot, but I made a sort of deal with myself. If the first bird to fly overhead went east, I'd come."

"You see! People reach many decisions through auguries, though frequently they don't realize it or remember doing so. They are tapping the universal spirit for information. In the same way, astrology is a tool for calibrating and utilizing our connection with the stars."

"It's worth considering," said Philip politely. But he was forced to ask himself why he had let a bird do his planning. *Stop it! You were tired of having to think everything out.*

The dinner served by Bob and the other tough, Bill, while Fat clapped his little hands in delight at the eaters' appreciation, was everything the count had claimed for the chef. Cold crayfish in a spicy mango sauce, a clear broth ("Chicken?" Philip inquired; "Dove," cooed Fat) containing the twelve astrological signs in pasta, South American venison *au poivre* and flaming with cognac, baby artichokes with hollandaise sauce, arugala salad ("The dressing *must* be virgin olive oil, lemon juice, garlic, salt, and pepper," the count insisted), twelve different kinds of cheese served with rolls Fat had baked, papaya pie, *petits fours, café filtre.* Philip had never seen the delicious wines, five of them, at a Chicago liquor store and doubted he ever would.

During dinner, they talked about astrology and nothing else. "Did you see the piece about Telly Savalas? I clipped it," Canny Koster said.

"Canny's always clipping things. You should see his files," Ari put in.

Canny went on. "Telly Savalas played the spaghetti circuit in Europe. He was a *nothing*, for Chrissake, until he gets this part in a movie, and his horoscope tells him his best thing is his head. He should draw attention to it. So he shaves it, and look what happens!"

"His horoscope predicted he'd become a big star if he did?" Philip wondered.

"You wasn't listening, Archy," Canny rebuked him. "His horoscope tells him to *use* his head, if you get me. It helped him make the right choice, which is different from prediction."

The moment of silence seemed strained. "The truth is," observed the count, "that we Cardinals—"

"Excuse me?" said Philip.

The count's face was slightly self-conscious. "We call ourselves the Cardinals because our birthdates represent the four cardinal signs whose origins lie in the solstice and equinoctial points of the zodiac. They are associated with the ideas of primal cause, initiative, and action. But we Cardinals don't think the same way about astrological predictions. Canny isn't high on them—he's a numerologist who specializes in character analysis. Libby is a *horary* astrologer—she works on the basis of questions asked at a given moment. Libby shies away from specific predictions too. Cappy is a *mundane* astrologer and we rely on him to catch the drift of coming economic and political events. He believes astrology can provide accurate predictions in such matters, as do I. My own discipline is called Uranian astrology, a rather complex form of natal astrology, using higher harmonies of planetary motion, with larger numbers of planets. Eight, to be precise. All undiscovered, though they will be someday. I feel Uranian astrology yields accurate prophecies about individuals."

"Tell him how you predicted Nixon's downfall," Marie-Celeste prompted.

"Nixon? Oh, that was interesting. With his sun opposite his Neptune, he obviously doesn't know who he is. Too much self-deception and self-delusion. Too great a need for authority, power, and prestige. His Pluto's in the tenth house, a troubled placement, and natal Mars is opposite his Pluto, both in square to Admetos, meaning a scheming trait, which is self-defeating. Had I been his astrologer, I would have told him to be terribly cautious before the Watergate period, because of Neptune's August 1973 station aspecting his natal sun and his Washington ascendant. In 1974 an approaching eclipse on his tenth house, Pluto, square to Admetos, did not bode well for him. But, not knowing the astrological situation, he panicked and covered up, which led to his fall."

"But isn't what you say about Nixon after the fact?"

"Ari said he predicted Nixon's fall from power a year in advance!" Marie-Celeste crowed, then pouted. "I wish I could do it. You Cardinals have such powers!" She stared at the gorgeous blond. "Tell Philip how you analyzed Elizabeth Taylor."

"All right," Libby said. "Pluto is difficult to deal with. It's given Elizabeth Taylor much trouble."

"Tell him why," Marie-Celeste urged.

"Well, you have to understand Liz. She's *such* a pleasant person, but she has troubles too. Like money and weight. Liz feels poor because she has only several million dollars. The darling! I am sorry for her, I really am. Why, she's trying to sell the delightful diamond Richard gave her, for two million plus. Imagine, having to part with it! I'm tempted to put in a bid. . . ."

"Now, now, you have other uses for money," said the count in a fatherly way. "Go on about Elizabeth Taylor."

"There's the sun in Pisces, also very good for an acting profession. Pisces is like the sea—it has all the elements in it, all the signs. A Pisces actor can play anybody! She has Mercury in Pisces conjuncting the sun—that's the ability to communicate who she is, in subtle ways, through Pisces. She's an emotional thinker—I've done her horoscope, of course, though she doesn't know it—who never reasons things out; with her it's sheer emotional reaction. She's compulsive, with Libra rising—a social sign: she has to be harmonious with her environment, she *needs* peace. Poseidon conjuncting the ascendant gives her a very original personality and yet she can simulate a sort of normal life, like an adaptable, old-fashioned married lady. She plays roles. Pluto's in there, which gives her a drive for power and career which ultimately takes over, no matter what she intends. She wants *importance*, as what woman does not! Probably, as a child, she felt put down, so she overcompensates, if that's the word, Philip. . . ." She smiled at him with her bow mouth.

"It'll do."

Libby went on explaining Elizabeth Taylor's personality in terms of her signs. For Philip, it was a peculiar exercise, reasons for behavior were being supplied, just as he, analyzing the actress as a psychologist, would have found reasons, only very different ones. . . .

He tore his eyes from Libby—Marie-Celeste was watching him, he felt, and listened to the calm deep voice of Cappy Morales, who had been asked, by Ari, about President Carter.

"Not a bad man, for a North American politician," Morales was saying. "They have, in general, profound limitations. Material versus idealistic ambitions cause tremendous problems among them. In a past life, Jimmy Carter was a minister—perhaps a priest in Central Europe or Germany. A hellfire-and-damnation preacher—perhaps Martin Luther himself! He has the mailed fist and the velvet glove—the fist is Saturn rising in Scorpio. Scorpio is the most powerful sign, Saturn the strongest planet for character. But he has a gentle, weak Libra ascendant, which reduces his power. He is too concerned with ideals, to the exclusion of practical matters, though he tries to solve the problem by applying his religious beliefs—that's all in his horoscope. Neptune in his mid-heaven makes it difficult to put his religious ideas to political use. He's bound to suffer feelings of great discouragement and disillusionment because his goals are too rigid, impractical. With his moon in Scorpio, he is a disciplinarian and would like to discipline others—the moon stands for other people—but he vacillates. His Mercury is heavily afflicted, which means he gets into trouble for what he says. He will take strong stands then realize there is another side. That his sun and ascendant are in Libra account for his lack of consistency."

"Will he be given the nomination?" inquired the count.

"That I cannot tell you yet."

De Vaucresson said, "Coffee? A cigar? Liqueur?"

The long cart that was wheeled to the table must have carried fifty varieties of liqueurs. Philip accepted—and loved—what Raymond said was an unusual one, called Saba Spice. "I must say, your kind of astrology sounds different from what you read in the newspapers."

"Sun-sign astrology!" Libby said. "It's amusing, perhaps, but not to be taken seriously. You wouldn't make important decisions based on it, as you would with the real thing."

"What kind of decisions?" Philip asked.

"Oh, *any*. A sex partner. Marriage, certainly. How many divorces could be avoided if people studied each other's horoscopes in advance! Or business decisions. Even committing a crime," Libby offered.

"A *crime*? How would astrology help you?"

"By character readings. Were I a criminal, I'd obtain the birth data of those I planned to, ah, victimize. If you know who someone *is*, it follows that you know what they'll *do*. And from my own horoscope I'd have a sense of how things would turn out for me in relation to them. That's how I'd operate, were I in crime," Libby said from her demure mouth.

"Character *is* prediction. Can you argue, Philip Castle?" the count demanded abruptly.

"No, not really."

"*I'd* want to look for weak places in a plan if I was a crook," said

Canny, snapping his fingers as though to a secret beat. He took a cigar
from a box. "The numbers in my birth force would show them. I'd
wanna make sure my defects don't get in the way. Everybody's got
defects, even me."

"You?" said the count in feigned surprise.

"And surely," said the man they called Cappy in his formal way, "you
would wish to know what future environment you would be operating
in. Whether there might be unsettled conditions, shortages, crop
failures, wars, revolutions, inflation . . . Such might alter one's plans
considerably, if one had intentions of certain sorts, is it not true?"

"His prognostications have been remarkably accurate," Ari said. "Oh,
not always, but the Tall One is shrewd. Do you anticipate from the
horoscope any important impending developments in the Caribbean,
Capablanca?"

"The government of Grenada will almost certainly fall in the middle
of this month," said Cappy's soft deep voice.

"We can only wait and see. And my kind of astrology, as I said, is
quite good at prophesying what people will do, including myself, whom I
study constantly. Suppose my Jupiter and the sun were in opposition;
that might produce overconfidence, the basic reason for committing
errors. I should know, being an Aries." The count employed the first-
person singular a good deal, Philip noted. "I would want a well-placed
Saturn to ensure caution. Or I might decide not to move at all. I might
wait for a period when Mars and Saturn are in trine, giving me
practicality and courage. I'm oversimplifying, in view of our new friend's
lack of acquaintance with the subject."

"You people seem awfully interested in crime," Philip said guardedly.

The count looked eagerly around the table. "Shall we tell him? Why
not? What have we to lose? Philip won't talk—that he can be trusted
shows clearly in his horoscope—and, even if he did, who would listen?"
He stared at Castle. "You are at this very moment in a nest of crooks.
Shall I go on? Yes? Ha! We four are behind the smuggling in the
Caribbean—liquor, guns, et cetera, though our slice of the drug trade is
very limited. Cappy is the executive officer in the business—we three
might be thought of as the board of directors. We make decisions on the
use of capital and assist in the forward planning. It is jolly good fun and
immensely profitable. Does that shock you?"

"I suspected something like it, as a matter of fact."

De Vaucresson chastised Marie-Celeste with his finger. "The girl reveals too much. But you won't tell anyone, will you, Philip? It wouldn't be friendly."

"It's your business, not mine."

"Does it interest you that we are somewhat nefarious characters?" the count seemed to tease.

"I suppose it does, yes" Castle admitted.

"We hardly conform to the cherished ideals of the good middle class, or to the stereotypes of organized crime, either," Raymond went on. "Of course, I suppose we are more on the entrepreneurial level than the underworld is. As a psychologist, you have read about the criminal mind, but we are hardly typical. You might find us rather unusual, Dr. Castle. It is *Dr.* Castle?"

"I'm never quite sure a Ph.D. counts."

"Oh, that you're a full professor at Northwestern with a Ph.D. from the University of Chicago certainly counts."

"How—?"

"I like to know the credentials of my guests. I'm looking forward to reading your book *The Psychology of New Nations*." So! Ari had checked on him, which wouldn't be hard. The book was in a catalog. Philip's name appeared in professorial listings—they wouldn't carry his birthday, the real one. *Who's Who* would, but the volume with his biography hadn't yet appeared. No, Ari wouldn't make a point of asking when Philip was born. For all the prudence the Cardinals undoubtedly exercised, they simply didn't expect a person to fib about something so commonplace. Besides, the count was probably an impatient sort who wouldn't bother himself with details unless forced. "Special guests, I should say."

"Thank you, but I don't deserve it, I'm sure."

"I admire your modesty," returned the count. "I can even tell you the name of the medal you won in the Korean war—the Distinguished Flying Cross."

That information wouldn't be hard to find, either. The Arizona papers had played him up as a war hero. His birthday wouldn't have been mentioned, only how old he was. And a private eye, if that's who de

Vaucresson had contacted—he must have moved quickly—wouldn't be looking for vital statistics, only corroboration that he *had* been in the war. It occurred to Philip to admit, there and then, that he'd lied about his birthday, but he had the peculiar sensation that the Cardinal's interest in him would abruptly end. So might Marie-Celeste's. Besides, he was having too much fun. "You're thorough," he said, flattered that the count had been studying him.

"I've been through your horoscope with a fine-tooth comb," said the count with controlled intensity.

"What can you predict about *me?*"

"Let me see. Something not too distant. You have an estranged wife, from what Marie-Celeste tells me. I will venture that within three weeks she will arrive on the island of St. Jean looking for you."

"What are you saying?"

"You will learn if I am right or wrong. That is—how do you Americans put it—sticking my neck out, isn't it?"

"It sure is. She could look for me in Chicago, where I'll be tomorrow."

"No. I saw a person reentering your life in a watery place, which must be the Caribbean. That person has to be your wife! I venture that she will be sad, filled with regret at a hasty, ill-advised action, but you will have embarked on a new, far more fulfilling life by then. You have, you know, completed your career in psychology—you sense that, I am sure. If you continue, you will only repeat yourself, which is not in your nature. You have lost interest in your profession, and will never regain it. It is time to do something more, ah, amusing."

"It's true," said Libby.

"Yes," Cappy said.

"Yup. *Che sarà, sarà,*" Canny chimed in. "Speaking of which, gotto split." He stamped out his cigar and scurried from the room.

Libby, still complaining about her lower back, went to bed. Cappy had correspondence—or was it correspondences, astrological ones?—to take care of. Marie-Celeste vanished. Philip found himself alone with the count in the library.

Ari unlocked a cabinet and produced an antique egg-shaped bottle. "Absinthe," he remarked. "Almost impossible to obtain today.

Throughout the world absinthe is illegal because, being made of wormwood, it causes blindness. But it also produces joy, and, taken in very small quantities, is perfectly safe." He poured a drop in each of two silver shot glasses containing Finnish vodka, he said, and passed one to Philip. The count raised his. "To the voyage."

The licorice-tasting liquid prickled Philip's tongue. "Have a good time on your cruise."

"*Our* cruise," the count protested. "Philip, you are a mature, responsible individual, which is hard to find. With a sense of humor, too. I like you, and wish to know you better. You have depths. I want you to join us on our little trip."

Outside, a car drew up and Philip heard Canny's shrill voice. "It's very nice of you," he said, shaking his head, "but I'm going to Chicago."

The count responded as though he hadn't listened. "The yacht is a dream boat. You'll enjoy her. And it will be a rare opportunity to visit some of the less-frequented islands, which are lovely. Frankly"—the spare man leaned forward in his leather chair—"you will be doing me a favor. We Cardinals will be occupied by business, and you and Marie-Celeste will be free to be tourists. You will be a companion for the girl. Is it agreed?"

"Thanks."

"You're coming, then?" said Raymond with a delighted smile.

"No"

"Philip, *Philip*." De Vaucresson patted Philip's knee, and his voice assumed a metallic quality. "You are *forbidden* to refuse! I *insist!* You're an adventurous soul—Sagittarius the traveler. You will come. We'll only be gone a week or so."

"I'd like to, but . . ."

"Philip, please trust me. The girl informed you I was fascinated with your horoscope, yes? I wish to test my theories—and you are a rare opportunity because your configuration is quite unique. You may be marked by an unusual propensity for danger, which you have suppressed for years. I want to see how your Mars—your warlike, aggressive side— would operate if freed from self-imposed and social restraints."

"Warlike?"

"Yes. Also competitive. For me war and competition have similar roots. If you are what I suspect you are—I shall have to see—I may have something wonderful to suggest, the chance of a lifetime. You may be marked for riches. Have faith in me. Can you refuse?"

Philip had to admire the nerve of the man, but the idea of bunking alone on the ship while Raymond slept with the leonine girl repelled him. "Sorry," he said.

"Listen! Do you think we are wicked persons because of our—how shall I say it—avocation as smugglers? Don't be naive. It is a means to an end. We have a much larger purpose. There is a powerful, evil man in this world of whom you will hear more; we intend to bring him to justice. Perhaps you can help. Perhaps you will even find something to believe in with your whole being. You'd like that Philip Castle, admit it! You're awash on the shoals of indifference—don't tell me otherwise. It is a universal disease, for which the cure, the only cure, is action. You must return to the struggle. But we shall discuss this further, I am sure." The count smiled pleasantly and called, "Marie-Celeste?" As if by magic she appeared, wearing chinos. "Isn't there a spare cabin on Canny's yacht? Next to yours?"

"Yes, there is."

"Good! Philip will use it. I'm so glad you've accepted, my friend. We depart in two days' time."

"But—"

"And," the count interrupted, "Marie-Celeste will drive you home now. I have a fearful headache. Good night!"

When they reached the VW, Castle thought he heard a woman— Sansa?—cry out in one of the small buildings. In pleasure, or could it be pain? No, he was a little drunk. He let Marie-Celeste lure him into bed and was grinning triumphantly when she finally left.

15

As he had the morning before, Philip rose at dawn. Chirping birds brought him to the terrace, where his eyes fastened on the airstrip below. He went inside quickly, returning with field glasses.

Yes, the woman was Sansa—he'd thought so from her walk. She was across the runway, heading back, probably toward the base of the hill, where she lived. What did she clutch in her hand? Leaves? No, it looked like money, American money. Had someone left it there for her, or did she have a cache buried in the ground?

As she stepped slowly on the airstrip, Philip saw at the opposite end of the runway the props of the twin-engine plane whirling. The sound reached him as the plane leaped forward. Sansa must have seen the racing machine at the same time. She was in the center of the strip. She stood uncertainly for a second. The plane gathered speed as it thundered down on her. She visored her eyes against the morning sunlight. It was already too late for the pilot to brake; he had to get up, and fast. Sansa ran back just as the pilot changed direction. *Duck*, Philip screamed to himself, but she didn't. A wing tip bore down on her like a giant scythe. The head rode on top of it briefly, as if to observe the body, which fell, spouting blood from the neck in a torrent. The money scattered in the propellor wash. The red Aero Commander lurched skyward while the head bounced down the runway. It came to rest in the sand by the sea.

Philip retched over the railing, then lay on the deck, breathing hard. When he drove the Moke down the hillside, people had gathered at an ambulance into which Sansa's remains were loaded. The Aero Commander was parked down the field: the pilot had landed again. The count was with him.

"*Terrible, terrible,*" Raymond was saying to a gendarme as Philip tried to follow his rapid French. ". . . my pilot . . ." He gestured toward the white-haired man, who looked hunched and old. ". . . avoid hitting the woman . . . but . . . she was out on the field. Why, I don't know . . . ran straight toward the aircraft . . . there was not time for him to . . . drugs perhaps? . . . a suicide? . . . bizarre? . . . We had come down to give something to my pilot to bring to Grand Cayman . . . I did not witness . . . not pilot's fault . . . he will return for an official investigation, if needed . . . thank you, officer . . . a tragedy indeed . . ."

It was only as the count walked away that the gray gaze, hooded, furtive, menacing, met Philip's. *Do you know anything? If so, you will not talk,* they seemed to say. Or did Philip imagine the malevolence? And what *could* Philip report? That the count had lured the foolish woman onto the strip, that his pilot had murdered her? Could he prove it? Who would believe him? And it really *might* have been an accident. The count was muttering in a small, nervous voice, "I have never been so upset. Why did this have to happen? If only I had prepared her horoscope—what was the woman's name? Perhaps something can be done for her family."

Philip went back to the house, prepared a *café filtre,* and decided: he would leave—now. Maybe the killing had not been intentional—his liberal instincts wanted to believe that—but if there was the slightest chance that she'd been murdered, he wanted out, Caribbean cruise or no, Marie-Celeste or no. He didn't wish to enter the "zone of death," as the Frenchman Durkheim had called it. Durkheim had been a father of modern sociology. Somewhat romantically in Philip's view, Durkheim postulated that people entered the zone of death willingly; one way or another they laid themselves open to it. He would not. The image of the count's spare, tightly stretched face at the runway suddenly reminded him of a skull.

He needed all of ten minutes to pack. There was a nine-o'clock flight to St. Martin. He got to the airport an hour early.

He bought a beer and sat until the window opened at eight-thirty. He produced his ticket, which the clerk put a tab on, indicating the flight. It was all so casual. Right on time, the Sea Otter came in through the V, landed, and taxied back. The passengers debarked, and Philip started through the gate with his hand luggage. He was thinking distractedly about how to contact Marie-Celeste from Chicago, when the shirt-sleeved gendarme— the same one who had admitted him—scrutinized him and said in English, "Your passport, please."

"Passport?" Entering had been so easy he hadn't expected to be asked for it. He fumbled in the breast pocket of the city jacket he carried over his arm and produced the dark blue booklet. The gendarme riffled the pages. "You have no entrance stamp."

"Stamp? Jesus, nobody said anything about a stamp."

"Since your passport isn't stamped, you have not been here, so how can you leave?"

"Nonsense! Who needs a stamp on St. Jean?"

"You do, m'sieu." The man glanced away.

"Okay. How do I get one?"

"You must go to the prefecture of police."

"I can't take this flight, then?"

"I am afraid not. Not without an entrance stamp."

"I see." Philip tried to control his temper. "Are they open?"

"Every day. But I must tell you, in cases of illegal immigration like yours, the stamp might require a week."

"A *week!* Come on."

"It is necessary to contact Guadeloupe and then Paris as to your status. We are part of metropolitan France, you know. Are there people on the island who can identify you?"

"Count Raymond de Vaucresson knows who I am," Philip said stiffly.

"M'sieu de Vaucresson could be a big help. Why don't you talk to him?"

Some help Ari would be.

* * *

Philip went to the café around noon, when it opened. Joe Martinez polished the bar with a white cloth. He seemed subdued. "To walk out on that runway was a pretty crazy thing for Sansa to do," Castle said at once.

"Planes don't usually take off so early in the morning, here," Joe's bass voice said.

"But this one did. And Sansa panicked. I saw it happen."

"If that accident had been avoided, there would have been another one. I predicted trouble," Joe said with baleful brown eyes. "I knew there would be with your new friends."

"But why would Sansa be in trouble with *them?*"

"That long-distance phone call must have *concerned* one of them. She was lucky to have gotten through, or unlucky, I should say. Her action was very ill-advised. Not that I am truly sorry for the woman. She worked for the wrong people. She claimed to have other reasons, but money was the real one."

"And *they* found out about the telephone call?"

"I would assume. Through Cappy's ties in El Parador, to which the call was placed. He was probably notified on the count's telex. Then, I imagine, one of them talked to her, induced her to come to the strip."

Canny had been with Sansa last night. Perhaps the cries he'd heard indeed had meant pain. Maybe Canny had tortured the East Indian woman for information. Perhaps the count had arranged to pay her off at the strip to lure her there, to kill her before she talked, departed in his jeep before Philip woke. Maybe. But an accident seemed equally likely. "How did you find out about the call?"

"I know what happens here. What I don't know is what those four people are up to."

"They're sailing in the big yacht in the harbor. They plan some business, en route." Philip trusted Martinez for some reason. "Smuggling, I guess."

"There is more to it than that, I tell you. I wish you could find out."

"I've been asked to go along."

"You *have?*" The proprietor seemed astonished. "Are you?"

"I sure wasn't as of this morning. I tried to get out of here, but a cop wouldn't let me." He related the incident about his passport.

"I've never heard of such a thing!" Martinez cried. "De Vaucresson has influence. He must be very eager to have you accompany him."

"He says he's on the side of the angels, Joe."

"But which side?"

He ought to decline, he knew, but felt divided, now that the shock of
Sansa's death had begun to wear off. He drank his beer and watched the
bay through the open part of the barroom. He really wanted, he had to
admit, a luxurious Caribbean cruise—never would a chance like this
come again. It would be interesting to study these self-styled Cardinals,
learn why he might be "marked for riches," as Ari said. (No! Don't
dream about that!) And Marie-Celeste—M-C as he'd started to think of
her—would be there. Hardly out of mourning for his marriage, and
possibly on the rebound, Philip was enamored. He wanted to stay with
the girl as long as he could. The mane of hair, the gold-brown eyes, the
creamy skin, the . . .

Come on! What's the real issue? That you don't really care what
happens? You're even more adrift than you let on to yourself, with a past
that doesn't add up and a future not worth fighting for. Your inner life's a
turmoil, a shambles. You haven't conquered your problems and you never
will. You're so tired of dealing with reality. You long for something
different, and here it is.

No! Don't go! You shouldn't nest with crooks. Have nothing further to
do with any of them, including Marie-Celeste.

On the other hand (quit qualifying, damn you!), maybe the count did
stand for justice and human betterment. Maybe he did want to bring a
bad man to justice. Inside Philip, perhaps there was an idealist struggling
to get out—he hadn't felt committed to anything for so long. It would be
good to try: the Count was right.

Martinez muttered, "Watch yourself," and moved down the bar.

In the doorway Philip saw a man in a tie-dyed shirt with a camera. He
took a stool near Castle and ordered a beer, in French. "Have one on
me," he said to Castle in slightly accented English.

"Okay."

"Been here long?"

"Rounding out a week. Great place. I could stay forever," Philip
replied enthusiastically.

"It looks splendid, yes. I'm on a cruise boat." The man had a tattoo on one arm. It said "I Love." The object of affection wasn't specified. The man drank from his beer glass. "Tourists learn so much."

"Do they? I thought tourists never learned anything. It's a sort of definition of tourists, isn't it?"

"But I would have thought, after a week, you'd find out many things. Drugs, say. Tourists often want drugs."

"You?"

"I wouldn't mind a little dope to take on board."

"Sorry, I'm not a user."

"Let's suppose . . . know how to play 'let's suppose'?"

"About hypothetical things?" Philip drank beer.

"Exactlee! Let's suppose the government of France were interested in smuggling, the drug trade. Let's suppose the natives of a certain isolated island would say nothing. Let's suppose a citizen of . . . America, say, were offered some large bills in his own currency, merely for divulging what little he had learned about smuggling and drugs on a small island. Enough to pay for his trip? A little more perhaps? No official involvement? Let's suppose this foreigner had information that might help France. Our two countries have been allies for a long time—ever since your revolution."

"Okay, let's suppose."

"Let's suppose you have heard things. It would be most useful if you were to divulge them. The term Sûreté is familiar?"

"Let's suppose that was the French police."

"Let's suppose I am one." The man with the tattoo took a card from his wallet. It had a typewritten name, his picture, and an official seal.

"Let's suppose I could help. How?" Martinez had his back to them; they were alone.

"I made myself clear. There are individuals acting against the laws of France, of which this island is part. Let's suppose you have heard or seen something."

"Okay. Smuggling goes on here—I *know* it! There is a dock on the far side of the island."

"A dock." The Frenchman sighed. "Who uses the dock?"

"Why, liquor smugglers! It goes on all the time. I couldn't believe it when I learned."

"But *which* smugglers? Have you met anyone involved?"

"Me?"

"It has come to my attention that you made acquaintances, dined in a certain home. Was nothing said about illegal activities?"

"You mean Count de Vaucresson? You must be joking! A man like him!" Philip sounded shocked.

"I do not joke, m'sieu. Please! Search your memory. Were not statements made about smuggling throughout the Caribbean? It is of the utmost importance that you remember."

"How could I forget? It was only last night. Nothing was said along those lines, no. Believe me, I would help you if I could, but I can't. Surely the information about the dock . . ."

"The dock," the man repeated contemptuously. "Very well, then." He stalked out.

Martinez stepped up to him. "I've seen that man, but I don't remember where. What was it about?"

"A test, I think."

"I think from your face that you must have passed."

A folded newspaper perched on the end of the bar. It was a daily from Puerto Rico, dated Monday, March 5, 1979, yesterday. A tourist must have left it. Philip hadn't seen a paper since he'd reached the island on March 1. He glanced at it without interest—the roiling world seemed too remote. Time enough to catch up on the news when he returned. The paper had an astrological page for the month. He checked the prospects for his real birthday, the 21st, the first day of Aries. "In Aries, the sun is at its most splendid. You are fiery and brilliant with a great sense of adventure and an aggressive, pioneering spirit that rises to challenges. You are original, seizing on new ideas, and you are ambitious, with the daring practicality to realize your ambitions." Oh, yeah, *what* ambitions? "You stand as a personality exalted, and you, as a highly interesting personage, must never forget that it is your privilege to lead the procession. At your worst, you are primarily cocksure, but at your best you are exceptionally able to inspire confidence. Empty intellection, idle speculation, and ideal considerations are all tiresome to you unless they lead directly to action, to freedom from social conditioning. But never forget that you were born on the cusp between two signs. That is a dangerous place, and those who inhabit it must be extremely careful."

Philip closed the newspaper as Marie-Celeste ran in. "A change in plans! The yacht leaves this afternoon, as soon as they can finish loading," she said with excitement.

"Anything wrong?"

"Wrong? Not that I know of. They huddled with their horoscopes and decided today was the best time. All set to leave?"

"My things are."

Her mouth was incredulous. "Scared?" she taunted.

In fact, he was—the sense of danger was palpable. Yet enjoyable, too; he'd been a sedentary so long—him, an "aggressive, pioneering spirit." And still another argument in favor of going emerged in his mind. Crazily, Philip Castle wanted to take on Ari, Count Raymond de Vaucresson, and triumph. In the end, perhaps, the pros and cons weren't important. He just had a feeling he ought to take the trip.

"I'm coming," he said. It was a turning point, he knew.

The ship's captain waved cheerfully when Philip came on board. "I Love" was tattooed on his arm.

At two A.M., all lights extinguished, a daggerlike shape hove to near a promontory on St. Jean. Rubber rafts went noiselessly over the side and men with blackened faces climbed down into them. Reaching shore, the men clambered up a shallow hill to the large house with a small sugar mill for an entrance. Lamps burned in the interior.

"Rough them up a little if they resist, but none is to be seriously hurt. And no rape. Understood?" whispered a man with braid on his cap above the visor.

The house was unlocked. The sailors from Hernandez' navy entered with drawn guns, knife handles protruding from their belts. They divided into groups, and moved silently. A scream came from somewhere in the interior. The men quickly reassembled in the living room. One had a dripping wound in his arm. He pointed to another, a man with saffron skin, black mustache, and a large hairy mole on his cheek. Knife drawn, he was about to deface a painting of a maiden and a ram.

"Him! He stuck me! It was dark back there. He must have mistaken me for one of *them*."

"Not me," said the man with the mole. "You're crazy."

"Enough," said the officer. "Whoever used the knife was in violation of orders. No! Do not touch that painting! We must leave no sign, in case we have to return. Back to the ship. Report to the infirmary at once, sailor." The men returned to their rafts.

A surreptitious check of the outer harbor revealed that the large yacht supposed to be moored there had departed. The commander broke radio silence, as instructed, reporting in code. The answer arrived in the morning when the warship was at sea: "Bear south."

PART III

16

Philip Castle stood in the stern, watching the gap widen between St. Jean and the *Zodiac*, flying the Panamanian flag. *What* was he doing here with four sociopaths bound to get him in trouble sooner or later? It was all because of Marie-Celeste. *La belle dame sans merci* hath thee in thrall. He, who knew the futility of escape, was engaging in precisely that activity.

Ellie, who had bragged that Richard *(damn him!)* would set her up in an expensive apartment with a maid, take her on trips. If she could see Philip now! *He*, not her, traveled on a multimillion-dollar yacht with a three-star chef on board, he, Castle, sporting an ever-darkening tan. He, Philip, the quiet, responsible professor, had bedded a young woman who could easily have been featured in an article about beautiful people. He, Philip, had embarked on an adventure a travel agent couldn't supply. It was delicious, and all because he had lied about his birthday in a frivolous moment on the beach. He laughed out loud.

"What's so funny, Archy?" a sharp voice demanded suspiciously. Canny-the-crabman stood at his side, holding a cigar.

"Oh, I was only thinking that maybe I was dead and dreaming all this."

153

"The dead don't dream," said Canny. "C'mon, I want to show you the ship. The swimming pool I can cover with plates for a dance floor, or even a copter pad. For a *little* chopper, which don't take up too much room with them blades."

Fingers snapping, eyes darting, Canny quickly provided nautical vital statistics and history so rapidly that Philip had a hard time following. *Zodiac* had been built, and later modified, for greater speed and range by Lurson, of Bremen, which made motor torpedo boats in World War II and still did. She was 160 feet long. In her huge engine room were two MTU engines, with 9,000 horsepower together. A third screw engine between them had been replaced by a gas turbine booster. She could make 40 mph, enough to pull water skiers, and with the booster could go even faster for short distances. Her normal cruising range was 4,000 miles.

The *Zodiac* had a flying bridge in addition to her wheelhouse. A long, narrow Cigarette speedboat covered with canvas hung from davits on the upper deck. Video cameras monitored all functions in the engine room, which were also printed on a computer terminal in the wheelhouse. Other TV cameras were mounted outside as well. The ship carried a crew of six, usually, but for reasons Canny did not explain, there were ten this time, plus the Cardinals' retinue. Except for the captain, a former officer in the French navy, the crew was German.

Further modifications had been made in Israel, but Canny wouldn't specify which. He had a way of talking freely but mysteriously at the same time.

Cantiere Navali de Chiavera of Italy had reconstructed the interiors, designed by some Italian fag, Canny said. "I told 'em, none of that cornball nautical shit—fucking nets, wheels with spokes, a mounted swordsfish, like I seen on other yachts. Except I wanted a little pirate stuff."

The main salon was fifty feet long. Interspersed by ceiling-to-floor mirrors, studies of numbers by major artists ("like Motherhole and Warwell and Robert Illinois", proudly said Canny, who'd commissioned them) hung on olivewood panelings. Behind one was the film bank, behind another a safe. A red-white-and-blue carpet hugged the floor. The furniture, large and comfortable, bolted down, was leather with chromium frames. The grand piano stood on a chrome base.

The "pirate stuff" was mounted on a varnished board—swords, cutlasses, grappling hooks, flintlock pistols, a flag with a skull and crossbones. Canny took down a saber and flailed it. Philip wondered about Canny's fantasy life. The luxurious yacht was the antithesis of a pirate ship.

A spiral chrome staircase led down to the twenty-by-twenty dining salon, with mahogany paneling, mirrors, eighteenth-century English pilasters, a round leather table with a raised rim. "If I want to make the dining room a casino, a roulette wheel goes in the middle of the table," Canny said.

Next to the dining salon was the library—with hundreds of volumes lining the walls. Philip checked quickly. Most of the books, some ancient and in many languages, were about the occult.

Each of the six staterooms was differently decorated. The largest, Canny's, was in pale apricot with a gray pickled finish on the bulkheads. Ari's contained English "Regency" chairs, and Oriental rugs. Next to Ari, with a connecting door, was Libby's nautical-blue chamber. Across the passageway from Canny was Cappy, whose lair had studded white kid walls. The walls of Marie-Celeste's cabin, next to Philip's, were of rich orange velvet. Every stateroom had linen curtains over the portholes, beds on raised platforms for storage space, built-in banquettes, TV, stereo, spotlights with rheostats, bathrooms in lacquer with heated towel racks and heatlamps over the showers, and air-conditioning control. Everything seemed to have been selected with the greatest care, down to the large handles on the curved closets and doors.

"Hey, Archy, what do you think of her?" Canny asked almost anxiously.

"Terrific," said Philip, uncomfortably envious again.

"Next year, maybe I get a bigger one."

Canny left Philip in his cabin, which had a red ceiling and cork-lined walls covered with lovely color shots of the Caribbean in Kulicke frames. He cracked the door to Marie's cabin—she wasn't there. He wondered if the one between Ari and Libby was unlocked too. He turned off the central air conditioning and opened the large round porthole, staring out. Water rustled along the hull; a flock of birds squawked and dived, though land was nowhere in sight. Perfect, too perfect. What was the catch? Could the stateroom be bugged?

An amateur in such matters, he searched the room thoroughly for a listening device, checking the closet, the storage area under the bed, the antique desk, the lamps, including the fixture on the ceiling, telephone, unscrewing the mouthpiece. He found nothing.

He unpacked his few belongings and stood for a moment with his dark blue passport in hand. The passport! It carried his real birthdate. Suppose somebody wanted to look at it? Philip got a chair and removed the plastic grate over the air-conditioning duct, putting his passport inside.

The radio was tuned to the St. Jean frequency and he switched it on. Then the classical music stopped, and the announcer shouted, in French, "Aries, Taurus, Gemini, Cancer, Leo, Virgo, Libra, Scorpio, Sagittarius, Capricorn, Aquarius, Pisces . . ." Hypnotically, the chant was repeated three times before the music returned. It was the same litany he'd heard on Jamaican radio his first day on the island.

The *Zodiac* had already moored off Saba when dinner was served, with Fat beaming from the galleyway. Again the food was superb— moray-eel soup, grouper poached in fish stock with mysterious, redolent spices, papaya in a flaming sauce. The liqueur cart came—Philip tried Framboise this time. Raymond said, "Cappy has a horoscope update regarding the political situation on Grenada. We shall have to hurry a little, especially since we're likely to have minor difficulty en route."

"Storms?" Libby asked, looking horrified.

"Because of her delicate balance, Libby gets seasick easily," Ari said to Philip in a confidential tone. He stared into the beautiful woman's eyes and patted her white hand, fingers covered with golden rings. "No, the captain tells us . . ."

"Tells *me*. I tell you. He's *my* captain," Canny said.

"Of course! The captain told Canny, who told me, that the weather will be almost perfect. But an enemy may attempt to interfere."

"Enemy?" said Philip.

"I'm afraid so." The count seemed to examine a spot on the arm of his long-sleeved silk shirt. "How, is difficult to say. By air perhaps, but by sea is more likely. There is water in the picture. Do not fear, Philip, we shall prevail, as we always do." He smiled genially at the other Cardinals, who nodded.

"But who is this enemy?"

"I see no reason not to explain. The enemy is—"

"General Hector Antonio Juan Hernandez Garcia, dictator of El Parador," Cappy spat out.

Ari went on, "Tell our guest what sort of man Hernandez is, Cappy."

The dark moody face turned to Philip. "I am from El Parador. Hector Hernandez is a long shadow on the hopes of my people. Political prisoners are kept in holes so small they cannot stand up or stretch. They are released once a day for fifteen minutes. Sometimes they're forced to drink their own urine with hairs cut from their heads put in it. Many die. But many more die outside prisons—from malnutrition, disease. The peasants are brutally whipped. The situation will not be tolerated much longer—the country is ready to rise up. Only a little push is required to topple the dictator. And then . . ." Morales trailed off.

"You are too modest, Cappy. I'll finish for him. And then Capablanca Morales will become President of El Parador," said the count excitedly. "He will bring democracy, justice, and equality. The Tall One is a hero at home—it is he who has armed and guided the guerrillas who fight Hernandez right now. And then, assisted by us, Cappy can begin the job of bringing the Caribbean nations closer together. His horoscope predicts that he will succeed."

Joe Martinez seemed to have the same objective, but Le Boucan's proprietor didn't trust Cappy. Why? Philip wondered. Maybe Joe was wrong. He, Philip, would prefer to believe in the count and Cappy—they seemed sincere and straightforward. He was stirred by their rhetoric, he confessed to himself. He might even come to like the Cardinals. Except that Sansa's death disturbed him. And astrology. Maybe astrology was only a foible with them. Plenty of good people had eccentricities. He wanted to suspend doubt. "Is the trip involved?"

"Very much so," Ari said. "En route, we shall be visiting personages of local importance, to explain Cappy's ideas and to convince them Hernandez is through. If we can promote a *cordon sanitaire* against the dictator, it will further weaken his position. Hernandez will find out, but it can't be helped. Everywhere in the West Indies he has spies. You met one."

"Sansa?"

"The unfortunate woman, yes. I have wondered since the accident if

Sansa was on heroin that morning—Hernandez routinely supplies his agents with it as a form of control. No matter. There will be others who report our progress, and Hernandez may attempt to retaliate—how, we don't yet know, but we believe ourselves resourceful enough to take care of whatever challenge he offers, don't we, Canny?"

"Sure," said Koster with a frown.

"And you, Philip, may be exactly the right person to have around."

"Me? Why on earth. . . ?"

"Psychology, my dear friend! These islands are mostly new nations, your very subject! How absolutely marvelous that we should have found you, but not a coincidence, I declare. Our meeting was destined, I'm sure. Perhaps from time to time you will be generous enough to offer us your keen advice." The count chuckled. "But enough of serious matters for the moment. Would you like to know our itinerary? Tomorrow we shall visit Saba, St. Eustatius, St. Christopher, and Nevis. The next day, Antigua and Montserrat. The third day calls for—we'll bypass Guadeloupe and Martinique; they're not within our purview this time— Dominica and St. Lucia, reaching Barbados at nightfall. On the fourth day we land on St. Vincent, and then we stop briefly on the islands of Bequia and Moustique—Moustique was named for the abundance of mosquitoes there, though not now; there are only rich whites, some of whom might be persuaded to be valuable allies someday—on our way down the Grenadines to Grenada. Then we shall stop, I hope, at Trinidad and Tobago. We had hoped, originally, to visit Curaçao and Aruba this trip, but the schedule may be too tight to permit it. I *must* be back on St. Jean in time to arrange a flight—a very important private flight—on the twenty-first." He stared at Philip almost provocatively. *Little does he know, but that's my birthday. The real one, that is.*

"To repeat what you already know, I *must* be on Grenada on the twelfth to prepare for the thirteenth, which will be a turning point," said the man in black.

"Guaranteed? Are you certain of success?"

"Guaranteed," said Morales.

Canny was snapping his fingers. "Friday, I want to hit Montserrat first and Antigua second."

"Impossible," the count replied. "The itinerary calls for Antigua to

Montserrat to Dominica, which we'll reach that night. As you're aware, I do not deviate from schedules. It is one secret of my success."

"Well, the secret of *my* success is to stick to the numbers. I need a couple of hours on Antigua."

"During the day won't do?"

"No, in the evening. It's a must."

"Is it a woman you want, my dear chum? I do not know why you Americans believe that sex must take place in the evening. The daytime hours, when energy is high, are most delightful. But I am a European, after all. If you insist on pleasures after dark—yes, yes, you nocturnal creature, you would—you can easily arrange a girl on Dominica tomorrow night. We can set it up by radio."

"Look, I need Antigua, not a broad."

"But why, Canny?"

"I'm going to get real lucky at the Antigua casino. The numbers show it. Pay for the whole trip, for Chrissake."

The count guffawed. "As if that mattered! Why won't the afternoon do?"

Canny said sullenly, "Naw, I got to gamble in the evening. That's what the numbers tell me. Not to follow the numbers is real bad news." Canny hunched his shoulders stubbornly. The shifty black eyes glared. "It's *my* boat."

Ari said irritably, "Would you like us to jump off?"

"Now, boys, be good," said Libby, serene.

The count appeared disconcerted, but only momentarily. He laughed and said, "Oh, we shall have to indulge you, I suppose. In a pinch we can eliminate a small island like Moustique."

"No!" Libby insisted. "I have a friend I must visit on Moustique. She's going to introduce me to Princess Margaret, who's there."

"Your meeting Princess Margaret is hardly vital," the count said coldly.

"Ari, I do as I want."

"Who is the leader here?"

"Don't push me around."

The count fondled the stem of his liqueur glass. With a flick of his wrist he hurled the contents into Libby's face. The woman snarled, then splattered Ari's face with sticky liquid too. Ari reached for a plate.

"Stop! My good china!" Canny yelled. "Bob, Bill, finger bowls, for Chrissake. Watcha say we see a flick?"

In the main salon they watched *Nine Hours to Rama*, an Indian film in which the police suspected that killers would try to assassinate Gandhi at an astrologically auspicious moment. Philip fell asleep in the comfortable chair before the picture ended.

Marie-Celeste shook him. "They've gone to bed. So should we. Come look at the moon first."

The full moon shone over Saba's extinct volcano, rising like a cone from the sea. "Tomrrow you and I will climb it."

"The volcano? Why?"

"Why *not*? It's there, isn't it?"

"I never thought that was much of a reason."

"It isn't a reason. That's what's good about it. Philip, you were right. You're too old for me."

"Can the count climb it?"

"Sure! He's done so several times."

"Lead the way," Castle said grimly.

"I will! We'll start early."

Standing in front of their respective cabins, they chorused, "Good night!"

Minutes later, the door between Marie's stateroom and his swung open and she stood naked in the suffused moonlight from the porthole. "Can we really get away with this?" he whispered.

"Nobody would hear me if I screamed."

"Don't. I want to open the porthole." It had been closed in his absence and his bed had been turned down by a steward, he supposed. "I hate air conditioning."

"So does Ari. More and more I have the feeling you two are a lot alike." She lay on the bed.

"I wouldn't throw *us* together if I were he. I thought you said Arians were supposed to be jealous."

"He doesn't suspect we'd—"

"He *has* to suspect. He just doesn't care." Philip started to undress.

"Oh, he cares, or would if he knew," she said. "He trusts me and he has a lot on his mind these days. He's preoccupied. Besides, Raymond was born at the end of the Aries cycle. It dilutes him a bit."

"I bet." Philip was feeling agreeably mean. "What about Libby?"

"Oh, shut up. Though it's true I don't see much of him when she's around."

"Leos are jealous too, you said. Aren't you jealous of Libby?"

"Not this time." She rolled into his arms.

"Saba—Unspoiled Queen," announced the license plate of the taxi that brought the party from Fort Bay to the only flat place on the island, a town called "The Bottom" even though it was eight hundred feet up.

Philip gazed at the steep hillsides. "It's beautiful," he said, "but why did people choose to settle in such a desolate place?"

"To escape religious persecution in Europe," Cappy said. "The settlers had piles of rocks which they rolled down on invaders, but the colonial powers defeated them anyway, usually by trickery. They always won, and you think you will, too."

"America's a colonial power to you?"

"Yes, in a way. It exploits the producers of raw materials and it relies on their inability to protest effectively. Of course, the Europeans used force to keep control, while the Americans do it with money and democracy. Democracy is a crippling force in the less-developed world. Elections are the curse of the Caribbean. Look!" He pointed to a building covered with slogans. "Only a thousand people live on these five square miles and they can't agree on anything. It's typical of the islands. And you call this the democratic process!"

"You don't believe in democracy?" Philip asked.

"Certainly he does," the count said hastily. "But he thinks there must be a temporary phase of consolidation and unity, don't you, Cappy?" The Tall One nodded as the cab drew up in front of what an antenna identified as a radio station. "We'll be leaving you now," Ari continued, as he, Libby, and Cappy, wearing his panama hat, got out. "We have business here—we have to renew our supply of Saba Spice!—so you two go on. The cab will leave you at the bottom of the steps and come fetch you. But don't be too long. We have a big day ahead!" The count's smile wrinkled his eyes.

"What are they doing here?" Philip said.

"Oh, just little things."

"Visiting personages of local importance, Ari told me."

"That's it."

"How big a climb?" Philip asked the driver when she offered nothing further.

"This here's Windwardside," he said, gesturing at the small attractive town. "It's eighteen hundred feet up. The top of Mount Scenery's thirty-eight hundred. You climb the difference. It's not much."

After an hour and a quarter of climbing slippery stone steps through the dripping, flower-filled rain forest, Marie and Philip panted on the crest. The cloud that habitually capped the volcano swirled about them. Sometimes it parted, revealing isle-dappled sea spread below.

"It's worth the climb," Marie-Celeste said.

"Think so? I won't be able to walk for a week."

It took forty-five minutes to get down. The driver was there.

"Two-hour round trip," he told them. "Not bad."

"How long does it take you?" Philip asked.

"'Bout twenty minutes up, seven down, on a slow day."

"Jesus." And the man had gray hair.

Philip could feel the *Zodiac*'s power beneath him as the ship cut the distance between Saba and St. Eustatius. During lunch, served on deck, Cappy said in his low, deep voice, "Before the American Revolution, Statia was probably the richest island in the whole world, despite a lack of arable land and a decent harbor. The Dutch, English, French, and Jews here lived on trading. They had massive dikes, great warehouses, mansions, paved streets, fancy-dress balls. The sea road was packed with ships from everywhere, trading sugar, molasses, silks, coffee, rum—and guns. Statia was a principal source of arms for your rebellion. In seventy-six, one of the few American warships came here and the Dutch fort fired a salute—your *first* official recognition. Admiral George Brydges Rodney then blockaded the island, finally capturing it. He destroyed the sea walls and deported the population. He flew the Dutch flag over the port, tricking merchantmen into stopping and then seizing them. He held an auction of captured goods—people traveled from all over the Caribbean for it. Ironically, the French and Dutch captured his personal treasure ship during the return voyages, and his fleet stayed at Statia for so long that the French were able to blockade Cornwallis into surrender. You can almost say that St. Eustatius won the American Revolution."

"Greed," the count remarked merrily, "is the undoing of so many. The wise man finds virtue in restraint, the containment of selfish impulse."

"Listen to him," Canny cackled. "Ari's got his sixteen million at least—he can afford to talk. What about pikers like me?"

"Canfield Koster, you are a prime example of a greedy person. Eight million—that's minimum, isn't it?—ought to be enough for anyone."

"It wasn't for you!"

Said the count, "I couldn't help it. I simply couldn't. Besides, I'm twice your age, and therefore I should have twice as much money."

"I'll catch up," Canny vowed.

"Would it be impolite to ask which of you is the wealthiest?" Philip asked, sure that it wouldn't be.

"Why, me, of course, as the leader of the signs. My holdings are in Florida real estate," Ari said gravely. "It may surprise you, but Capablanca Morales is second. That is because he had the perspicacity to acquire a gold mine in South America. Let us hope they do not expropriate it, since his holdings are principally in that country. He has assets of more than eleven million. Was that all right to say, Cappy?"

"Certainly. I am not ashamed of being rich, and they will not expropriate."

"Low woman on the totem pole," Libby said with a trace of bitterness. "It's a man's world when it comes to making money. I'll surpass you all, wait and see."

"I'm sure you will, Elizabeth, when you figure out how to crack the computers of the Federal Reserve. Why, we shall all be coming to you for handouts, right, Philip?" The count winked. "Meantime, our Libby is almost a charity case. She only has five million or so. Hardly enough to keep her in diamonds."

Sixteen million plus, plus eleven million plus, plus eight million plus, plus five million plus, added up to forty million plus, Philip calculated. Jesus! And they worked together. The Cardinals weren't the Bank of America, but they were still in business, and those assets could be expected to grow. They might be quite a potent force—unless they were lying. He didn't think they were, especially when the count said: "It took us a time before we revealed to each other how rich we were. We had to gain confidence. It's a mark of our confidence in you that we have told you so much." De Vaucresson smoothed his wavy hair, tousled by the breeze. "Do you have aspirations toward riches, Philip?"

"Me? You have to be kidding. Unless an ivory tower is worth something. I'm a professor, remember?"

"What about your book, *The Psychology of New Nations?* Won't it make a mint?" The count formed his canted grin.

"Really, Ari, you are in terrible taste," Libby said.

"Why? Philip knows that his book, even with the superb notices it will doubtless have, will be lucky to break even, unless it is picked up as a text. Then he might pull down twenty thousand a year on it, which is fine, by other people's standards, but not ours. Tell me, Philip, how much money would you like to have?"

Nobody had asked such a question of him before, nor had he ever considered it. He said lightly, "A million would do."

"Ah ha! You're not greedy, like Admiral Rodney! A good sign. But a *little* acquisitive, perhaps? If you had, say, one hundred thousand, I could parlay that into a million, I believe. Through clever investments in real estate."

"I don't have a hundred grand," Philip said.

"Then you must get it! Surely there is a way . . ."

The license plates on Statia claimed "Golden Isle." The black people—Philip had to admit to a bias, the *women*—were striking. Marie-Celeste and he wandered around through ruins of ancient walls and sugar mills while the Cardinals visited the radio station and held a lengthy confabulation with a small group of animated islanders.

This island had a volcano, too, and lovely views of the sea, but a lot of shanties, abandoned cars, and rusting machinery. The count exclaimed as they departed, "You see, the Golden Isle is a junkyard! Those good people need help."

A whirlwind stop at St. Christopher, usually called St. Kitts. Philip and Marie-Celeste were too tired to climb 4,314-foot Mt. Misery in any case, but had no time to do any more than taxi to Brimstone Hill, an elaborate fortification in remarkable preservation, nibble on succulent fish in the harbor of Basseterre, and watch the last sailing lighters in the

Caribbean, forty-foot open boats crudely rigged with masts raked forward
and booms pointed up. Once more the Cardinals vanished on their
rounds.

A short spin to neighboring Nevis. That made four islands in one day;
Philip was beginning to be dizzied by the impact of so many cultures.
Again the furtive Cardinals left them to the business of being tourists,
trying the thermal baths, standing solemnly before a plaque that told
them Nevis had been the birthplace of an illegitimate child named
Alexander Hamilton, inspecting houses made of cut-coral blocks that
dated back to the eighteenth century, and stroking two magnificent old
brass cannon in the harbor. "Two of a kind," Philip said.
  "If you mean us, forget it!"
  Philip seized her arm with urgency.
  "Easy," she said.
  "Listen, what's wrong with two of a kind?"
  "We're not, that's all. You're one kind, I'm another—astrologically
and otherwise. Can you imagine *me* as a faculty wife—or mistress?"
  "I didn't ask you to marry me."
  "I wouldn't, even if you had. But you *will* remarry, your horoscope
says."
  "You'll be a tough act to follow. You've spoiled me for other women,
I'm afraid."
  "So you say now, but you'll marry again. Somebody just like your
wife. They all do."
  "All?"
  "American squares."
  They were not alone, Philip was suddenly conscious. Two young
black men had appeared in the dusk. Each jumped up on a cannon
barrel before them. "Havin' fun?" one said, voice truculent.
  Philip said, "Until you spoiled it."
  "*Us*, man? We is *for* fun, not again' it. But that lady don' look like she
havin' fun."
  "Bug off, guys," Marie-Celeste said.
  "Yeah? Maybe we bug *in*, pretty gal."
  "Don't pretty-gal me."
  "Let's leave," Philip said.

"Not yet! This lady need *sizable* enjoyment which maybe you don' *provide*, mister." The man rubbed himself provocatively on the barrel. We's jus' a little bigger'n you. Want to find out?"

The men were inching toward them astride the cannon, smiling hugely. There was no one else on the parapet. Philip had a vision of assault and rape. He started to say, "Let's run," but didn't. He was deeply angry. He muttered, "Fuck off."

"What kinda talk is that? It ain't *nice*. It ain't *right* to insult the local people. It's our island, not yours. You got to pay a price for sayin' that. You take care of him, I'll go with her first," said one to the other.

The young guys had reached the cannon butts, faces eager. The first one had his hand on the zipper of his fly. Marie-Celeste was backing away uncertainly, moving to a position behind Philip, who let his hands hang limp. *When they leap down, feint, swing right. Aim for the nose. Break it. Step back. Crouch. The other guy'll be on top of you. Step on his foot. Aim for his solar plexus with your elbow. Then come up with the other hand. But watch out for the shoes with sharp points. If he kicks, grab the ankle. Pull up. Pound his head on the pavestones. Get the other one with your knee.* . . . "Want something? Come and get it," Philip said. He must have communicated resistance of powerful intensity, like a force field, because the two young men, seeming to signal each other reluctantly with their eyes, got off the cannon and left without a word.

"Good show," Marie-Celeste said. But after all, he'd left them with no alternative but murder, a pretty stiff rap.

In his cabin before dinner Philip turned o.. the radio. Soon he heard, "Aries, Taurus, Gemini, Cancer, Leo, Virgo, Libra, Scorpio, Sagittarius, Capricorn, Aquarius, Pisces, Pisces, Pisces, all of them, and you, right here on ZIZ, the voice of Nevis!" He fiddled with the dial. "Aries, Taurus, Gemini, Cancer, Leo, Virgo, Libra, Scorpio, Sagittarius, Capricorn, Aquarius, Pisces, all of them, and you, right here on radio Statia!" He heard the chant again on Saba's scratchy signal. It seemed to be a pitch for astrology, though nothing was offered for sale.

After another of Fat's remarkable productions, coffee was brought to the main salon. Philip carried his Berger Blanc. Canny picked up the telephone, said, "Yeah, speak," and put it down again. He reported, "During the meal, captain got a coupla peeks at a ship on the radar screen. He had one earlier, too. Looks like she might be hitting the same islands we are. It's a big boat and it don't act like a freighter. No tourist ships around—we checked."

"Danger at sea! Cappy?"

"Hernandez has a warship. He must have dispatched it. It must be looking for us. The chances of trouble have definitely increased, according to our composite natal charts on acetate. Transiting Uranus approaches the midpoint of our collective sun-mid-heaven. The solar eclipse of February 26 has left its mark. Yes, I had intimations before, but today I feel even more certain that we shall be attacked on or about the lunar eclipse, March 13, the very time I anticipate a profound change in Grenada."

Philip said, "What are you talking about?"

"Oh, simply that Cappy expects a naval engagement between ourselves and our enemy," Ari said calmly.

"A *what?*"

"A battle. I thought I had made myself clear."

"A *battle?* Who's at war?"

"Why, we are, I suppose. Canny, does the captain think the warship spotted us?"

"Probably not, since we're moored offshore, and it went behind another island. But it will."

"I'm supposed to believe this?" Philip muttered.

Morales' dark, fathoming eyes turned on him. "Predictions based on the lunar eclipse must not be ignored. Let me provide you with merely one example out of many. In seventy-two, Senator George McGovern was nominated on the day of the solar eclipse. Was that a good omen for his party? I think not, in view of events. The lunar eclipse, inexorably, occurs two weeks later. On that very day, Senator Eagleton was revealed to have suffered from mental stress, effectively killing what chances poor McGovern had left. What do you make of that, my friend?"

To Philip the idea of a naval battle was too absurd to contemplate. Surely they were putting him on. He considered the McGovern incident. Assuming Cappy was right about the dates, it was just one more of those coincidences people loved to make larger than life. If something bad happened on Friday the thirteenth, that proved it was a bad-luck day. If nothing happened, nobody noticed. Astrology couldn't prove, much less repeat, its results, like science could. "McGovern lost, that's all," he said.

Ari waved his hand impatiently. "Libby, what's your view?"

Libby, in a blue velvet suit, opened a mahogany panel. A computer terminal was concealed behind it—Philip read the name of the manufacturer: Wang. She pressed buttons, standing up, and a horoscope appeared on the lighted screen. "Mars is prominent. Luncar eclipse is featured, as Cappy says. Quincunx hostile. The opponent will be eager to fight." Libby seemed nervous. "Do you really think we should go ahead, Ari? Shouldn't we get under way at least?"

"Yeah," Canny said. He reached for the phone.

"No. If the auguries turn unfavorable, we should head back, but not before. In the meantime, let's stick to schedule. We have business here in the morning."

"Whose horoscope is that?" Philip asked into the silence.

"Our enemy Hernandez. Canny?"

Canny replaced Libby at the terminal; numbers flashed. "It seems okay for the next few days. I can't tell anything beyond. You know I don't believe in long-range prediction." The numbers faded and a horoscope appeared. "Looks good for me at Antigua tomorrow, though. That's *my* horoscope, Archy."

"I didn't know astrology was computerized."

"Libby programmed it. Easy to work. Want to see yours?" Another horoscope replaced the first. Koster studied it. "Tell me something, Archy. Ever change your name?"

"No."

Canny grumbled, "I still say Archy's nodes ain't right."

"Don't be an alarmist, Canny. You tend that way."

"But I don't figure the square. There's opposition," said Canny.

"Technical terms," Raymond explained to Philip. "An 'opposition' is an unfavorable aspect, or can be, but not in your case." He said to Koster impatiently, "I've been over his chart a dozen times. He is *favorable* as far as we're concerned. Highly so. You're confused, Canny. It was you who changed your name from . . . what was it?"

"Cut it out!"

"I have it. Yes, from Kotlowitz, Herman Kotlowitz. Too Jewish, eh, for a crab?" The count tittered. "Canny likes to put on airs, don't you, my boy?"

"Up yours," Canny howled, puffing furiously on his cigar.

"The coming lunar eclipse makes us short-tempered. We must watch ourselves. Perfect judgment will be required," Libby said.

"She's right. Calm down, Canny. Entertain us with one of the horoscopes you cast for famous visitors to your plush hotel."

Canny's pout cleared. "Oh, all right. How about Frankie?"

"Sinatra will be fine."

"I didn't tell him *everything* that was in his horoscope, natch. You don't, you know—not the bad stuff. Sinatra was born December 12, 1915, at 3:03 A.M., in Hoboken. Has Leo on the mid-heaven with Neptune. Neptune's the planet of the imagination, music . . . creat . . ."

"Creativity," the count filled in.

"Yeah. He got Jupiter in the fifth house—the performer's house—and Mars in the tenth, which is the best place to have Mars if you want a big career."

"How can you remember all that?" Philip asked.

"All us Cardinals got just about total recall when it comes to horoscopes. Frankie's Mercury and Sagittarius conjunct the sun in his second house of self-worth, meaning dough. Lot of push on money there. Libra's rising. Shows the desire to be a big shot, popular. Got the first meridian house in Scorpio. Gives him the idea he's a tough guy, but Neptune squared in the ascendant makes you connect with the wrong people sometimes. That's because—"

"All right, all right!" the count interrupted. "Very smart, Canny. Don't you think so, Philip—as a psychologist, I mean?"

"Sure. Except it sounds like Sinatra's hand was dealt at birth."

"To a large extent it was," Raymond replied smoothly. "Both heredity and environment are shown on the natal chart; one's character is formed by them. The trick is to find out *who you are* in terms of what the stars decreed in the first place. I, for instance, *found* my destiny. What a pleasant sensation—to be what you were meant to be."

"Or what you *wanted* to be," Philip suggested.

"Wrong! *Had* to be, if you were open to the possibilities. Take

yourself. You were willing to come with us, though a large part of you
didn't want to. But the *right* part of you did."

"Look. I flew to an island I never heard of, met Marie-Celeste by
accident. You offered me a trip and I accepted. What's star-crossed about
that? It was completely accidental."

Ari looked pained. "How can you say accidental? Why, the coincidences that brought you on board this vessel defy all laws of pure chance.
The cosmos always has a purpose: you are here for a reason."

"To enjoy myself."

"No, there is more. You are exploring an uncharted part of your
character. You are learning how your destiny fits with ours. And we with
yours."

"But why?" Philip demanded.

The count shrugged his lean shoulders. "It is unclear as yet. We shall
have to see what happens." He smiled wanly at his fellow representatives
of cardinal signs. "When we are pure spirits, we will be able to do
without sleep. But not yet. Shall we go to bed? We'll be up long before
these two—we have a big day tomorrow." He touched his forehead. "I
have a headache."

"Ari, you overdo it," said Libby, getting up, poached blue eyes
twinkling. "You must give that high-powered brain of yours a rest."

"Yes, when these fateful days are over."

The Cardinals departed.

"What did he mean?" Philip asked Marie-Celeste.

"I don't exactly know, except the stakes are very big."

Waiting for her, Philip spun the dial on his cabin radio.

"Aries, Taurus, Gemini, Cancer, Leo, Virgo, Libra, Scorpio, Sagittarius, Capricorn, Aquarius, Pisces, Pisces, Pisces," babbled voices in
the night.

17

The morning light penetrated the rustling porthole curtains and the flimsy defenses of Philip's eyelids. Useless to try to sleep again; dawn anxiety mounted as his mind poured out questions. His new friends seemed to speak openly, but so much was left unsaid.

Philip felt he had to be careful: for whatever reasons, the Cardinals spun webs of intrigue and mystery to catch him in. What better way to lure an adventureless city man like him? But why? Sooner or later he would learn, and if he didn't like the answer, he could leave the ship along the way.

In the meantime, the cruise was certainly pleasant—he had no complaints, far from it. He squeezed the muscular bottom next to him, hoping for a response, but there was none. Little wonder. That he felt desire at 6:52 A.M. after such a night as they had had seemed incomprehensible. Was Fat putting an aphrodisiac in his food?

Philip rose, went to the porthole, pushed back the curtains, and thrust his head into the day. They were still moored off Nevis. A strong breeze chopped the sea. Stretching his neck, he could see the stern. A dory was tied there with a black man inside.

Curious, Philip put on his robe and, in bare feet, padded down the carpted passageway until he reached stairs that led to the main salon. The glass rear doors were open, and he could observe what was happening on the aft deck unseen.

Ari, Canny, and Cappy stood by the narrow swimming pool, Bob and Bill behind them. Across it were a pair of black men in bright-colored clothes and shiny shoes. One held an airline bag. They looked apprehensive, as if sorry they'd come.

Cappy leaned forward on his cane. His voice was barely audible. "So! You wish more, then?"

"Spent what you give us."

"Oh, yes, I know, señores. Nothing escapes me—you must believe this. But what did you spend it *on?* Hah!" Philip had never heard Cappy laugh before—it was a strange sound, utterly humorless. "You have squandered it on drink, women, gambling, clothes! Is it not true?"

"But—"

"*Do not interrupt!*" The men shrank back as though Cappy's words were blows. "You were given money for a reason, and you used it for frivolous purposes. I abhor weakness and self-indulgence. I shall teach you a lesson you will never forget. There will be far worse if you do."

The Tall One twisted the goat's-head handle of the cane and from the end a shiny metal object protruded. It resembled a little hoof. He moved rapidly, with the same hopping gait Philip had seen at the airport. Dark eyes glittering with something like lust, he swept powerfully around the pool and the cane shot upward sharply. *Thwack.* Philip could hear the steel hoof strike bone. Crying out, the man sank to the deck. *Thwack.* The other went down, too.

"Next time I will break your knees," Cappy said.

Jesus! Philip recoiled.

In his cabin, Castle peeked out the porthole again. The toughs, Bob and Bill, lowered the groaning men over the side with ropes. The dory sped away with its bruised cargo.

The *Zodiac* was under way, bound for Montserrat, bow slicing the swells. Philip sat morosely in a deck chair, wishing he'd left the ship at Nevis. He'd skipped breakfast, served by the pool. Marie-Celeste showed up after a while. "What's the matter? Seasick?"

"I don't feel good," he said.

"It's a little rough. Sure that's all that's the matter? You seem preoccupied."

"I'm not cut out for this."

"You have to get used to cruising. A lot of empty water, empty time. Good for thinking."

"I've been doing a lot of it. Tell me about Morales. He looks nasty sometimes."

"He could make black hats crawl."

"Black hats?"

"Canny's word for Mafia."

"Speaking of hats, why does Cappy usually wear a white one?"

"Oh, a sort of Capricorn stunt. You know—goats."

"I don't *know* goats," he said irritably.

"You *are* on edge."

"I got up too early. Goats. White hair on their heads?" She nodded. "What about that black suit he never takes off?"

"He *must* have more than one of them. He's in mourning. For El Parador. He's sworn not to remove his weeds until his country's free from the dictator."

"All right. Why does Cappy limp?"

"He has arthritis in one knee. Typical of a Capricorn."

"Huh? What's being a Capricorn got to do with arthritis of the knee?"

"You never heard of the zodiacal man?"

"I guess not."

"Well, the signs are related to parts of the body. Aries is attached to the head. It's why Raymond gets dizziness and headaches."

"I have one, too. No wonder," he muttered.

"Well, the upper thigh is the Sagittarian weakness, not the head. Libras have problems with the kidneys. Libby does. Her Pluto's angular in Leo, meaning the buttocks and lower back problems. Libby has them. She has a slipped disk."

"Or slips them. She works with computers, doesn't she? What about Canny?"

"Chest pains. Nothing serious, I think—just gas. It's the things he eats. Did you know he loves raw fish? I don't mean Japanese style, either. I saw him eat half a fish before it had stopped breathing, or whatever fish do."

"So then physical problems are supposedly related to their signs! Talk about self-hypnosis! Tell me, if an astrologist—"

". . . er."

"*Er*, for Christ's sake." Ellie coursed through his thoughts and was gone. "If an astrologer wanted to dish it out, would he or she pick on the part of the body that was astrologically his or hers?"

"I don't get you."

"Suppose Cappy wanted to punish someone. Would he go for the knee?"

"I never thought of it." She looked at him straightforwardly, without blinking. She wasn't lying, he decided. She didn't know about the incident on deck. Maybe he was naive, but he felt certain she wasn't privy to the Cardinals' real secrets. "Why do you ask?"

"Just curious."

Marie-Celeste lay bare-breasted on a matress by the pool, sipping from a tall glass, while Philip stayed on the sundeck over the main cabin, in his boxer trunks. He had taken a volume from the library and was scanning it indifferently when Libby said, from the chair beside him, "What are you reading?"

People landed like aircraft, Philip thought. Some powered in noisily—big jets. Others made their presence known with a kind of sigh—turboprops. Libby was a glider. She made no sound at all. "A book on astrology—by . . ." He flipped back. "MacNeice."

"Oh yes. Charming. Louis MacNeice. A leading English poet. That was his last book before he died."

"Never heard of him, I'm afraid."

"What? You've heard of Auden?"

"Sure."

"Well, Auden, Spencer, MacNeice . . . they're in a class by themselves. Very famous, I assure you. You're not much on poetry, I gather."

"I used to like it, as a matter of fact. But I don't get time to read anymore, except what I have to—journals, reports."

Libby didn't answer immediately. She wore a bikini of what he guessed was expensive synthetic material. Blue, of course. She undid a hook between her breasts and slid off the halter. She stretched her legs—

fuller, whiter, than Marie's lean, tanned ones, with plump toes descending evenly in size. Dimples in both knees. Prominent *mons veneris*. Little bulge at the middle—a gentle female swell, not fat, though Libby had to watch her weight, he suspected. Breasts smaller than M-C's, but more rounded, less pointed. Small pink nipples. Not a glisten of sweat on her. Seemingly oblivious of him, she began rubbing lotion on her bosom, palming the nipples slowly. She purred, "I used to write poetry. I hope to again someday, but I'm too busy now, just like everyone else. Industrial society has destroyed romance—nobody has the time or inclination. Look at the great psychologists—Freud, Adler, Ferenczi, Carl Jung—they were great romantics, interested in *everything*. Ever read Jung on astrology?"

"Well, no. He wasn't in my field of study."

"*He* believed in it. He thought some coincidences were simply too hard to explain by ordinary rules of chance, too improbable to be understood except in terms of correspondence between earthly events and planetary and astral cycles. He developed a theory he called synchronicity."

The hands moved down the expanse of soft flesh, coming to rest on her lower belly, fingernails tucked just under the bikini bottom, thumbs touching above it.

"Synchronicity?"

"He meant there was a relationship between some events that couldn't be accounted for by mere coincidence, that outside forces in the universe had to be responsible, which is what Ari has been trying to tell you . . . You're not listening, Philip. You seem distracted." Their eyes met. Libby licked her lips.

"Who me? Can two people be synchronous?"

Libby smiled blissfully. "You mean, can an attraction be so strong that only an outside force can explain it? Of course, if their signs are right. Female Libra, male Sagittarian—those are double signs of duality with qualities between them that defy definition. There's seldom a quiet moment where those two are concerned. They don't bore each other . . . sextile vibrations. Libra's air fans Sagittarius' fire." The woman lit a cigarette and blew smoke at him. "It takes air for fire to burn."

Philip felt the beginnings of an erection, even under her watchful stare. Sagittarius rising . . . but he wasn't a Sag, he was an Aries. Aries rising . . . *Cut it out.* He crossed his legs. "I should be taking notes."

"Libra doesn't like it when Sag makes fun of her. Libra gets sore."

"Sag is sorry."

"Sag should be punished by Libra."

"What kind of punishment?" he asked, too quickly.

"You're blushing. Sagittarians are the blushers of the zodiac. Let the punishment fit the crime. Libra stands for justice as well as truth. Is Sag attracted by Libra?"

"Must Sag tell the truth? The answer is yes," Philip said reluctantly.

She seemed to draw back. "The archer is . . . too flighty. Libra the balance is too measured, careful."

"*Are* you so careful?"

"Oh, very. Libra is careful about what she sees—she hates ugliness. Libra must have an equilibrium. Libra considers all sides of a question: she has clarity of thought. Libra doesn't wish people to know her business. She regards herself as a secret she must keep."

"From whom?"

"Why, from everybody, unless she trusts them. Which is rare, because she's easily taken in. I trust you for some reason, though. I hardly know you. But then, I know you very well."

"Do you?"

"You're not one of those cheap people who use sex to bolster their infantile egos."

"We all do a little of that, I'm afraid."

"Yes, I suppose," she said reluctantly. "You interest me—Libra requires mental stimulation."

"Thanks."

"I like the straightforward way you deal with things. Marie-Celeste is like that, too. She has a kind of honest intensity, don't you agree?"

"From what I've seen," he said cautiously.

"I think she's sexy," Libby murmured. "So young."

"She's not all that much younger than you."

"But she is, spiritually. I'm an old soul. She's new on the horizon. I doubt she's been reborn. She might be from the future, though."

He didn't want to scoff openly. "Does Raymond believe in reincarnation, too?"

"For sure! Ari started as a priest in Babylonia."

"And you?"

"I was a queen if you must know."

"You and Ari must get on well."

"We do! But only for a short while," she said. "Aries is too demanding, too aggressive, too violent, for Libra in the long run. He becomes an annoyance to her. They argue."

"Do they argue over Marie-Celeste?"

"They both *like* Marie-Celeste. Libra could teach her things. You too," said Libby

"Such as?" he murmured.

Her plump toes found his calf, her toenails scratched lightly. "Things you deserve."

"Philip!" It was Marie-Celeste calling at the top of the metal ladder from the afterdeck. "Montserrat. We're here!"

Montserrat, the "saw-toothed mountain," another volcanic discharge floating on the Caribbean Sea. Philip learned from a pamphlet in the main port, Plymouth, that among the waves of European settlers had been the Irish, who in a fit of transatlantic nostalgia had called Montserrat the "Emerald Isle," and bright green it was. Another Irish legacy: red-haired natives, though Philip didn't see any.

There were two stations: Radio Montserrat and Radio Antilles. Ari told a taxi driver to take them to one. As the Cardinals got in the cab, he said, "You can catch a swim at the black beach, but that's all the time you'll have."

The "black beach" turned out to be of volcanic sand, dark as night, edging into pale green water. Marie-Celeste was wearing a bikini underneath her shorts and blouse. Philip hadn't brought a swimsuit. She took a ball of cloth from the bag she carried and threw it to him. "Put it on," she commanded.

"But . . ." he cried.

Though there was hardly anybody on the beach, he went behind a palm tree. He emerged, a lot of white skin showing where his boxer trunks had covered it. Marie-Celeste said,"That's better! You can throw out the other trunks."

"I feel like a stripteaser!"

"For that you need an audience."

Philip's lioness looked great, with her tawny hair and golden skin against a background of licorice sand. But there *was* an audience: an audience of one, a black man with reddish frizzled hair. Something twinkled between his fingers—a razor blade. Philip sat up and said, "What do you want? I'm not in the market for scar tissue."

"Your money," said the man with the slightest Irish brogue. "Your wallet."

"My wallet? There's hardly a farthing in it, pal," Philip said. *What's got into you? Ought to be terrified, yet making smart-ass remarks. But maybe it'll work: he looks surprised.*

"Come *on*," said the red-headed black man. "Your wallet. I means it." He jabbed at Philip with the razor blade.

"Give him the wallet," M-C advised quickly.

"You can have the money if you'll leave the wallet," Philip said. He wanted his credit cards.

"Yeah."

Philip stood, seized the Air France tote bag Marie-Celeste had brought, and emptied the contents on his towel—clothes, her suntan lotion, rattail comb, mirror, bandanna, a piece of fruit, the battered leather billfold he'd had longer than he could remember. The man bent and stuck the wallet in the pocket of his jeans with a smirk.

"Why, you . . ." The rage that freed him from fear was oddly exhilarating. He dived for the towel, rolled, and came up with the rattail comb, which had a long, sharp, strong point. He advanced; the thief had his back to the sea.

"You crazy, mister?" the man said warningly. He still had the razor blade between his fingers.

"Philip!" Marie-Celeste cried.

"That's right, crazy. Nuts. Just got out of a mental hospital," Philip said, waving the point of the comb.

"Get back, you hear?"

"When I'm through with you you'll be wide open. You'll get a sunburn of the guts."

Alarmed, the man retreated a few steps toward the sea. "You gonna be hurt, mister."

"Crazy folk don't feel pain, know that, you black mick? Maybe you'll cut me a little, but you won't have any eyes left."

"A loony," said the thief. He seemed to search for an escape route, but Philip was too close. Shifting his feet uncertainly, he reached in his pocket and threw the wallet on the sand. "Okay?"

"Okay. Scram." The thief ran off.

"Philip! You *are* crazy!" M-C cried.

The *Zodiac* had just emerged from the harbor when a long gray shape appeared from behind a point some distance away. "Warship," the captain called from the bridge. "Frigate, Dealey class. No flag or visible identification."

"In Montserrat waters, too," said Cappy. "She's after us."

Libby said, "Let's go back. We'll be safe on shore."

"No, they'll send in a party at night. We have to run. Head south."

"But Antigua!" Canny wailed.

"We'll get out of radar range and double back," the count said. Canny gave the order.

Philip hadn't experienced the *Zodiac* at full speed. The gleaming yacht trembled slightly as the engines revved up. She shot through the waves, sending up a cloud of spray and leaving a boiling wake. The other ship was long out of sight when Ari said to Philip, "You know how to use a gun, I understand."

"Me?" He was instantly sorry he had told Marie-Celeste. "I haven't fired one in years."

"Let's find out. I thought we might have target practice—for diversion."

Canny Koster named the weapons lugged on deck by the wordless Bob and Bill: Colt .45 automatic pistol, Smith & Wesson .38-caliber pistols, Savage pump shotguns, and Beretta and Browning automatic shotguns, XM-22 Stoner assault rifle, Danish Krag 8mm rifle, a Mauser hunting rifle, a pair of M 14's. A squat gun with a long clip was an Ingram M 11 submachine gun.

"It's an arsenal!" Philip said.

"Canny likes to have guns on board," the count said in a confidential tone. "They make him feel secure."

"Not me."

"Try one," Ari urged.

The ship's speed was reduced, and the target—a human figure made of plastic, braced on a tripod and standing on pontoons—was let out from the stern on a rope. Marie-Celeste and Libby fired first, using pistols. Holes in the Styrofoam indicated hits, Libby's in the pelvis, Marie's in a plastic arm.

"Philip?" said the count, handing him a Smith & Wesson. He squinted down the barrel, aimed at the bobbing target, and missed all six shots.

"I *am* out of practice," he muttered.

The target was let far out for Canny and Cappy, both holding rifles. With three deft shots Cappy knocked off a Styrofoam leg.

"Let it out more. C'mon," Canny commanded. He laid a round cheek and a beady eye on the stock and squeezed twice. "How'd I do?" He grabbed the field glasses. "Two hits in the heart."

"There's only one," said the count, who also had binoculars.

"Second shot went through the hole the first one made."

"Philip?"

Again Philip failed to hit the target.

"You'll catch on," the count said. He seized the Mauser. "I'm more comfortable with European weapons," said he. He wore a hunting jacket with a pad over the clavicle. He put the butt to his shoulder, placed his long, straight nose close to the barrel, and fired once. The head of the target fell into the sea. "Personally, I would shoot an individual only in the most extreme circumstances. As for killing, let our servants do it for us."

Philip missed with the shotgun, too. "I'm not in your class."

"Shoot the Ingram," the count advised. "A truly marvelous weapon. It weighs less than nine pounds and holds thirty-two rounds of nine-millimeter ammunition. It can shoot single shots, at forty rpm, or multiple bursts at a cyclic rate of one thousand rpm, more or less, and an automatic rate of ninety-six rpm. Its effective range is a hundred twenty-five yards, but it's really at its best close up, which is why intelligence units favor it, that and the effective silencer. Fire!"

The submachine gun whirred quietly. The bobbing target displayed no new destruction.

"Perhaps you'd prefer a bow and arrow," the count said. "Philip, you're too impatient. Place your shots in short bursts. You don't want to exhaust the magazine too quickly. Remember that. It might be useful someday."

But Philip hardly heard the words.

Annoyed, he aimed carefully. The target dropped into the sea.

"Atta boy, Archy," said Canny. "You get the gold metal. We go down Antigua now."

Late that afternoon both Montserrat stations carried the familiar "Aries, Taurus, Gemini, Cancer . . . Pisces, Pisces, Pisces . . . All of them, and you, right here on . . ."

Philip found de Vaucresson in the library, volume on his lap. Before him was a tray with crackers and caviar, at which he nibbled. "Care to have some?"

"No. Raymond . . . Ari . . . I'm leaving the ship."

"What did you say?"

"I want to get off at Antigua."

"Aren't you having a good time?"

"For how long? The target—suppose that had been a *person?*" He had decided not to reveal that he had witnessed the incident on deck.

"So?" the count asked.

"That's what I thought—it *could* have been a person, couldn't it? We're being followed."

"Not any longer. We've shaken them."

"For now. What if they find you again? Look, what's it all about?"

"I thought it was clear. The dictator Hernandez sent a warship after us. He wishes to eliminate Cappy. I would imagine he expected to capture the Tall One on St. Jean, but we, ah, foresaw that move and departed in time, we later learned. The frigate has continued the chase, to no avail."

"But why a ship? Why didn't he just try to have Morales assassinated?"

"Cappy is too elusive. Besides, Hernandez would like to take him alive so he could kill our friend himself. And then . . . well, he suspects the Tall One has accomplices, namely us. It would be a prize for Hector Hernandez to capture all of us at the same time."

"You make it sound like we—I mean, you—are a bunch of pirates! Well, I don't want any part of it."

"Don't worry. We'll be all right," the count said with a bland look.

"According to you. Do you sell life insurance?"

"You're entirely too apprehensive," said the count, eating caviar from a spoon. "The signs are entirely in our favor, so far at least."

"Maybe Sansa thought the same thing about herself."

The count's expression was guileless. "I *hope* you're not suggesting anything. I said it was an accident. She was crossing the runway to collect her pay for an evening with Canny when the plane took off."

"You claimed she was a spy. The phone call had nothing to do with it?"

"You know about that?" the count said with surprise. "It was perfectly true that Cappy wished to learn what she had communicated, and used Canny to find out, which he did. A little force was required; the money was intended as an apology, and a guarantee of future silence. The information Canny got accounted for why we left St. Jean so abruptly: we thought Hernandez would come after us. Satisfied? Those are the facts." The count raised the volume from his lap. "By the way, I admire your book very much."

"My what?"

"*The Psychology of New Nations.*"

"How did you get that?"

"I was afraid you'd ask. Naturally, Marie-Celeste told me you were the Astrotwin of the dead pilot. Curious to know more about you, I had the bound galleys specially delivered from New York even before we met. I would have said nothing if I didn't like the work, but I do. Your notion that new nations act like small group animals—needing each other's support and company—while older countries are far more autonomous makes excellent sense. You'd make a good adviser to new nations in their dealings with the established ones."

"Thank you." Philip was flattered again.

"Yes. Your insights, coupled with astrological—"

"Forgive me, Ari. I have trouble accepting astrology."

"Perhaps tonight will make a convert out of you. Canny is sure he will win—I have a similar premonition. I hope you'll come along and watch."

"And if he loses?"

"That would say something about astrology, wouldn't it? Perhaps it would confirm your desire to leave the ship."

"Fair enough," Philip said, despite himself. He started out, then turned. "Why are the astrological signs broadcast all the time? Did you put them there?"

"Guilty," the count said after a pause. "The same campaign appears in island newspapers, too. It's really very innocuous. We believe the Caribbean will be fertile soil for astrology—we'd like to see it replace that old-time religion the West Indians love so much—and we're planting the seeds."

"But why?"

"If one believes in something, one wants other to believe it, too. It's a perfectly normal attitude. We might even publish a book on astrology designed for the Caribbean. Or start an Institute for Occult Studies down here." The count's gray eyes filled with glee. "If it's all right with you."

Antigua. Philip and Marie-Celeste taxied fifteen miles from St. John, where the *Zodiac* was moored, across the island to English Harbour, once the major British naval installation in the Caribbean. The fortifications, the cannon, the facilities at Nelson's Dockyard, where men-of-war were refurbished and repaired from 1707 to 1899, when ships became too big to negotiate the harbor entrance (Philip gleaned from an inevitable tourist brochure)—the place brought back the days when Europeans contested continually for supremacy, not just over each other but, in the long run, over the trade routes and dominion of the sugar islands, and their sweetening of superstitious slaves. It seemed so long ago. . . . A black tourist carried a portable radio. Philip heard, "Aries, Taurus, Gemini, Cancer, Leo, Virgo, Libra, Scorpio, Sagittarius, Capricorn, Aquarius, Pisces, Pisces, Pisces, all of them, and you, right here on radio Antigua!"

Canny Koster refused to leave the ship until he had run a series of numbers through the computer—his "progressed numeroscope," he said—and then studied his horoscope. Nor would he arrive at Castle Harbour casino before eleven or touch a card until eleven-thirty sharp. Instead of his snappy nautical whites, Canny wore a flowered sport shirt, wrinkled pants, and sandals. He looked nondescript. "Pretend you don't know me," he ordered the others.

The casino was crowded. Canny went to a high-stakes blackjack table and edged himself in until he was right behind the players. At a few minutes after eleven he slid into the number-one seat and took from his pocket a large roll of bills tied with a rubber band. Rather conspicuously he peeled five one-thousand-dollar bills from the roll and handed them to the dealer for chips. The dealer's head turned slightly. Another man, in evening clothes, arrived behind him. Canny had been noticed.

He ordered a drink—a double Scotch; Philip, standing across the table, heard his loud voice distinctly—but failed to play the first few hands, though the dealer waited for a bet. The drink came. Canny slurped from it noisily, looked at his watch. At the stroke of eleven-thirty he put a striped chip on the table—the maximum. He took a hit at fifteen, and lost.

Canny lost eight out of the next ten hands. Fifteen minutes later, he was down four thousand dollars, and by midnight, nearly ten, by Philip's count. Slurring, he ordered another double Scotch and bought more chips from the seemingly endless roll. He won a few hands and began to lose again to another dealer. Just before one Canny needed more chips.

He demanded to see the manager; he wanted higher stakes. A hurried conference took place behind the table. Smooth-faced men in evening clothes looked Canny over, while his black eyes darted back and forth. A crazy, Philip could almost hear them say; a druggy *and* a supplier. Who else has that kind of cash? They moved Canny to a separate room and gave him a new dealer, a black with a foxy face. The two bosses followed, as did others, among them the contingent from the *Zodiac*. Nothing was said about limits at this table.

Canny bought twenty thousand in chips. The dealer shuffled and Koster cut the cards, which went back in the shoe. It was exactly one o'clock. Playing alone against the house, Canny bet the twenty thousand, and hit blackjack. The dealer shoveled over the chips, and looked questioningly when Canny stayed motionless. "Let 'em ride," Canny said in a shrill voice.

Canny hit blackjack again. Another whispered conference. Canny became so agitated that he upset his drink. More chips were brought and given to Canny. "Let 'er ride," he said thickly as a waitress mopped up.

Canny got blackjack for the third time in a row. Canny got plaques this time. One of the men in authority stepped forward, about to close down the table, Philip guessed, when Canny shouted, "I'll let 'em ride!" The man nodded.

"Is he really drunk?" Philip whispered to Marie-Celeste.

"He's faking."

Close to a hundred grand waited on green felt. Another dealer, a white woman, arrived, and shuffled carefully. Canny cut. The bulging eyes never left her slender, flowing fingers as she dealt from the shoe. Canny got a king. The dealer got a face card too. As the woman gave herself the down card, he cried, "I want a new deal. Don't fuck around dealing seconds with me. C'mon!" He reached over and flipped the hole card. It was an ace.

The man Philip took to be the manager came quickly forward. "Surely,. sir, you're not suggesting . . ."

"C'mon. I want to play. *You* deal."

The other guy must have been the manager's boss. He had a dark, pocked face and a narrow mouth. His head tilted slightly. He had icy eyes. The eyes said that Canny couldn't get blackjack four times in a row. And Canny was betting the whole pile. Disaster lay that way.

The cards were shuffled, cut, and dealt again. A curtain of silence fell around the table. Canny received an ace, the dealer a ten. Then Canny had two aces; Philip *knew* the dealer had a face card in the hole. Twenty. Canny needed another blackjack to win and didn't have it. The dealer waited.

Koster took his time, puffing on his cigar. Very deliberately he separated the two aces. He divided his steak between them. The dealer placed a card on the first ace. A jack. He gulped a little, then dealt the second. A king—a double blackjack! Canny had won about two hundred thousand dollars, more money than Philip had ever seen.

Canny rose swiftly, without a trace of unsteadiness. It was precisely one-fifteen. "Got to scram," he said. Bob and Bill flanked him as he scuttled to the cashier, who offered a certified check. Canny demanded banknotes, and after an argument was given a stack of bills. He watched the cashier count them. Bob and Bill followed him out.

"What do you think of astrology now, Archy?" Koster said on the way to the launch.

Arthur Herzog

"Never heard of blind luck, Canny?"

"Luck! You got to be kidding, perfessor. The reason I started winning was because it's the tenth of March. The king of diamond's day. The king's top dog in my suit. And the moon's in Leo. Leo's the gambler's sign. The moon's transiting over my Mercury-Pluto conjunction in Leo." He clapped Philip on the shoulder. "Pluto for plutocrat!"

The count said softly, "You'd like to win, too, wouldn't you, Philip? Perhaps you should take another look at astrology. In any case, I hope you'll stick around awhile."

18

Waking with a start, Philip chased the sun to the porthole. He dreaded finding another small boat tied to the stern, but there was nothing. Maybe the Cardinals had finished with drumhead justice; maybe they didn't want to be cruel on the Sunday Isle, even though it was Saturday.

Christopher Columbus had named the "Sunday Isle"—Dominica—because he had discovered it on a November Sunday in 1494, Philip learned from a postcard in the capital, Roseau. The shore party had come in on the *Zodiac*'s trim Cigarette launch. Urchins, sharing the streets with goats and chickens, besieged them for handouts, which Cappy forbade the group to give. "They've been dependent long enough. The Caribbean *must* learn to be self-sufficient. It must be *taught*. This island has the best agricultural potential of all of them. Anything grows here. Even better than Montserrat it could feed the whole West Indies— properly led."

The market was piled high with produce of all kinds. Philip took pictures while the Cardinals disappeared into a dingy office whose windows were placarded with election posters.

Philip and Marie-Celeste had time to taxi to a grotto, fed by a waterfall, lined by giant ferns. Bright birds sang everywhere, incredible flowers bloomed against a jungle so thick with vegetation as to be impenetrable. Much of the rain-forested island had only been seen by the Carib Indians who had defied the Europeans with poisoned arrows, the driver told them proudly. He had a little Carib blood, he said.

"Are there still Caribs here?" Marie-Celeste asked.

"A few. You never see 'em."

But a little later they did. When they returned from the grotto, the driver had vanished. Three bow-legged brown men with flat faces surrounded the cab. They carried staves.

"What do you want?" Philip said sharply. He was emboldened by his successes with the other intruders.

Philip's watch and camera, the Caribs indicated.

"Speak English?"

"A little," an Indian said.

"Let's reason together, then."

The Indians shook their sticks and looked mean.

"If I give you the stuff, will you go away?"

The Indians nodded.

Castle removed his Timex and held it up, as though to inspect it. He said casually, "You know, M-C, I've had this watch for five years. It's always kept perfect time—never stopped running. I sure hate to lose it. Say, what do you fellows plan to give in return, a rain dance?"

The Indians muttered.

"Nothing for nothing, I say." Philip threw the watch on the dirt, ground it with his heel, and kicked it toward the Indians. Next he raised the camera over his head as if to drop it too.

Shaking their heads, the Indians disappeared into the forest.

"At least I kept my camera," Philip said.

"You sure take chances, professor," Marie-Celeste observed.

Philip spotted a movement in the bushes. "Okay, driver, you may come out now. Brave man!"

The Zodiac's horn was sounding the call to return when the taxi reached the port. The great white yacht was surrounded by tiny vessels, like a whale under attack by perch.

Breathlessly Marie-Celeste told Ari about the incident with the Caribs, just as she had reported the two previous near-assaults. "Odd," said the count blandly. "I've traveled the islands for years, and I've never heard of any such trouble. I told you you had a propensity for danger, Philip!"

In his cabin, Philip switched on the radio almost out of habit. On the Dominican frequency he heard the usual: "Aries, Taurus, Gemini . . ."

The *Zodiac* didn't stop at Martinique (as Guadeloupe had been omitted: the islands were part of metropolitan France; too hard to get a foothold there, Ari said obscurely. One day . . .). There were eight satellite islands, just south of it. Off a smaller one, which appeared uninhabited, the yacht came close to shore, in shallow water, so that Marie-Celeste could water-ski without danger from sharks. Nonetheless, Bob and Bill sat in the stern with loaded sniper rifles while the girl slalomed behind the ship.

"Good chance for you to practice with the Ingram," said the count to Philip. "One of the crewmen will throw bottles from the side. See if you can hit them."

Philip agreed, to his surprise. Surprising himself was becoming habitual. Ari spoke in German, and the guns and a boxful of empty beer bottles appeared. Bottle after bottle was thrown in the air, but he missed them all.

"The curse of your sign," the count said acerbically. "Sagittarians are clumsy, and lazy, too, which comes from being too good-natured. You require a serious challenge to perform."

"Thanks, Ari. You try it."

"Oh, all right." The automatic shotgun shattered every bottle in the air. "I have an advantage with scatter shot," the count said. "Still, you have the Ingram's fantastic rapidity."

But Philip continued to miss. He wouldn't let a crewman help him, but insisted on replacing the magazine himself, with effort. He had wasted thirty-two rounds and felt foolish.

The captain cried from the bridge, "Unidentified ship heading toward us."

"*Merde*," said the count. "Pull in Marie-Celeste!"

The yacht slowed abruptly, throwing her forward on the one ski. She fell in the water.

A dark back appeared on the surface behind her and vanished.

"What is it?" Philip cried.

"Dunno. Dolphin?" Canny said.

"Or a shark?"

"Search me. Pull her in, for Chrissake!"

Bob and Bill tugged frantically on the rope, which the girl clung to. She was two dozen yards from the boat when the fish surfaced again. The dorsal fin left no doubt.

Canny screamed, "Shark!" She looked back and let go of the rope. She drifted. "Swim!"

That, Philip thought, was a mistake. The shark seemed to follow the splashes.

"Swim, for fuck's sake!" Canny screeched. The fin came on. The yacht moved forward slowly, turning to starboard.

From the bridge the captain yelled, "It's the same warship!" Glancing quickly, Philip saw it. The yacht had moved offshore now. In the pale mist that hung over the ocean, the gray shape looked huge even at a distance. No other craft was in sight.

"Marie-Celeste, please hurry!" the count shouted hoarsely.

She grabbed at the rope. Bill and Bob jerked at it. She seemed to have it but lost it again. The fish vanished. It reappeared, circling, near the ladder on the port side.

Something flashed in the mist. A blinker. The warship was warning them to heave to, the captain reported. Heads on deck turned automatically.

Marie-Celeste trod water while the shark moved astern. She headed cautiously toward the ladder. An eternity seemed to pass; the warship loomed larger. Bob and Bill fired and the shark dropped from sight.

"Now! Come!" Ari cried.

The next flash in the mist was colored red. A shell! Water spouted not far away.

"Radio the French navy," Canny screamed.

"No!" Ari countermanded.

The next shell dropped closer. It seemed to bring the shark to the surface again, on a trajectory that would intersect Marie-Celeste just before she reached the ship. It swam rapidly now.

"Help me!"

The shark was alongside, making for the girl, who had stopped swimming and watched it openmouthed. Philip seized the weapon he had set down. He didn't have a chance to raise it; he fired the full magazine from the hip. Blood spurted from the sea. The shark went under.

He grabbed her cold hand when she was on the ladder and pulled her aboard. "That's my archer," she said weakly. "Thank you."

"I thought I'd lost you, darling. I love you," he whispered.

"I love you, too, I really do," she murmured, and collapsed.

"Good work, my boy," said the count ebulliently. "I told you Sagittarians need serious challenges! You came through! I trust you'll do as well next time—if there's to be a next time."

Zodiac sped toward rain that fell upon the sea. A final shell from the warship sent spray on the deck. An hour or so later, the captain reported them out of the frigate's radar reach.

Philip stood alone at the bow, watching green water part and flow along the hull. Between the whitecaps the sea was clear yet fathomless— how many wrecks littered the bottom, victims of mishaps, mistakes, miscalculations, storms, war, greed? The *Zodiac* might easily join them.

Of course, the Cardinals weren't fools—mad maybe, but not fools. The *Zodiac* had to have defensive capabilities other than speed. But he wouldn't be around to find out. He'd leave the ship at the next port of call, St. Lucia. The wind bore dread. Suddenly a sea battle seemed entirely possible. Why, he'd heard about an environmental group which, loving whales, had a boat that actually *rammed* the ships of illicit whalers. If anything, progress had made the world even wilder— conspicuously failed to tame it, at least. Shots had been *fired* at them, right off a French island, with impunity. If the warship found them again, the great white yacht would certainly be sunk.

But suppose the Cardinals wouldn't let him debark? Suppose he was compelled to remain with the ship? What if, when he elected to stay on land, they pretended he was drunk or sick and brought him back? Such speculation was nonsense, he presumed, but it served to raise again the question of why they wanted him aboard so badly. They wouldn't tell him yet, he knew, but would give him evasive answers, like how, when the time came, Ari would make an important proposition. It *would* have been interesting to find out what de Vaucresson wanted . . .

Soft footsteps sounded on the deck behind, and Libby appeared, wearing a slicker. She said huskily, "You'll be drenched."

He put one hand to his hair. "I didn't realize there was so much spray."

"Preoccupied, eh? And no wonder. It isn't every day that a ship and a shark attack."

Philip laughed. "And I was invited on a pleasure cruise!"

"Oh, don't worry, we'll survive. And the surprises are amusing—admit it!" Cappy, who frequently paced the deck, passed by at that moment, hands behind his back, nodding gravely. "What would be truly surprising would be no more surprises, knowing us."

"Which I'm afraid I won't, not really," he said.

"You will—better than you think." The blue eyes widened suggestively. It was the same expression he'd seen yesterday on the sundeck. *Was that only yesterday?* "We'll come to know you, too."

"I thought you already did."

"You may have qualities you hide, even from yourself."

"Such as?"

"Well, we can't be sure. You *appear* to be an honest, upstanding man, well-intentioned, honorable, cautious." Libby laughed gaily. "Is there more to it? I bet there is. Much more."

"Who knows what evil lurks in the hearts of men?"

"And women. How many Philip Castles are there?"

"Depends on who's counting."

"You're a sophist! Well, we'll learn the truth about that, you'll see. In the meantime, the spray's getting under my hat. Take my arm, will you? I'm afraid of losing my balance."

Arm in arm they entered the main salon. Marie-Celeste was about to change a record; when she saw them, her hands went to the narrow hips of her tailored denims. "There you are," Libby said. "I was hoping to find you. Darling, my hair's a mess. Would you set it?"

M-C's face showed teeth. The two women went to Libby's cabin.

Philip returned to the deck. He was seated in one of the fighting chairs beneath an outrigger pole used for trawling when Morales approached, pacing slowly. "Excellent shooting," he said.

"Well, I could hardly miss at that range."

"But you could have! You might easily have become rattled, especially with the warship out there. You displayed remarkable presence. You're an ex-soldier, and it showed."

"Pure luck, really."

The dark countenance turned toward the horizon, seeming to ignore him. "We need good soldiers to fight against Hector Hernandez. He must be defeated. Hernandez must not be permitted to go into exile in Florida, or in Mexico, or in Switzerland, or in the Bahamas. Do you realize he owns half our country? Even now he is putting his property in mortgage and taking the proceeds out, just in case. What sort of creature is it who will remove millions on millions from a small, impoverished land? Somoza, Hernandez—they are all the same. Are they patriots? Clearly not. Hernandez deserves to die—brutally." Morales' eyes glistened. "I would enjoy killing him myself, though it is not in the stars."

"Killing's not in my stars, either," Philip said, realizing too late that he had misunderstood the Tall One.

Morales faced him. "There are times when killing is mandatory, my friend. When there is no other way."

"Maybe in war. Aside from that I'm pretty much a pacifist," Philip said.

"But this is war! As we've told you. But even outside of war, killing is sometimes required," the man said, soft voice harsh. "For reasons of discipline and disloyalty as well. And to rid the world of evil people who ought to die.

"Have you killed people, Cappy?"

"Certainly. And so may you."

"Only in self-defense, and even then—"

"Your horoscope predicts that you, Philip Castle, will kill." Cappy limped down the deck without another word.

Rain squalls intercepted them as they neared St. Lucia. They had sailed toward Barbados to trick the slower-moving warship, then doubled back on a different course. The frigate would continue to Barbados and, failing to find them, leave.

Or so Ari predicted. He, Cappy, and Philip were in the library.

"You hope," said Philip.

"It's more than hope. My horoscope would make serious trouble apparent."

"Did your horoscope tell you the frigate would show up today?"

"I studied my chart immediately afterward and found what I missed at first. Anyway, we avoided disaster, didn't we?"

"Marie-Celeste nearly died."

The count shrugged. "But she escaped harm, that's the important thing. Her horoscope wasn't *wrong*. My dear boy, just because astrology isn't a precise tool doesn't mean it's not accurate."

"The count is correct," said Capablanca Morales, who was always deferential to de Vaucresson, and to him alone. *(Why? Because he's in awe of royalty?)* "You should have such a—how do you say?—track record as we Cardinals do."

"Me? I'm always wrong. I'm worse than the weatherman."

"On the contrary," said Ari admiringly, "I believe you may have psychic gifts."

"Like when you kept the Ingram by your side. I wondered at the time if you had foreknowledge you'd need it."

"I didn't. I don't believe in premonitions."

"No? Never had one? Most people have."

The plane crash? But that had been déjà vu. *That someone had been killed in it? Somebody almost had to be. That Marie-Celeste would come over that night, after they'd met on the beach? That she'd make love with him? But he had clues; he was a professional psychologist, after all. That the man at the bar had been testing him—but Martinez had tipped him off.* He reached back to the death of his mother. *You knew what it was the second the phone rang. But she was sick; you'd been expecting the call. It's all explainable if you look hard enough.* "I don't buy parapsychology either."

"Don't you have a *hunch* you ought to stay with us despite your desire to leave?" asked the count with a sly look. "I hope you put your logic aside for a change and follow your instincts. You ignore them too much."

"What do you think I desire so desperately?"

"That, you must let your instincts tell you. Riches? Freedom?" suggested the count.

Philip shook his head. "No."

"Then what?"

"I don't know."

He decided to say on board until Barbados.

The yacht, rolling in rough seas without a creak, rounded the southern tip of St. Lucia, passing the village of Vieux-Fort. The passage between the island and St. Vincent teemed with distinctive-looking fishing boats with sharp ramming bows, copied from the Carib war canoes. "The Helen of the Caribbean" St. Lucia was called because she had been responsible for so many colonial wars. The island was shaped like a tear.

The *Zodiac* moved up the western coast toward a pair of towering peaks, over a half-mile high, rising straight from the waves that crashed against their bases. They looked like loaves of hard-crusted bread. These were the Pitons, the remains of extinct volcanos. Not far beyond, a sulfurous gray cloud identified Soufriere, a dormant volcano which had never erupted in recorded history.

The yacht put into the main port, Castries, where they cleared customs, hoisting their "Q" flag. A uniformed official came aboard at once, and passed them through respectfully. The Captain moved *Zodiac* to be refueled while the passengers were on land. Castries was one of the best-protected harbors in the Caribbean and what the fighting on St. Lucia had been all about. It was a lively place, with a noisy Saturday outdoor market and raucous squares.

Carnival was about to arrive, and the streets were filled with festivity. Ari (adhesive on his cheek; he had cut himself shaving), Libby, Cappy, and Canny vanished, while Philip and Marie-Celeste watched revelers in painted faces and garish costumes form an impromptu parade, joined by a steel band. Suddenly the beat quickened, and space was cleared for four men in white face, carrying bamboo poles. They crossed the poles, each man holding the ends of two of them, so that a square was formed in the center. The poles clapped together, a few feet off the ground. A painted male dancer jumped easily in and out of the aperture when it opened and before it closed.

"Looks simple, huh, dude?" one of the men in white face said to Philip.

"Not at all!"

"You want to try?"

"Me?"

"Come on," M-C challenged. "Show them how fast you are."

Philip found himself inside the square formed by the four poles the men carried. A crowd was assembling. The steel band played. The square contracted and Philip jumped out.

The box opened and he jumped in again. When it closed, he leaped out.

The beat of the music, he could hear, was quicker; so were the poles. They clicked together hard as he jumped out of the box. He didn't *have* to jump back in again, but *she* was watching. *Jump, click, jump, click, jump, click* . . . if he wasn't fast enough the bamboo poles could break his legs. *Jump, click* . . . Sweat covered him. He *wouldn't* quit.

"Enough!" he heard her shout. The white-faced blacks grinned and moved on. "You should have stopped earlier. You're nuts!"

"I was more worried about my knees."

"Ha-ha."

He took her hand. "I wouldn't have been hurt, I'm sure, but you got upset because you love me, didn't you?"

"You're laughing at me. I can't bear it."

"I was laughing at *us*. Hey, you're blushing! I thought Sagittarians were the blushers of the zodiac."

"Who told you that?" she asked sharply.

"Why, Libby did."

M-C wrenched her hand away. "You're making a fool of me. I'm a free spirit, I tell you. I'm just doing my job, which is to keep you amused until . . ." She stopped speaking.

"Has it been a chore? Anyway, I thought I was supposed to keep *you* amused. Until what?"

"You'll find out."

"You make me so irritated I could slap you."

"Don't try it. I claw. I bite."

"This morning you loved me and now you're just doing a job that has side benefits."

"I loved you for a moment out of gratitude because you saved my life. I meant nothing beyond that. I'm Ari's woman, and don't forget it."

"Ari's woman! M-C—"

"Marie-Celeste," she said coldly.

"How can you be Ari's woman, the way you are with me?"

"I just *can*. You're with *me* and yet you're always playing up to Libby. Footsie on the sundeck. Walking arm and arm. You'd like to sleep with her, wouldn't you?"

He smiled. "You're jealous!"

Her freckles faded as she flushed again. He registered down on her upper lip. "Of you and her? Never. I'm out for kicks, that's all." She hesitated. "I could sleep with her as easily as you could."

"What are you saying? If you're trying to get back at me, don't. Libby's attractive, sure—"

"Oh, she thinks you are too! Those languid looks—"

"That's just a reflex action. Libby sees herself in the mirror of other people's eyes. It has little to do with me personally. And it doesn't mean anything's going to happen. People can feel attractions without acting them out. It's a mark of mature behavior. We're all *potentially* capable of . . ."

He sounded like a college professor again, and knew it. "So you *are* attracted to her. You two will make out, just wait." She strode off amid the dancing and singing on the street.

When he got back to the wharf, taking his time, the count and Libby sat on a bench, M-C between them, a hand on the leg of each. She laughed, but shot Castle a cold stare.

Libby slipped and almost fell as a crewman helped her down into the launch. For a moment Philip thought she would slap the man, though the fault was hers. "Stupid idiot!" she shouted. "I hate fools."

Two transmitters operated on St. Lucia, Philip learned, and as soon as they were under way from Barbados, he tried both. Before long he picked up the familiar astrological chant.

The Cardinals played bridge. Marie-Celeste sunned by the pool. Philip decided to put off packing—he had plenty of time before Barbados. In his cabin he leafed through some astrological books from the library, making notes on a pad. He was curious to see just how closely the gang of four corresponded to their astrological descriptions; and he wanted to compare his own analyses with the astrological ones. He wrote:

ARIES: March 21–April 20 (male)

The most positive sign for good and evil. Leader of the zodiac, yet infant of the universe. Wants to be in charge. Bossy. Ambitious. Strong. Belligerent. Great personal magnetism. Determined. Stubborn. Short-tempered. Talkative. Needs challenges. Likes to win. Indomitable will but lacks caution. Engages in large enterprises but tends to rush them through. Careless about details. Frequently overly optimistic about the chances for success. Makes good teacher, leader.

Original, inventive, sometimes clumsy. Blind to faults of friends. Keenly intuitive. Remarkable predictive power and fond of forecasting events. As a rule not anxious to marry. With so much energy, puts too much strain on weakest parts of body. Prone to fevers and headaches. Highly emotional, though conceals the fact. Strives for the kind of superawareness which, ultimately, is "consciousness," the final purpose of the universe as far as he's concerned.

So much for astrology. And not bad, Philip noted reluctantly. It *did* sound a good deal like de Vaucresson—his leadership, magnetism (which Ari had, all right), intuition (he'd *known* Philip would come on the voyage), recklessness (as with the warship), temper (the blowup with Libby), rushes over details (Philip's birthdate!), need to win, headaches, clumsiness (he'd cut himself shaving that morning?).

But *who* was Ari? Philip tried to dig to the essential man. He seemed dominated by a massive drive for success. Such a person, Castle believed, had deeply unsatisfied emotional needs which he sought to fulfill, always failing, because he lacked emotional resources. Ari sought to prove himself but never could because no matter how much money he made, he'd always tell himself he needed more.

He'd turned to crime because it seemed to offer a solution. Like many criminals, Ari had a streak of omniscience—he thought that he knew best, because he believed himself superior. *In the end, Ari wants power. He'll do almost anything to get it.*

What about Canny? Astrologically . . .

CANCER: June 21–July 21 (male)

Sensitive to the point of seeming eccentric. Yearns for sympathy and hates disapproval. Capacity for self-sacrificing love, but prone to morbidity, avarice, moods that don't last. May lack emotional maturity, exhibits flashes of adolescent behavior. Deeply fears poverty and craves riches. Having achieved them, will hold on with the tenacity of a crab. Curious habit of hoarding.

Selfish. Pessimistic. Possessive. Cranky. Susceptible to self-pity. Soft, but can be forced into a role of aggressive self-sufficiency. A cardinal sign of leadership, though conceals the quality. Often unduly feminine and overemotional, from strong maternal influence. Marriages frequently unhappy. Can be sly, but intensely loyal. Activity and passivity frequently conflict.

Congenial occupation: working with the public.

Essentially psychic and attracted by all things occult. Symbolizes the primal water and stands for our ancestral origins, all life having begun in the sea.

Canny, the selfish shellfish. Runs a hotel. A little feminine. Sensitive, easily offended. Flashes of juvenile behavior. Possessive—"It's *my* boat"—but utterly loyal to Ari. Emotionally disturbed. . . .

Philip's mind went back to the evening before Sansa's death, when, as he and M-C were leaving, he had heard the woman cry out. Had Canny *raped* the East Indian? Somehow he thought so. After Canny extracted information.

If Canny had raped one woman, it was probable that he had raped others. And rapists suffered from mental and emotional disorders. Sex offenders frequently had stern, cruel, sadistic mothers who made the boys scared of women and insecure with them. Their personalities could often be described as passive-dependent. The gambling? Maybe a substitute for masturbation.

Canny as a criminal—Philip thought he must be a big-time Las Vegas cheat—probably had a strong unconscious desire for punishment. Crooks ran the risk of being caught, and rapists were masochists as well as sadists; the rapist wanted to hurt himself as well as the woman. And Canny was pseudo-aggressive. Expressing the aggressiveness had led him to crime, but underneath he was emotionally weak.

A definitive knock sounded at the door. Philip opened it. Ari stood there.

"May I?"

"Sure."

In white ducks, the V of his printed shirt showing gray hair, Ari strode in. He looked quickly at the pad on Philip's bed. "Writing?"

"Notes for my lectures."

"Ah, yes. You intend to resume teaching, then?"

"Did I say I wasn't?"

"I had the impression that your interest in academia had faltered." The count sat in the chair. "We arrive in Barbados in a few minutes." Lord! Philip hadn't packed. Where had the time gone? "It's a pity our stay will be so short. I detest rushing like this—it's contrary to the Caribbean spirit—but appointments have been set up all down the line and we have to keep them. Once this trip is done, I look forward to a few weeks of taking it easy." His gaze seemed to glide over the books on Philip's table. "I don't envy you if you plan to return to Chicago. The temperature there is below zero, with two feet of snow. Do you like the cold?"

"No. I came from the Southwest."

"How about Chicago?"

Philip shrugged. "It doesn't feel much like home anymore."

"My home is where I happen to be," the count said. "The beauty of my work is that it permits me to travel so much. I adore traveling. I always have. Do you?"

Philip wondered what Raymond was getting at. He laughed ruefully. "I haven't really traveled enough to know. My work keeps me pretty pinned down."

"It's especially nice when you can fly around in your own plane. Which reminds me. My pilot is thinking about retiring." The count smoothed the side of his head with his palm.

"Oh?" Philip sat up on the edge of the bed.

"Yes. Would you consider taking flying lessons?"

Castle said in surprise, "Why do you ask?"

"I might need a replacement. You'd have to do some brushing up, I expect."

There it was! The count wanted Philip to be his pilot. Or was that all of it? "I, ah, don't want to fly a plane. It's bad enough being a passenger."

"Come on, Philip," the count said gently. Once a pilot, always a pilot."

"I'm a full professor! That's my career."

"Actually, it might be good for you to have a change of scene. The work's easy, with plenty of time off, and you'd visit a lot of places. As for the money, I can easily match what you earn now, and then some. You'd be able to continue your—how shall I say—friendship with Marie-Celeste. Could you swing a sabbatical? You could try it for a year and see."

"I've got a sabbatical coming, as a matter of fact," Philip replied automatically. "But, sorry, I'm not an airborne chauffeur."

"No offense intended. I was just sounding you out. I like you, and I find you dependable, enterprising, and intelligent, rare qualities! Oh, I probably ought to add that the job could entail some business responsibilities, at even higher pay. I'm carrying too large a load for a man of my age."

Nonsense! He doesn't think of himself as old. "I'm sure you will have plenty of candidates."

"Yes," said the count in a disappointed voice. The ship's horn bleated. "Here we are." He rose. At the door he turned and said, "I'm going to buy a new plane. I wanted a Learjet . . ."

"A Lear! You're talking about millions!"

"The price doesn't matter," said Ari. "The problem is that such a plane needs too much room for the usual Caribbean runways. I'm in the process of selecting another aircraft. I know a few things about them. Let me know if you change your mind."

"I won't."

Ari closed the cabin door and opened it again. "You were thinking again about leaving the cruise, weren't you?" he asked almost apologetically.

"You must be a mind reader, Ari."

The count chuckled. "I am, in a way. Oh, there's something on Barbados I want to show you."

Again curiosity got the best of him. "Okay," Philip said. He'd quit the ship at St. Vincent.

Barbados, the Spanish word for beard, after the bearded banyan trees in which monkeys climbed and brilliant hummingbirds darted. Philip had to remind himself it was still March 11. This was the third island that day.

Marie-Celeste had hardly spoken to Philip since St. Lucia. With Libby Harris she took a taxi to the Animal-Flower Cave, grottoes filled with sea anemones that were exposed at low tide. The men went straight to the TV and radio stations, where Ari took ad copy from his beige gabardine jacket and paid to have it aired. The TV commercial was a little longer than the ones Philip had heard. Ari handed him a copy without comment.

"Aries, Taurus, Gemini . . . Pisces. Yes, folks, the twelve signs of the zodiac. What's in them for you? Plenty. Know yourself better. Make more money by finding the right job. Pick a mate who was meant for you. Learn about your future. It's all in astrology, yes, astrology. Study it. Follow it. Believe it. Aries, Taurus, Gemini . . . Pisces, Pisces, Pisces . . ."

"You think that'll win adherents?"

"Oh, yes. Especially when repeated enough. The whole Caribbean's talking about these ads. Where they've been aired, astrology books are sold out."

They went to a café and took a large table. "We'll be seeing important locals now," said Ari. "Cappy is their contact. In this way we are gaining support for the cause—the overthrow of Hernandez and the unity of the West Indies. Libby usually keeps a record of the proceedings but I'll be secretary today. Canny acts as our, ah, bursar. You are the first outsider ever permitted to witness one of our little meetings," the count said conspiratorially.

Koster took a sheaf of envelopes from his shoulder bag while de Vaucresson produced a notebook. "You've had these meetings before this trip?" Philip asked.

"Oh, yes. This is our third swing through the islands in less than a year. Now, where are the Bajans, as the people here are called?"

"Goddamn stinking niggers are always late," Canny said.

They waited in silence until a shabbily dressed black man appeared. He seemed nervous. Cappy introduced Philip as "a new member of the organization," which the newcomer accepted indifferently. Then Morales asked, "Are things moving along?"

"Oh, yes. Just fine."

"You are gaining recruits?"

"Each day, yes."

"You have talked to members of the government I specified?"

"Every one."

"And they listened?"

"Think so, yes."

"*Think?*" said Morales.

"*Know.*"

"What do you hear from our people in St. Vincent?"

"A little trouble in St. Vincent, I hear. Some folks ain't doing their jobs."

"But you are," Cappy said insistently.

"Oh, yes, suh," the man replied.

"What are the identities of the troublemakers on St. Vincent?" The man provided two, and Ari wrote them down. "They shall be contacted this afternoon for a meeting at the usual time tomorrow. Here is your literature." Cappy had carried a large bag. He removed a large packet of what seemed to be astrological pamphlets and handed it to the man. He asked for details about the local political situation, which the man provided. Then Canny inspected the names on the envelopes and gave one to the man, who took it eagerly.

"You may go," said the Tall One.

Another Bajan waited to take his place. Ten people appeared in the next hour and a half to receive pamphlets and envelopes and answer Cappy's terse questions. All gave pretty much the same replies.

"There was money in the envelopes?" Philip said as they returned to the wharf.

"Yes. We're spending a fortune, but there's no better way to assure loyalty than hard cash," Ari said.

In the main salon the soft beat of Fat's gong announced dinner.

The Cardinals seemed edgy; maybe the morning's encounter with the warship was responsible, but they paid scant attention to the finny feast Fat laid before them—mousseline of wahoo, dolphin chowder, fresh tuna steaks.

"I wish," said Count de Vaucresson to Canfield Koster, "that you would cease snapping your fingers. The sound grates."

"Hear, hear," Cappy said, a sardonic smile on his dark face.

"*Ingrates*, you mean," Canny retorted. "I can do what I want on *my* boat."

The count sighed. "I am tired of being reminded you own this vessel."

"We're in this together," Libby said.

Canny's bulging eyes swiveled back and forth, as if seeking a target. They settled on her. "Don't lecture me, you bitch. Where's the five hundred you lost at bridge today."

"I quite forgot," Libby responded evenly. "I suppose you'd like me to fetch it from my cabin right now."

"Yeah."

But Libby didn't move.

Canny raged, "She's always forgetting what she owes or borrows. What did you do with the books you took from the library? Throw them overboard? They're not in your stateroom."

"Do you always break into the rooms of your guests?" Libby cried.

"Only when they're out."

The count said softly, "If you mean the astrology books, Philip has them." How observant the count was!

"We have a believer?" Canny rasped.

"I'm on the fence," Philip said.

"Leaning our way?" Libby asked. Philip shook his head. "You *are* hard to persuade."

Coffee and liqueurs were served in the main salon. Philip tried a Mirabelle this time. He was growing fond of liqueurs. "Don't they ever speak?" he asked when the wordless bull-necked Bob and Bill had left.

"What a very strange question to ask just at this moment," Ari said. "Bob and Bill are English boys. They have been thoroughly trained, at my direction, in the martial arts. They are my bodyguards, and utterly devoted to me."

"What's so strange about that?"

The count seemed to enjoy creating suspense. "I read about them in a

London paper seven years ago, when they were fifteen. Both were born on the same day, June 7, which makes them Geminis with Taurus rising—Taurus probably accounts for their large necks. Not only do they look alike, but both were in the same institution. Both are orphans and mutes, the latter being one reason I adopted them. Both had tuberculosis—a Gemini disease—which was cured because of me. I found your question curious since we were talking about astrology, and Bob and Bill are living proof that—as an American ad has it—the stuff works." He smiled.

Philip plunged. "What about death? Can you predict that?" he challenged.

"One's chart would show if one had the ability to forestall death. There's a formula . . ." The count closed his eyes.

"Ari, Philip knows nothing about the incident," Libby said. She put her hand lightly on Philip's shoulder—he saw M-C's golden-brown eyes follow. "Ari's wife . . . well, she died in an automobile accident and he's never forgiven himself for not predicting it, which is silly of him. Ari, I don't mean to be cruel, but you know perfectly well that predicting death is virtually impossible and always will be, because the universe will not permit us to be as gods. Don't forget Guido Bonatto of Florence."

The count's eyes opened quickly. "Of course! The astrologer. Bonatto, having stated that he could foretell the precise moment of his demise, was killed the very next day by robbers. Dante put him in hell with his head turned backward for the sin of having the temerity to predict the future—a sin of pride, Dante thought. But what about Pierleoni of Spoleto?" He turned to Philip. "Having foreseen from his horoscope that he would die by drowning, Pierleoni took every possible means to avoid water, even turning down a lucrative job in Venice because of the canals. Still, he ended a suicide. He jumped in a river."

"Did he will himself to drown? Maybe the thought of drowning became an obsession, so that he had to do exactly what he dreaded most. It's not uncommon."

"No, no, professor of psychology, I am certain that Pierleoni died because he failed to read his horoscope correctly. Had he done so, it would have told him to avoid water during certain periods, that is all. Astrology always offers choices if one looks into it deeply enough. Take the signs of the zodiac. Aries is supposed to be, typically, a bold, venturesome, active figure, but a person can be the exact opposite of his sign. An Arian can be modest, careful, cautious, even timid. How I wish I had developed my personality more along those lines! I am rash, you know, impetuous—to a fault! I do not ponder things sufficiently." The count hesitated. "Had I done so in the case of my wife's destiny, I would have learned that on certain days she should not drive a car!" The count choked a little and his trim face sagged into deep lines.

"Ari, darling, don't blame yourself! You have no idea how susceptible to guilt Ari is," Libby whispered to Philip. She said to de Vaucresson, "Didn't your wife make a strange prediction about you?"

Ari wiped his eyes. "You're right. She claimed that a rival with a configuration similar to mine would come along, meaning a male Aries, whose identity would be disguised. She warned me that I would be vanquished if I were not vigilant. All these years the threat has haunted me, but no such individual has come along. Or perhaps, because they might be Arians, I have deliberately avoided serious competitors without being fully aware of doing so. One's unconscious can reach such decisions, Philip, don't you agree?"

"What? Certainly." What would Raymond do if he learned a secret Aries was aboard the ship?

"Aries, Taurus, Gemini, Cancer, Leo, Virgo, Libra, Scorpio, Sagittarius, Capricorn, Aquarius, Pisces, Pisces, Pisces . . ." The door from Marie-Celeste's cabin opened and he turned off the radio. "Where have you been?" he asked.

"On deck talking to Libby. Not that it's any of *your* business."

"What's the matter? Why snap at me?"

"I don't know. Why do we always sleep in your cabin instead of mine?"

"Because we started that way, I guess. I'll be happy to move to your bed."

"I'm freer like this, come to think of it. I only have to get up and go." She was cool with him that night; his lioness was afraid of being caged.

19

Sunday morning off St. Vincent. A calm, cobalt-colored sea. A square-ended craft was tied up at the *Zodiac's* stern.

Philip crept up to the deck and hid behind the funnel. Two blacks, a young man and woman, stood on one side of the pool, the three male Cardinals on the other. The Geminis were positioned by a garbage can that contained a wet burlap sack. Something moved inside. Fish?

Cappy said in a stentorian voice, "You have chosen to defy us! You have failed to follow directions, given lip service only to our cause, gone through the motions of activity, accomplished nothing—"

"But—" the woman protested.

"*Do not interrupt!* This is not a court of law—the verdict is already in, and justice shall be done. Nothing you say will prevent this! Insubordination is the first charge against you, the second is graft. You have lined your pockets with money given to you for political purposes. Now you shall pay the price!"

Cappy gestured, and one of the powerful Geminis took a heavy stick with a kind of rubber noose at the end. He thrust it into the burlap sack and moved it around until he seemed to catch hold of what was inside. It took both Bob and Bill to lift it out.

Philip gasped. Drawn from the sack on the bending pole, caught by the clamp just under the head, was a snake, fully eight feet long, with a body as thick as a human leg.

"No . . ." the woman screeched as the two men carried the reptile toward her.

"A Pacific sea snake, far more venomous than a rattler, a coral, a bushmaster, a cobra, an Australian taipan," Cappy told them. "You shall share the pool with it." The Geminis waved the writhing creature before the terrified blacks.

"Please," the man begged.

"Too late for entreaties! Have you informed on us?"

"No!" the two shouted at once. "We swear!"

The faces of the three Cardinals were admixtures of cruelty and glee. "How about a dip, folks?" Canny cackled.

The snake's tongue flicked in and out. It looked like an import from hell. The woman dropped to the deck; she had fainted.

"Lord, Lord, Lord, Lord," the man moaned. "Please. Mercy."

"What?" asked Capablanca Morales.

"Mercy, mercy."

"Mercy what?"

"Mercy, master."

"Again!"

"*Massa mercy.*" The man fell to his knees.

The Capricorn Cardinal loped across the deck, reached down, grabbed the prostrate woman, and threw her overboard. The Tall One bent again, seized the heavyset man, raised him in the air, forced his face close to the darting tongue, hurled him into the sea as well.

"I believe," said Cappy, "that we shall have no further problems on St. Vincent."

That settled it. He'd quit the ship at St. Vincent before Cappy killed someone. After M-C had gone upstairs for breakfast, he threw his gear in his suitcase and worked on his notes until he heard the engines of the launch. He was out in the passageway before he realized he'd forgotten his passport.

Where had he put it? *Think.* The specter of the snakes had unnerved him, left him confused. He took everything out of his bag again—

nothing. He looked in the breast pocket of his city jacket. He examined the soft-cover mysteries he'd brought, hoping the passport was inside one.

Then he remembered—the air-conditioning duct! He got on a chair and pulled out the plastic grate. Nothing. The vent was empty.

In a fury Philip ran on deck, ready to throttle the count. But the launch had departed, carrying the Cardinals and M-C.

"They were in a hurry," the captain explained. "The launch will return for you. Ah, there it is now."

Philip didn't take the bag—he wouldn't be able to get off the island without a passport. He went ashore filled with hate.

In Kingston, the capital, he saw police resplendent in dress uniforms with white helmets, white jackets, Sam Browne belts, dark pants set off by white stripes. He thought of stopping one and reporting a theft, but it wouldn't have done any good. Where were the Cardinals?

At last he found them, minus Marie-Celeste, in the rear of a second-story restaurant. He waited impatiently until the black man Cappy had been interrogating rose. He rushed over. "Ari, where is it?"

"Where is what, my friend?" the count said.

"You *know* what! My passport. It isn't in my cabin, where I left it."

"Are you sure?"

"Sure I'm sure.

It occurred to Philip belatedly that he was on extremely hazardous ground; if the count had his passport, he might have looked at the birthdate, in which case Castle was as good as dead. But Ari merely spread his hands in a placating gesture. "I have nothing to do with it, I assure you. Canny, did you see Philip's passport?"

"Me?" Cappy and Libby shook their heads in response to the same question. Libby looked slightly amused.

"I'm certain your passport is still on board," the count said. "Perhaps Marie-Celeste has an explanation. She went to visit St. Mary's. Now, if you'll excuse us, people are waiting." He gestured to someone across the room.

St. Mary's, a Catholic church, was an almost eerie maze of balconies, turrets, arches, spires, courtyards, and fancy touches in stone. It had been designed by a Belgian monk in the 1930s, the plaque said. Philip stormed down stone corridors until he located M-C on a battlement.

"Where is it? It has to be you, unless the others are lying. You know what I'm talking about."

"I do?" she said blandly.

"My passport. I hid it in my cabin. It's not there anymore."

"You're accusing me?" she said, eyes steady.

"The others deny having anything to do with it."

"Me too. Lay off, will you? What's the screaming need for the passport?"

"I want to get off the yacht."

"You do?" She examined the balustrade. "Libby will miss you."

"Libby again!" he said. "For a person who isn't jealous, you give a good imitation."

"I'm *not* jealous! Libby can have you if that's the way it's supposed to be."

When they returned to the ship, Philip went straight to his cabin. Maybe he'd shoved the passport farther back into the duct than he realized; maybe in his haste he'd overlooked it. The chair was in front of the vent where he'd left it. Removing the grate, he saw the passport just by the opening.

"Jesus," he said out loud. He *hadn't* overlooked it. Somebody had taken it. To keep him on board.

The knock on the door was Ari's. Philip opened it. "Good! I see you found your passport," he said genially. "I learned what happened. Yesterday a crewman was inspecting the air-conditioning system and found it. I suppose he thought it might have been there for a long time— who knows? He forgot to give it to the captain until this morning, after you'd gone ashore. The captain told him to put it back. That's all there is to it. Why did you hide the passport in the first place?"

"So nobody could stop me from leaving," Philip growled.

"Hoisted by your own passport. Ha! Really, Philip. I wish you would trust me. You can depart anytime you want, my boy. At any rate, airline service out of Grenada is far superior."

Philip asked himself if anybody had looked at his purloined passport for his birthdate. Evidently not. His luck—if such it could be called— held.

*   *   *

The dozens of islands along the sixty-five-mile route from St. Vincent to Grenada were called the Grenadines. Bequia was first, but the *Zodiac* paused only briefly. Again forced to taxicab tourism, Philip and Marie-Celeste were given a glimpse of Moon Hole, a cave that passed through the tip of the island, with a fine stone-and-concrete house built directly inside it. Other mansions were perched on the cliffs around. Signs announced a private development.

White people, Americans mostly, owned the houses. The driver was light-skinned himself, a descendant of New England whalers who pursued their catch as far south as the Grenadines and, loving the climate, never went back, the driver said. Who could blame them?

In Port Elizabeth, Marie-Celeste bought scrimshaw, Philip a model Bequia whaler—a locally built small boat—mounted on a coconut husk to give David. David! How seldom his only child came to mind.

The *Zodiac*'s horn summoned, and soon they were at sea again.

Ari and Libby renewed the argument about stopping at Moustique. Libby still wanted to meet Princess Margaret, while Ari insisted that Moustique, a private island almost entirely white, was valueless to them, who *had* to be in Grenada that afternoon. An obscenity on Princess Margaret, the count said. Libby Harris returned with something vile.

The ship's captain got on the radio telephone at Morales' suggestion. Princess Margaret was in England. Libby regained composure instantly. The *Zodiac* proceeded on her way.

Off Moustique lay the French cruise ship *Antilles*, which had run onto an uncharted rock in 1971. All aboard had been saved, but the wreck reminded Philip that somewhere behind a warship lurked.

He stayed in the bow, identifying the passing islands from a sailing book from Canny's library, *The Yachtsman's Guide to the Windward Islands*: Savan, Petit Cannouan, Tobago Cays, Mayero, Union, Palm, Petit St. Vincent, Petit Martinique, Carriacou, Saline, Frigate, Large, Diamond, Les Tantes, Ronde, Caille . . . island after island, mostly less than a mile across, rounded humps, dry but gleaming greenly, sparsely or not populated except by goats and birds.

Carriacou had an airstrip. Saline, just south of it, appeared deserted. *A perfect place to hide out. You could fly into Carriacou, get rid of the plane, buy a motorboat, come in for supplies* . . . What a ridiculous fantasy!

The two thousand-foot mountains of Grenada were in sight.

Grenada. Ironic that Christopher Columbus, who named it "Concepción," didn't land, although his mandate was to find spices, and later Grenada became known as "Spice Island" because they grew in abundance.

Cappy, in his dry voice, lectured Philip before they went ashore. "Please! Do not stray far, because we must be on the yacht before sundown. On this island very unstable political conditions exist. Leave your camera—you must not take pictures. Do not talk to strangers—*anything* you say might be construed as anti the present government. Grenada is dangerous, and don't forget it. For the slightest indiscretion we could be placed in custody."

"I'll try to be a good boy. How long is the stopover?"

"If nothing untoward happens to us?" Ari asked. "Until the morning of day after tomorrow."

Tomorrow, then. No hurry. The airline offices in St. George's, the capital, were closed, but why should he bother going to the airport? He'd depart on Monday surreptitiously. So, in the scant hours available, Philip and his chilly companion sampled the sights.

Fat's dinner comprised local delicacies—two soups, urchin and calaloo, made out of crabs, okra, garlic, onions, and pork fat; fresh-caught kingfish in guava sauce; ice cream topped with nutmeg on a bed of papaws. "I have been thinking," remarked the count as one of the Geminis served liqueurs—Philip ordered Apry. "Assuming we succeed tomorrow, perhaps it is time for a gala affair. I spoke of giving Fat a serious gastronomic test? Very well, I have an idea, subject to our host's approval, of course. It's *his* boat, though it's *my* chef." He winked at Canny Koster. "Bill, would you fetch Fat? Fat is versant with astrology, too, which is almost as popular with the Chinese as with the Indians." Fat arrived at the table. "Chef, I have a challenge for you. Tomorrow evening I'd like you to prepare an astrological banquet."

"A *what?*" Fat cried.

"A stellar feast, with a course for every sign."

Fat's grin twisted into consternation. "But what serve?"

"Let's invent a dish for each of the twelve symbols."

Fat gulped. "All twelve? What for Alies?"

"Aries," the count corrected. "I keep telling Fat not to confuse *l*'s and *r*'s. The Aries course must be identified with the ram and higher intelligence," the count said easily.

"Taurus?"

"Taurus-the-bull clearly calls for beef."

"Beef Wellington?"

"A little too obvious, I think. Let your imagination go mad. I'll join you presently, to help plan. Fortunately, the locker's filled with exotic foods that I had flown in—my contribution to the voyage. Whatever else is needed can be obtained on shore, but it would be better to do your shopping in the morning." De Vaucresson watched the little Chinese depart, head bent. "Poor Fat! He'll be up all night."

Philip wondered what they fed the snake, down in the hold. He wanted to ask about the reptile, but the time was wrong.

"It's an absolutely thrilling idea, Ari," Libby said.

"It's not quite original, I'm afraid. Petronius Arbiter, in his *Satyricon*, wrote of such a feast, but surely with modern culinary arts we can do better. Do you approve, Canny?"

"Maybe we could start an astrological fast-food chain when we get back," Canny said.

"Not bad. It would have more romance than Pizza Hut or Sambo." He turned to Morales. "What's the matter, Cappy? You look unhappy."

"Because I foresee serious trouble on Tuesday. I am worried."

"All the more reason to celebrate *now*. Let us worry about Tuesday on Tuesday." Cappy excused himself in his grave manner. Ari continued, "Seriously, Philip, romance *is* lacking in our lives. I don't mean romance of the boy-girl sort, which quickly sours, but the sense of wonder, deep mystery. For most people it is all pretty cut and dried: school, career, marriage, kids, mortgage, probably divorce and remarriage, tax troubles, retirement. . . . How many ask, as the grave beckons, 'What did I miss?'"

Philip had to confess his own life had seemed pretty pointless when he arrived on St. Jean—when was it? Twelve days before. Twelve turbulent days. He was almost grateful to the Cardinals for exposing him to a different world, but if cracking kneecaps, scaring people to death with Pacific sea snakes, and maybe committing murder with an airplane wing added up to romance, it wasn't for him. And he was much too poor to travel in the private yacht set or keep a girl like Marie-Celeste. He found himself wondering what he would do *had* he millions like the gang of four. What pleasures would he award himself? What secret dreams would *he* act out?

Libby moved into Cappy's empty chair next to Marie-Celeste. Taking her arm, she said, "I have a splendid thought." Libby whispered into M-C's ear.

"We have a magical relationship with the universe, but we've forgotten it," said the count.

Canny Koster must have heard this before. "I'm going to watch a porn flick. I got dozens on board. Anybody?" He scuttled off.

"The universe is not a piece of dead machinery," the count continued.

Marie-Celeste's grin spread. "Uh-huh."

"We need a return to beliefs of a bygone age when man, society, and the universe operated under the same laws. In a world dominated by realistic philosophy and technology, a romantic revolution will be required."

"Wouldn't that be fun?" Libby breathed.

"Think what astrology could bring to the earth—breadth, simplicity, order, a sense of man being one with eternity."

"Where shall we do it?"

"Why not my cabin? We wouldn't want anyone to watch."

"How will we find what we need?"

"We'll improvise!"

"Poverty, recessions, wars, could be eliminated with a farsighted leadership tuned to the zodiac."

"What are we waiting for? Shall we tell them?"

"Why not?"

"We've decided to design costumes for the banquet! But we won't tell you what they are even when we know ourselves!"

Ari looked at Libby with glazed gray eyes. "Even more amusing! Where was I? To accept astrology is more important than to believe in it, so essential is it that the role of the mythic be restored. . . ."

The women left, arm in arm. In his dry, clipped voice, Ari droned hypnotically, while Bill replenished Philip's glass. He was drinking far too much again—he'd been temperate on the ship. Something bothered him. Was it a foreboding that he wouldn't get off the yacht in the morning?

"We offer hope," Ari rhapsodized. "Consider a rainbow. Beautiful yet ineffable. A perfect creation of gossamer, an arch in heaven. If we could pass through a rainbow and learn what lies beyond . . . who knows but that rainbows are gateways to the stars? Yet when we approach a rainbow it vanishes. Though supreme knowledge is like that, we must come as close to it as we can."

"Mmmm."

The count finished his diatribe and went off to find Fat. Philip *knew* M-C wouldn't be there when he returned to his cabin. The door to hers was locked, and a note on his pillow said, "Don't wait up. See you tomorrow."

Good-bye again, Marie-Celeste. Tomorrow I'll be gone.

Despite the liquor, he wasn't ready to sleep. He continued his notes on the Cardinals:

LIBRA: September 22–October 22 (female)
Artistic, beauty-loving, and often beautiful. Possesses strange foresight. Can face adversity unruffled but first must overcome many doubts. Doesn't like to act until ready. Difficulty in making up mind.

In some Librans the sign of balance is warped into pettiness and criticism. Careless of belongings and frequently fails to return what has been borrowed. Averse to handling money herself.

Superior intelligence, but impatient with mental inferiors. Gentle on the surface, but inwardly tough. A leadership sign. Ability to smooth tempers and help people to work together. Sociable, cultured, courteous, repelled by coarseness and vulgarity, though can be vulgar herself. Hates violence and bloodshed.

Exhibitionistic. Languidly sensual but experiences sex more as art than animal passion. May be so delicately balanced between the sexes as may not be one or the other, resulting in homosexuality.

Makes good mathematician or artist.

Sees goal of universe as Supreme Intelligence, omnipresent, omnis-cient, omnipotent.

Well, that astrological description seemed to fit too, when he got right down to it, from what he knew of Libby: intelligent, balanced, a peacemaker, yet tough, petty, self-indulgent. About her amorous proclivities he would only wonder: Libby seemed to have suggested she was at least bisexual. Her attraction for Marie? Good Lord! The two were in Libby's cabin. He hastened to another thought: could Libby be a well-concealed split personality? Suppose she was the victim of an unresolved Oedipus-Electra situation—sexually driven toward her father, and because that attraction was forbidden, had turned to women instead. Part of her might be fixated at an early narcissistic period of her development, might live in a world of which she was the center, a world whose reality was only words (or mathematical symbols) without emotional content, like a computer.

Astrology? By fashioning herself according to her sign, Libby might find a perfect outlet for narcissism. Libra the balance. Inorganic, remote. Perfection in her own eyes.

And Cappy?

CAPRICORN: December 22–January 20 (male)
Towering practical ambition. Leaps over adversaries and obstacles in the climb. Hardworking, punctilious, reliable, with tremendous drive and initiative. May come into his own comparatively late in life.

Cautious, conservative, with deep respect for authority. Strong attach-ment to family. Reserved. Rarely engages in superficial words or activities. Preconceived notions of right and wrong, and stubborn in sticking with them. Not especially original or creative. Low adaptability to change. Frugal and farsighted. Hates filth.

Might make a brilliant speculator or politician. Managerial talents and organizational skills.

Iron constitution and great powers of endurance. May have recurring moods of depression. Faint aura of melancholy and loneliness. Grave, dignified demeanor.

Chief desire, to be above the common herd, and contemptuous of inferiors. Longs to associate with the aristocracy, and obsequious toward

them. Appreciative of respect, but may abhor flattery and demonstrations
of affection when meant as courtesy.
This type can be cold, indifferent, cruel. If poverty threatens, may sink
physically.
Self-knowledge is thought by him to be the highest principle of the
universe.

That *did* sound like Cappy, with his austere, detached, even
ponderous manner . . . physical power . . . solitary pacing of the deck
. . . political ambition . . . deference toward Ari, the aristocrat . . .
dislike of empty gestures (he wouldn't kiss M-C at the airport) . . . the
cruelty he'd displayed on deck . . . .

Capablanca Morales was supposed to be a revolutionary, and Philip,
from what he'd heard, had no doubt the dictator Hernandez should be
overthrown. But those avid eyes when the Tall One assaulted the men
with his cane and held another's face against the snake! Cappy was
dominated in inner forces. He might always have harbored deep
resentments for which Hernandez (vile as he sounded) provided a focus.
The essential murderer acted out his impulses, no matter how well-
rationalized his motives were. He operated *against* society even though
he claimed to have noble ends. If Philip were right, Morales could be
interpreted as a person with homicidal traits, carefully controlled. The
man in black was a killer.

20

Monday morning. Marie-Celeste wasn't there when he reached out to touch her. He went to the porthole, then raced up to the sundeck again, gripped by dread. In the dawn light, the three male Cardinals stood on one side of the pool, with four black men across from them. Two garbage cans stood before the Geminis.

These blacks seemed different from the other victims. They were big and fierce-looking, with bulging muscles. The scar on the face of one ran from lip to ear. Another wore an eyepatch, the third a dirty stocking cap. The fourth held a switchblade.

They failed to daunt Capablanca Morales. "So you have chosen to defy me! I have asked that you join our side—the *right* side—and you present me with outrageous terms, with which I cannot comply without losing my honor, nor can I trust—"

"You puts up or shuts up," snarled the man with the scar.

"Yeah," said eyepatch. He nodded meaningfully toward the knife.

"*Do not interrupt!* I had hoped to come to terms with you, and in return I am blackmailed! You have tried to take over *my* operation! You have spied for my enemy, the dictator. I can see that dealing with you is hopeless. . . ."

"We don' have to take dis, y'know," said the man with the knife.

"But you do! Bob! Bill! Disarm him!"

Philip had never seen karate, or whatever it was, outside of the movies. No hoarse shouts. No gestures of menace. No palms upraised in anticipation of combat. The Geminis moved quickly. Bill placed himself before the knife-holder, just out of reach, while Bob went to the rear as one of the other three whirled. Bill's gesture was so rapid as to almost defy credulity. He feinted with his left hand, stepped backward, crouched, sprang, the fingers of his right hand extended. Three bunched middle fingers struck the knife-wielder's solar plexus like a club. The man gasped, sagged, struggled for air. Bill shouldered him roughly into the pool. The knife dropped from his hand.

Stockingcap pulled a gun. Bob leaped into the air, as if propelled by a spring, brought down the edges of two clasped hands on the man's nose. There was a sound like cardboard crumpling. Stocking cap turned, trying to aim, waveringly. Bob kneed him in the groin, pushed and tripped him. As Stockingcap went down, Bob gave him a kick on the base of the neck. The man's head struck the metal rail with a hollow pop. The gun sailed overboard.

"He dead!" yelled Eyepatch. "Whatcha wan to—"

"Want to lose the other eye?" Canny yelled.

Scarface lunged at Cappy, whose cane was ready, little hoof extended. He struck Scarface brutally in the knee, and as the man reached for it involuntarily, pushed him into the pool with his foot. Eyepatch gaped.

"The snakes. Now," Morales hissed.

The Geminis emptied the contents into the water—two long thick snakes that twisted frantically on the blue bottom. The men cried out and attempted to hoist themselves over the side, but Bob and Bill forced them back.

Something happened below the roiling surface of the pool. The blacks seemed to try to levitate themselves out of the water, kicking desperately. Moans emerged from the contorted mouths. After all too short a while they ceased to move; their features became rigid, then placid. They floated peacefully on their backs, rolled over, noses down. No more than a few minutes had elapsed.

Cappy said to Eyepatch in a low voice, "Go. Tell your friends. I want no interference today. Get out of here." He kicked the fallen man, who moaned. "Take him with you."

Eyepatch scrambled down the ladder to the small craft. The semiunconscious man was lowered on a rope to the dinghy, which raced off.

"Drain the pool. Retrieve the snakes," Cappy ordered.

Suddenly the count called up, "Philip!" Castle realized that in his shock he'd stepped from concealment. "Don't be upset, my boy. I'm sure you wish to know the facts. Cappy had these creatures trapped off the western coast of Central America. They were brought on board not as instruments of death but rather as means to intimidate the most recalcitrant. You saw that no one was harmed on the last occasion they were employed, yes? But these four, well, they threatened us physically. The men were murderers and they deserved to perish. Perhaps I should add that the two died quite painlessly. . . ." The count's look was expectant, as if he hoped Castle would agree with him.

Without answering, Philip went below.

What was happening? After witnessing Sansa's death he'd retched, yet two men had just been killed before his eyes and he hadn't raised a hiccup.

Maybe he had become hardened to atrocities, and lost the capacity for moral outrage which, for him, distinguished civilization from barbarism. Now he worried about a change in himself.

"You saw no one was harmed on the last occasion," Ari had shouted. He's *known* Philip was there before, yet said nothing. Was it an obscure test? Was Ari trying to make Philip an accomplice?

He could still see the Cardinals' expressions as the men floundered in the pool—pitiless, hard, the faces of fanatics, of petty tyrants amusing themselves. Joe Martinez had been right—beneath the fancy trappings of wealth the Cardinals, except, Philip hoped, for Libby Harris, were scum. Crazy, too, for all their high-sounding astrology. He knew that once and for all. Capable of anything. He hated them. If a way came to punish them . . .

Hearing a heavy splash, he went to the porthole in time to see a weighted body disappear into the water. The other corpse followed. Philip's cabin faced the sea; the burials wouldn't have been noticed on land. There would be, then, no justice unless he . . .

He considered pounding on M-C's door, but that would have been a panicky act: he had nothing to gain by waking her. It was still too early for the shore party to depart, and he didn't want to confront the Cardinals before he had to. He lacked any interest in breakfast. He put his clothes back in the suitcase. He'd leave the swimsuit M-C had given him behind; he'd take as few memories as possible.

In trousers, a white shirt with a button-down collar, and brogues that felt heavy on his feet, he lay down on the bed to wait. Switching on the radio, he found Grenada, but hearing "Aries, Taurus, Gemini, Cancer . . ." turned it off. Unbelievably to him, who woke several dream-tortured hours later—Philip Castle slept.

He went on deck to learn that the Cigarette launch had left for shore; so had the Boston whaler used by the crew and Fat for shopping. In the wheelhouse, he confronted the English-speaking French captain.

"I want to get off this ship right now."

"Sir?" asked the man with the "I Love" tattoo.

"You heard me."

"There's no transportation, as you can see," said the captain.

"When do the boats come back?"

"Well, the dink the chef's using ought to return soon, but in any case it is impossible for you to go on shore today. Mr. Koster's orders."

"Why?"

"For your personal safety. They are expecting trouble on land."

Philip became exceedingly angry. But the man merely followed orders. It was nothing personal or arbitrary as far as the captain was concerned. "Is there an American consulate on the island?"

"I wouldn't know, sir."

"Find out, will you? Please? You have a radio."

"I'm not permitted to use it, not today. Except in emergencies."

"But this is an . . ." What was the use? "Is Miss Rombachet on board?"

"No, sir. She went ashore too."

He was a prisoner.

The ship had inflatable rafts, but he would be prevented from commandeering one. He stood glumly by the railing. It was too far to swim. Maybe he could signal a passing ship—no, ostensibly polishing, but obviously keeping tabs on him, was a crewman in white. Anyway, nautical activity in the harbor was scant.

Philip paced the confines of his cabin restlessly. Then he put on his scanty bathing suit and went to the sundeck, to find Libby anointing herself with lotion.

"I thought you were ashore," he said, startled.

"I didn't feel up to it," Libby said cheerfully. She lay on a mat. "Marie-Celeste went in my place." Under a napkin on a small table near her were a coffeepot with two cups, rolls, and butter. "Have some," she offered.

Castle had vowed he would never eat again aboard the *Zodiac*, but the rolls smelled delicious. He buttered one and poured coffee, standing up. "Beautiful day, isn't it?" she said.

"It's always a beautiful day down here."

"You've gotten quite a tan. You're brown as a cocoa bean. *This* is as dark as I get."

He stared at the empty pool and stopped chewing. "Oh." He chewed again.

"Didn't you sleep well?" she asked.

"Yeah, fine. Libby . . ." He wanted to bring up the murders, but suppose Libby didn't know of them? "I'd like to get off the ship today."

"Too late, Philip. You'd have to turn back by the time you got there. There may be fighting on the streets soon."

"So this is a revolution!"

"Yes—a coup. We'll learn the outcome tonight."

Could Cappy Morales have predicted horoscopically a revolution to the very day—March 13? No! Unless the Cardinals' cash had helped to foment it. Philip gazed at the green island, so near, yet so distant. Never had he felt so isolated from the real world as at that moment, on a gleaming pleasure yacht gently rising and falling like a cork on Caribbean swells. "When will the others be back?"

"Not until after lunch. We have plenty of time." She stroked the mat next to hers.

We?

He sprawled out, one arm shielding his eyes from the sun. Libby shifted her body.

"Well?" she said.

"Well what?"

"You know damn well what."

Strands of hair tickled his shoulder, lotion reached his nostrils, breath played on his forehead. He waited, immobile. Soft skin rubbed against his upraised palm—breasts! Fingernails—long, red, sharp, he could imagine them—traced a delicate, slow, meandering course across his chest, skating down to his stomach, circling his belly button, moving maddeningly on his lower abdomen, reaching the boundary of his swimsuit, passing beneath. She gave a shuddery sigh. "Come on. God I'm hot.

He hesitated a moment, mind racing, astonished by her boldness, trying to absorb the information that *he* had been granted a goddess. Did she have no scruples at all? They hadn't even *kissed*. No matter how "liberated" some women were these days, you had preliminaries, courtship routines, byplay, foreplay, and always you kissed beforehand, except maybe with whores. And, if only ritualistically, the man started it even when the outcome wasn't in doubt. Marie-Celeste was far from shy, but he'd had to arouse her. . . . And him? He was very curious about Libby Harris but he would be loyal to his lioness, whom he loved.

"I'm sorry. I want to, but I can't."

"Bourgeois morality?" She glared at him.

"I guess so."

He rose and went below. In his cabin he lay on the bed, eyes closed. He heard the door open, like fate, and then Libby was beside him, nude. A bare breast hovered above him. She rubbed a pointed nipple on his lips. "Undress. Quick," she commanded.

There was nothing else to do. Philip pulled off his trunks.

Unlike Marie-Celeste, with her enthusiastic, frankly animalistic ardor, Libby was deft, expert, controlled, controll*ing*. It was she who started kissing him, soft and slow, establishing mood and tempo from the outset. She sucked his tongue, rubbed the inside of his lips with hers, pulled his ears, tugged his hair, pushed the sole of her foot up his inner thigh, while her sharp fingernails ran lightly down his neck and spine, and retraced the motion. She toyed with him, permitting penetration only little by little.

She rolled on her side, he with her, accepting him fully at last. Had they danced, Libby would have led, undulating easily, directing his hot body with her cool one, forcing him to follow her rhythm to please her. She cupped her breasts, pinched her sharp nipples as he held himself up on his arms, forced up there by her arched back.

He was *not* going to climax before she did—if she could. Her forehead furrowed as if her organism made an intense but unsuccessful effort. The luminous blue eyes were only half-shut. Libby had to remain a detached observer of the proceedings, he decided, opening his fitfully, which made him detached too. He wanted those eyes to close so that his could be as well. Without cerebration—his mind was melting down to a bright flame at the center—he desired to *make* her respond fully. He flung his body at her, faster and faster, harder and harder. Beads burst from her upper lip, she who never seemed to sweat. The eyes snapped shut, his too. She moaned. Her hands brought his torso to hers and her talons scratched his behind, hard enough to hurt. To punish him for pleasing her? he wondered dimly. She screamed and he cried out in pain and passion—he wasn't sure which, and didn't care.

They lay very quietly. "You're terrific."

"Thank you." She stared at the ceiling. "I enjoyed it, too. I don't usually come with men. I don't usually make love with *men*."

Philip took that in. "Not even Ari?" They were back to reality.

"None of your business. Anyway, I've known him a long time and we're kindred souls. He doesn't make demands on me like you would."

"Would?"

"If we made a habit of this. You're straight—I'm not. I can't help it. But thank you for a wonderful time. You really got to me."

"And you me," he said, echoing her mood.

At least he'd been with a goddess.

21

The shore party returned later than planned and went to their cabins to rest—even the indefatigable count appeared exhausted. Marie-Celeste, in a cotton shirt and jeans, gave Philip a hostile look. He wondered if his face reflected his experience, but maybe he just felt guilty.

He decided to swim in the sea because the pool was empty—remembering the snakes, he doubted if he would have used it anyway. He discovered flippers, face masks, and snorkels in a box on deck. With them, could he make land? But there was no point in drowning or being eaten by a shark. Besides, a crewman was watching him.

A metal ladder hung from the side. He lowered himself into the water and, treading water, put on the equipment. Not a confident swimmer, he stayed close to the ship. Circling the vessel slowly, he found what appeared to be a trapdoor on the stern. Standard equipment for a yacht?

When he hauled himself up the ladder, the crewman disappeared. He dried himself with a towel and went through the silent passageway to his cabin. A bundle lay on his bed. A note said, "Wear it. Main salon, 7:30. M-C."

It was his Sagittarian costume—cape, breechclout, leggings, a toy bow and arrow of plastic.

He wondered what she would say if she knew about Libby. What *he* would say to Ari, Canny and Cappy? Could he sit down to dinner with killers? All in all, he concluded, he could—the banquet might be a memorable occasion. As for the dead men, they were strangers, after all. Maybe, as Ari said, they'd gotten what they deserved. . . .

Stop it! Murder must not be condoned! And he had no further doubt about Sansa.

Ari wore a crown of nutmeg leaves from which two little horns stuck out (a certain irony there, Philip thought), and a long flowing robe of red for Mars, his ruler. Canny-the-crabman had on a flat cap whose visor partly concealed the beady eyes, and a shirt with a scooped-out front that showed his overdeveloped chest, hairless as a carapace. He held lobster crackers, which he clicked with vicious enjoyment. Libra's ruler was Venus, she explained, which seemed to account for the white toga that exposed one breast. She carried a small scale from the galley. Cappy-the-goat sported high leather boots, tight black pants, and a black shirt, like a nimble Spanish dancer. He carried a whip because Capricorns were supposed to be disciplinarians. Libby explained all this for Philip's benefit.

M-C, the lioness, wore a gold robe (for the sun, Leo's ruler), and on her head a mop dyed yellow for a mane.

Ari looked at his watch and turned on the radio. "The announcement ought to come any minute now," he said.

It did. An urgent voice said briskly, "This is Radio Free Grenada. The criminal dictator of Grenada, Eric Gairy, was overthrown by the New Jewel party today. A curfew is in effect. Obey the orders of members of the People's Revolutionary Forces. They can be identified by the red-and-white emblem of the People's Revolutionary Forces, headed by Maurice Bishop. The PRF has suffered no casualties. Two of the former government's secret police—the notorious Mongoose Gang—are missing and may be dead.

"Tourists! You are in no danger, but remain in your hotels for your personal safety.

"We repeat: the criminal dictator, Eric Gairy, has been overthrown . . ."

"My God," said Philip. "It really happened!"

Ari switched off the radio. "Bill! Champagne!"

Corks popped. Raymond turned to Morales and raised his glass. "A toast, Capablanca! Without arms provided by you, the revolution could never have succeeded! The Gairy clique will blame the Cubans. So much the better. To the lunar eclipse today, which helped us."

They drank. Philip too, captured by the festive spirit. Then Cappy said somberly, "Danger arrives tonight, according to the signs."

"The warship!" the count muttered. "Canny, find out what's on the radar screen."

Canny spoke into the telephone, then lifted his head. "Captain says a boat's parked about twenty miles out. A big one. He don't know what it is."

"I do, and it waits," said Morales. "For us."

"Well," asked de Vaucresson, "what now?"

"Get the hell out of here. It'll never catch us in the dark," Canny said quickly.

"Correct," Libby joined in. "Why should we risk our necks? You can speed back to St. Jean. By the time Hernandez learns where you are, you'll have finished there."

"You?"

"Well, I can fly home from here. I have business in New York." Libby glanced away. "You can do without me."

"Very reasonable, and very self-serving," said Ari with contempt. "What do you say, Cappy? Braver words, I hope."

Morales' eyes seemed to become opaque, as if he contemplated a private vision. "Hernandez has exactly one warship—to sink it would be a terrible psychological blow. Let us do so. We are not helpless."

Ari said, after a silence, "Hernandez is desperate. He knows that we are his mortal enemies. He is angry, threatened. His spies are ubiquitous. He'll quickly find us on St. Jean, grab us, with his warship. No, I too say fight. We cannot avoid the inevitable."

"Because you want to fight, to prove yourself," said Libby.

"You will make me lose my temper. What color is tomorrow?"

She replied thoughtfully, "A white day."

"You see!" The count turned to Philip. "A black day is when rashness, lack of skill, miscalculations, mechanical defects, and so forth threaten the success of an enterprise. One should attempt heroic actions only on white days. And, Libby, we need your predictive abilities as much as ever."

"Oh, all right," she said, tugging at a tuft of blond hair.

"Canny?"

"I won't buy it, and it's *my* boat."

"Canny, Canny." Ari put his arm around Koster's shoulders. "Be a good boy. We are a majority, you know. Three to one."

"Let me check the numbers," Canny said reluctantly. He marched in his sideways fashion to the library, followed by the rest, Philip in the rear. Canny looked at a book and pressed buttons on the computer console. "We got a chance, and that's all."

"And that's enough, dear chap!" shouted the count. "Agreed?"

"Agreed," Koster said sourly.

"Good! The banquet can commence!"

This floating pleasure palace against a destroyer escort? They're mad! Philip Castle was resolved to leave the yacht that night if he had to swim, darkness, current, sharks, a revolution, and all.

The service was solid gold, the array of different-sized glasses heavy crystal. At each place setting lay a stiff card with "ZODIAC" embossed in green letters, the menu in neat script (Marie-Celeste's, as it turned out), and a date at the bottom—March 13, 1979.

> *BANQUET ASTROLOGIQUE*
> *L'amuse-guele Cancer*
> *Les hors d'oeuvres Aries et Gemini*
> *La Soupe Taurus*
> *Le poisson Pisces*
> *Le viande Leo*
> *L'entr'acte Scorpio*
> *Le gibier Sagittarius*
> *La salade Aquarius*

Les fromages Capricorn
Le dessert Virgo
Le divertissement Libra

"What does *amuse-guele* mean?" Philip asked Marie-Celeste, who sat next to him.

"Something to whet the appetite," she said without looking up.

In a starched white jacket with braid, Bob carried in a silver tray, raised on one hand. He lowered it to the side table, where Fat stood chuckling. On it were six small round tarts, pale green, with tiny shrimp on top.

"Florida land crab," the count said. "Philip, can you explain the symbolism? This one's easy—it's for openers."

"Cancer-crab. *Land* crab because people walk on land?"

"Why are the tarts green?"

"Because there's tarragon in them?" Philip ventured.

"Yes, but green is Cancer's color, my boy! Cancer is ruled by the moon—don't the tarts look like little moons? Shrimp come under the moon, too." He tasted the cold concoction Bill had served him. "Fat, superb!" Philip agreed.

The white wine poured for the tarts stayed on the table for the first hors d'oeuvres—an ivory mound dotted with capers the size of marbles, lying on a bed of ferns. "Philip?" the count challenged.

"In the first place, what is it?"

"Sheep brains, of course."

"Well, sheep for ram, brains for Aries."

"The most intelligent sign! You are learning. You couldn't know this, but ferns fall under Aries—Fat spotted these fiddle-heads at the market. They are edible ferns. The capers were my idea. Capers fall under Mars, which rules Aries—a nice touch, don't you think, considering my occupation?" The gray eyes glittered with deviltry. "About which you are mostly ignorant."

"Your humor is delicious, Ari," Libby purred. "And so is the dish." Philip forced himself to taste the brains. Good they were.

A frothy new Beaujolais was served with the next course—silver bowls each containing an egg with two yolks. "Eggs Meurette Gemini.

'Muerette' refers to the red-wine sauce," the count informed. "Philip?"

"The double yolks must stand for Gemini, the twins. I've never seen eggs like that."

"Were we lucky to have brought them, or did I predict to myself an astrological occasion? Some hens lay only double-yolked eggs. I regard them as a culinary conceit—wit and antics are ruled by Gemini's patron, Mercury. Small birds like chickens fall under Gemini, an air sign."

"Is everything ruled by something?"

"Everything rules everything else, as the natal horoscope displays influences from all the planets, signs, and houses, and as all things are one, but things do not have equally powerful relationships. Some influences are stronger than others, hence they are termed rulerships. Please forgive me if I sound pedantic sometimes." He laughed. "We are having fun, aren't we?"

Soup Taurus was consommé served from a china tureen shaped like a bull. Fat had scrounged it from a tourist shop on Grenada, Philip was told. Delicate pasta cut into shapes resembling bulls' heads floated in the rich, dark broth. It came with a glass of sherry, which Philip sipped.

"You have a marvelous appetite," the count told him.

"I skipped lunch."

"Have you had an enjoyable day?" Ari wondered.

"It didn't start off so hot. I had a bad dream about snakes that killed people in a swimming pool." He looked sharply at Marie-Celeste, whose face was impassive, as was Libby's.

"How upsetting," the count said blandly. "Do you analyze your own dreams?"

"Sometimes, but not this one. It was so real it didn't seem like a dream at all."

"Do you have bad dreams often?"

"No. Except on this ship I have. A little after dawn, usually."

"Indigestion, I expect. Perhaps the fare aboard is richer than you're accustomed to. But this is no evening to hold back."

"Yeah. This might be the last supper," Canny said gloomily.

"Canny! We have a triumph to celebrate! We, ah, pulled it off! But here is the fish."

Bob carried one handle of the heavy silver tray, Bill the other. On it was a plump barracuda with spikelike teeth. Philip asked himself what they did with the leftovers. Fed them to the reptiles in the hold? "I wasn't aware barracuda's edible," he said.

"Extremely, when properly prepared. Fat! Pisces is two fish, not one," the count scolded.

"Impatience!" Fat cried. He deftly lifted a flap cut into the side of the barracuda, revealing a smaller fish inside. "Baby mako shark!"

"Brilliant, Fat. A mako shark, and facing in the other direction, as the Pisces hieroglyph does. Makos are among the tastiest of fish. What is the sauce?"

"Choron," Fat replied.

"A type of béarnaise with a touch of tomato," the count said with confidence. "Ah, the *big* burgundy—Corton Charlemagne seventy-three. Excellent. There is very little around." He added, "People who insist on white wine with fish are gastronomic imbeciles."

Wineglasses were being replaced with bewildering speed by the well-trained Geminis. Philip was becoming light-headed, though maybe an abundance of food caused it. Would the repast ever stop? He longed for a rest, but it was not to be. When the fish plates and another in the long rows of gleaming utensils had been replaced—even Canny did not have sufficient goldware for a feast like this!—Fat arrived, bent from the weight of a wood carving board that held a standing roast in the shape of a crown, over which was a tangle of shining cellophane, with walnuts and parsley. The tips of the bones were adorned with sections of oranges. "Doesn't *that* look good," bubbled the count, whose appetite seemed insatiable. "Can anyone tell me what the meat represents? Another of my ideas."

"Is it lamb?" asked Libby.

"Yes. Next?"

"The crown stands for the king of beasts," Cappy said thoughtfully, "but the lamb is not a wild animal. Leo is."

"Ah, but in the higher realms of duality the lamb and lion lie down together, do they not? And the spun-fried cellophane noodles? Take a guess, Marie-Celeste, since you are a Leo."

"The lion's mane! And citrus is Leonine, as are parsley and walnuts."

"You win the prize. Shall we dig in, as the Americans say?"

The lamb, as the Americans said, melted in Philip's mouth, but he was ready to die when he'd eaten it. Inquiring of the laconic Leo to his right about the "entr'acte," he was told it was meant to cleanse the palate for the next "tribute."

Fat brought a bottle coated with ice, which he chipped away with theatrical gestures. The bottle was phallically shaped. Inside the clear liquid was a large insect, tail curled.

Libby bit a finger. "A scorpion!"

"Local produce," joked the count. "The vodka is special Russian." One of the Geminis ground pepper into each glass.

"Scorpio's the sex symbol, obviously," Libby said, "and pepper's an aphrodisiac. But the bottle is a little *too* much, if you ask me." She pretended to shudder. "Why is it sheathed in ice? For decor only?"

"The quintessential duality of the hieroglyph," Ari replied. "Sex can be cold as well as hot, of course." He blinked at her knowingly.

They took an intermission then. Libby went to the bathroom—she did so quite frequently. Was the bladder ruled by Libra? Philip was tempted to do the same, to regurgitate, Roman-style, to make room, but he cornered Marie-Celeste instead. "Were the Cardinals really responsible for the Grenada coup?"

"They think so. Listen, I don't really want to talk to you, after today especially."

"But you *are* talking to me. What's today got to do with it?"

"I bet you were busy."

"Me?" he said with apparent surprise. "I did nothing but laze around. I could get used to it."

"Used to *her*, you mean. I told you I was intuitive." M-C walked off, impervious to his protestations.

The Geminis displayed the gibier—a saddle of venison with perigourdine sauce. Piped potatoes in the shape of a bow around it. A bundle of asparagus tied with a strip of red pimento. "Tell us what this signifies," the count urged.

"Sagittarius," Philip said promptly. "I see the bow and arrows. Sagittarius must have felled the deer."

"On target!"

Salad Aquarius proved to be watercress with tomatoes and white grapes. "Aquarius the water pourer—watercress," said Canny, snapping his fingers. "The vineyards belong to Aquarius—grapes. And the tomatoes had to be grown in water . . ."

"Hydroponically," muttered the count, seeming disappointed.

Capricorn was easy—goat cheese, four varieties from mild to strong, fresh, slightly aged with soft ends, rolled in ashes, wrapped in grape leaves. Served with crisp French bread Fat had baked that morning. The table was cleared and dessert arrived, much to Philip's relief.

"What is it, Fat?" the count asked the chef, who was pouring liqueurs into a chafing dish.

"Truffle ice cream."

Philip tasted the white wine—Château d'Yquem, 1921—and understood ambrosia. Steaming goblets formed of ice were brought to each place. The vanilla ice cream was crowded with what Philip took to be the truffles. Said the count, "Let me see if I can unravel this concoction. Virgo-the-virgin, is pure—what can be purer than the finest vanilla ice cream? The wafers suggest chastity, perhaps the hymen itself. White truffles from the Italian Piedmont . . . truffles are of the earth, and Virgo is an earth sign. The ice goblets will melt—Virgos like to finish things. And the virgin is cold. She has not yet been ignited."

"Light the virgin, set her on fire!" cackled the chef as he applied a match to the chafing dish. Blue flame rose and he poured the molten mixture into the goblets.

"Fat, you are wonderful," Ari said. The count gave a thousand-dollar bill to the rotund little chef. "That was a feast beyond belief," said the count contentedly. "Will we taste its like again? Yes, after the ultimate victory. Let us have our *divertissement* Libra."

One white-jacketed Gemini brought a small balance scale from the galley. The other arrived with a cutting board, on it arranged a sharp knife, six silver reeds, an antique box of printed porcelain, and a mirror. The paraphernalia was laid before the count, who opened the box and withdrew plastic bags. When the toughs had left, de Vaucresson placed the bags on the scale with a weight on the other tray. "Exactly two ounces. The scale is balanced, like Libra herself."

"Yes," Libby said with soft enthusiasm.

"Detachment, visions, supreme clarity, the highest qualities of Libra, and the results of the finest cocaine."

"It better be good at eight grand for two lousy ounces," Canny said. "Don't nobody sneeze."

"Ah, but I paid for it. It's *my* coke. Nonetheless, my contentious

Cancer chum, you shall have some—if you are good." Ari laughed. He carefully poured the bright powder on the mirror, slicing it again and again with surgical precision. "Libra mirrors herself," said the count chattily. Complete silence ruled the dining room as he divided the cocaine into six exactly even rows. "Didn't I hear you've never tried coke, Philip?" *Did M-C tell him everything?* "It's a simple procedure. You cover one nostril and inhale with the other." He put a silver reed to his nose and sniffed up part of a powdery file. He did the same with the other nostril. "Ah. Libby?"

Philip was at war with himself once more as the cocaine neared. He'd assiduously avoided hard drugs all these years, and was just as leery of them now. And he'd need a clear head for his escape that night. Yes it would be fun to try just a little cocaine; after all, this bizarre interlude would soon be ended, and who knew if or when coke would be offered again? He thought he could handle it. He sniffed through the silver reed, watched the white row dwindle, felt the dry, chalky substance in his nose. "Hey, take it easy there, pal. That's strong stuff," Canny warned.

"I spoke of the ultimate victory," the count went on a little dreamily. "Philip, the three wise men from the Bible, do you know why they traveled west? Jupiter and Saturn in Pisces—oh, yes, they were astrologers, certainly—heralded for them the birth of Christ, meaning the dawn of a new era. We Cardinals . . . we can perhaps play a parallel role for the modern world, usher in the astrological age . . . of course, our tools must be honed . . . astrology must become a science of itself . . . neglected for hundreds of years . . . computers will assist us . . . astrology can function for psychology . . . predict the future with a certain precision . . . guide humanity toward a better life . . . but we need help to carry out our mission."

"Why are you looking at me?"

"You may be the one. You might be able to render a significant service, which is why you were invited along, of course."

"I told you I didn't want to be your pilot." He heard a buzz in his ears.

"My pilot," the count said disdainfully. "No, no, the task is more important than that. But I *wish* I were more certain of your character. There is something hidden about you."

"I thought you said I was pretty much out in the open."

"Almost, but not quite." With his head the count declined the cocaine Libby offered. Philip sniffed just a *little* more. "Sagittarians are truth-seekers, but, as I've told you, the obverse quality of a sign may prevail. Sagittarians can hide their bad qualities."

"Meaning?"

"Well, among other things, you might have the configuration of a *thief.*"

"A thief," Philip said indistinctly, conscious of five pairs of eyes.

"Did I say that? I merely remarked on a possible tendency. But I suspect that only a quirk of fate stopped you from being a criminal, albeit a petty one. You might be capable of stealing from *us.*"

Philip gripped the edge of the table. "Just because you're a crook doesn't mean everyone else is!"

"You are more volatile than you admit, Philip. Because of your Mercury. You anger easily. You might have a violent streak," the count said in an even voice.

"Come *on!* Everyone does. It's what we learn to control—unlike you with your killer snakes!"

"I'm going above," said Marie-Celeste, walking off unsteadily. *Hear no evil. But Libby knows—she didn't bat an eyelash.*

He heard de Vaucresson say through an icy veil that must have been the cocaine, "Come on, Professor Castle, climb down from your tower. *Be who you are.*"

"I am what I am," he said sullenly.

"I don't think so. You are afraid to accept the implications of astrology. Perhaps, like many people, you are religious underneath, and you don't wish to change allegiances."

"There's nothing to astrology! It's a static system, a throwback to the days when there wasn't any conception of progress and change. People were *fixed* like the universe itself. Astrology is nothing but fatalism, which is wrong! People can change, do change, every day of their lives. And they can change for the better, if they try. What does personal change mean to you?"

"Nothing," said the count, seeming bored. "Less than nothing. The point isn't to change, but to be as you were *created.* Don't you understand? It is the part of you that you have suppressed which interests us. We need very special qualifications, of which you have many. Like being a warrior, even a man who can kill. *Didn't* you kill someone, or try? I don't mean in aerial combat either. Answer!"

Castle said nothing.

"Listen, if I can be sure you are willing to play the game, I am prepared to offer you a fortune."

"I won't join you! Never!" Philip tried to keep hysteria out of his voice.

"A chickenshit," said Ari relentlessly. "I have no use for cowards. Especially a man who's as good a pilot as you and is afraid to fly."

Philip gave the count a fierce look—he could feel it on his face—and rushed up, through the main salon, where Marie-Celeste danced by herself to disco, and out on deck. He stared at the star-swept water and beyond the lights of St. George's. *You won't make it, not in this shape, stuffed with food, drunk on wine, high as a kite. You didn't think one snort of coke would hit so fast and hard. Maybe you don't even want to leave. The son of a bitch called you chickenshit. You could have slugged him for that.*

He remembered that he'd been a kid with a terrible temper, the kind that overrules fear and pain. He remembered how badly he'd beaten Eulalio, then remembered the captain. . . .

Even after the crash landing at K-2, they'd wanted him to fly again, because of the heavy casualties among the pilots. But he wasn't superman. He was bushed, almost wished he'd been wounded. When the captain said lightly, "Don't be chickenshit," the word festered. Him, a war hero! He got smashed in the officers' mess the night before he was supposed to fly. The captain saw him. The captain had to have been crazy, too, because he said "chickenshit" again, this time without a smile. It was Eulalio all over again, but worse. The captain was unconscious when they pulled Philip off.

They sent Philip to a hospital in Japan. He was interviewed by a psychiatrist who told him that nobody would press charges. He'd be honorably discharged but they wanted him to go to a military hospital in the United States. "Call it battle fatigue," the psychiatrist said. There was another psychiatrist in the states, a civilian. Philip had begun to fear he was mentally ill, like his sister. The civilian shrink said no, but he advised Philip to go into psychotherapy because of unresolved problems. Philip did so, became interested in psychology, majored in it, went on to a Ph.D. But he'd never ceased to worry about his demons, always kept himself under strict control, until now. . . .

He smiled grimly into the darkness. He was free! Or almost. His controls had been too tight. *Relax, follow your instincts, and it'll be okay. . . .*

Okay . . . okay . . . okay . . . The word reverberated in his mind, louder and louder. . . .

De Vaucresson materialized on deck. "Philip? Are you all right?"

"Yes. Okay . . . tomorrow . . . I'll help if I can. That's all I'll guarantee."

"Why, that's splendid!" The count's eyes wrinkled in the gloom.

Marie-Celeste entered his stateroom, like a reward. She undressed quickly, got into bed before he could take off his clothes, wanted him to hurry. Again she was passionate, Libby seemingly forgotten, and he was passionate too, despite Libby.

She slept but he couldn't, mind tossing with worries about tomorrow's battle. He switched on the bedlamp to look at her. The sheet was pulled down. Faint marks appeared on Marie's rump, as covered his own.

The bitches! . . . Philip's anger became pain, then perplexity. For to tell Marie-Celeste that he knew the origin of the scratches would be to identify himself as a fellow culprit. It was a labyrinth, like everything aboard the yacht.

He cradled her in his arms and made himself forget about Libby. She didn't matter now.

22

Philip woke at first light, and leaving M-C behind, went to the main salon, where the three male Cardinals drank coffee from a cart—Canny in nautical white, Cappy in funeral black, the count in cordovan shoes with rubber soles, lightweight tan trousers, sharply creased, and karate shirt tied with a sash. "Just because we can't spot the warship on radar doesn't mean she can't see us. Her mast is higher, after all."

Ari nodded at Philip, who asked, "Where are we headed?"

"Trinidad, if the frigate doesn't show up."

The telephone burred. Canny raised it, listened, put it down. "Target to the northwest at twenty-five miles on an intersect course. Might not be the frigate."

"I fear it is," said the count. "How long will it take for her to reach us?"

"Less than an hour if we stick to this course. This might be the last chance to run."

"My dear Canny, we settled that," said de Vaucresson with a sigh. "No, we shall fight and we shall win."

It was still very early. The women were on deck now, Marie-Celeste in tightly cut overalls without a shirt beneath, Libby in a blue jumpsuit open at the neck. The group milled around, watching the haze on the slack sea.

For Philip there was a surreal quality, as if they were alone in the world. When the sun appeared low on the horizon, the haze began to vanish, but it was still dark to the west, where the enemy steamed toward them. "They will have a visual sighting of us before we see them, which should be any minute now," said the count. He waited. "There she is!"

He passed the binoculars to Philip, who saw a wreath of smoke and under it a mast with a crow's nest that grew taller. Canny rattled off what the *Zodiac*'s captain, using *Jane*'s, had told him: The American Dealey-class destroyer escort was built in the early fifties. It was better called a frigate because it was not an escort, but a real warship, with four three-inch guns, triple torpedo launchers, twin forty-mm antiaircraft guns which could also shoot horizontally, rocket launchers, and depth charges. She displaced 1,900 tons compared to the yacht's 120, and carried a crew of one hundred or more. She might or might not have been refitted with a modern radar tracking system that locked the guns into a computer for greater accuracy. Philip prayed it hadn't been.

"What's her speed at present?" Ari asked.

"Thirty-five knots, faster than she's supposed to make from the specs."

De Vaucresson shrugged. "Why should the military tell the truth?"

Crewmen removed the tarp over the Cigarette and brought equipment wrapped in canvas. "The men seem to know what they're doing," Philip said.

"They are specially trained and highly paid. They're good, the captain especially. He had to resign his commission in the French navy because of a scandal—a murder, I think, though he was acquitted—but the captain's superb when it comes to modern naval warfare."

"You were expecting this occasion well in advance?"

"We knew it was possible, yes, from our charts. And it pays to be ready for all contingencies. You might wonder why we didn't simply abandon the ship instead of equipping her with, ah, modest defenses, at enormous cost, which we bore together. The answer is that we needed the yacht, for pleasure as well as business. One must never neglect the pleasure principle, life being as short as it is."

The *Zodiac* stayed on course, sailing at moderate speed. The two ships were alone on an empty ocean. "We shall ignore her as long as possible," the count said. "That way, the frigate's skipper will think we are—how do you Americans say?—sitting ducks. He will hold his fire, believing that he can overpower us easily, or that we will surrender, until the vessels are close together, which is exactly what we want. He has no idea we have the capacity to fight."

"With what? Sea snakes?" Philip asked.

"Your sarcasm is out of order. The Pacific sea snake does not belong in the Atlantic Ocean. Did you know that the ecological consequences of a Pacific-sea-snake invasion has been one strong reason for the opposition to building a new sea-level canal to replace the Panamanian one? No, no, we are conscientious environmentalists. The snakes will be returned to their native habitat. We would never harm them. . . ."

Canny interrupted from behind field glasses. "I should have mentioned the fucking frigate can carry a chopper, and here it comes."

A horn sounded.

"We should go inside," Ari said. "There's nothing we can do here for the moment, so why risk our necks?"

Steel plates covered the swimming pool and the portholes of the main salon. Canny shut a metal door behind them—it had been hidden behind paneling. "The walls are lined with steel, too," he said. "We ought to be safe here unless there's a direct hit, or unless the scow sinks, which it probably will."

The count seemed not to hear. "Anyone for a drink? Well, a little gin and burnt bitters would taste quite good." Behind the brown leather bar, he heated a spoonful of bitters with a match, ignited it, and poured the flaming liquid into two fingers of gin. "Cheers."

"Cheers my ass," said Canny. He twisted dials on the TV, switching from one outside camera to another.

"I'm terrified," Libby said. "If you're wrong about the outcome, I shall never forgive you."

"Oh, perhaps you will in another life." Ari laughed. "Really, Libby, don't be alarmed. This is a white day—you said so yourself."

The helicopter came into focus on the sixty-four-inch color TV screen, flying low over the water, nose pointed down, Plexiglas canopy shining in the sun. "A Hughes Cayuse," Philip said softly. *What in hell am I doing here?* "Flies at one fifty knots, if I remember right. Carries five-inch rockets and miniguns. It moves like a dragonfly, hovering back and forth."

"You know your stuff!" Ari said with admiration. "I'm not surprised!"

"I . . . subscribe to a few aeronautical magazines. That's a deadly bird."

"We'll see," said the count placidly.

Philip decided he was still high from the cocaine. This *couldn't* happen—the chopper's image belching smoke from her guns, the *flap-flap* of her rotor blades sounding through the baffles that encased them as she moved into position to fire the rocket that would make the *Zodiac* part of the sea bottom. The long curved outrigger poles over the fighting chairs on the afterdeck (shown by another camera) turned in tandem, seeming to follow the copter as it darted toward the ship. The cabin lights dimmed, the tips of the poles became incandescent, emitting two narrow, bright beams. The TV set went crazy.

When the screen cleared, the burning helicopter plunged toward the ocean. The cabin lights shone as before.

De Vaucresson patted his high shiny forehead with a linen handkerchief. "Thank God for an Israeli military secret. With the lasers, we knew we'd be safe from such an attack, though I must confess, even with the extra generator we had enough power for only one burst. Well, I had no doubt we would bring it down, not one. Shall we go on deck again? We'll be safe enough for a while, and I should like to see the sinking of the warship in three dimensions."

He really believes we'll get out of this alive, Philip thought.

"I'll remain here," Libby wailed. "Marie-Celeste, stay with me. Please." The lioness nodded reluctantly.

Several miles to the west, closing fast, the knifelike frigate loomed ever larger and more menacing through the binoculars Philip held—tall mast bristling with electronic equipment, bulky bridge, sharp bows sending up plumes of spray. When the frigate was about five thousand yards off, her three-inch guns began to fire. Three inches, he reflected, did not seem especially impressive, until he saw the spouts the shells sent up. Fortunately, the gunners were inaccurate: the shells landed far away. The *Zodiac* picked up speed and changed course. A second salvo, and a third, came no closer.

Activity on the yacht had centered on the Cigarette, long, sleek, equipped with two powerful twin-screw engines, capable of sixty knots or better, somebody said. The Zodiac, meantime, was headed in a wide northerly arc that carried her toward the warship's starboard beam, maintaining the same distance. Again the three-inch cannon fired; this time, spray reached the ship. The great white yacht began to zigzag across the sea. What must her skipper think when he saw that the yacht refused to run?

A funnel cracked open, revealing a uniformed crewman in a bucket behind a cannon. He wore a headphone. As the yacht veered toward the frigate, the Zodiac's cannon began to fire. Philip put his hands over his ears. Smoke rose from the frigate's superstructure. "A hit! A hit!" Canny yelled, pounding Cappy on the back. The Central American smiled uncomfortably.

The Zodiac's course brought her well to the stern of the frigate. The crewmen had just started to lower the Cigarette launch from the davits when Philip, borrowing Ari's field glasses again—despite himself, he was actually starting to enjoy the contest; it reminded him somehow of an Errol Flynn flick—saw that tubes were being swung out from the warship's side. An object leaped into the water, then a second, and a third.

"Torpedoes!" said the count, snatching the glasses. "Fools! Even I, far from skilled in such matters, know that torpedoes run too deep to bother us."

They waited silently by the rail, seeing nothing. Then a torpedo appeared, lunging toward them. Philip could see the wake with his naked eyes.

"Merde, a surface runner," de Vaucresson shouted.

Philip gasped. There would be no survivors if the projectile touched the ship, as it surely must. It was headed directly toward them in a shroud of spray, only the dark nose exposed. The situation had become desperately real, not at all like an episode in a harmless movie.

A shrill whine sounded below, and the ship lurched forward so rapidly that Philip had to grab a rail to keep from falling. He thought the Zodiac had been at full power previously—it hadn't. The bow rose; the ship seemed to spring from the sea. But the torpedo was still on an intersect course. It had begun to porpoise now, jumping in and out of the water, coming rapidly nearer. The yacht turned hard right; Cappy went down on his arthritic knee and bleated. The wind whistled in Philip's ears. And then, just when a collision seemed inevitable, the torpedo sped past the stern.

All of them were breathing heavily. Philip ran a hand down his cheek—it seemed incredible to have a hand and a cheek. He found himself thinking that he hadn't shaved that morning. "Whew!" Ari said. "The gas turbine booster was meant to be saved as a little surprise for the enemy, but oh well. We have a few others, but we must get nearer to effectuate the battle plan. That will be the dangerous part."

"The torpedo wasn't?" Philip said.

The *Zodiac* had rounded the frigate's stern and was on a parallel course, with her gunner firing continuously, scoring minor hits. To Philip it seemed miraculous that the yacht had thus far escaped damage, but the frigate's crew wasn't trained to fight an opponent that moved with such speed. He wondered how long the yacht's fuel could last. Abruptly the sleek vessel slowed until it almost drifted, and the frigate's gunfire straddled them. The Cigarette dropped in the water and sped off, twin screws churning. One man was at the wheel, the other in the bow holding a long tubelike weapon. Both wore goggles.

"A three-inch recoilless rifle," said the count with pride. "That ought to do some damage, especially at close range. I envision a large hole in the warship's side, perhaps a direct hit in their ammunition bay . . ."

Madness. Pure madness. Ari's overconfidence is absolutely manic! What wouldn't you give to be in Chicago right now?

Machine-gun bullets swarmed through the air. The Cigarette swerved, seemed to skate on the water, regained its heading. The machine guns followed as the speedboat roared toward the warship over the calm sea. Abruptly it slowed and began to circle aimlessly, offering a perfect target. The man at the wheel slumped over it, Philip saw through the glasses he and Ari passed back and forth. He had been hit. His companion left the recoilless rifle, scrambled back to the cockpit, and wrestled for the wheel. More cannon fire. A violent explosion, and smoke.

"But this is a white day!" said the count, looking gaunt.

"Color it gray," said Canny, snapping his fingers.

"Let's go forward," Ari said.

They arrived in time to see crewmen lift panels on the deck and an object wrapped in canvas emerge on a platform. It was a small rocket launcher. Five-inch rockets several feet long lay in tiers, with a crewman in a headset operating the equipment. Ari muttered, almost as though to himself, "This better be good." One by one the rockets blasted off as the count watched through the glasses. "*Merde, merde, merde, merde, merde,*" he swore. "They all missed. Damned computer."

Computerized guidance or not—not, Philip concluded—the frigate's missiles did no better, but after all, the two vessels were engaged in a fairly long-range duel. Sooner or later, though, the warship's heavier armament would destroy them. Then Cappy spoke to the count, with the deference he reserved for the aristocrat. "It is time to engage."

"I had thought we would have disabled the enemy by now," said the count. "But you are quite right, Capablanca. It is our only means of obtaining victory. Don't you concur, Canny?"

Canny raised his arms as though to defend himself. "Do we have to?"

"We shan't be sunk."

"Promise?"

"I promise, my boy."

"And now," Cappy said, "let's go inside."

Gently but firmly Morales took Ari's elbow and led him to the main salon. Both women had drinks. Canny picked up the phone to the bridge. "Okay," he said with a grimace when he hung up, "I gave the order. Here we go."

The yacht picked up speed. Water pounded against the forward hull as the *Zodiac* completed a circle around the destroyer escort, bringing her once more on the warship's starboard side, only nearer than before.

The yacht shuddered. Canny raised the phone. "Damage report," he shouted over the uproar outside. A frown took possession of his sallow face as he listened. He came back and said uncertainly, "We took a hit in the hull just over the water line. Nothing serious, but we can't go at top speed. Maybe we should—"

"No!" Ari barked. "This is a white day, I tell you. Send the sub quickly."

"*Sub?*" asked Philip.

"Don't you speak English?" the count said impatiently. "Sub—for submarine."

"Yeah," said Canny. "We got a baby sub in the hold. I just hope one of these tricks works."

"One *will*," said the count. "Do not forget this is a . . ."

The yacht's stern appeared on the TV screen as Canny pressed buttons. Under the *Zodiac's* midsection a trapdoor opened from what must have been a watertight compartment. Out of it, as though the yacht gave birth, popped a long clear plastic cylinder, with a man stretched out inside. A periscope protruded above the surface. "The sub is nothing more than a delivery system. It has a compact electric engine. Reaching the warship, it will attach a magnetic charge on the warship's hull and return. Boom! So much for the enemy," said the count.

Again, it was not to be. The *Zodiac* began to maneuver, to avoid the warship's fire. A few minutes after the sub had been launched, the TV screen showed canisters flying from the frigate's stern. The yacht shook. The sub suddenly surfaced, then sank quietly. "Depth charges. They spotted it," said the count. "We have now lost three men. A real pity."

The phone burred. "Four," Canny reported. "Our topside gunner's been killed."

"Oh, dear." For the first time Ari seemed to have lost confidence. He rubbed his slightly wrinkled hands together mournfully. "The warship is playing cat and mouse." He stared at the screen. "She's coming after us." Indeed, the gray hulk sped toward them, guns silent. The *Zodiac* lay dead in the water, as though disabled. Perhaps she was, for all Philip knew. "If she rams, it's finished. We shall have to employ the bird. I, for one, intend to watch the action on deck. If the bird fails, it will make no difference where we are."

They trouped after the spare figure.

The panels over the empty swimming pool had been removed. At the bottom, steel doors rolled back and hydraulic jacks raised a small drone helicopter to the level of the deck. "My God," said Philip, "where did *that* come from?" No one answered; their eyes darted back and forth between the rapidly approaching frigate and the unmanned aircraft. The captain must have been punching buttons in the wheelhouse. The drone's miniature jet engine screamed into life. Almost immediately the rotor began to turn, and the machine lifted gracefully from the deck, with a phallic object hanging between the landing gear.

"The copter carries one wire-guided missile, which will be enough, assuming it gets a direct hit, which it shall." De Vaucresson's optimism had returned.

"Sure," said Philip.

Just over the sea, the drone helicopter raced toward the frigate, puffs of smoke surrounding it as the warship's ack-ack opened up. The chopper reared vertically, plummeted . . . yes, it was over . . . no . . . the tiny machine flew. Down to the water the craft plunged, then up, barely clearing the frigate's deck, then down again. The missile had been launched! From the warship came a red flash, a second, a third, seeming to rip out her guts. The frigate was burning—she had been mortally hit!

"We did it! We did it!" the count said. He hugged his partners in turn, and they each other, even the reserved Cappy. M-C winked happily at Philip. Ari turned to him, and shouted, as if to all the skeptics upon the earth, "What do you think of astrology now? The frigate sinks!"

"Congratulations," Philip said, more excited than he was willing to show.

"A sizable bonus for the captain and crew is definitely in order," the count was saying as the helicopter landed on the plates over the swimming pool.

Philip picked up the field glasses. "It isn't over. Look."

Two gray launches crowded with sailors came into view from the far side of the frigate. "If they mean to board—I suspect they do—they shall be repulsed." As if on command, crewmen lugged heavy machine guns on tripods on deck. "Canny, fire a burst in the air to warn them away,"said the count.

Shipboard protocol seemed to require that while the count gave most of the actual orders, Canny yelled them to the captain. He relayed this one. A machine gun rattled, but the launches kept coming. Ari shook his fist. "Idiots! I do not wish to harm defenseless people, but if killing a few men is necessary, we shall."

A white flag waved on one of the launches. "What do you see?" Ari asked Philip, who had the glasses.

"There about fifteen men on each launch, some obviously hurt."

A voice shouted in Spanish over a bullhorn. Cappy said quietly, "They want to be taken to Trinidad, where they assume we're headed. They claim many are badly wounded."

"I don't like it," Libby said.

"Me neither," Canny said. "Fuck 'em, I say."

"However," Cappy said quietly, "if we refuse to assist, some at least will get back to El Parador and will spread the word that we turned our backs. I want friends there, not enemies."

"Yes, I think the humanitarian as well as strategic choice is to assist," de Vaucresson argued. "What's the weather prediction?" Canny checked with the captain, who said high winds were expected. "That settles it, as far as I'm concerned. We must help."

"Suppose they have weapons?" Libby asked.

"Cappy, tell them anyone possessing a weapon shall be shot instantly. Tell them to throw their weapons overboard."

Morales asked for a bullhorn and spoke Spanish into it. A few pistols dropped in the ocean.

"I still don't trust them," Libby warned.

"Let's compromise," said the count. "Suppose we take the wounded on board and tow the others in the launches. Off Trinidad, we put the wounded back on the launches and leave. We shall tell them to say they had an explosion at sea—who would believe otherwise? All in all, that is the wisest course. Agreed?"

Libby nodded glumly. Canny said, "I'm gonna have the small arms brought on deck, in case."

Cappy bellowed instructions over the bullhorn; the gangway was lowered, with the machine guns on tripods stationed over it. The first launch approached. As it reached the yacht, a man lying in the crowded thwarts suddenly reared up and threw something. "Grenade!" Canny screamed.

Philip fell to the deck with the others. Shrapnel pounded the ship's superstructure above him. The crewmen at the machine guns were down, weapons upended. Fierce-faced sailors raced up the gangway, holding pistols and knives. A few had superficial wounds. The second boat was coming up quickly.

The cache of small arms was neatly stacked between where the six had dropped and the gangway. Philip dashed. He reached for the Ingram M 11 and, standing straight up, fired a short burst, as Ari had taught him. He must have missed, because nothing happened. He fired again, saw a man on his knees before him, holding his stomach, yelling at him. Obscenities, he thought, from the face. He saw a big man bounding up

the deck, waving his arms like a crazy savage, take a shot that doubled
him over so that he staggered and fell forward over the rail and out of
sight, and behind him a flock of sailors from the enemy ship, screaming,
started to fire at *him*. No clarity, just a blur, and lots of desperate voices.
A burst of fire sounded at his ear. He turned: he must have moved
toward the gang, because the cache of small arms was behind him now,
and M-C held a pistol. Said something to him. Smelled like gunpowder,
as though she used it for perfume. Fired again at the attackers. One had
righted a heavy machine gun, twisting it toward them, kicking the
prostrate *Zodiac* crewman out of the way. Philip squeezed the trigger
gently, amazed at his own composure. The enemy sailor threw his arms
up, went forward as in a dive, landed on top of the crewman, who had to
be dead—Philip saw the blood. More shots came from behind him—
Cappy and Canny held rifles and used them, though not Libby or the
count. Libby retreated hastily. Ari held the Beretta but didn't seem to
want to fire it. Philip saw the look on the lean handsome face and
instantly figured it out—the count was scared, petrified. At least when it
came to close combat, he, not Philip, was the coward!

Amazing how quickly the battle focused in a single strategic objective—control of the gangway. The gangway was vital to the hopes of both
sides; nobody had to say so—they all knew it as a matter of military
instinct. If the attackers won clear possession of the gangway, the little
war was all but over. The combined forces of those remaining in the first
launch and those in the second, zooming up, water bubbling behind it,
would be too great for the defenders to handle. But if the defenders could
deny the enemy further access to the yacht, then they could pick off the
sailors already on the yacht, and those in the launches would become
easy targets.

Philip just didn't know how many enemy sailors had already come on
board. It had happened too fast, and it was all too confusing. Besides, his
vision was too constricted, huddled as he was against the superstructure,
above his own cabin, unable to see what was happening elsewhere.
Shouts and shots sounded above—the yacht's captain and crew must
have been fighting enemy sailors up top. He saw Canny scuttle toward
the bow, rifle in hand—Canny would be protecting their rear in case
attackers were circling the vessel. He saw Cappy raise to his full height
and fire down at the second launch. One . . . two . . . Cappy counted.

Then cursed. The launch must have vanished below the protective lip of
the deck where Cappy couldn't shoot at it without foolishly exposing
himself at the rail.

When Canny screamed, Philip whirled. Canny had taken a bullet in
his big forearm. He clutched it, dropping his rifle, out of action. He
squatted against the superstructure, blood appearing on the sleeve of his
white uniform, face ashen. The man in black stalked forward to replace
him—their flank had to be protected or they would be killed. Philip's
self-appointed and, he knew, vital task was to keep a bead on the
gangway, firing a quick burst whenever a head appeared. Marie-Celeste
was beside him, but her weapon wouldn't be of much use at this range.
The count had the only remaining rifle, but Philip had lost all
confidence that he would actually use it.

Philip had begun to hope that the defenders might prevail for one
reason alone: the attackers only had pistols. Those in the launches must
have been writhing in frustration, hoping the sailors who'd boarded
would be able to clear the way. Philip heard M-C cry, "Look out!" She
raised her pistol and fired. A shape fell from the deck above, struck, and
rolled toward the railing, where it stopped, still holding a gun. An enemy
who'd been about to shoot down on them. M-C had got him; she looked
numb. Then a grenade, lobbed from below, rolled on the deck, well out
of reach. Philip, Ari, and M-C tried to bury themselves in steel. The
weapon exploded, harmlessly, at least for them, but not for the huddled
forms near the gangway, which took the shrapnel.

Philip spat out curses. In the intervening seconds two enemy sailors
had bounded over the platform of the gangway and raced down the deck
toward the stern. He got one in the leg, but missed the other. The first
one limped onto the afterdeck. Marie-Celeste's gun roared ineffectually.
The count had the barrel of his to his cheek, but nothing happened. He
hadn't even released the safety catch!

Philip had brought two spare clips—all there were—with him from
the cache. He'd already used up one. Swiftly he inserted the fresh
ammunition and faced the gangway again. Firing still sounded above;
Canny remained on the deck, whimpering softly. Then the count said it.

How obvious yet how elusive! Why hadn't the captain thought of it?
Because he, in his wheelhouse, must have been under attack. Why
hadn't Philip thought of it? Because the entire battle had consumed a

matter of a few minutes and his brain had been fully occupied. And after all, the first grenade had taken them completely by surprise. Still, that the count had not come to it immediately, or any of the rest of them, said much about the errors to which the human mind, under stress, was liable.

For the count muttered, "Raise the gangway."

"Where are the controls?" Philip shouted.

"There's one at the head of the gangway, but you'll be ambushed." Philip noted the "you'll." "There's another in the main salon, beside the rear door."

There was a porthole behind him, but it was locked. So was the door to the interior—Libby must have done that, damn her. She was probably barricaded in her cabin.

Clutching the Ingram, Philip moved down deck, with the count promising to cover him and Marie-Celeste, who came part of the distance to be nearer the gangway. He crawled through the maze of mangled bodies, through a pool of blood, which he could feel warmly through his T-shirt.

He decided to enter through the rear, because if an enemy lurked, Philip would be in a better position to shoot him. He looked inside and saw no one. Sliding back the glass doors, he entered. He found the controls, clearly marked, where Ari had said they would be, but wasn't quite sure how to operate them. Then he heard a slight scuffle of feet. Turning abruptly, Philip saw the man he had shot in the leg. He had saffron skin, a black mustache, and a large hairy mole on his cheek. He had been hiding behind the chrome base of the grand piano. He held a knife.

Philip raised the M 11 in haste and mashed the trigger. The gun jammed. He retreated, grasping the submachine gun like a club. The limping man came after him, knife weaving, light glittering on the blade. The man advanced, face sullen.

Philip found himself pressed against the paneling, where wielding the submachine gun was harder. Near him was the board on which hung Canny's pride and joy, the collection of pirate weapons. He was counting on surprise. *Is this you? YES! But you don't have to kill him. Wave the saber, that ought to be enough. NO!* As he waited, the sailor lunged. Philip dropped the gun, grabbed the handle, and brought down the blade, chopping deeply into the sailor's cheek where the mole was. The man crumpled.

Cappy said you'd kill somebody, and you've killed more than one. Jesus! The guilt! The guilt! Where is it?

He was vaguely aware the firing on the upper decks had ceased.

He wondered afterward what they would have done with wounded enemy sailors, but all those aboard the yacht were dead. The ones in the launches, though, remained very much alive; shouting in Spanish, which Cappy interpreted, they begged for mercy. The wind was coming up.

The Cardinals' justice was merciless and swift. The *Zodiac* moved off, turned, spurted toward the two launches, which had stayed together; her prow sliced through them. All 160 feet of her passed over the men in the water, and yet—how, Philip didn't know—some still lived, clinging to bits of wreckage, waving their arms, thrashing.

Marie-Celeste, leaning weakly over the rail, saw the sea snakes first, announcing them with a weak cry. The snake tank must have been situated where a shell had blown a hole in the bow. The confused reptiles slithered out, one after another, five or six in all, dropping into the ocean, swimming just under the surface toward the men.

"Oh, dear," said Count de Vaucresson. "I fear we may have brought an ecological problem to the Caribbean."

The frigate sank as the *Zodiac* turned north.

The yacht moved slowly ahead because of the hole in her side. The rumble of pumps sounded continually.

The few remaining crewmen gathered on deck, and in the absence of Canny, who was with the captain below, Ari congratulated them for bravery. "You will be amply rewarded," he told them.

"What about me?" Fat asked.

"You, Fat?" the count said in a jocund voice. "May I inquire as to your contribution to the battle?"

"I killed an enemy with a creaver!"

The dead, friend and foe, were given to the sea. "We have to think of something good to tell the families of my crew," said Canny, who had appeared. His wound was superficial, though he carried his bandaged arm in a sling. "We don't want an investigation."

"Oh, don't worry. We'll come up with something. Perhaps we hit a submerged wreck or an unmarked reef that showed up too late on the fathometer. The unfortunate crewmen met their ends in various ways. There were no bodies. One was attacked by a shark while inspecting the hull for damage after the accident. Another fell overboard during a freak storm. Still a third . . ." De Vaucresson trailed off. "People are easy to fool."

"Including me," Philip said. "Nobody's yet told me the truth about why I'm here."

"Yes, some explanations are definitely in order. Can we wait until this evening? It has been a strenuous morning and I have a headache. All that noise."

That night, over coffee and liqueurs in the main salon, the count, natty in a blue blazer with solid gold buttons and an ascot, leaned toward Philip and said, "I want to commend you on your courage. Without you, we might have failed, white day or no. Of course, that statement is tautologous, since we were aware from the charts that your presence would be vital to our victory. It still is."

"Go on."

"Well, I shall begin at the beginning, insofar as there can *be* beginnings. Life is a process, not a concatenation of unrelated events. You materialized on St. Jean almost the moment my pilot was killed in a wreck, and revealed you were a pilot, too. I was interested, as Marie-Celeste knew I would be—what the world considers coincidences are, for me, often signals that *spiritus mundi* shows its fine hand again. The girl encouraged you to meet her on the beach, to learn more about you, and a most astonishing fact emerged—that you and the dead flier had the same birthday!

"I simply *had* to know the exact time of your birth, to cast your horoscope properly. Having done so, I was impressed—perhaps over-whelmed is a better word. You had perfect qualities as far as I was concerned. You would be a strong, dependable ally. You had sufficient bravery to undertake a dangerous mission. Imagine how I felt when I learned you were not only a pilot but a war hero! A superb fighter pilot! I also arranged some little tests to see how you would act under pressure.

They weren't very good, but I had to improvise. The men on the cannon, the one with the razor blade, the Carib Indians on Montserrat—I sent them all."

"What about the stick dancers?"

"My idea," M-C said cheerfully.

The count went on, "But I did not judge you in a vacuum: I saw you in relation to me. I have a soft spot astrologically. My natal sun is in twenty-nine degrees Aries—the last degree. I am not a perfect Aries because I require support. You come along. Your sun is also twenty-nine degrees—of Sagittarius. It is precisely trined to *my* sun—a fire trine. More than ever I was sure I could count on you. That you and I would get along was also indicated by your Venus opposition to my Mars, in the house of friendship. And your moon is trine to my tenth house Pluto, also meaning that you and I can be close—how do you say it?—buddies. You will tend to support my position." The flesh around the count's eyes wrinkled. "I should also observe that in a past life—I know this from the position of your south node in Leo; it might have represented treachery, but thank God it did not—you served royalty well.

"But! There is always a 'but.' I told you last night that you had a hidden side. *'Only last night?'* I told you that the nature of your twelfth house perplexed me. I told you that you had a streak of criminality you did not reveal, not even to yourself. To me, this was a two-edged sword. Would you work with me in the end? I might say that had you been an Aries, and gotten this close to me (which you would not, unless by trickery), I should have eliminated you because you would have been a serious threat, as my late wife prophesied.

"But even as a Sagittarian, you might have turned against me because of the twelfth-house problem. What I need most of all is loyalty, which you proved today beyond doubt.

"Philip Castle, I will make you a proposition. We Cardinals have a plan in which you can play a vital role. But I shall not tell you what it is unless you elect to join us. If you do not, when we reach St. Jean you shall receive the sum of twenty-five thousand dollars cash as a reward for your heroism. No strings, although there shall be no further contact between you and any of us, including Marie-Celeste." Philip looked at M-C, who nodded. "But if you decide to throw in your lot with us, the reward shall be far greater. However, you must agree to do *exactly what I tell* you. You may not back out, once you say yes.

"Perhaps your acceptance of this condition is the final sign of your faith and trust in me.

"Please! Do not answer now. Sleep on it. Good night!"

PART IV

23

Sleep on it! What a joke! You ought to be exhausted from yesterday's activities, but it's three in the morning and you haven't so much as dozed. You always sleep when you and M-C have had sex, but not tonight. You can't wake her and try it again. It wouldn't be fair.

Ari's proposition keeps you up, of course. "You must agree to do exactly as I tell you." Who in his right mind would accept such terms? He could order you to rob a bank or murder someone, but he wouldn't. You wouldn't be his choice for such assignments. No, he wants you to fly. Where? What for?

Common sense tells you to take the twenty-five thousand and run. Ari says he's willing to give it without strings. It's blood money, but so what? You earned it—you were instrumental in the victory. The victory! Jesus. Over a hundred men died, and for what?

He'll give you a lot more if you join them, but money doesn't mean that much to you, even though it might be nice to have a little Caribbean home, maybe a small boat . . . No! Resist such dreams.

So why do you lie here, eyes open? Because you're furious at M-C? You have every reason. She was the count's instrument. He used her to attract

257

you, get information, bring you to dinner, lure you aboard the yacht. She
probably made love to you because the count told her to, the whore. Well,
even if that was the reason at the start (was it?), people can't feign
passion for long. The woman likes you, loves you. As you love her.

You don't want to lose her, but that's not the reason you can't sleep,
either.

You and the count—that's closer. You're oddly attracted to the man—
he has spirit. Maybe you and he are more similar than you think. More
than anything you'd like to go against him and win! Wouldn't you? YES!
It's been like that ever since Marie-Celeste told you about him. Why? Do
you want to obey him, then surpass him? Oh, God.

You can't sleep because you're terribly mixed-up. Against all reason
you want to accept his offer. But if you do, you'll have to fly, and you're
afraid. Afraid to fly. You hate that in yourself—it's humiliating. You
don't want to be weak, but you'll be obliged to fly again if you say yes.

"Yes," Philip said in the morning when he found Ari alone in the
ship's library.

"Yes?" said the count, arching his eyebrows.

"I'll do it. Whatever it is."

"Good! I want you to fly a mission for me."

The count's apparent interest in Philip's book, his mention of a role
for him with the Cardinals (not that he'd have taken it), the talk of
Philip's usefulness in interpreting the new nations' psychology—all that
had been sheer nonsense. The count had wanted him to fly a mission—
that and only that.

"I guessed."

"You'll be glad to know I've already ordered the airplane by radio from
Piper in the United States, a brand-new one. I have a line of credit with
them. It's being flown here via Miami, arriving this afternoon."

"This afternoon?"

"Yes. There is no time to waste."

"What kind of plane is it?"

"An Aerostar Six Hundred. A marvelous piece of machinery. It is the
nearest thing in a private plane to a fighter."

"Fighter?"

"In the sense of maneuverability and taking punishment. The man who designed it also designed military aircraft."

"Ted Smith. He just died. He designed the A-20 Havoc, which was probably the best low-altitude attack bomber in World War II. And the Aero Commander—your planes."

De Vaucresson did not pursue that subject. "Yes, but the Aero Commander isn't sufficiently versatile for the mission. The Aerostar is. They tell me the airframe can take an eight-hundred-mph dive. It is the fastest of the light twins, I believe. And . . ."

"And?"

The count appeared to examine his white patent-leather shoes with gold buckles. "Well, the very name of the plane might be a good omen. Smith, you see, thought of the name while star-gazing. It seems so appropriate, in view of my chief interest." Ari trailed off, then went on firmly. "Seven days from today you fly. It *must* be on the first day of Aries. In the meantime, you will have to get in shape for a long, arduous trip, as well as learn to operate the equipment. The pilot who brings in the Aerostar will stay and train you. He's on loan from Piper. I will tell him you are my pilot. He will not know that you don't have a current license. That is no business of his and he will not ask. But don't reveal that you haven't flown a plane in a long time."

"Will there be a copilot?"

"I'm afraid not."

"For God's sake tell me what the mission is!"

"In due course," replied the count.

Philip rose to leave—in a few minutes the Boston whaler would take them ashore—then turned. "What if I'd refused? What would you have done about a pilot then?"

"Oh, I'd have found one. But, to be truthful, I never considered another pilot from the moment I studied you. I *knew* you'd take the job."

Seven days. The casual Caribbean had corrupted his sense of time. Not until Philip had driven the Moke to the house on the hill did he deduce that the appointed flying time was not just the first day of Aries but his birthday!

He would have five full days, starting tomorrow, to master the specifications, operating and emergency procedures, instrumentation, and performance data of the Aerostar. And to climb into the aircraft and fly it. That would be the hardest part—going up in the air alone.

As Raymond had said, he'd need to be in good shape for an extended flight, especially as there might be hazards. Beforehand, he'd need plenty of exercise and sleep. He and M-C had already agreed to stay apart that night. She was tired and planned to get to bed right after dinner.

He worked up a sweat with calisthenics on the terrace. He'd improved his physical tone the first week on the island, but inactivity aboard the yacht had slackened him again, and Fat's high-calorie cooking had put a little flab on his stomach. In his bathing suit he drove to the beach and ran two miles on the packed sand by the water.

He nibbled a little lunch from a doggie bag he'd taken from the ship, then napped. He hadn't been asleep more than fifteen minutes when a sound woke him—a low-pitched whistle he hadn't heard before. He went quickly to the terrace and saw an aluminum gleam in the sky. The Aerostar! He recognized it by the needlelike nose. The plane was factory-rough aluminum. De Vaucresson must have wanted it in a hurry. The pilot circled the strip twice before making a perfect landing through the V in the hills.

The count must have seen it too—he was at the airfield when Castle drove up. "Philip!" he said enthusiastically. "Meet your mentor, Gus Tretino."

They were standing by the aircraft that looked as though it was ready to leap into the sky. Tretino, in black trousers, a white shirt with breast pockets and epaulets, and dark glasses not unlike the ones Philip wore, was long and skinny, like the machine he'd brought.

"Good trip?" Philip asked.

"Yeah, but I'm bushed."

"How'd you come down?"

"Miami . . . Andros . . . San Juan . . . coast of the Dominican Republic. Spent the night in Puerto Rico. Got a girl there."

"Gus would like to log some beach time while the sun lasts and start showing you the ropes tomorrow," Ari said.

"Okay with me. I'd prefer to start out fresh," Philip said. He examined the Aerostar. It seemed bigger and sleeker close up. The nose cone with the windshield high up reminded him of a snout. He noticed the plane's identification—N 5 DV. "N"—U.S.; "5"—DV's lucky number.

Tretino was watching him. "It'll take you wherever Mr. Vaucresson wants to go, which must be a long way," he said. He handed Philip a brown leatherette ring binder book, an inch thick. "This is the Aerostar manual, if you want to start studying."

"Thanks. I will."

"Gus is staying at the beach hotel, which will be convenient, since he can walk to the strip in a few minutes. I think he'll find plenty of—how do you Americans say it?—action. Come on, Gus. I'll drop you off." They got into the striped-top VW Marie-Celeste had driven.

Gus and Philip agreed to meet at nine in the morning.

Philip spent the rest of the afternoon with the Aerostar flight manual, memorizing the instructions, evaluating the craft. He was about to drive to Le Boucan when a taxi came up the hill. The driver called, "M'sieu Castle?"

He went outside and looked into the backseat. "Jesus!"

"Hello, Phil. I wasn't sure it was the right house."

"Ellie, Ellie . . ." he said.

"It's me," she said, face both elated and nervous. "I missed the last plane from St. Martin, so I hired a speedboat. I decided just to show up when you didn't answer the messages I sent from Chicago. Why not?"

"I didn't get them. I was away. Ellie, oh Lord."

"Phil, would you pay the driver? I don't have any funny money."

"Sure." He went and returned with French francs. The driver had opened the trunk, and passed Philip two new and expensive pieces of luggage. They were heavy.

She followed him inside, saying, "Where were you?"

"Cruising the islands."

"On a yacht?"

"Yes." He set down the bags in the living room.

"Aren't you going to kiss me hello?"

Philip put his hands on the familiar trim waist and kissed her mouth. Ellie's lips were soft. *Ari predicted she'd arrive.* "I can't tell you how surprised I am."

"Me too. I can't believe I did it. Whose yacht?"

"I have some new friends."

"I'm dying to meet them." She glanced around. "I had the impression the Waller house was bigger."

"Depends on what you're used to. It's fine for me.

Ellie took a step away from him. "It should have occurred to me that you might have somebody staying here."

Not true. She'd thought it over carefully. "I don't. Why isn't Richard with you?"

"I left him. Christ it's hot. I'd like a drink."

"Gin and tonic?" She nodded and walked out on the terrace to wait.

Philip's heart pumped and his mind raced. The purpose of his trip to St. Jean was to rid his system of Ellie, and thanks to M-C (and the Cardinals, he supposed), he largely had. He thought of her only infrequently, and without self-pity and sadness. The change had happened so quickly that he hadn't had time to assimilate the transformation, but the torment had left him. And here Ellie was, ready to reenter his life, he knew. He understood her so well. She would anticipate that he might have found a girl, that his hurt pride would have to be assuaged, that she would have to humble herself a bit—nothing she couldn't handle. His devotion to her was clear—look what he'd put up with—nor would she expect him to be different. For her, Philip would be the same creature of habit and routine as before. She wouldn't believe that he could refuse her. Indeed, could he?

She was seated rather primly at the terrace table, arms folded, one foot lightly tapping the deck. He brought a gin and tonic for both of them, seating himself across from her. He was still in shock; he hadn't seen Ellie for almost three months, and hardly dared look at her. She wore pumps, stockings, a long skirt, wrinkled from the voyage, a flowered blouse that showed her bra and sweat at the armpits—she had removed her jacket. She had put powder on her nose, which always shone when she was overheated. He didn't know if the dark circles of rouge on her cheeks were the result of style or carelessness, but he didn't like them. Ellie had gained a little weight and a line or two on her face. She remained physically attractive, though not in a class with M-C or Libby—not many women were.

"So what happened?" he said.

"What happened?" She'd been smiling at him with a kind of fixed gaiety, but her mouth dropped. "Richard . . . turned out to be a jerk. Sometimes you have to live with a person to understand something like that. I guess I got spoiled being with you." She tried to resurrect the grin but failed.

"That's all there is to it?" he said, sounding more suspicious than he meant.

"Well, no. Richard wanted to have a baby. I don't want another baby. I'm too old to have a baby—it isn't safe. But Richard wanted to anyway."

His eyes went to the diamond on her finger. "What about the ring?"

"My engagement ring. He gave it to me so I kept it. Why not?"

"We're divorced, then?"

"You've only been gone a couple of weeks! No, we're not divorced. We're still married, thank God." She started to cry.

He didn't do anything, just sat there, face opaque, he sensed. After a while she took a handkerchief from her pocketbook and dabbed her cheeks. "Is my mascara running?"

"A little. Nothing serious. Where are you living?"

"I moved back into the house last week."

"The breakup is new, then?"

"Yes, but final. Don't *stare* at me like that. I'm going to work at the end of the month, though I'm not looking forward to it."

Philip permitted himself to be snide. "Things didn't quite work out like Zoltmann said they would, did they?"

"Stop! Don't rub it in." Consternation crept into her face. "Tell me about you." She appeared to examine him from the bottom up, inspecting his bare brown legs—the hair on them was becoming blond from the sun; he hadn't noticed before—his shorts with a loose hem, his T-shirt with a torn sleeve. "You look darling with that long hair and tan. Your female students would climb all over you if they could see you like this. All you need is a guitar and a chain with a medallion around your neck."

"You can dress as you want down here."

"Have you been lonely?"

"No."

She peered at him. "You can be honest, Phil."

"I am. I told you I made new friends."

"Is there a woman?" Ellie's green eyes widened when he nodded. "Is she young?"

"Yes, but that doesn't make any difference."

"Is it serious?"

"I'm not sure. It depends," he said laconically.

"On me, I suppose." He said nothing. "I'm not the person I was, Phil. This experience grew me up finally. You know, I'm thinking of therapy."

"Might be a good idea, Ellie."

"How calm you are!"

"Because I'm loafing. It's nice not to work so hard. I like it."

"You wouldn't for long, Phil. You're programmed to work."

"I wonder. Anyway, it hasn't been so calm. And I'm certainly not calm right now."

"You seem distant, too. Harder. You've changed. I don't blame you."

"Don't blame yourself, Ellie. Besides, I think I've changed for the good."

"I'm sure! Speaking of that, I've great news. David's coming home."

"David?" He shook his head as if to clear it. He went on quickly, "Doesn't he like the commune?"

"No. He hates it. He wants everything like it was before. The three of us. Phil?"

"Another drink, Ellie? I am."

It was turning dark. She didn't ask if he wished her to move to a hotel—the house had only one bedroom—nor did he suggest it. She unpacked only enough to change clothes for dinner, yet left her toothbrush in the bathroom. He was unable to send clear signals because he was far from clear within himself.

He was still angry for the pain she'd inflicted, yet not vengeful and disposed to get back at her. Somehow he was stronger than he'd been— Ellie was his litmus paper. She was forced, he could tell, to reappraise the man who sat opposite her in the restaurant. *This* Philip was far less harried, distracted, worried and anxious, more purposeful (he didn't know why or about what), more confident, better able to thrust and parry, to resist her blandishments. He was bolder—he had learned from experts, dislike the Cardinals though he did.

"Next week is your birthday, or have you forgotten, now that you're a middle-aged hippie?"

"I haven't forgotten."

"It would be nice to celebrate your birthday at home. Do you think we might do that?" She was being vaguely deferential.

"I don't think so, no." But he had only answered part of her question.

"You'll be forty-six. Four years after that you'll be fifty. Do you really want to be alone?"

"Why should I be alone?"

"You don't *have* to be. I certainly don't mean that. But this young thing of yours—how long will she last? She'll drift out of your life as fast as she drifted in."

"Maybe. So?"

"You take her to Chicago, you won't want her anymore. You know how it is—you buy a souvenir and when you get it home you don't like it. A native drink tastes great in the tropics but lousy when you try it up north."

"Maybe I won't go north."

Ellie gaped. "You'd stay in the islands? Don't be silly. How would you earn a living?"

"I'd find buried treasure or something. I'm tired of the grind. I really am."

"But, Phil, how can you talk that way? It's taken years to get where you are. You can charge patients what you want! You have a fine reputation! You'd throw all that away?"

"I might."

"When your book comes out you'll be famous." She was pushing him hard. "You can write another one."

"I guess I have nothing left to say. The world isn't as pat as I thought. As for fame . . . Listen, Ellie, I'll never be famous. Maybe I don't want to be."

"What *do* you want?"

"I don't know. That's the beauty of it. I can find out."

Of course, he thought, Ellie's greatest appeal was the stable, conventional life they had lived, whose limits, dimensions, and rules were familiar and comfortable. This new existence had no fixed positions. It was like a compass without points. But Ellie reminded him of winter, and he was becoming addicted to the sun.

He might have slept on the couch, but that seemed silly. Perhaps he still possessed a tattered hope that she would ignite fires, rescue him. In bed, though, he knew with finality that they had reached the end. Ellie was warm and affectionate—he had no complaints—but he longed for M-C. Within him Ellie had died, and during the night her ghost passed out.

He told her so in the morning. He'd take her to a plane later in the day if she wanted to return to America—she did. She said she appreciated his straightforwardness.

He gave her the Chicago house as an outright gift—she appreciated that, too—and the Bequia whaler model for David. Then he went off to the Aerostar.

Gus Tretino said, "Where'd you learn to fly?"

"I flew small planes in Arizona. After that I flew for Uncle Sam— fighters." He was careful not to specify how far back *that* was—there was no point to alerting Gus, and the pilot didn't ask. "I need some air time with the Aerostar is all."

"You'll get it. We'll work a day and a half or so on the ground, to familiarize you with the plane, and then we'll go up. Two, two and a half days in the air ought to do it."

"Okay. I want to be complete."

"De Vaucresson's been a good customer," Tretino remarked as they walked toward the Aerostar. "This is the third plane he's bought from us. One crashed, I heard. Pilot error."

"Who said that?"

"De Vaucresson."

"Oh."

"Wonder what he needs so many planes for."

"Business, I guess."

Philip didn't need a crystal ball to know what was in Tretino's mind: Colombia. Drugs. Yes, it would appear that way. Maybe it was. He gave what Tretino would take to be the right answer. "He hasn't told me yet where he wants to go. I'm new here."

But what the plane was used for wasn't Tretino's concern. Gus said, "You'll be his regular pilot?"

"Looks like it. But he's never seen me fly. I expect he wants an opinion from you."

"Huh? Vaucresson told me you had plenty of hours."

"Sure. And I used to do stunts."

"Well, not in this ship. It isn't certified for acrobatics."

"I can't even roll it?" Philip said with a laugh.

"You could get away with a *few* tricks if you're good enough."

"Quit grinning. I am—or will be." He carried the flight manual aboard the plane.

They worked on the ground. In the cockpit, Gus pointed at an array of switches and gauges. "The gear and flaps are hydraulic and mechanically actuated—not electrical. If you lose hydraulic pressure, the gear is spring-loaded to the down position . . ."

"It's fucking hot in here," Gus said, swatting at a fly.

"Let's keep on."

"Okay. Engine failure after liftoff. Props?"

"Forward."

"Throttles?"

"Forward."

"Gear?"

"Up."

"Flaps?"

"Up."

"Engine?"

"Feather."

"Mixture?"

"Idle cutoff." He hadn't heard these terms in *years*.

"Boost pump?"

"Off."

"Fuel selector?"

"Off."

"Mags?"

"Off."

"Alternator?"

"Off."

"What then?"

"Get down as fast as you can."

"Okay. How about an engine fire?"

"Mixture—idle cutoff," said Philip, glancing at the manual.

"Fuel selector?"

"Off."

"Hydraulic shutoff?"

"Closed."

"Prop?"

"Feather."

"Mags?"

"Off."

"Alternator?"

"Off."

"Brake-system failure?"

Philip winced. "Use nose-wheel steering and opposite rudder to maintain directional control for one-wheel braking."

"Low-fuel warning?"

"I'll get a light." Philip yawned. It *was* hot sitting on the ground.

"It's practically five. Okay we quit? I got a date with a fish."

"Go ahead, Gus. I'll stay awhile."

He remained in the cockpit until after dark, familiarizing himself with the plane's time and distance computer, the VOR receivers, and the ADF radio. Tomorrow he'd check them out with Gus.

Sometime during the day he had put Ellie on a Winair flight and said good-bye. "What will you do?"

She seemed to vacillate. "I don't know. Maybe I'll patch it up with Richard."

"Why don't you try? He loves you?"

"Worships."

"Maybe you can talk him out of the baby. Does he know you're here?"

"No. He's off on a business trip to China."

"I thought he planned to retire!" She lowered her head. "Win a few, lose a few. I wouldn't tell him about your expedition."

"I won't." The hard lines on Ellie's face softened. "Phil . . ."

"Ellie, what you said in Chicago was right—I'm not what you want anymore. Listen, I'm going to make a long flight. I'm sure it'll work out, but there is an element of risk. No questions, please! If you haven't heard from me by . . . let's see . . . March 24, contact the State Department, okay? Maybe they can trace me. If not, I haven't changed my will. You and David inherit what little there is."

"Are you being melodramatic?" she demanded.

"Probably." He took her arm. "You'll miss your plane."

He showed up at Le Boucan that evening after more work with the flying manual and a long run on the beach. The place wasn't busy. Martinez said from behind the bar, "Home is the sailor, home from the sea. Thought you might come in last night."

"I had a visitor, who left."

"Where's the big yacht? I hear it was damaged."

So even Martinez didn't know about the sea battle. The *Zodiac* had gone immediately to St. Martin to be repaired after discharging its passengers. Everyone who had been on board had been pledged to secrecy, which Philip wouldn't violate. An official investigation might easily prevent him from flying for de Vaucresson, which he was determined to do.

"We hit a submerged wreck, they said."

"Anybody hurt?"

"No." The deaths hadn't been publicly admitted yet.

"Funny. An El Parador warship blows up about the same time. No survivors. Was the yacht anywhere near?"

"Not that I know of. I hadn't heard about the warship." Lies came easier and easier. "Well, it was quite a jaunt."

"I bet it was. The usual?" Joe picked up a square brown Cointreau bottle. Philip nodded: he'd graduated to regular customer. "Enjoy yourself?"

"In a manner of speaking. It wasn't exactly uneventful. The . . ."

Philip started to say "Cardinals" but stopped himself; Martinez wouldn't have understood. ". . . group was very busy on the islands, spreading the gospel."

"Gospel?"

"They're fanatics, Joe. Their religion is astrology."

"I heard that recently. Strange."

"They want to proselytize."

"They *what?* That's the most ridiculous thing I ever heard of."

"Those birds are pretty effective when you see them in action. They claim they want to help the area."

"Do you believe that?"

"Not any longer. And they may have another objective, too. Something to do with El Parador. I'll try to let you know when they tell me. I'm sticking around a little while to do a job for them."

"That's why you're messing around with the new airplane?" Joe asked suspiciously.

"I'm going to fly it."

"That's why you're taking lessons from Tretino? He was in here."

"Yes. Don't ask me what the job is. I don't know that either."

Incredulity appeared in Joe's deep-set eyes. "You're making a flight without being told of the purpose?"

"Or the destination," Castle confessed.

"That's dumb, Phil, don't you think?"

"I couldn't agree more, but there it is. Oh, Joe?"

"Yes?"

"I have a queer suspicion they'll want me to fly money around. Seems logical. I have a sort of, well, not plan . . . idea. I might need help."

"You know where to come," said Joe Martinez. He picked up a glass and seemed to study it in the light.

The VW with the striped top stood in his driveway, and he dashed inside, delighted. He found the lioness in the bedroom unpacking a suitcase. Seeing him, she frowned.

"What's the matter?" he asked.

"As if *you* didn't know. You've had a woman here."

In case Marie-Celeste showed up, he'd scoured the place for clues of

Ellie and was sure he'd left none, but maybe he'd missed something. "What makes you say a screwy thing like that?" he protested.

"I can smell her." M-C pouted.

"Come on! You can't!"

"I meant smell *psychically*, and you just confirmed it. There *was* someone. Who?"

If she'd pointed a gun, he wouldn't have confessed. Ellie was *his* business, though he couldn't help wondering how M-C had guessed the previous presence of another female. He said stolidly, "Lay off, will you? Why the clothes?"

The golden-brown eyes seemed to take his measure. "Stonewalling it, huh? Well, she's gone and I'm not. I'm moving in for a few days if you don't mind."

"Mind? I'm ecstatic. What about Ari? Is he?"

"Ari and I decided together that I should come."

"To make sure I don't duck out?"

"Of course not." Her blinks gave her away. "To make sure you go to bed early."

"I'm for that if you're in it. I just wish you weren't whoring for the count."

M-C bit her lip. "I'm here because I miss you, goddammit!" she shouted. "I told Raymond so."

"And he accepted *that?*"

"Listen, there's nothing between Ari and me anymore. Not for a long time. Why do you think he slept in Libby's cabin?"

This time Philip believed her. He kissed her. "What happens when I get back? *If* I get back?"

"Let's not think about the future," M-C said.

On Friday afternoon, with Tretino in the right seat, they flew for the first time. Gus went through the checklist methodically, for Philip's benefit, hitting switches, starting the engines, warming them up at 1,400 rpm, and then he guided the Aerostar down the runway into the sea breeze and soared over the bay, rising rapidly, clearing the hilly promontory.

"That's a pretty short strip," Tretino remarked when they were at cruising speed and circling the island, "especially if you have a heavy fuel load."

Philip looked down. "Yes," he said a little apprehensively. It felt new and strange to sit in a cockpit, like the bottom would drop out, like the world would spin away, leaving him dangling in space. But the powerful purr of the engines reassured him, and the surroundings seemed comfortable and familiar again. "The bird has plenty of power."

"That it has. Want to take over?"

"Not for a little. I'm enjoying this."

He did take over eventually, arms tense as he worked the controls, circling, gaining and losing altitude. Gus watched him carefully but kept his hands in his lap.

It was a cloudless day, with unlimited visibility. At ten thousand feet the islands looked like a tiara of emeralds. He flew the plane for two hours over the sea, with Gus advising him. Finally Gus said, "Let's go through the stall series before we knock off. Tomorrow we'll shoot landings and takeoffs."

With Tretino at the controls first, then Philip, they went through a number of operations designed to show how the Aerostar handled as it approached the danger zone—moving too slowly to sustain flight—under various conditions that could actually occur when the plane was landing or taking off: power on, both engines, clean (flaps up, gear up), flying straight ahead, turning right and left; same thing, with one engine out; power on, gear up, flaps down (dirty), a departure stall, an approach stall . . . One by one they went through the whole stall series.

Ari was a Scheherazade, spinning out the story of the mission.

After dinner at the villa, with the other Cardinals and the lioness listening, he said, "I will acquaint you with the details, but not all at once. The less you know, the better, at least until the last minute."

"Why?"

"Oh, security reasons." The count flicked a crumb from the sleeve of his velvet smoking jacket. "Your journey will be about twelve hundred miles."

"The distance to El Parador."

"You've been studying maps! Yes, somewhere in El Parador."

"Not the capital, El Parador City, then." Raymond said nothing. "El Parador's stretching the limits of the aircraft, you know."

"It will be all right."

"What will I carry?" Philip asked after a moment of silence.

"A passenger, and two pieces of cargo."

"I have to know the gross weight."

"Details are such a bore! The passenger is a big man, and the cargo weighs about four hundred fifty pounds."

"Can I refuel en route?"

"No. You may not land until you get there, under any circumstances."

"What do I do then?"

"Why, refuel and fly back."

"That's the deal? Fly there and fly back?"

"Safely." De Vaucresson looked at him. "You must fly back immediately—before the enemy gets wind of you, so to speak. The airstrip is shorter than this one, but you'll have left your cargo and the passenger with the guerrillas. I foresee no problems. You'll be in splendid shape, aeronautically as well as astrologically."

How about physically? Jesus. It'll be more than a dozen hours in the air, almost nonstop. A lot of flying for a man who hasn't even earned his wings again. Can you do it? He began to wonder. "I'll have the autopilot, at least."

"Yes," said the count a little reluctantly. "But it will be necessary to avoid El Parador coastal defenses and Cuban radar before that. The Cubans are touchy about air space and we can't *afford* to have you shot down." He glanced at his fellow Cardinals. "You must fly very low. One hundred feet ought to be about right."

"Meaning I have to stay alert for downdrafts."

"You can rest when you get back." Ari paused, as if sensing Philip's discouragement. "Oh, I haven't told you the fee. It will be one hundred thousand dollars—not bad for a day's work, eh? But well worth it to us because the mission will be in such capable hands. Gus Tretino tells me you are doing excellently. You will be ready."

"I hope so. I'll have to dope out my flight plan. You want me to file it?"

"Certainly not," snapped the count. "This will be a journey that never happened as far as the international authorities are concerned."

"Okay. I ought to depart early—say, three A.M.—when the air is cool. I'll be going out at max gross weight and I'll need all the lift I can get. I should reach El Parador midmorning. That'll bring me back before dark, if all goes well."

"We'll have a reception for you," Ari said. The other Cardinals murmured encouragement.

24

Saturday they flew again. "Let's start from the begin-ing," Gus said.

"Preflight inspection completed. Seats, doors, landing-gear handle, flap handle, brakes, flying controls, parking-brake switches—okay. Props full forward . . . mixture . . . battery on . . ."

"Throttle?" Tretino said.

"Woops. Idle cutoff . . ." He watched the gauges move as he flicked panel switches.

Philip guided the plane down the runway, gathering speed. The green-blue bay rolled nearer. "Pull her up," Tretino said sharply. On the beach beneath, faces lifted as the plane passed over, a little too low.

Philip was also a little low coming in through the V in the brown hills. A road ran through the V almost to the foot of the runway before it turned. There were cars. For a split second he feared his landing gear would hit one, and then he was safely down. "Thought you might make a convertible out of that sedan," Gus said.

On the next approach Philip was too high. He chopped the power and dropped in, bouncing on the touchdown.

"This isn't a helicopter," Gus said.

"I know, I know, it isn't a seaplane either."

He was getting better. After a dozen landings and takeoffs Tretino said, "Good." It was five o'clock already. Gus asked about a restaurant to take a girl to. He had a date that evening.

"Make it on the late side? I want to practice night landings."

"No lights on the field," Gus reminded him.

"There's plenty to see by down here. The stars at night are big and bright. . . ."

The moon wasn't up yet, but he didn't need it. He used, as navigation aids, the town, the houses, the lighted boats, the white windmill atop one of the hills. He passed over them, headed out to sea, turned, and landed from the ocean side, using the V to line up his approach.

Then, over Gus's protests, he took off again and threaded the Aerostar through the V and touched down gently.

Countenance pale in the faint glow from the control panel, Gus said gratefully, "Whew! Thank God that's over. I don't know if I would have tried that myself. I have to hand it to you. You're a quick study. Tomorrow you do it alone. Can I go out to dinner now?"

Sunday. With both fuel-injected Lycoming engines idling, he sat for a moment on the apron, battling fear. It was one thing to fly with the comfort of Gus at his side, another to go up there alone. He thought he'd conquered the terror, but he had not, would not, could not. It clutched his throat like a clamp. *Enemy jets are waiting to shoot you down. You'll come in through the V on fire, gear damaged, brakes out. You'll nose over, blow up . . . you're chickenshit . . .* Through the side window he saw the faces: Tretino's with a long, sharp nose; Libby's blue eyes wide open, beautiful bow mouth slightly parted; Cappy's gloomy; Canny's greenish, ironic; M-C's worried; the count's haughty, challenging. He applied power, moving to the end of the strip, taking off, climbing steeply over the hills that fringed the bay.

You did it! Once he was up, handling the yoke, fear became calm, then confidence, then joy. It was all he could do not to engage in a few wing-overs and rolls, to show off his refound skills to the watchers below, but dismissed the urge as, if not childish, then certainly premature. He still had much to learn about his aircraft; he had to know it inside and out. For the next few hours he dutifully shot landings and takeoffs, practicing and perfecting his short-field techniques.

Tretino was alone when he came down—the Cardinals and M-C had departed. The rangy pilot laughed and said, "Okay, fella, that's good enough for me. You're a real flier, but don't forget: nothing fancy now— no barrel rolls or Cuban eights. I'll check out the plane for the last time. Luck, and have fun in South America."

"I'll try," said Philip.

After dinner at the villa, Count de Vaucresson led Philip to the library, poured Cognac for them both. "Gus Tretino tells me you're a first-rate pilot, though still a bit nervous."

"I'm almost over it. I'll fly for you, don't worry," Philip said.

"I'm *not*. I have complete confidence in you and in your abilities. You wouldn't fly for me if I didn't—I will take no risks. The mission is far too important. The fate of a nation hangs on it! Incidentally, I must ask you, before you fly, not to speak to *anyone* unless Marie-Celeste or one of my other associates is with you. Is that satisfactory?"

"I guess so."

"Now, then, do you know about the situation in El Parador?"

"What I've been told."

"You are aware of the massive inflation? Discontent and inflation are like lips and tongue—they work together. The government will topple." The count cupped his snifter in both narrow hands and inhaled the fumes deeply. "We, the Cardinals, will be instrumental in the downfall of Hernandez."

"Exactly how?"

"As Fat says, impatience! I must confess the idea is not entirely new. The Germans did it in Greece with British pounds. I have heard the Americans used it against the Chinese Communists, but that may be only rumor. I know *for certain* that the CIA advocated that the scheme be employed against the North Vietnamese, but your Treasury vetoed it, on the grounds that the same trick might be tried against America, once the precedent had been established. Governments are most conservative on such matters. But we are not a government—we can do as we like." The count stared into his Cognac. "In any case, the CIA would have failed because of faulty economics."

"I don't understand what you're talking about."

"Why, counterfeit money, of course! It's absolutely necessary if Hernandez is to be overthrown. You see, the CIA proposed dropping counterfeit North Vietnamese money all over the country. The theory was that the peasants would find the money and spend it, causing huge shortages and inflation, but the idea had a fallacy: there was not enough to buy, and the peasants would simply have hoarded the . . . may I call it bogus bread?" The count grinned broadly. "We have been far more adroit."

Raymond rose and began to pace. "No, the counterfeits have to be *spent*. They have to enter and increase the money supply. For that, a mechanism is needed, and we developed one, an organization which is called 'money shops' or something like that in Spanish. Actually it is a loan association with offices everywhere in the country. You have such businesses in the United States. Its ostensible purpose is to make loans to the struggling middle class and the poor. But, were the El Paradorian government less stupid, it would quickly see that very few questions are asked of the borrowers, and almost no attempt is made to collect on the loans. The money shops make no profit—in fact, they lose. Well, they do not really lose very much, because the money they lend is counterfeit. Are you following me?"

"So far."

"That is not all. In El Parador, as in most Latin countries, many dissident Catholic priests exist. Considerable currency has been given them—the guerrillas, called Gonzalistas, distribute it. The priests dole out the money to the urban poor, who spend it. The money is all in small bills, and is counterfeit."

"Do the Gonzalistas know this?"

"About the counterfeit money? Yes, so does the government—now. It didn't for a long while. You see, the counterfeits are practically perfect— by El Parador standards at least. The notes are printed for us in the Cayman Islands by American experts. One more infusion of them should be enough. This time, the money will be in large bills and fed into the banking system, with the help of—why hide it?—the Minister of Finance, to be precise. Inflation will jump once more, and even greater numbers of people will join the dissidents. Soon, Hector Hernandez will drop, like ripe fruit. All signs point to this outcome, including astrological ones."

"Very clever. What's it got to do with me?"

"You will fly the counterfeit money."

"The government won't interfere?"

"Well, if you're spotted coming in, you may run into jet fighters coming out."

"Lord," Philip said.

"On the other hand, we've never used an aircraft to deliver the counterfeits before. We've relied on boats. Hernandez won't be expecting a plane. Nor is the dictator sufficiently vigilant. He is also a horoscopist. According to our sources, he finds the aspects favorable to him."

"And you don't."

"Hernandez is a rotten astrologer." The count peered through the window at the bright stars. "Imagine! He thought he could fool *me*."

"Oh?"

The gray eyes turned harsh. "He attempted to foist a spy on us. Having learned the man's birthdate, I detected him because I realized the solar eclipse would hit his ascendant. Looking further, I saw a dragon's tail . . . No matter. The spy mailed a letter, which I retrieved, sealed again, and sent, knowing it would increase Hernandez' anxiety when he received it. It meant risk to us, but I was certain we would triumph."

"What happened to the spy?"

"He was the pilot who crashed in the bay the day you arrived on the island."

"*What?*"

"Yes, yes. A faulty landing gear was responsible. The green lights were on when he landed, but the gear was not locked down. He tried to take off again, but he could not gain altitude quickly enough. I *knew* he wouldn't be able to. Above all, I hate betrayal," Ari said softly. "The counterfeit money you will carry was aboard my Aero Commander. Perhaps you saw the lights. Another Cognac?"

"No. I'm in training." Philip remembered the nighttime activity around the plane—Bob and Bill undoubtedly had been retrieving the counterfeit loot. Another murder.

"You needn't tell Marie-Celeste about the pilot—she is ignorant of the matter, which is why I speak to you privately. The dear girl is not aware of the lengths to which we've gone. You're fond of her, aren't you?"

"Yes."

"Good! She's fond of you too. She'll be waiting for you when you return. You will return, of course, for your payment. Also, should anything go wrong because of you, I would have to assume Marie-Celeste had a hand in it. That's enough for the moment, isn't it? Let's rejoin the others. Philip, do you play bridge?"

"Sorry. I don't know how."

"A pity. I would have enjoyed the challenge."

The next morning, after an early jog, Philip went to the airport to say good-bye to Tretino. "Thanks, Gus. You're a hell of an instructor."

"Same for my former pupil." Tretino squinted at him. "You hadn't flown for a real long time, had you?"

"It showed that much?"

"Yes. Frankly, I thought De Vaucresson was out of his skull to hire you as a pilot. I'd trust you to fly me now while I was making out in the backseat. If you ever want a job as a company pilot, look me up." He handed Philip a card. "I almost forgot to give you the keys. De Vaucresson's got the other set, and the papers. The plane is registered in the name of a bank. Is he having trouble financing it?"

"He owns the bank."

Philip watched the De Havilland Twin Otter take off. Then he remembered the count's injunction. He'd violated it already, leaving M-C asleep and going to the airport alone, talking to Gus. Oh well. He threw the keys in the air and caught them with the same hand. In his T-shirt and shorts, he sauntered to the Aerostar, removed the chocks, unlocked the door, and climbed on board. He put the key in the ignition, started the engines, and revved them up. There was no control tower to clear with. He taxied to the runway and was aloft moments later.

He hadn't intended to fly that morning, but somehow as he sat in the cockpit, the aircraft took possession of him. It was as if she asked him to put her through her paces, open her up. She was a dream, that plane; she had all the spunk he could have asked. *She* wanted to show off.

First he buzzed the field. He shouldn't have, but no commercial flights were scheduled for the next hour. Faces lifted on the beach, a man shook his fist. Noise pollution! To hell with it, just once. *You're acting like a teenager. You felt like this flying the Stearman.* He wagged his wings, to interest those on the ground. Then ceasing became impossible. He performed aileron rolls and loops for his growing audience; cars stopped on the road, people got out, necks craned. He zoomed straight up, dived, pulled out over the sea. He did an Immelman, climbing, turning, rolling out in the opposite direction. He rolled and flew upside down for a few seconds, then pulled smoothly through in a split S.

It was crazy of him. The plane wasn't built for aerobatics. Did he dare a Cuban Eight? He dared. He dived to pick up airspeed, rolled over in a half-loop, finishing cockpit-up. Enough! Soaking wet, he landed with a big smile on his face. He had brought a small crowd to the airport.

The count rushed to him. "Philip! *What* were you doing?"

"I was having a few laughs. I'll be a good boy now. If you'll forgive me, I have to work on the plane."

"Work? What work?"

"I'll remove the passenger seats. That'll save me a hundred pounds. I'll take out the second navcom and transponder—I won't need them, and that's twenty pounds less. I have to lose weight. I've gone over the numbers, and the margin on the return leg with the prevailing winds against me is tremendously close."

"There won't be a *problem*," the count insisted. "The signs are perfect."

"Does a horoscope provide flight statistics?"

That afternoon Philip wandered the streets of Pointe-de-Mer. After looking at the window of a duty-free shop, he went inside, Marie-Celeste at his heels. He asked for the watch, examined it, and told the clerk he had a sale.

M-C grabbed the watch as Philip signed traveler's checks—it was all the money he had left. "An Omega Flight Master. Is it heavy! The watch must cost a fortune in the States. What's so special about it?"

"Besides keeping perfect time? It has two hour hands. You use the orange hand to measure elapsed flight time from the moment you pull the chocks."

"And the blue one?"

"You set that at Zulu."

"Come *on*. What's Zulu?"

"Greenwich mean time. Used for flight planning."

"GMT is astrological time, remember?"

"May the zodiac be with me." He slipped the stainless-steel band over his wrist. "I want to stop at Le Boucan."

Joe Martinez said from behind the bar, "Quite a performance you put on! Reminded me of *Dawn Patrol*. The island's talking about the mystery flier."

"Did they enjoy the show?"

"They did, despite themselves. Peace and quiet's the credo here, other-worldly as it seems. Say, you're quite a pilot!"

"I try." He touched M-C's shoulder. "Would you leave us for a little?"

"I'm not supposed to do that, Phil."

"But would you? The ladies' room maybe?"

"Well . . ." she said uncertainly.

"I need to talk to Joe for a couple of minutes. Trust me."

"Hmphf!" The Lioness stalked off.

Philip waved away the Cointreau Joe offered. "I've learned where I'm to fly tomorrow. El Parador."

Joe made a sucking sound. "That's a long way. Why, for God's sake?"

"I'm a delivery boy. I'm carrying two parcels and a passenger, who's got to be Morales. I'm leaving them with the guerrillas, in theory. Morales is to lead the revolution to victory."

"Well, the rebels hold the Tall One in high esteem."

"They shouldn't. Morales has the others with him. They work as a team. They'd take over the country, for whatever reason."

"They'd be as bad as Hector Hernandez, if you ask me. They ought to be stopped. The rebels can win without them."

"Especially with the counterfeit money I'm bringing." He briefly explained the plan. Joe made the sucking noise again. "If I can somehow leave the counterfeits and bring Morales out, would it make a difference?"

"A tremendous difference. It would give me time to alert the Gonzalistas before Morales can get back. After that it might be too late."

"Okay, I'll try. Christ knows how I stumbled into this mess, but I'll need a gun. Have one?"

"A twenty-two, for protection. It's not much of a weapon."

"Is it here?"

"Yes, and loaded."

"Can I take it?"

Joe reached under the bar and came up with the cloth. He pushed it to Philip, who felt the object underneath, glanced around, and slipped the gun in his pocket. "That's all?" Joe said.

"I . . . you don't know me very well, Joe."

"Well enough."

"I want to get out of this alive. I'll need to refuel when I return."

"You plan to come back *here?*"

"I have to. Otherwise you wouldn't know if I'd succeeded. And . . ." He glanced at the rest-room door.

"They'd make her pay?"

"The count hinted at it. She's been so close to me he'd figure she was in on it, though she isn't."

"I can get the key to the petrol pump."

"You'd have to have it when I land." The ladies' room door was opening.

"You want me to be there, then."

"I'd like it. I'll also need help with the two stooges, Bob and Bill."

"I hate those punks. You can count on me."

"It might be dangerous," Philip warned. "And it'll mean trouble for you after I take off again."

"Don't worry. I can take care of myself." M-C sauntered toward them. "You've worked out where you want to go?"

"I think so, yes. There's an airstrip in the Grenadines . . ."

Philip stopped speaking as Marie-Celeste approached. He still thought of her as the count's accomplice, and the lioness was unpredictable. "What are you two whispering about?"

"Crime in the Caribbean," said Joe.

M-C said she wasn't feeling well, so Philip went alone to the count's, accompanied by one of the Geminis, who had taken up residence on the terrace. It was to be, he felt sure, his final repast at the villa.

Dinner, served at the ungodly (Ari complained) hour of six P.M. because of Philip's early departure, was simple: filet mignon, white asparagus (from France), hearts-of-palm salad, pastries. Sparkling red and white wines were served. The count, in a nubby linen suit, beige-colored, went to the point.

"I will give you the remaining details now. When I am finished, you will understand your future better."

"Such as it is."

The count pointed his pastry fork. "Philip! You have a marvelous opportunity. A new life awaits out there. You have only to fly safely and return. You have guessed who your passenger is. Yes? You will carry Capablanca Morales to El Parador and leave him there to guide the revolution to its final stage. He will have the counterfeit money and—"

"Are you certain you should tell him this? Even the Gonzalistas don't know," said Cappy, his somber dark eyes examining Philip with a hint of distrust. "I have gone over his horoscope again. The twelfth house—"

"Cappy! What has made you apprehensive? If we do not have full confidence in Philip, will he have confidence in us later on?" Morales lowered his eyes. "On board the airplane will be a chest containing gold worth a million dollars."

"A million," Philip repeated without visible emotion. The count watched him.

"Cargo weighing two hundred fifty pounds. Gold is a heavy metal." The count waved for the table to be cleared. "I might add that the bullion is insured by Lloyd's of London against transportation risk, but not against theft. That is why you must be careful with it. The gold belongs to us."

"What's it for?" Philip asked.

"Bribery. The gold will go to El Parador's Minister of Finance . . . I forget his name."

"Dr. Enrique Cordova Astacio Sanchez," Cappy said.

Ari shooed a mosquito away. "Astacio is trying, not very effectively, to remove the counterfeit bills from circulation and launch a stabilization program. For a million he will—ah, how do you Americans say it?—snafu the government even further through red tape. To bribe him is a contingency measure—the revolution would succeed without him—but it does no harm. Besides, we will get the money back. We see it as a sort of loan, even though Astacio will not. But he lacks time to take it out of the country."

"How will you get it back?"

"Oh, a few threats should be enough. After all, we will control El Parador. Do you know what that means?"

"To the rebels?" Philip said, declining coffee and liqueurs.

Ari sighed irritably. "The rebels! What are they good for besides shooting and dying? No, no, I meant to El Parador. With our brains and skills, the country will flourish. Think of our experience and assets! Capablanca's superb political abilities plus a smuggling operation that can be augmented easily. El Parador will benefit. Libby here is a top computer specialist. The country will be the first fully computerized one in Central America. Canny's forte, of course, is gambling, which shall be legal. We shall make El Parador City as Havana was before Castro."

"I get the brothels, too," said Canny.

"I will put the country's economy back on its feet," the count went on. "I will manipulate the currency. I can make money stand up and do tricks! I will parlay what little there is in the national treasury plus what we Cardinals lend El Parador—as a short-term measure—into enough to improve its credit rating. We shall secure development loans as soon as it is obvious the nation is moving at last. The United States will be delighted at having a stable, freedom-loving country in Central America. America will help, you'll see! The country has much potential— unexploited minerals, gold for instance; excellent hydroelectric opportunities; bauxite; large deposits of oil, most likely. And uranium. Never forget El Parador's uranium. There appears to be lots of it. Do you have *any* idea what uranium sells for?" "We don't need an atomic bomb, but I foresee the day when we *threaten* to build one. That should make headlines around the world."

"Come on, Ari . . ."

"How did a little country become so *strong?* they will ask. And grow so quickly, for with our improved standard of living and job opportunities, people will flock there. The country will be a pivotal West Indian force, especially with the mercenary army Cappy intends to establish. The area is weak, splintered, in ferment. It will become completely Marxist without a strong countervailing ideology—not America's, but astrology. Yes! Our campaign for horoscopy will continue, this time backed up by a Caribbean power. We shall make the Antilles astrological throughout, unify the islands.

"Begin to see the picture, Philip? The destinies of the Cardinals unfold toward the ends we desire—in this life at least. Right, Canny?"

Click, click, click, sounded Koster's fingers, like a rattle of chips. He wore the usual starched nautical whites. "Yeah. I want to run the show, not them black hats. *All* the casinos I can get my hands on. I want to control Vegas, Atlantic City, Covington, Antigua, St. Martin, Monte Carlo, Nice . . . I'll have a big piece of Resorts, Caesar's and the rest. I can do it, too, the numbers say."

"You, Libby my dear?" said Ari.

Libby Harris said dreamily, "I pose the question to myself, right now, will I be among the richest women in the world? The answer is indisputably yes. Who can stop me? I will have the banking system of the whole Caribbean to infiltrate—I am that good with computers. I shall be a queen again, at long last." Libby's nipples were erect beneath the clinging blue chiffon.

Said the man in black, unassumingly, "I have cast the horoscope of the Caribbean. It shows without doubt that one man shall soon rule, a Capricorn, born on the same day as me. He will be just but strong, able to take whatever measures prove necessary for public good. But he shall also serve another." Cappy bowed toward the count.

"And I," the count responded, "shall be a person of vast and unusual influence—a power such as the world has never seen. Philip, have I told you of Alfonso, King of Spain? Alfonso was the only known ruler since antiquity who relied on astrology to govern. Alfonso shall live again, in me. Oh, I have time. I am not destined to die for many years. I have frequently stated my desire to make astrology a science. There is only one means."

Philip's new watch told him it was time to leave, but he couldn't, not yet, not before Ari finished. "If astrology is good now, consider what it would be if we knew the moment of *conception!* Conception! That precise instant represents the fusion of the earthly and the divine, when the astral presence is most powerful. But to clock it for the perfect horoscope—one in which both the personality and the future can be shown with utter accuracy—requires conditions of, I shall say it, controlled breeding. We *must* be aware precisely when the egg has been fertilized. Perhaps men and women should live apart until the decision is made for them to mate . . . perhaps one-way mirrors or sophisticated

electronic equipment can be used to record the second of ejaculation
. . . details tire me, but it can be accomplished. And then, at last,
mankind will have mastered its ancient enemy, uncertainty, and can
face the future with confidence."

"Confidence," said Philip.

"As to your future," said the count, "obviously you can rate high in
the pantheon of astrological leaders. You will be powerful and rich—
riches tempt you, confess! But there is more. Philip, you and I are much
alike despite the disparity of our signs. There must be a reason, though I
don't know what. Let it pass. Philip, I may be wrong, but from what I
can read, you are destined to succeed me! You, when you have mastered
astrology, may be in fact a leader—perhaps *the* leader—of the *world!*"

Ari started to laugh. Canny laughed, as did Libby and Cappy.
Probably hearing the laughter, Fat came out of the kitchen and began to
laugh. Bob and Bill appeared—they laughed too, silently. Everybody but
Philip was laughing, bending over, slapping the table or each other in
mirth. Why? The Cardinals' imminent success? In appreciation of their
own superiority? Or perceiving the futility of human dreams, especially
ones as grandiose as theirs, did the Cardinals mock themselves? Or did
they laugh at Philip, who, apparently taken with Ari's blandishments, sat
with his mouth open? Because he was a toy in their hands?

A Gemini in the other seat, he drove the Moke back to the house on
the hill. M-C, in a bathrobe, worked with circular charts at the coffee
table. She looked up sharply when he entered and said abruptly, "Philip,
don't fly. I'm warning you, and I was right before."

He sat down. "What do you mean?" But he knew. Intuitively he had
reached the same conclusion.

"I've matched your chart with Raymond's. Phil, when you get back he
intends to have you killed by Bob or Bill—I can't tell which, but Gemini
is distinctly unfavorable. You think they trust you? They don't—they
don't trust anybody, no matter what they say. Not even me. I may be
killed too, according to my horoscope."

"Because of me?"

"Yes. They want no witnesses. They'll call you a suicide. You were in
pretty rotten shape when you came down here, remember?"

"Not anymore."

"Who's to believe that? You shot yourself with the twenty-two Joe gave you, they'll say."

"You saw the gun?"

"Think I'm a fool? I found it after you left. I want you to *live*. Me too. We could hire a boat and get out of here tonight."

"We'll live, M-C. We have a future ahead of us, though not the one Ari told me about. I'm flying tomorrow. I need sleep. Come with me."

"I certainly hope so," she said with a sad smile.

25

It was 2:45 A.M. and the moon whitewashed the night. The striped-top VW stood by the Aerostar while the Geminis put a box on board. They reached inside the jeep again, but Morales waved them away. Bad leg and all, he raised a metal chest and stowed it in the cabin, though he told Bob and Bill to lash it down.

Limping on his cane again—the knee seemed worse since he'd fallen on the *Zodiac* during the battle—Morales went over and gravely shook hands with the other Cardinals and Marie-Celeste. Then he squeezed his long frame into the cockpit, dropping the cane and the panama hat in the rear.

"Now it's up to you, my boy. Better take these along. Dexedrine." Ari gave Philip a vial, and pressed his hand, as did Canny. Libby kissed him on the cheek, and Marie-Celeste threw her arms around him.

"You get back safe, hear?"

"I aim to. So long, M-C." He patted her rump. In the canvas jacket the count had lent him against the late-night cool, a tote bag hanging from his shoulder, he made the final pass around the airplane, climbed inside, making sure that water, food, and an inflatable raft had been put on board.

He strapped himself in, making sure Cappy was too, and hit the starter. The engines caught easily; he taxied down the runway. At the end of the 3,500-foot strip, he turned, braked to a stop, and applied power, checking the magnetos carefully. *Go!* He pushed the throttles smoothly forward, listening to the engines' throaty roar, and released the brakes. They were off, at three A.M. sharp, right on schedule. *No turning back!* The Aerostar surged forward as the wheels folded and the flaps ground up silently.

The plane climbed away from the strip in a graceful arc. Phosphorus shone in the bay's gentle waves. Philip pulled up the gear and flaps as they rose over the hills—he could see the five-form of the Count's illuminated pool: Ari conferred good luck, no doubt. Philip set a course almost due west for El Parador.

He "cleaned up" the cockpit, turning off the boost pump, closing the cowl flaps, following the after-takeoff checklist. He pulled the throttles back to twenty-two inches, set the props at 2,200 rpm's, and leaned out the engines for maximum endurance cruise. The left engine hiccuped slightly, and Philip moved the mixture level up a hair. He adjusted manifold pressure and rpm's, setting the aircraft on cruise power.

Almost compulsively—remembering the skills the best fighter pilots were supposed to have, aggressiveness, consummate skill, cunning, he added another quality to the list: compulsiveness—he reviewed the flight plan once more. To the El Parador coast, 1,170 nautical miles, with another fifty or so to the jungle airstrip. Make land partly by dead reckoning, check the course on the automatic direction finder. He'd have to rely on Cappy—asleep already, dark head leaning against the door—for the crucial headings after they got to the coast. The Aerostar's maximum range to dry tanks was 1,367 nautical miles, which left him a safe margin, especially as he counted on the trades to provide a quartering tailwind of twelve to fifteen knots. They ought to arrive over the jungle field with an hour's fuel to spare. But if they failed to hit the strip dead on the nose, the extra gas might not mean a lot. He had to assume Cappy could find it.

He used the weak beam of St. Jean's radio to establish his drift and ground speed—about 220 mph. Later, he would cross-check on the automatic directional finders at San Juan, Santo Domingo, and Kingston, Jamaica. By then he'd be down to one hundred feet, to avoid being tracked by radar. He'd be on his own after that until he picked up El Parador radio. Though he'd be relying on the ADF again, they could still be in the soup if the trade winds picked up or if he got an offshore breeze as they approached Central America. He could be blown substantially off course.

Yet he wasn't really worried about this leg of the trip. He'd been through something like it before. In Arizona, coming home on his first solo cross-country flight, he had thought he was lost. Panic descended, black as the rain clouds ahead of him. He'd remembered the words of his instructor: "Just maintain your heading and fly out your time. Keep checking your chart and you'll find yourself." Good advice! It almost sounded like Ari, except the chart wasn't astrological but navigational, with the established features of earth. The good old globe, securely mapped. It wasn't always easy to know where you were from the air, and the ground below could be dangerous, but at least geology and civilization had provided physical landmarks. He'd reached his destination then.

The Aerostar flew smoothly. A thermos of coffee had been put beneath the seat. Letting go the yoke, he poured himself a cup without danger of spilling it. Cappy snored beside him. *Do goats snore?* He studied the flat features in the gray light. Even in sleep, when lines relaxed, Morales had savage creases in his cheeks, furrows on his forehead as though a plow had crossed it. A rough face of the land. Very shortly, Cappy would be his mortal enemy.

It occurred to him that Morales, though he looked older, was about the same age as himself. *Jesus, this is your birthday! You're forty-six! Happy birthday, Phil! What a way to celebrate! What kind of present are you giving yourself? What are you letting yourself in for? This guy, bad knee and all, picked up a 250-pound chest filled with gold. You saw what he did to the blacks with the cane, the snakes in the pool. He has a level of anger—and power too—you'll never match. Go against the beast? Don't try it. Leave him in El Parador.* Dawn seemed to illuminate the precariousness of his position.

Philip reminded himself that the Cardinals were a menace—sociopaths if not out-and-out loonies. But suppose they succeeded in their plot to take over El Parador, using it as a springboard to undermine the Caribbean and grabbing control? What then? Astrological enclaves everywhere with big political followings? Was the world *really* that secure from myth and superstition? Destabilization of the hemisphere? Atomic bombs? He *had* to risk his neck.

The sun was rising behind him; he could almost feel the cool trades that blew little whitecaps on the water below. *Wind coming up a bit. Almost halfway there. Correct right with the seat of your pants to compensate for the freshening breeze. Time to get down from one thousand to one hundred feet. Everybody's radar will soon be in range.*

There wasn't much to do except stay on heading, though he couldn't afford to become careless, even for a moment: he had the ship on automatic pilot, but vigilance was necessary with the plane skimming the surface. The cockpit was becoming warmer. He turned off the cabin heat. Cappy still slept, and Philip, for the first time, longed to do the same. No! He considered adjusting the mixture, but that was merely an impulse to find activity, to watch needles move.

The monotony of long-distance flying caused his thoughts to float free, jostling with each other for attention. Out of the turmoil, his mother emerged. His mother, who back in Bisbee had practiced astrology of sorts, though not with the artistry of the Cardinals. His mother read the astrological column in the paper every day, subscribed to magazines, held evening sessions with the neighbors, cast horoscopes. As a kid, he'd felt his mother neglected him, then Ellie had taken up the stuff, contributing to the resentment that led him to lie about his birthday on the beach. Step by step, he'd been brought to where he was, a hundred feet above the indigo Caribbean, a sleeping killer next to him. He had to smile. He'd forgotten most of what he knew about astrology, but he wasn't *quite* as naive about the subject as he'd let on. He wasn't totally ignorant of houses, signs, planets, and the rest. He'd played possum with the gang of four and M-C. It wouldn't help, but he was amused all the same.

The plane dipped in a downdraft and Philip pulled on the yoke. Cappy's head snapped up and turned immediately toward the metal chest in the rear, as if to reassure himself it was still there. He spoke for the first time on the flight: "Where are we?"

Philip punched numbers into the ship's computer. "Past the eastern end of Jamaica." It had been full daylight for a while now. Philip looked at the Omega: 7:30. "About two hours left."

The cabin was starting to get hot, even with the ventilation on. Hot, sweaty, and boring to fly hour after hour. A numbness in Philip's backside. Both men undid their harnesses again. Cappy reached back and came up with the food—fruit, milk, hard boiled eggs, chicken sandwiches. They munched silently. Watching the whitecaps, Philip adjusted his course slightly.

Cappy's wakefulness returned Castle to reality: he still hadn't completed his plans. His first notion had been to return to St. Jean an hour or so after takeoff, telling the goat man the plane had mechanical troubles, pulling the gun on him after they landed, exchanging his hostage for Marie-Celeste. But the scheme had too many flaws—what if a Gemini put a hole in a tire, where would Philip be then? Besides, quixotic as it seemed to him, Castle wanted to fly the distance and deliver the counterfeit notes, not only as his contribution to what he vaguely conceived of as social justice—the overthrow of a bad man—but as a test of his new-found confidence. He had a peculiar conviction he could succeed in this venture if he could handle Morales. Yes, Cappy was the question. The answer was to ditch him in El Parador. First, of course, Philip had to refuel. That was primary, whatever came after— having gotten in, Castle had to get out. He was sure there would be an interval while Morales and the rebels talked; the Tall One would reconnoitre before he removed the bullion from the plane. And, when he did, he'd require elaborate security arrangements. The counterfeit money, surely, would leave the Aerostar first.

Philip would need Cappy on board when he began his escape from the jungle airstrip—he doubted if the guerrillas would risk their leader's life by turning guns on the plane as it taxied to the foot of the runway. He would force Morales to climb out; Castle would take off alone. If it happened quickly, the rebels wouldn't grasp what was occurring in time to shoot. The scheme was so crazily unexpected that it might work.

Castle repeated the rewards to himself. And, when he got to St. Jean, he'd tell Martinez the details of the Cardinal's schemes, so Joe could warn the rebels. . . .

Morales collected the remnants of the meal and put them in the box, almost daintily. It seemed odd that a man so large could be so fastidious. "Flying is a bore, no?"

"This kind is, with nothing but water to look at hour after hour." He looked at a string of cumulus clouds trailing downwind to the west.

"Being so close to the sea makes me nervous. It will be good to be on land."

Capricorn-the-goat. An earth sign. A land animal. "It won't be long now."

Cappy peered through the windscreen. "Do I see the shore?"

"We're way off course if you do. Just ocean." "I'm certain I see the land. Give me the binoculars."

"Between the seats."

"You're right," said Cappy. "Wishful thinking."

Wishful thinking. The Cardinals excelled at that. What about you?

"If you can't find me a heading when we reach the coast this trip will be wishful thinking."

"The field has been used for smuggling, and I'm familiar with the area. My wife's family comes from the region."

"I didn't know you had a wife."

"She's in Costa Rica, seriously ill." Cappy tried to stretch his bad left leg, but there wasn't room. Instead he rubbed the knee, wincing. He said finally, "She may not live."

Philip felt a trace of compassion. "Do you want to be with her?"

"Very much. But I have no choice. Her destiny is hers, mine is mine—to lead my people. This is the hour. I must be present or the victory will not occur."

"Why can't the guerrillas succeed without you?"

"Why? Because they are not sufficiently disciplined or farsighted. They are a stupid rabble."

Compassion faded. "I'd have thought a revolution doesn't depend on a single person—the man on horseback. I mean, don't the rebels work together? Does one individual matter so much if people are united in a cause?"

Cappy said coldly, "*I* make the difference, believe me."

"But . . ."

"Please do not interrupt! In history forces exist. I am one." Cappy pulled on a long brown ear reflectively. "Without me, the Gonzalistas will fail. I am responsible for El Parador's destiny. I have to urinate."

Philip was sorry Morales had mentioned urination. It made him want to pee too. "Not far now," he said.

Cappy continued with intensity: "The stars focus their light through the prism of the heavens on a few. When the light falls on a person he cannot ignore it: it is a command. I cannot avoid my preordainment. I did not ask for it, but who am I to refuse? I must do as destiny instructs. I told you the rebels are children. They must be strongly led. Killed if they do not obey."

Castle concentrated on the horizon, changing from a hazy blue line to a smoky brown one: peasants burned the jungle to clear it, as they always had. *Killed if they do not obey* . . . The water was becoming a murkier color. Should Philip leave this murderer among his people? No—Philip refused to consider bringing Cappy out for more than a moment. It would increase fuel consumption: he'd made an allowance for the gold but the Tall One's presence would further strain the margins of safety. And Cappy would vastly increase the difficulties at the other end where he intended to make Ari prisoner, swapping the count for M-C, not mentioning that he had the precious metal, keeping them away from the plane.

He found El Parador radio. A voice spoke clearly in Spanish, and Castle altered his course again. Finally he said, "There it is. Welcome home."

The verdant coastline organized itself into bays and peninsulas. Cappy sat erect. "Yes! I recognize the landscape. That is Capa St. Maria." He indicated a promontory with a large hand.

Philip checked the Admiralty charts—he was only fifteen miles off intended landfall, and, the Omega told him, ten minutes early. He too glanced at the gauges. Plenty of fuel left. Not bad. No aircraft in sight. "Where to?"

"Wait." Philip couldn't spot any distinguishing landmarks except for the promontory, but Cappy was watching the muddy shore and the coastal swamp behind it. Low hills appeared in the distance. "There."

Changing the heading, Philip flew over the hills. A river appeared abruptly. Following Cappy's gestures, he banked left, then right. A narrow dirt strip no more than 2,500 feet long lay directly ahead.

Philip shoved the mixtures and props up, dropping the nose to gain airspeed, and buzzed the strip. A wrecked DC-3 cluttered the far end but he saw no one.

"They are here," Cappy said calmly. "They know we are coming. They wish to be certain it is me and not a ruse."

"It couldn't be a government ambush?"

"Impossible."

The runway looked firm, without ditches or potholes. Philip raised the plane into a tight left-hand chandelle; rolling out at the top, he lowered his gear and flaps and slowed before turning back to the runway. The Aerostar dropped neatly over the trees and rumbled over the hard-packed earth, coming to a stop near the end of the strip. Opening the cockpit door to the jungle heat, Philip taxied where Cappy directed, toward a few dilapidated buildings along the edge of the trees. There were a broken-down jeep and some rusty fuel drums. As Philip shut down the engines, he noticed that the dirt was stained dark black from other refuelings. It was precisely 9:20.

Cappy undid his shoulder straps and harness, put on his dark coat with difficulty in the small cockpit, reached back for his panama hat and cane, and struggled with the locked door handle. Philip unstrapped, leaned over, and opened it for him. Morales climbed out stiffly.

Young men and women in battle fatigues ran from the trees armed with rifles or pistols. Crying out in joy, they surrounded the tall man, who raised his hand to greet them, like a religious figure. Philip left his cockpit door open. Behind a tree, he urinated and squatted. There was toilet paper in his tote bag. The motionless air was hot and damp. An old truck rattled toward him down a trail. He returned to the plane, and the truck pulled up to it. Four fifty-gallon drums stood in the back. A man in faded khakis said something Philip didn't understand, handing him a funnel with a piece of gauze stuck in it. Philip frowned; he hadn't considered contaminated fuel. He put the funnel into one of the tanks and held the nozzle while the guerrillas took turns cranking the pump. Hands loosely touching the shoulder of two rebel soldiers who looked like midgets beside him, Cappy limped inside the shack.

Philip watched the gauze for dirt or water. Slow, silent minutes passed—if the guerrillas spoke English, they gave no sign of it. He filled all three tanks, topping off carefully, and jammed extra gallons into the fuel vent space—that gave him over thirty additional miles: he would need every drop of gas he could throw in. He clicked the fuel caps into place and flipped down the locking tabs. There were cans of oil in the truck—he put in six quarts.

Castle looked at his watch: 9:50, ten minutes before takeoff time. Where was Cappy? Morales emerged, walking with his hopping gait, using the cane, surrounded by his followers. He pointed to the box with counterfeit money in it, which the guerrillas removed and put in the truck. Morales watched, then turned toward the plane. Philip had counted on Cappy's proprietary attitude toward the gold once more. In the same way he had loaded it, Morales would insist on removing the treasure chest himself.

Philip stood behind him. He took the .22 from the tote bag and put the muzzle to Morales' ribs. "Tell them to stand back."

"What?"

"This is a gun."

When Morales hesitated, Philip prodded. Cappy gave orders. The rebels milled and moved off. The truck also retreated.

Philip closed the cabin door and said, "Go to the other side of the plane." He herded the goat man with the pistol. "Climb in."

"You will never succeed, you understand."

"Never mind. Quick."

That the fuselage concealed Cappy and Philip was his only advantage, because if the rebels were to shoot, the moment was then, with Morales climbing into the cabin and Philip on the ground. But the guerrillas didn't grasp what was occurring, couldn't believe their beloved leader was being spirited off under their noses, didn't know about the gold, couldn't comprehend what motive the pilot could possibly have. Then he was in, with Cappy sitting in the right seat, holding the cane. Keeping the gun on him, Philip started the engines with one hand, stabbed the right brake and wheeled down the runway, wondering if it were long enough; the wreck of the DC-3 at the other end looked ominously close.

As he turned for takeoff, Philip could see the rebels waving fists and guns. The truck bounced toward the runway, an intervention Castle had not foreseen. Was there time to dump Cappy? Only if Philip acted at once. Why then did he hesitate, as though paralyzed? Because . . . . *Killed if they do not obey.* Because he couldn't leave the beast with these unsuspecting people. If they were to win their revolution they could do so without the Tall One. Philip knew that he had already decided to take Cappy out when he jammed the extra fuel in the plane. He ordered Morales to strap in, and did so himself laboriously with one hand, pointing the gun with the other.

Now! He dropped the flaps and applied full power—the Aerostar shook against the brakes until Philip released them and the heavily-laden ship rolled down the rough surface, gathering speed—20 knots, 40. . . . The truck! It was on the runway; those aboard it apparently thought they could force the Aerostar to halt if a collision were imminent. Philip couldn't have stopped even if he'd wanted. He pulled the plane as close to the foliage as he dared, and increased speed. The wingtip barely missed the old vehicle. Eighty-five knots, 90. . . . *Wheels! Wheels! Get up!* The gear tucked into the ship and they were airborne, climbing slowly on the edge of a stall, both engines screaming as Castle held the throttles full open. The wreck leaped at them. The trees behind it were small. The Aerostar's belly cleared them, barely.

Cappy glared but there was nothing he could do unless he could fly the plane himself. Castle made sure the boost pumps were off, that the aircraft was trimmed for normal flight. Routines could not be ignored. Routines kept complicated machinery working. Routines made humans conscious of their own potential for error, and Castle could not err once. The return leg would be longer because of headwinds and because he would fly slower—162 mph—to conserve fuel. Even so, the trip would test the Aerostar's maximum endurance and Philip's too: the journey would consume almost nine hours. He listened to El Parador radio, to be sure he was on course, while he watched the coast slip by under his wing.

The shadow over the water startled him—Philip had thought he would have nine hours of peace. He strained his head upwards and recognized the snub nose instantly. *Jesus!* An F-86 Sabrejet. The fighter had spotted him. Perhaps the pilot had been training or target practicing with a T-33 that dragged a sleeve when his base radioed. Maybe somebody on the ground had seen the Aerostar, believed it carried drugs. Maybe there had been a leak. But the result was the same: the F-86 was after him, no doubt of that. The jet orbitted, made "follow me" passes from the side, veered off. Stubbornly, Castle maintained his heading. The Sabre was on top of him; splashes erupted in the water. Warning shots. The F-86 wagged wings—the command to follow.

Philip recalled Korea. Adjusting mixture and props—Cappy, expressionless, watched his every move—Castle pushed up his power. The Sabre returned. Philip rose rapidly to 5000 feet, reversing course. He wanted to get behind the F-86, prevent the six .50 caliber machine guns from being aimed effectively. *Rattle him. Maybe he's green.*

The maneuver must have confused the F-86's pilot. He broke off and climbed, to come in from another direction and ended on the Aerostar's tail. *This will be a tight circuit.* Philip did a shuddering Immelman. He rolled out on his original course, forcing the other pilot to do the same. *He knows he can't stay with you long at this low altitude; he'll run out of fuel. Pull the power.* The jet, overshooting him, raced by, did a graceful cloverleaf and was coming back, ready to fire. Cappy jabbed his finger at the Plexiglas in warning. Philip slowed the Aerostar to near-stalling speed and began a spiraling dive for the water. For the enemy, Philip had temporarily vanished from the gun sights.

"Give me the altitude. Quick!"

"Where do I find it?"

Philip pointed at a dial without removing his eyes from the rising ocean.

"Three thousand . . . two . . . one . . . eight hundred . . . five . . .," Cappy said hoarsely.

Morales didn't have to shout against the slowing revving engines, the hiss of air rushing by the plane. *The enemy is flying in relation to you; you hope he doesn't realize how low he'll be.* Philip dropped the flaps as a spurt of a .50 caliber rounds splashed into the sea below him. *On your tail. Good! Pray.* Just over the water Philip pulled out of the dive, leveling off. *You're right on deck, skimming the waves. Where's the Sabre? Yes, too close? Traveling at the speed of sound, he's in a stall, fighting the controls, trying to get up. He'll never make it—he hasn't time. Just like Korea. . . .* The jet passed him; a wingtip touched the sea; the Sabre cartwheeled and exploded; smoke and debris marked its passage.

Philip augmented power and pulled up the flaps. Worried that the Sabre had a wingman, he made a few turns but saw nothing in the sky. Fear was an after effect. Panting, he regained his course with the aid of the ADF. *What did that cost in fuel?* The dogfight had consumed less than three minutes, but he had been forced to climb and his margin for navigational error was virtually infinitesimal even before.

"Thanks," he said, ridiculously, under the circumstances. Cappy, slumped in his seat, head bent, did not answer. Philip thought of the Dexedrine. *No, not yet. You'll need it later.* He put on the automatic pilot and tried to rest. Fifteen minutes passed, thirty, an hour, two, three. He tuned the radio to Kingston, one hundred miles to the north. The sound of the Morse-code identifier filled the cabin, and Philip set to work locating his position. Twenty minutes later he congratulated himself. Though not totally precise, the bearing confirmed his dead-reckoning estimate of where he ought to be. And the winds against him were no stronger.

The wake below belonged to a yacht almost as large as the *Zodiac* heading into Jamaica. *Zodiac.* . . . Trying to account for his triumphs— the sea battle, abducting Cappy, luring the jet into the sea's embrace— Philip could summon only empty phrases: *Christ, you've been lucky. So lucky you almost can't call it luck any longer. Like the odds favor you so completely as not to be odds. As though, because meant to be, success is certain. It isn't! Don't fool yourself!*

Cappy sat up, "Where are you taking me?"

A fair question. Philip realized he could touch down at St. Croix or Haiti. Given his apparent luck, the customs people might not look inside the chest. He could refuel and fly to Carriacou, where he and the gold might be safe. But he couldn't land with Morales in the ship. How to dispose of him? Only one answer. Shoot him, put the plane on auto, wrestle the body out. Would he do that? No! He had to return for the lioness. "St. Jean. If we get there."

Cappy's sardonic smile, announced that he, Cappy, personally would take care of Philip when they landed. No doubt he contemplated how to hurt Philip the most before he killed him, just as Philip was thinking of how Morales could be immobilized. How weird—two men side by side in a cramped cockpit pondering how to inflict bodily harm on each other.

"And then?" Cappy said.

"We'll see."

"Why have you done this?"

"How about a million bucks in gold?"

"It was not in your horoscope, though I suspected something was the matter."

"You were right."

How would Raymond react when he learned Philip was an Aries? Castle looked forward to telling him, to watching the surprise. Surprise would still be important; consternation might give Castle a little time. He could almost hear the count's dry voice asking why he had been betrayed. The answers were obvious, and yet, Philip thought, perhaps there were deeper reasons, ones he didn't, might never, understand.

His body ached from sitting too long in the same position. He washed down a chicken sandwich with coffee. Midafternoon, he picked up a commercial station in Port-au-Prince for another fix, but the signal kept fading. He learned that a thunderstorm hung over the south coast of Hispaniola, accounting for the poor reception. He waited for San Juan, where he got a good fix, altering the course a little. He'd promised himself to keep his eyes off the fuel gauges, but his resolution wasn't strong enough. He tapped one, frowning.

At 5:30, he went down to fifty feet and stared ahead intently. St. Croix and the other Virgin Islands were just over the horizon, and he wanted to be sure that the control-tower operators didn't pick him up on the scopes. Soon, through the afternoon haze, he spotted the low hills and white buildings of Christianstad. He banked slightly to the right and kept away from shore. *No point letting anyone have a peek at you.*

Less than an hour to go, and Castle was becoming extremely tired. Time for the Dexedrine. And then he smelled it—a fecal odor, growing stronger, filling the cockpit. He looked sharply at Cappy, whose eyes were shut. *Jesus, he's crapped in his pants! Goat shit. Ugh. Awful . . . And Cappy hates filth! He'd love to kill you right now!*

Philip's palms were wet as he watched the gauges drop sharply toward empty. Fifty minutes to go. If they ran out of fuel, he'd have to ditch the plane at sea. Would he be able to manhandle the gold onto the inflatable raft? Cappy might interfere, the plane might break up in the four-foot seas running beneath them. If the gold sank, would the water be too deep to dive for it? *Probably. Stay on course. You'll be all right.*

Where was St. Jean? *Where is it?* Philip knew his position was good, but the island wasn't there. It refused to appear. *Patience.* He ought to be in range of the island radio soon. Tuning the ADF, he heard, a few minutes later, the St. Jean station. The astrology pitch! Of all things! But it wasn't the usual one: the message had been altered. Instead of "Pisces" being repeated three times, "Aries" was repeated twice. "Aries . . . Aries . . ." the announcement began. Why the change?

Philip, making a slight adjustment that would bring him into St. Jean head-on, tried to grasp the significance of what he was hearing—the message was being aired over and over again. Was M-C responsible? Was she attempting to communicate with him? If so, "Aries—Aries" meant something . . . had to refer to de Vaucresson and . . . himself? Two Aries. Had Raymond learned that Philip shared his sign, that his ultimate enemy had at last appeared? *Two rams on an intersect course. . . .*

Castle sucked in his breath. If he interpreted the signal correctly, Ari would be ready. With surprise eliminated, his only assets were a puny .22, an extremely dangerous hostage, and Joe Martinez. *Lord, suppose Joe doesn't show up?* Philip considered an alternative to the airstrip. He *could* ditch the plane at the mouth of Pointe-de-Mer harbor and turn himself in to the cops. He might be safe that way, would merely risk prosecution by the French government. But Ari's men would dive for the gold, and M-C would be left in de Vaucresson's hands. No! He would land at the strip.

He examined the fuel gauges again—empty. How many minutes left? Then out of the darkening sky he saw hills in the distance. He pulled on the yoke, trading airspeed for altitude, climbing to two hundred feet. He changed his heading again, to pass directly over the field and make his approach from the sea.

Number one engine began to miss. Fuel starvation. He jammed the mixtures forward, but the engine sputtered and died. Instantly he feathered the prop, hoping number two would hold. He shoved up the prop on the right engine and increased the power a little to compensate for the loss of power on the left side. As he turned into his dead engine at low speed, the other quit too. He was forced to try to glide in through the V.

Don't panic. He switched on his landing lights and lowered the silent airplane's sharp nose. The headwind seemed to have stiffened, and helped to hold him aloft. The craft handled beautifully. He put down the gear, dropping half flaps, sliding down and through the notch, past the windmill that gleamed dully in the twilight. The tires sounded on asphalt. Braking slightly, he let the plane roll, turned, came to a stop past the squat terminal. At least he was down.

Philip had positioned the gun on the window side throughout the voyage. He pointed it and said, "Unstrap and duck down in your seat, out of sight. Don't mess around."

"You haven't the slightest chance."

"We'll see." Philip fingered the trigger, and Morales huddled. *Keep Ari guessing in case he knows about your birthdate.*

Through the windscreen he could see figures approaching slowly, perhaps cautiously: the Cardinals, the Geminis. M-C hung back; something about her face seemed strange, but he couldn't make out what. *Is Martinez here?* Philip opened the cabin door and stepped down, grateful for the fresh air. He ordered Morales to follow him.

The Tall One squeezed through the opening. His long face appeared relieved when his feet touched tarmac, as though the ground revived his confidence. *Killed if they do not obey.* Glaring, he twisted the goat's head handle of his cane; the metal hoof emerged. At the same moment, Philip bent, lunged, smashed the gun barrel on the man's arthritic left knee as powerfully as he could. Cappy bellowed in a high pitch, dropped the cane, and followed it to the apron.

In a brown battle jacket with a red scarf tied around his neck, Ari trotted past the tail section. Seeing Cappy, he cried, "What in the world?"

"The gold," Cappy said weakly. "Still on board."

"What about the counterfeit money?"

"Delivered," Morales moaned.

Libby rushed up. "What's happening?"

Hatred punctuated the count's spare countenance. "Philip has managed to injure our companion. Apparently he planned to steal the gold—how, I don't know, and frankly do not care. He shall not succeed."

"I told you we shouldn't trust this guy," Canny said angrily.

"It's all right, my boy! The fool has brought the gold back. Astacio will be notified about a brief delay—he will understand. Cappy will be on his feet in no time. This little interruption is for the best. I have learned something of vast importance."

"Where is Marie-Celeste?" Castle asked. "I just saw her."

"You may talk to her when you have surrendered your weapon, Philip."

The Geminis separated, each moving toward either end of the plane, hard eyes on Philip, who aimed the .22 at the count. "If there's trouble I'll shoot."

De Vaucresson showed his palms. "But you won't. It's not in your character—the Arian one."

"You found out," Philip muttered.

"Just in time, too. A Chicago paper carried a flattering article about you because of your forthcoming book. Congratulations! One of my people sent me the text on telex after you left this morning. Your *real* birthdate is mentioned. Happy birthday! If you wish to celebrate another, I suggest you be sensible: give up, have a good night's sleep, return to America tomorrow. I'll see that you'll have no problems with your passport—I really *should* have looked at it when we took it from the duct. And you've earned your fee—the counterfeit money reached its destination. Since neither of us likes bloodshed . . ."

Where is Joe? Keep Ari talking. "How about the prediction another Aries would beat you?"

"That's what is important. I spent the entire day on our horoscopes. Yours with the accurate natal information showed clearly why you chose to lie, but let's skip the astrological details. Mine tells of certain victory in this enterprise, even with another Aries in contention, and it became plain to me at last that my late wife was wrong. Your position, my Arian rival, is totally untenable. *Philip, you cannot win!* So much for the prediction which has haunted me all these years. Even good astrologers, like my wife, sometimes make mistakes. I demand you give me that gun."

Marie-Celeste wriggled under the belly of the Aerostar with a bruised and swollen face. She yelled, "Phil, watch out! Bob and Bill are armed."

De Vaucresson shouted, "I told you to stay back. Haven't you made enough trouble already? All right, show your weapons, fellows."

The Geminis produced heavy revolvers that must have been stuck in their belts, behind. "Point those things and I'll shoot your boss," Philip threatened.

The count sighed. "Philip, Philip, try to understand your position. Suppose you shoot me, what then? The Geminis will shoot you They are excellent marksmen: they will only wound. They will leave the job to Cappy, who, I am quite sure, would like to kill you himself in the most painful way." Morales' incoherent mumbling conveyed lethal eagerness. "Have you heard what he did with a dozen lemons to a man? Quite a story—I'll tell you about it sometime. And Marie-Celeste. She will also die because of her role in your misadventure. Canny will see to that as a favor to me, won't you, Canny? Something excruciating. As a crab, Canny likes to work on the chest. Remember when you had a man's breast bone crushed with a sledge hammer, Canny? Ha-ha. What do you suggest?"

"Cut off her tits, one at a time, then both boobs, with one of Fat's cleavers," Canny suggested, eyes darting.

"Oh, God," M-C said.

"But these are merely speculations! You won't fire, Philip," said the count with a saintly smile. "You see, you can't. You are really quite helpless, Philip. You are far less willing to die than I am, because, though you do not believe you will live again, I do: I wanted to accomplish more this time but for me there will be another day. I will go on and on, and in that certainty death means little. So you are helpless, Philip, because of your compassion for Marie-Celeste. . . ." He inched nearer, hand extended. ". . . and because of your dread of death. Helpless, yes, quite helpless."

The coward, Philip thought bitterly. He'd seen how the count avoided combat on the ship. *He's as frightened of dying as I am!* But Ari was right, for a different reason. On the yacht he'd been able to kill because the battle was the counterpart of war. To shoot Ari would be murder, and murder wasn't in him. Maybe it would be if he could save M-C, but to fire at the count might ensure her mutilation. Raymond had him, trapping his eyes in a gray stare. The Geminis would raise their weapons—in moments Philip would be dead. *Bargain for M-C's safety.* If only Joe had shown up. *Jesus, you made that incredible flight for nothing, nothing! Except to endanger your girl's life, and yours. Give Ari the .22 and hope. . . .*

"Good evening," said a hearty bass voice. Joe Martinez poured from the gloom. Bob's gun swung toward him and Philip, acting purely on instinct, held his gun hand out, elbow stiff, sighted, and fired. Bob winced, dropped the gun, and clutched his wounded arm. "Nice shot," said Joe. "You saved us from a murder rap—the boys would have killed him."

The boys moved in, surrounding Martinez. They had been lurking at the nose and tail of the Aerostar. Joe's sons! Big fellows! Good! They advanced on the Geminis. Bill looked at Ari uncertainly. The count lowered his head.

Joe's sons were on the Geminis, kicking them savagely until they went down. "Large families have advantages as well as drawbacks," Martinez observed as he watched.

"You cut it pretty fine," Philip said.

"Sorry. They were at a soccer game and I couldn't get them to leave."

"A soccer game!" He laughed. "Joe, would some of the boys push the plane to the pump? Did you bring the key?"

"Yes, sir " Martinez presented a mock salute.

"Ari, you owe me a hundred grand."

De Vaucresson looked up bleakly. "Under the circumstances, I hardly think . . ."

"I earned it, you said."

"This is theft!"

"That's a good one, coming from you."

"I don't have that sort of cash lying around. I'll have to obtain it from St. Martin tomorrow."

"Does he have it, Marie-Celeste?"

"I don't think so, not on hand. But Canny does. The loot he won at Antigua."

"I put it in the bank."

"He's lying! I'm sure I know where he keeps it. In an astrology book I saw him take from the ship. It must be in his room."

"Is that right, Koster?" The beady black eyes stared back defiantly, but the fingers stopped clicking. "Get it, M-C, will you? I want a hundred thousand, no more and no less, please. And bring your passport and jewelry."

"What about my clothes?"

"We'll get you some new ones."

M-C scurried toward the VW. Some of the boys had pushed the plane to the pump and were gassing her. The others guarded the Geminis, who sat on the runway, appearing dazed. Philip said to Martinez, "They had a master plan, after all. It wasn't just El Parador they wanted, but the whole Caribbean. They intended to soften it up with astrology, then use El Parador as a power base to make the area a sort of astrological empire, with them in charge."

Martinez' expression conveyed incredulity. "Repeat that." Philip did. Joe chortled wildly. "Preposterous! They would *never* have succeeded. The West Indies are much too strong to be subjugated like that."

"I saw them bribe local officials."

"The locals were suckering them, that's all."

"What about Grenada? They predicted the revolution."

"They must have had inside information. It would have happened exactly the same without them." Joe stared at de Vaucresson with contempt.

The pep pills had made Philip euphoric. He said to the count, "Seems like your late wife's prediction was accurate after all. An Aries has licked you."

Ari said tremulously, as if dazed, "But . . ."

"No 'buts' this time. We're both Aries rising, but my sun's in the first degree, yours the last. I'm a young Aries, you're an old one."

The count took a few steps backward, brushing his head against the fuselage as he did. His wavy hair seemed to shift, revealing whiteness of skull. A toupee! The count was bald on top! He looked pathetic with his hairpiece awry.

The villa wasn't far away, and Marie-Celeste soon returned, waving a manila envelope. From it Philip removed a stack of hundred-dollar bills. "Seed money." He handed the rest to Martinez. "For you and the boys. M-C, we're all set. Let's fly."

"Ari . . ." Marie-Celeste said softly, but the count stared fixedly at the first stars.

"It stinks in here," she said when she strapped in.

"You should have smelled it before. Morales had an accident."

Philip went through the preflight checklist, turned on the engines, and taxied off. He had what he hoped was his last glimpse of the Cardinals, in the lights from the plane: Cappy, supine, pounding asphalt with a fist; Canny hovered over him, snapping his fingers; Libby comforting the count, who stood with slumped shoulders and a haggard mouth.

Over the field, though they probably couldn't see it from the ground, Philip wagged his wings.

Elation filled him as the Aerostar sped south at seven thousand feet—furtiveness was no longer necessary. "How's your face? What happened?"

"Raymond was furious when he learned you were an Aries. He planned to kill you when you landed. I paid the radio announcer to change the message. You heard it?"

"Thank God. I'd intended . . . Lord knows what I'd planned, but at least I was ready."

"Ari heard it too, on his car radio. I knew he'd listen, but I'd hoped he'd think the announcer made a mistake. He's shrewd. He beat me up—for real this time. He'd have done worse once you were out of the way."

"Were you surprised that I'm an Aries?"

"Flabbergasted. And you know something about astrology, don't you, you big liar? How?"

"My mother was an astrologer, of sorts."

"What?"

"Yes. She was a believer. I didn't like her for it because she spent so much time with astrology that she neglected *me*, which was like being abandoned, I suppose, to a childish mind. . . ."

"The professor!" M-C teased again.

"Not anymore. But I perceived a weakness in the Cardinals. Call it inflexibility. They were so *convinced* that everything would happen as their horoscopes predicted that they made no allowance for the unforeseen. The trouble with zealots and madmen too—your ex-friends are a little of both—is that they're rigid. They really expect things to turn out as they wish, and they're not ready when things don't."

"Mmmmm," she said.

"I don't know very much about astrology, by the way," he said, sensing her disinterest in his explanation of the Cardinals' defeat.

"Do you know enough to understand why I was attracted to you in the first place? Because your moon's in Gemini and I have Gemini rising.

So does Libby." She stared at him sharply in the soft glow from the panel lights.

"Sounds like a song, but your Mars is trine in mine, or vice versa. That means harmony and enthusiasm between us, doesn't it?"

"I'm not sure about the harmony, but there's plenty of enthusiasm, especially as we're both fire signs." She sighed. "I still don't fully get it. You were so much *like* your horoscope—the Sag one, I mean. And then you turn out to be someone else completely."

"A rare case of parallel horoscopes, I guess. M-C, you played a pretty slimy role, luring me in."

"I'm sorry. I did what I was told."

"And I'm delighted." But he wondered about M-C's lures and deceits. Despite her bruised face, might she still be an ally of the count's, sent along to report back Castle's whereabouts? Was she truly ignorant of what happened to the pilot, to Sansa, to the men in the pool? "Do you know about the murders?" Philip asked abruptly.

"What murders?"

Did her see her blink? *Could* he trust her? Would he *ever* trust her? He didn't know. But she had tried to warn him, after all; she had returned with the money when she might have skipped. On Marie-Celeste he would take a chance. He was too happy not to.

Islands rushed by beneath them; calypso music and steel bands from the ADF radio filled the cabin. He longed for a shower, drinks, dinner, bed. It wouldn't be long, either; they ought to make Carriacou by nine. He started to descend when they reached Martinique; out of sheer exuberance, he let the airspeed build up until it nudged the red line. At 280 mph, the smooth air howled by the fuselage. When they reached St. Vincent, he slowed, and Carriacou was quickly beneath them.

"What'll we do with the plane, Phil?" she asked.

"Leave it. It's done its job. It's only a machine, though a lovely one." He patted the control panel as if thanking the Aerostar.

They could see the dark airstrip in the moonlight. M-C held the Admiralty charts and called out landmarks—Saline Island to her right, Mount D'Or one thousand feet below. He turned base leg over the Jack A Dan light, using the red and white beacons on the beach for his final approach. Landing lights on, he swept in low, dropped full flaps, and touched down. As he parked under a fringe of palm trees and cut the engines, he realized how utterly tired he was. For the last time, he went through the check list, making sure he had completed every item, as always. It was his responsibility. He left the keys in the ignition and the door unlocked.

Castle stepped into the evening breeze. It carried a hint of flowers, and of the sea.

Epilogue

So here you are living in a tent on Saline, with a million dollars in gold buried in the sand, pirate-style. Every day you take the launch you bought to Carriacou for supplies and to ask if a big yacht's been seen, or four strange characters. There has been no sign of them.

They won't be able to trace you through the Aerostar—somebody stole it.

What should you make of the whole surreal story? Did you invent it? Do you deal in dreams, purvey illusions? Have you crossed the line between reality and fantasy, substance and shadow? Touch yourself. Touch her, asleep on the cot. Remember what you heard on the portable radio—students and peasants stormed the presidential palace of General Hector Hernandez, who did not have time to flee. They killed him.

It happened, all of it.

Why? How?

You didn't used to think about luck, fortune, coincidence. To you these were empty words. Your neat and tidy world rolled on. You never worried about the unexpected and unforeseen. You could plot your course like a navigator. But suddenly you have questions.

311

Why did matters work out like this? Is chance merely a matter of dice? Is fate only random? Is there such a thing as destiny?

You have to ask because you won. You! You vanquished the Cardinals (or so it seems). You have what you wanted. You can go where you like, be what you wish, anyway up to the point that money buys freedom. You ought to be delighted with yourself. You ought to be satisfied. Completely. Yet . . .

The questions bother you because you don't really understand why you triumphed. You shouldn't have; the odds against you were staggering. Did you just get lucky, or was there another influence?

You don't care to believe that.

You shake your fist at the tropical sky and demand an explanation, but the stars aren't supplying one this or any evening. You must provide the answers yourself.

But no more yous, Phil. I have found my identity.

Well, ask again, what happened? For one thing, the Cardinals copied their signs, became them, down to the tiniest details, like having rings made of the stones governed by their hieroglyphs. Realizing it or not, they shaped themselves in their zodiacal images, tried to become the ego ideals their signs represented. It isn't all that unlikely; people imitate models— role models, in the sociologists' lingo—all their lives, and for the Cardinals, astrology provided them.

Mostly unconsciously, I did much the same—remaking myself in the Aries mold. I don't know how exactly, but I was down in my soul and needed, desperately, a change. And I was attracted to the so-called Arian qualities, the spirit of adventure, of triumph, of being a pioneer.

Which leaves . . . well, the question I have wrestled with almost from the start. For the odds against my involvement with the Cardinals seem high, to say nothing against those of relieving them of a million in gold. A quite remarkable number of coincidences had to occur, seeming to defy chance, or chance as we understand it.

Maybe there's another way to look at it. Maybe chance is bound to fit somewhere within the rules of logic. Everything, no matter how bizarre, is explainable even if you have to fall back on the notion that if people want things badly enough they can conspire to make them happen. When something is desired sufficiently, events may shape themselves in ex- tremely curious ways, coincidence heaped on coincidence, until the inner goal is arrived at. It's as though the deep desire, call it an inner absolute, makes a new dimension. The subjective self somehow works its way into reality and controls it. In some peculiar fashion, I became part of a set of circumstances in which events more or less had to unfold as they did, once I was part of the pattern I created. Up to a point, I intervened in my destiny. I, not the stars.

Of course, I'll never know—I can't go back and test fate by acting in a different way. But it is true that I wanted a new life and I found one.

Ari was right—I'll never be a psychologist again. I'd only be repeating myself, as he said. I won't return to Chicago, either. If there is a distinction between freedom and responsibility, I choose freedom.

It isn't a good distinction, though. Maybe a compromise is a better idea. Not freedom from, but freedom to.

Which brings me to the gold. I think my old self would be tempted to give it to the people of El Parador, since it isn't mine, in an altruistic and guilty liberal gesture. But I don't want to. I stole it and I'm going to hang on to it.

On the other hand (will I always reason like a professor?), I can't laze around the beach for the rest of my days. An active spirit—that's me. The Caribbean needs a dependable little airline, one that will carry freight, especially produce. A million bucks is enough to buy small planes, hire an extra pilot—like Gus Tretino. The business would need a capable executive, one who understands aircraft. I think I'll try out for the job.

The idea, of course, will prove a pipe dream if the Cardinals find us. M-C insists we're safe; she's studied the horoscope of their guiding light, the count, and she's sure he wants nothing more to do with Philip Castle. She's cast a new horoscope for me, which reveals that I am destined to marry a Leo and have two children with her. M-C seems to have changed her mind about marriage.

Am I building sand castles, Castle?

I wonder what will happen to all of us.

In 1981, Canfield Koster was poisoned, probably by the mob. When the convulsions started, he was on a catwalk in his casino and fell through an eye-in-the-sky onto a roulette wheel, where he died.

Elizabeth Harris, disappointed at failing to achieve dreams of untold riches, broke her own rule against stealing money and attempted to penetrate the computers of the Federal Reserve System, through which, every few days, passes enough money to equal the national debt. Sent to prison, she soon achieved recognition as a minor poet. She was killed with a broken bottle by a jealous lesbian inmate.

Capablanca Morales Ramon's ability to walk was increasingly limited by arthritis. His smuggling operation fell apart, and more zealous law enforcement in Latin America brought an end to various swindles. Investments based on his reading of forthcoming events turned sour and his gold mine was confiscated. He returned to El Parador, where the new regime, which survived, felt it owed him a debt, though the ease with which he had been abducted, plus certain accusations by the ex-Finance Minister, Astacio, who was attempting to get out of prison, cast doubts on him. Astacio claimed that the Tall One had stolen a million dollars of El Parador's gold. The story could not be proved or disproved, and Morales became a minor government functionary. He did not remarry.

The banking empire of Raymond, Count de Vaucresson collapsed following an investigation by Interpol and other police agencies. He was found to have used the assets of his private bank for personal investment. Accused of fraud, he was successfully sued for many millions of dollars while serving a jail sentence in the Cayman Islands. He went to the United States, where he wrote a syndicated astrology column. He died of natural causes at the age of 65.

The Geminis—Bob and Bill—were institutionalized in Great Britain for incurable sociopathic tendencies. Both died during a prison riot at exactly the same time.

Joe Martinez continues to run a cafe on St. Jean, helped by his children. Despite his sudden affluence he did not redecorate—the place looks the same as ever—but he did hire a chef, a small Chinese. Joe uses his money to pursue the goal of a Caribbean commonwealth and tours the West Indies making speeches. He often attacks the United States for its ungenerous and short-sighted policies toward the region. His influence grows.

Among Le Boucan's customers are Marie-Celeste and Philip Castle, who fly to St. Jean, from the fertile Caribbean island where they live and prosper, in their new Aerostar which Philip normally uses to fly produce. Sometimes they bring the two kids.